For Curt,
with love

ALSO BY LINDA BARLOW

Keepsake
Her Sister's Keeper

Published by
WARNER BOOKS

INTIMATE BETRAYAL

LINDA BARLOW

WARNER BOOKS

A Time Warner Company

WARNER BOOKS EDITION

Cover design by Dan Bond

Warner Books, Inc.
1271 Avenue of the Americas
New York, NY 10020

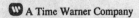 A Time Warner Company

Printed in the United States of America

First Printing: November, 1995

10 9 8 7 6 5 4 3 2 1

Acknowledgments

My deepest thanks to the many people who helped me during the writing of this novel, including Fran Busse Fowler, Rina Johnson, Henry H. Miller, Pamela Bleakney, David and Jean Ferris, Richard Currier, Larry Ellison, Jenny Overstreet, Raegen Rasnic, David Nathanson, Tina Moskow, Steven Axelrod, Dilek Barlow, and Curt Monash.

INTIMATE BETRAYAL

Chapter One

Annie Jefferson sent a quick prayer skyward. Standing in front of her was Matthew Carlyle, the one man who could save her company. She gave him a tentative smile, which he did not return.

"I appreciate your taking the time to meet with me," she said. "I know how busy you are."

"Do you?"

"Well, of course you must be, as CEO of Powerdyme. I really appreciate the way you're taking a firsthand interest in it instead of sending a vice president or somebody like that to talk to me."

I'm babbling, she thought. She smiled again, and this time he smiled back. Charlie always used to tell her that her smile was irresistible.

Ah, Charlie, my darling, I miss you so much!

"Sit down, please," Carlyle said, indicating a simple straight-backed wooden chair just opposite his desk. All the furniture would have to go when the office was redesigned, she thought wryly as she sat down on the hard, unforgiving chair. She felt like a prisoner in an interrogation room instead of a corporate designer addressing a prospective client.

"There are several things I'd like to discuss with you, Annie," he said.

Annie. Wouldn't it have been more professional to address her as Mrs. Jefferson? It wasn't as if they knew each other well. At least . . . *Don't think about that*, she warned herself.

"I presume you've reviewed my proposal," she said.

Matthew Carlyle had not sat down but was leaning one hip against the front of his desk. It seemed to her that he was closer than was necessary in such a spacious office. He was known in his business circles as a brilliant, ruthless, and intimidating man, and Annie suspected that he was quite deliberate in his posture and body language. How much simpler it must be to negotiate his multimillion-dollar computer industry schemes when he was able to establish complete and unquestioned dominance over his associates and competitors.

He was a good-looking man. Tall and lanky, without an ounce of fat visible on his body. He had to be at least forty, but he didn't look it, which was probably the result of rigorous exercise in some wealthy executive gym. His hair was dark brown and he had high, angular cheekbones. His eyes were a deep shade of green.

"I've reviewed your proposal, and I think it's excellent," he said.

"I'm delighted to hear it." Thank goodness! He was a difficult man to read, and she'd been starting to wonder. The fact that he'd invited her here for a personal meeting had been encouraging, but she hadn't wanted to set her hopes too high.

Still, it was hard not to hope. The proposal to design the new corporate headquarters of Matthew Carlyle's incredibly successful Powerdyme had been one of the most exciting she'd ever worked on. Annie had given it every ounce of her creativity and skill, and she was proud of the results. Her proposal was superb. If Carlyle didn't recognize that Fabrications could provide him with the best design at the lowest price, then he wasn't the businessman he was reputed to be.

She hoped he was able to recognize quality when he saw it. Because, much though she hated to admit it, she needed Matthew Carlyle. If she got this job, which would bring in more money than her last six projects combined, Fabrications would survive. If not, the company she had started with Charlie, her late husband, would very likely fail.

It was as simple as that.

Carlyle picked up a folder from the top of his desk. Her proposal. He leafed through it casually, nodding once or twice. "Your work is top-notch. I've worked with other design firms—much bigger and more famous than yours, in fact—so I know what's out there. As you may know, I've always taken a personal interest in such matters. The working environment I provide for my employees is vitally important."

Indeed she knew, and she'd worked with that in mind. One of the outrageously successful computer companies of the baby boom generation, Powerdyme was famous for the way it had combined high tech brilliance and ingenuity with the New Age ideals of the counterculture. You didn't go into Powerdyme with the same design solutions that you might present to General Motors or even IBM.

After all, Matthew Carlyle had started out as a slap in the face to corporate America. Together with a few other young high technology entrepreneurs of the 1970s and '80s, he'd turned inside out the old ideas of how an American corporation should be run.

"We are, as you know, an unconventional company," he continued. "This has to be reflected in our workspace. I've received several other serious proposals for this project, but I have to say that yours has the best solutions to our unique problems."

He lifted a page from the folder and examined it, smiling slightly and nodding. "Really, Annie, you've done a fantastic job."

"Thank you. I enjoyed it," she said in a heartfelt tone. "Most corporate design work is fairly routine, but this one has presented all sorts of exciting challenges."

"You enjoy challenges, I take it?"

"Oh yes." Although at this point in her life, she thought wryly, she would have been happier with fewer situations that were challenging and more that were secure and certain.

"What about risks?" he asked. "You enjoy them too?"

She was alerted to the new tone in his voice. "What do you mean? What sort of risks?"

"You know what I mean. Are you a risk taker? Do you love being out there on the edge, feeling your adrenaline pumping as you reach for the ultimate thrill?"

"Come with me. Don't think about it. Just come."

"I can't. Please, don't ask me."

"You can. You've come this far. Some things are meant to be."

Annie felt her cheeks grow hot. Was he too thinking about that magical, terrifying, far-better-forgotten weekend? Or had he put it out of his mind?

"I don't think I'm much of a risk taker, no," she said.

He tossed the folder that held her proposal down onto his desk. "Well, the fact of the matter is, neither am I."

Annie flinched deep inside. Something was going wrong; she could feel it. Her fingers clenched into fists. Was he going to turn her down?

"Your work is indeed excellent, but I've done some checking into the current status of your design firm. I'm afraid I don't like what I've learned. Fabrications is a small company—far smaller than any I've worked with in the past. It was quite successful in the mid-eighties, but the past few years have been increasingly lean, and the unfortunate death of your husband last year has been disastrous for the firm. You are not an architect, Annie. You're a designer, and no doubt a very good one. But the architect you're working with now is nowhere near as good as your husband was. And that fact is hurting your firm."

That fact was killing her firm, actually. But she'd been trying to hide it and certainly wasn't going to admit it now. "My husband was special," she said. "You're right that it hasn't been easy to replace him. But Sidney Canin is a good architect, and I have every confidence in him."

"He's mediocre, and you and I both know it."

Annie felt herself flush. "As a matter of fact, Sid won't be with us much longer, although that has nothing to do with his job performance. He's leaving for personal reasons—he's originally from New York City and he wants to move back there. I'm in the process of interviewing architects now, and I'm optimistic about the talent out there. I intend to hire the best."

He shook his head. "You can't afford to hire the best. In

fact, I doubt you can afford to hire anyone. Your firm is in serious trouble. Although your proposal was by far the best one I've received on this project, I don't believe you had any business submitting it, because Fabrications simply can't do the job that you've outlined."

"That's not true!"

"It's the way I see it, Annie. I'm sorry." He paused, then added brutally, "You're good, but you're not good enough."

"Wait a minute." Her hands were clenched so tightly that her fingernails were digging into her palms. Without the Powerdyme project, her company might not survive. "You're telling me that I'm talented and creative, that I've suggested ways to solve your design problems that occurred to nobody else, that my proposal is the best of the lot, and yet you're not going to hire my firm?"

"That's right. I don't think Fabrications is going to be around long enough for you to complete the job."

"Well, it probably won't be if we don't get this project!"

The moment she'd spoken the words she regretted them. One of the primary rules in this dog-eat-dog business was never to display your weaknesses to others. Bleed even a little, and the predators move in for the kill.

Oh God. Fabrications had meant everything to Charlie, and now that he was gone, it meant everything to Annie to keep it alive. If the company died, she would be failing Charlie, and she couldn't allow that to happen. It would be like losing him all over again.

"So what would you have me do? Take you on charity? That's asking rather a lot, even for a pretty young window. As I said, I'm not a risk taker, at least not when I have so much at stake."

And suddenly the present vanished and Annie could hear her own voice whisper, *"Oh, stop, please stop. I can't. I'm not a risk taker, at least not when I have so much to lose."*

She jumped to her feet, wanting to run from the room. *Bastard*! she thought. Any doubt that he recalled that night three years ago had vanished. He remembered, all right. And he was just as ruthless as everybody claimed.

But she already knew that. She'd known it ever since the night in England when he'd come so close to sweeping her off her feet. He'd known she was married. So was he. Francesca Carlyle, his wife, was a beautiful, well-known San Francisco socialite. But that hadn't stopped him. And he was such a charming and skilled seducer that it almost hadn't stopped her, either. He'd been a smooth-tongued demon, with the tempting abilities of the Devil himself.

As for her, she'd been weak and foolish, warm, fresh clay to be molded according to his desires. She had never forgiven herself for the way she'd acted. And when so soon afterward Charlie had shown the first signs of the cancer that had taken his life, Annie had felt as if it were a punishment for the adultery in her heart.

In the end, though, she had rejected Matthew Carlyle, which must have been a blow to his masculine ego. Now, she thought, he was getting even with her for that. He was punishing her. No doubt he'd been waiting for his chance to do so for the past three years.

Summoning every shred of dignity she possessed, she moved to his desk and picked up the folder containing her proposal. "Thank you for your time, Mr. Carlyle. I don't think there's anything more to discuss."

"Annie . . ." he said softly, but she ignored him, turned

her back, and moved toward the door. As she passed the wastebasket, she sailed the folder neatly into it.

She would survive in the corporate design business *despite* Mr. Matthew Carlyle.

After several minutes of staring blankly at his computer screen, Matt Carlyle rose and looked out his window. Somewhere down below, Annie would be getting into her car, feeling disappointed and angry. Scared, too, probably. Deep down inside she must know that what he'd told her about her architectural design company was true. Annie was an excellent designer, but her husband had been the firm's CEO and guiding force. Charlie Jefferson had also been an award-winning architect, and Fabrications would very likely founder without him.

It was a shame, because the city could use more small creative firms. It was unfortunate, too, that so great a personal loss should also become a professional one. *But life is tough*, he thought grimly. *No point in getting sentimental about it.*

Running a successful business was tough, too. Most small businesses failed. His own first one had bitten the dust after less than a year. Annie had nothing to be ashamed of. And if she had half the gumption he credited her with, she'd stand up, brush herself off, and find a way to start over again.

On the other hand, he reminded herself, she was both a woman and a widow. Not that a woman couldn't be successful on her own—but only a fool would deny that the old-boy network that was so instrumental in raising capital for new business ventures tended to favor men.

Staring out the window across the hills of San Francisco,

Matthew Carlyle let his mind wander. Those blue eyes of hers, flashing fire, that fine gold hair that curved so delicately around her neck and chin, that stubborn chin that tilted up just a smidgen when she was angry, the subtle yet alluring curves of her body . . .

Annie, a widow.

Whereas he, of course, was still married. . . .

He considered and rejected various options until finally he came up with one that seemed attractive no matter which angle he viewed it from.

He picked up the phone. A few minutes later, he hung up, satisfied. He'd done what he could. Now, maybe he could clear his mind of the memory of Annie Jefferson's anger and disappointment and instead remember her bright, hopeful smile.

Chapter Two

One Year Later

"He's very handsome, isn't he?"

"Who?" said Annie.

"Matthew Carlyle. Don't you think so?"

Annie shrugged, then managed a smile for Darcy Fuentes, her co-worker at Brody Associates, one of the largest architectural design firms in the city. They were standing together in the salon of Matthew Carlyle's yacht, docked in a slip in San Francisco Bay, watching several well-dressed couples swing dancing. Among them were Carlyle and his wife, Francesca.

Actually, he's not that handsome, Annie was thinking. Sam Brody, their boss, who was also out on the dance floor, was more conventionally good-looking with his amiable features, firm body, and perpetual California tan. Carlyle's long arms and legs gave him a certain awkwardness, and his features were more sharply defined than Sam's. It was like comparing Daniel Day Lewis with the young Paul Newman.

Besides, Annie couldn't even look at Matthew Carlyle without feeling a knot of hostility form in her belly. She just couldn't forget that if it hadn't been for him, Fabrications might have survived.

"I think Francesca's drunk," Darcy said. "She's swaying a little more than she ought to be, and her husband seems to be keeping quite a grip on her."

"Maybe she's depressed about turning forty," Annie said.

"Why should she be? She looks about twenty-nine. I hate her," Darcy added with a laugh as Carlyle and Sam Brody changed partners and Francesca moved into Sam's arms. "I should look so good when I'm forty."

Annie raised her eyebrows in amusement. Darcy, a luscious brunette of her own age, thirty-three, was attracting a lot more male appreciation than their hostess. "The birthday girl would trade bodies with you in a flash if she could," Annie said. "So would most of the women here."

"Fat lot of good it does me," Darcy said. "My love life sucks."

"Compared to mine, your love life is a veritable cornucopia of sensual delights."

"Yeah, but always with the wrong guy." She sighed. "Our Venus and Mars aspects are never compatible."

Darcy, a senior architect at Brody Associates and Annie's closest friend there, was a passionate believer in astrology and other New Age subjects. Before moving in next door to Annie in the North Beach district of the city, she had cast Annie's chart. "If we're going to be neighbors as well as co-workers, we'd *better* get along together."

The stars had ruled them compatible, and it certainly seemed to be true. Darcy was a top-notch architect—a woman who had succeeded in what was still pretty much a man's world. And Annie, who specialized in interior design, particularly for large corporate projects, loved working with her. Their talents meshed nicely.

"I'm a fire sign—Leo—full of energy and enthusiasm and lots of grand plans," Darcy had explained. "You're a Cancer, a water sign, and tenacious, sensitive, loyal, and attentive to details."

"If we're fire and water, how come we get along so well?" Annie had asked, amused.

"Well, we have several harmonious trines and conjunctions in our charts and only two squares, and I have Pisces rising, and you have several other fire signs to go with mine. . . ."

Whatever *that* meant.

People often commented that Annie and Darcy had complementary looks as well as jobs. Annie had tawny hair, blue eyes, and fair skin; Darcy's hair was black, her eyes brown, and her skin a deep olive that held a tan year-round. Annie dressed elegantly yet conservatively, in business suits with tasteful accessories. Darcy came to work in low-cut dresses that were tight and short. She wore thick, dark mascara and heavy eyeliner that made dark rims around her eyes. Her long nails were usually painted in deep shades of brown, purple, or red. Although Darcy never dressed in a "serious, businesslike manner," she had no trouble commanding the respect of the people she worked with, as far as Annie could tell.

"Well, I don't know about their planets," Annie said, scanning the crowd, "but I see some eligible types here tonight." She noticed that Francesca Carlyle was now giddily moving from one partner to another on the dance floor, while her husband had returned to his table to sip champagne. "How about that surfer type over there in the tight pants?"

Darcy shook her head. "This is San Francisco, remember? The good-looking single guys are all gay." Then she considered the surfer more carefully. "On the other hand," she grinned, "I suppose it wouldn't hurt to try."

"Go get him, babe."

As Darcy switched into her hunting mode and moved away, Annie wondered why she could not bring herself to do the same. Charlie had been dead for nearly two years now, and it was time to stop hugging the wall at social gatherings.

But it was one thing to tell herself that and another to do it. She still missed Charlie. He had been her rock, her teacher, her protector. Even though he'd been only five years older than she, he'd come from another world—a world of confidence, security, and hope. He'd convinced her that anything was possible if you worked hard and held on to your dreams. And she'd believed him because with Charlie, anything *did* seem possible. Until he'd been diagnosed with cancer.

He had been determined to beat the disease. When it became obvious that he couldn't, he'd taken comfort in his belief that everything his doctors learned from his suffering would help them to cure others. Charlie had always found the silver lining in the cloud.

In tribute to everything he'd taught her, Annie had tried her best to hang on to that optimism after his death. When she lost her company as well, the world had seemed very black. But perhaps Charlie had been right after all, because here she was a few months later, a professional designer with an excellent job, partying with other professionals and socialites on Matthew Carlyle's yacht. It was certainly not a scene she could have imagined a year ago, when Carlyle had shattered her dream of keeping Fabrications alive.

She had arrived late for the party, just as the yacht was about to begin its moonlit cruise in San Francisco Bay. The cruise had continued during the dinner served on board and for an hour or two afterward, but now they were back in the slip at the marina, allowing anybody who wanted to leave early to do so.

Annie was somewhat surprised that she hadn't left yet, since Matthew Carlyle was the last person she'd ever wanted to see again.

But she wasn't sure if he even knew she was there. It must have been Francesca who had put her on the guest list. The socialite and philanthropist was one of the leading lights of the building committee of the United Path Church, which had just hired Brody Associates to design and build a cathedral. Annie had gotten to know Francesca during the proposal and bidding process.

The United Path Church was Francesca's favorite charity. It was a fast-growing, interdenominational Christian sect led by one of Annie's dearest friends, the Reverend Barbara Rae Acker, whose work with battered women and AIDS victims was legendary in San Francisco. The UPC cathedral would be one of the largest and most magnificent building projects the city had ever known, and Annie was slated to be the project manager.

Although tonight's party was to celebrate Francesca's fortieth birthday, for Annie it was a celebration of her own astonishing success.

"Hi there," said Sam Brody, her boss. "You look radiant, Annie. Are you by any chance happy about something?"

His voice was mischievous, and Annie grinned. "You know why I'm happy."

"Might it have anything to do with a certain cathedral—for which a designer by the name of Annie Jefferson did most of the exquisite interior design?"

Annie hugged him spontaneously. She loved working for Sam. He was one of those people who seemed to bring sunshine with him wherever he went. Sam had blond hair that shone like newly minted gold coins, blazing blue eyes, and an air of distinction and old money about him. He'd gone to all the right schools and belonged to all the right clubs but he never displayed a hint of social snobbery; he was warm, charming, and very approachable.

"By the way," he said, "I found out yesterday that the Pressman project is in the bag. Al Pressman was so impressed with your designs for the cathedral that he jumped at the chance to hire us. You deserve a lot of appreciation, and I intend to see that you get it."

She cocked her head and grinned. "In the form of a raise, I hope?"

"I was thinking of both a raise and a promotion."

"Now that sounds like an offer I can't refuse!"

He smiled and in a courtly gesture took her hand and raised it to his lips. "I realized some time ago that hiring you was one of the best things I ever did."

"Thank you," she murmured.

As Sam moved away to continue mingling, Annie took a deep breath. Things were good! No more of this moping around, fretting about her work, fretting about her future. For the first time since Charlie's death, she was beginning to feel secure.

"Would you care to dance?" someone asked her a few minutes later.

Annie turned to see Sidney Canin standing somewhat hesitantly behind her. Sid had been her architect at Fabrications. She had been surprised when, after the company's demise, Sam had offered a job to Sidney as well. Apparently Sid's plans to move back to New York City had fallen through, and the ever-genial Sam had hired him despite his less-than-stellar reputation.

Compared to either Sam Brody or Matthew Carlyle, Sid was the sort of man you wouldn't look at twice. Medium height, medium build, unremarkable features, and old-fashioned horn rimmed glasses so thick that they distorted his eyes. He never had much to say for himself, and what he did say was always gloomy and petulant.

Still, not wanting to be rude, she agreed to dance with him, and was surprised when he turned out to be a good dancer with a fine sense of rhythm.

They spoke briefly about the triumph of winning the cathedral contract. Sounding negative as usual, Sid said, "We'd better not rest on our laurels until the thing is actually built." His eyes slid away from hers and he appeared more nervous than usual. Annie noticed that he was staring at Francesca Carlyle, with whom he had recently been dancing. He hadn't looked gloomy while dancing with Francesca—on the contrary, he'd been remarkably animated.

"With a project so big," he added, "things are bound to go wrong."

While this was undoubtedly true, it wasn't something that Annie relished thinking about. As project manager, she had a lot riding on the successful completion of the cathedral.

She and Sidney danced past Sam Brody, who once again had the now very obviously drunken Francesca in his arms. She was giggling and tossing her head. As Annie caught Sam's eye, he grimaced slightly as if to say, "get me out of here."

Annie grinned at him. Francesca in her sober state had personally contributed heavily to the building fund of the United Path Church, and she was chairwoman of the building committee. Without her support there would be no cathedral. So, Sam had to make nice.

Sidney glared at Francesca and Sam. A tiny suspicion stirred in Annie's head—was Sidney attracted to Francesca? In love with her? Involved with her? It seemed unlikely, but there had been rumors for years that the Carlyles' marriage was rocky.

As the dance tune finished, Annie smiled at Sidney and said, "Thanks, that was lovely." But as she tried to back away from him, he seized her hand.

"I'm worried about this project. Can we go somewhere and talk?" he asked.

Annie had no wish to be subjected to a long list of Sidney's unsubstantiated fears, but neither did she want to ignore a legitimate concern.

"What, exactly, are you worried about?"

"Just some details, but they could prove important."

But somebody was pinging a glass with a knife, calling for

everybody's attention. Annie was grateful for the interruption. When Sid got going on "details," he never stopped.

The glass-pinger was Matthew Carlyle, who had stepped up in front of the band to make an announcement. His wife was leaning against the wall to his left, her skinny arms wrapped around her middle. She looked a bit ill. Annie hoped she wasn't about to pass out or throw up.

"This is a special day for my wife, as you all know, and we're delighted that you could share it with us," Carlyle began. "Francesca, I know, is particularly happy to have so many of her friends here, and we thank you all for coming."

Sidney, standing right next to Annie, made a low sound in his throat. Annie glanced at him and noted that he was now glowering at the Carlyles. Francesca too was behaving strangely. As her husband spoke, she fidgeted and looked bored. In her business and charitable dealings, Francesca was invariably courteous and very much in control. But Annie had heard whispers about a drinking problem, and Francesca had certainly overdone it tonight.

Francesca and Sidney? Nah, she thought.

"When I first suggested we give this party," Carlyle went on, "my lovely wife was reluctant. The money could be spent in some more useful way, she said, and earmarked for a far worthier and less frivolous cause than, as she put it, a social-ite's meaningless birthday. But, as you're all aware, Francesca devotes so much of her time and money to worthy causes. She does so without fanfare and, often, without taking personal credit for the many people she helps. For that, she deserves something back, and on this occasion, at least, I believe a little fanfare is appropriate."

Francesca stepped forward, prematurely it seemed, since

her husband appeared to be about to continue speaking. Pushing in front of him, she glared at him and said, ''Oh, for God's sake, cut the crap, Matt.''

The room grew even more hushed than it had been. Carlyle took his wife's arm, as if to restrain her, but she jerked away from him. ''Let's stop kidding ourselves here. I'm sick of the masquerade, and I'm sure you are too.''

''Sit down, Francesca,'' Carlyle said in a starkly different tone. ''You've had too much to drink.''

Both his voice and his expression called up in Annie's mind the way he had behaved on the day he'd essentially scuttled Fabrications. Despite his fine veneer of courtesy, there was something ruthless about Matthew Carlyle.

His wife ignored it. Again she brushed off his hand on her arm, then raised her half-empty glass and announced, ''Indeed I have. I'm celebrating. But I would hate to have our friends get the wrong idea about why I'm having too much to drink. It's not my birthday that I'm celebrating, but my freedom. Not the fortieth year of my wretched little life, but the final year of my marriage to you!''

Darcy sidled over to Annie and whispered, ''Do you *believe* this?''

Before Annie could respond, Francesca went on. ''Yes, my friends, this sham of a marriage is over. In the morning I'm filing for divorce from the great Matthew Carlyle. You're all invited to stay tuned for the California Community Property Divorce Wars, which will no doubt begin shortly, since I'm advised by my lawyer that billionaire businessmen can be stingy when it comes to splitting up the marital assets.''

Matthew's expression had frozen, and even from across the room Annie could see a pulse hammering in his throat. She knew immediately that he was supremely angry and only barely able to control it.

He did not respond to his wife's comments, however. Instead he turned and stalked out of the room.

Francesca's high-pitched laugh rose over the low mutterings of her guests. Nobody knew how to react. Annie did not know the Carlyles well and had no idea whether their closer friends had had any inkling of this, but her impression was that most people present were profoundly shocked.

Sam came over, his face a little pale. He and Carlyle had been friends for many years. "Maybe we'd all better leave," he said to his co-workers. "Looks to me like this party is over."

The same conclusion had apparently been reached by all. Whispering their gossip, the guests began to move toward the doors. A few people gathered around Francesca, Sam and Sid among them, offering comfort, Annie supposed. She tried to gauge whether Sid was surprised by Francesca's announcement, but for once his face gave nothing away.

Annie scanned the crowd for her good friend Barbara Rae Acker, who was also Francesca's minister. This was exactly the kind of situation that Barbara Rae was skilled at managing. She knew when to listen and when to speak. Even better, she always knew what to say to calm people down.

Although she had been present earlier, Barbara Rae appeared to have left. Probably one of her parishioners had needed her.

After getting her coat, Annie approached Francesca and pressed her hand gently. "The party was lovely," she said sincerely, for it had been—up until the last few minutes. "Thanks for inviting me. Take care."

The woman was so drunk that Annie wondered if she would even recognize her. But Francesca looked straight at her, and for a moment her eyes seemed to clear. "You take care, Annie." Francesca smiled knowingly. "He's always liked you, my dear. Take my advice. Be careful."

Annie blinked, blushed, and immediately felt a flash of guilt.

"What did that mean?" Darcy demanded as they headed down the gangway to the pier.

"I've no idea," Annie murmured. "She was very drunk."

"I always thought they were such a happy couple," Darcy said. "Just goes to show—you never really know anyone, do you?"

The story was all over the news the following morning:

> *Francesca Carlyle, 40, wife of billionaire computer industry entrepreneur Matthew Carlyle, was found floating face down in San Francisco Bay this morning at dawn. An autopsy will be performed to determine the exact cause of death.*
>
> *Her demise followed a party held last night on the Carlyle yacht to celebrate Francesca Carlyle's fortieth birthday. There are reports that the deceased had been drinking heavily and that she and her husband quarreled in front of their guests.*

Matthew Carlyle refused to be interviewed, but he is said to be cooperating with the police investigation.

As, shocked, she read the papers and watched the news, Annie kept remembering the look of cold fury on Matthew Carlyle's face.

Chapter Three

Eighteen Months Later

"Wow, it's dazzling, isn't it?" Sam Brody said as he stood next to Annie in the Mission district of the city, across the street from the newest cathedral in San Francisco.

"Yes," Annie said simply. It was magnificent to see the new construction rising toward the heavens. Although she had worked on many construction sites over the past decade, she'd never seen one so huge.

Ground had been broken a year and a half ago, the foundation had been set deep into the ground, and the steel structural core of the building had been completed. Next had come the walls and the high vaulted roof of the modern Gothic-style building. The stonemasons had completed most of the work on the exterior, although there were still some intricate carved statues and gargoyles to be added. Meanwhile, the interior work was now proceeding—the design for which Annie was directly responsible.

The cathedral was designed in the most popular traditional manner, in the shape of a longitudinal cross, with the long central nave running from east to west. This section was crossed near the front of the building with the north and south transept arms and terminated at the east end in a semicircular apse, where the Lady Chapel was located.

The design was classic, but the building materials were, of course, modern. Contemporary techniques and equipment had enabled the contractor to build a structure in eighteen months that workmen of centuries past would have labored over for decades.

Annie, Sam Brody, Darcy, and Sidney Canin, all of whom had played major parts in the design for the cathedral, were on site today, along with two of the six members of the United Path Church building committee, for a tour and an update. As project manager of the job, Annie was there every day, but today she would have to fill the others in on her progress. She was a little nervous about the visit, since lately it seemed that they had been plagued with one small problem after another.

Annie's role as project manager was to oversee the entire operation. Her position was one of enormous responsibility, and it was pretty much a full-time commitment. Since she was under special contract to the owners—the United Path Church—she monitored the work both of the contractor, McEnerney Construction, which was in charge of all the structural work, and all the subcontractors who did the thousands of smaller jobs inherent in all big projects.

Since she was not an architect or a structural engineer,

Annie had occasionally encountered problems that challenged her technical know-how, but she'd tried not to let these upset her. If there was something she didn't know one day, she made damn certain she understood it the next.

In an industry dominated by men, she occasionally ran into a bit of macho "don't worry your pretty little head about that" from the contractor's office, but after a year and a half on the job, most of that patronizing had ceased. Annie was confident that she'd won the respect of *most* of the construction crew.

"Come on, everybody," she said. "Put on your hard hats and let's go inside."

"Hey, boss, did you authorize some folks from the church and the architects' firm to visit the construction site today?"

Paul McEnerney, owner and CEO of McEnerney Construction, one of the biggest building contractors in the Bay Area, puffed on a cigarette as he listened to Jack Fletcher, calling him on a cellular phone from the job site.

"Don't need to authorize it, Fletcher—you oughta be able to take care of that yourself." As the contractor's job superintendent, Fletcher supervised the scheduling and coordinating of the work of the many subcontractors, including the painters, plumbers, electricians, stonemasons, and woodcrafters. He was supposed to be on top of things.

"I didn't know they were coming," Fletcher said.

"Come on, man, you've told me a thousand times that the project manager broad—what's her name—Annie Jefferson—is over there all the time anyhow."

"She is. And so's that lady minister we're working for.

But this time they've got a whole slew of folks and are taking a little tour."

"Are they interfering with the workmen?"

"Not really, but you know how this kind of thing slows things up. There's been too damn much visiting."

"Hang on a minute, Fletcher." McEnerney put him on hold while he punched up the latest data on his computer screen. Until recently the numbers had been excellent on the cathedral job. He certainly didn't want anything to screw up the tidy profit he was making. He smiled. Tidy indeed.

Most of the structural work had been completed on time and under budget. It was the subcontractors who were dawdling. The interior work had been going slowly lately. Everybody was being so goddamn painstaking, for some reason. Maybe because it was a church—shit, no, a fucking cathedral—and they were awed by the greater glory of God.

McEnerney didn't believe in God. He considered the concept a stupid fantasy invented to counter man's natural terror of death. But he did believe in the power of superstition, and he'd seen it operating among the various crews working on the cathedral. Ever since one of the early excavations had unearthed a human leg bone or something, there had been a few guys moaning and groaning about the site being cursed.

McEnerney didn't like these stories. They made the construction crews nervous. And he didn't like nervous crews. When crews got nervous, things went wrong. Tempers frayed. Union troubles started to brew. Sometimes people got careless and accidents happened. Construction was dangerous work. Even though the company was insured up the wazoo for anything that might go wrong, there was no way to insure the goodwill and dedicated labor of the men on the crews unless they felt safe at the place. A lot of stupid tales about nuns, skeletons, and old rituals sure didn't help create that feeling of security.

McEnerney pressed the button to resume the phone conversation with Fletcher. As he did, it struck him once again that he didn't really know Jack Fletcher very well. He'd hired him on Sam Brody's word because Brody had insisted that he'd vetted him personally.

So far Fletcher had done a pretty decent job. Certainly he'd held all the workers to the schedule, which was crucial in a job this large.

"Listen, Fletcher, I don't like what I'm seeing on the recent delays," he said. "You're my man out there in the field on this one, and I expect you to tighten things up."

"Yes, sir."

"So get with whoever you need to. That blond designer from Brody Associates is their project manager, right? You and she oughta be able to manage things between you and get this mess straightened out."

"Right. I'll talk to her. She's actually been doing a good job. She's earned the respect of most of the people working on the project."

Has she now? thought McEnerney. And to think that this was a woman whom everyone had expected to be only marginally competent. After all, she was a designer, with little experience in the field and none at managing construction sites.

Brody too had recently remarked on what a good job the broad had been doing. Just goes to show, he'd told Sam, it doesn't pay to underestimate people.

"Glad to hear you and she are getting along. Let me know if you have any problems."

"Right, sir. I will."

You'd better, asshole, McEnerney thought as he hung up.

Fletcher put down the cell phone. He felt a tightness in his belly. He didn't like the way Paul McEnerney condescended to him. And he hated the way he, in return, had to kiss ass.

But he liked this job. He liked being in charge, ordering people around. He liked the way they kissed *his* ass when they wanted something.

Fletcher took a quick back-and-forth in the trailer he used as an office. It was parked in the vacant lot adjoining the job site, along with the other construction company trailers and subcontractors' vans and cars. He liked his trailer and thought of it as a cozy little home. He had a computer, a cellular phone, a small fridge where he could store sandwiches and beer, and a microwave to heat coffee and frozen pizza. There was even a narrow bed along one side, and a can in the back. He used both a lot more often than his employer realized. It was better than going home to that cutesy little apartment in the Castro. Never shoulda moved in there—the district was full of dykes and queers.

He reran through his mind the conversation he'd just had with McEnerney. The man was a prick, but Fletcher knew that he'd just have to bite back his anger and pretend to have some respect for him. But he wasn't ever going to forget that his first loyalty was not to McEnerney Construction but to the building's architect, Sam Brody.

Brody was all right. He'd done a lot for him, and, much as Fletcher hated to be indebted to any man, he had to admit that he owed Brody. He'd never have gotten this job if Brody hadn't taken a liking to him.

Brody had known about his trouble but had been willing to overlook it, which had astonished Fletcher at the time. After all, Brody was a golden boy—rich and sophisticated, the type you'd think would sniff in disgust when confronted with the brutal facts of a man's ugly past. What did a society boy like Brody know about life in the real world, the down and dirty world of black hearts and mean fists?

"I don't believe in judging men solely by their pasts," the golden boy had said. "What I want to know is this: Are you a stand-up guy I can trust right now—today, next month, a year from now? That's all I care about."

"I want to bury the past, bury it deep," Fletcher had replied. "If you'll help me do that, you'll find out that I'm one helluva stand-up guy."

"Okay," Brody had said. "You've got yourself a job."

Brody had kept his word. He'd never once thrown Fletcher's prison record in his face. He'd never even looked at him funny. He'd trusted him completely, and he'd gone to bat for him with McEnerney.

Fletcher considered himself Brody's man. He intended to do his damnedest never to let him down.

Fletcher went to the doorway of his trailer and watched Sam Brody enter the cathedral with the designer and project manager, Ms. Jefferson.

Annie Jefferson.

Annie.

Chapter Four

Everything went smoothly as Annie led the visitors through the site, pointing out to them the special details of the beautiful building. She was explaining about the installation of the handcrafted stained glass panels, when they all heard the sounds of an altercation down at the west end of the cathedral, under the scaffolding for the mammoth rose window that was going in at the traditional position above the cathedral's main entrance.

Two male voices were raised in anger, and, as they all turned toward the noise, a young man swung down recklessly from the scaffolding where he had been working. He made an obscene hand gesture to the man who was still high up on the scaffolding above the choir loft, then he stalked off the site.

"Any idea what that was all about?" Sam asked.

Annie explained that the rude young man was Vico, nephew of the older man who was still up on the scaffolding, Giuseppe

Brindesi, the Italian master craftsman and world-renowned stained glass expert. Vico was a wild, unpredictable ruffian, forever taunting his uncle, who had gotten him the job here.

When Giuseppe saw the party of visitors, he climbed down from the scaffolding—a long climb that most of the workers didn't bother with, instead using one of the construction cranes or aerial lifts to raise and lower themselves. But Giuseppe prided himself on his physical conditioning.

"I apologize for my nephew's behavior," he said to the group, shaking his head. Annie noticed that he looked quite upset. "Children today have no respect."

Giuseppe was a strong, stocky man in his late forties. Annie figured that he must have been a real heartbreaker about twenty years before. He had roguish eyes and boundless energy. And during the few moments each day when he wasn't completely absorbed in his stained glass work, he made sure that Annie felt the full effect of his masculine charm.

She'd originally met Giuseppe through Francesca Carlyle, who, as head of the United Path Church building committee, had highly recommended his work. Although he and his sister's family lived in San Francisco, Giuseppe spent a fair amount of time abroad, doing restoration work in the great cathedrals of Europe. In fact, he'd been out of the country for over a year recently, and Annie was thankful that he'd managed to squeeze this job into his schedule.

Giuseppe hugged Annie and smiled expansively at Darcy. "How is my little madonna?" he asked Darcy, who laughed. He had once told her that she resembled the Virgin in one of the most beautiful stained glass representations in St. Peter's in Rome. Darcy found it hilarious to be taken for a virgin, and an immaculate one at that.

"How is the work progressing?" Annie asked.

"It is satisfactory," he said. "There are some things I do not like, but that is not unusual."

Nothing was ever more than satisfactory for Giuseppe. He was not only a master but also a strict perfectionist.

"I've brought my boss with me today," Annie explained. "He wants to meet you."

Sam stepped forward and Annie made the introductions. When Sam put out his hand to Giuseppe in his usual friendly manner, Annie was surprised to see the older man hesitate. He was staring intently at Sam, a puzzled look in his eyes.

"Have we met before, signor?" Giuseppe asked.

Sam looked briefly surprised, then shrugged. "If so, I apologize for not knowing it," he said affably. "Put it down to my lousy memory for faces."

"Me, I have an excellent memory for the human face and form," Giuseppe said.

"And you re-create them exquisitely in the stained glass," said Annie. "We are very fortunate to have your talents. These will be the finest stained glass panels in the entire city!"

"In the entire country, if not the world," Giuseppe corrected. He was not a modest man.

"It looks as if you're almost finished with the rose window," Sid Canin noted.

"Yes. Tomorrow we start on the large panels over the doors in the transept aisle," Giuseppe said. He waved his hand toward the front of the cathedral, where there was a lot of hammering going on. "They are installing my scaffolding now."

"May I climb up there with you and get a closer look?" Darcy asked, squinting up at the rose window.

Giuseppe nodded and smiled. He seemed to have put aside the altercation with his nephew. "You are the architect, are you not, madonna? Yes, please, come up. There are several things I would like to show you."

"Be careful, Darcy," Sam called out as she started to climb.

Darcy turned and shot him a flirtatious grin. "Will you catch me if I fall?"

Sam laughed. "Hey, if you fall, I'm getting the hell out of the way!"

"You'd both better be careful," Sidney Canin said in his usual lugubrious tone. "If anybody falls and gets hurt on a construction project, we'll have OSHA breathing down our necks for the next decade."

When the tour was over and Annie emerged with her colleagues into the muddy lot where the construction trailers were parked, Jack Fletcher took her aside.

"We've got a problem," he said. "You saw what happened in there with Giuseppe and his nephew?"

Annie nodded. "Just the end of it, actually."

"We're going to have to let him go. For good this time."

"Ah, Jack, I know the boy is difficult, but I was hoping we could give him some leeway."

"Look, we've got no choice. The cops were here a little while ago with a warrant for Vico's arrest. It seems our boy has been running a cocaine ring on the side for several months."

"Dammit!" Annie said. No wonder Giuseppe had been so angry. He'd been trying to straighten Vico out for months. The boy was talented, too. But he'd been running with a gang since the age of ten or eleven. "Poor Giuseppe. He's such a hard worker and such a decent man. It must kill him to have such a reprobate nephew.''

''Yeah, probably. But we got no choice now, Annie. We gotta fire the kid.''

''You're right,'' she said slowly. ''Okay, let's do it.'' This was one aspect of being project manager that she really hated. Fortunately there had been very few firings on this job, but she worried about the workers involved every time it happened.

''It's got to be done,'' Fletcher said. ''I'll take care of the paperwork.''

''We were right, I think, to give him a chance, but we certainly can't employ fugitives from the law.''

Fletcher's expression changed. ''No, ma'am, I reckon one criminal associated with this project is more than enough.''

He was talking about Matthew Carlyle, she presumed, who was on trial for the murder of his wife. He was associated with this project since a significant portion of the building funds had been donated by him, via Francesca.

''Mr. Carlyle isn't technically a criminal,'' she reminded Fletcher. ''He hasn't been convicted yet.''

Fletcher blinked at her. ''Matthew Carlyle? No, he hasn't and he probably won't be. But all that proves is that the rich are different.''

Annie shrugged and excused herself. As she walked away, it struck her that there was something about Jack Fletcher that she didn't like. Although he was always polite, she didn't care for the way he deliberately tried to cut her out of the decision-making loop.

She had confronted him about it—in what she'd hoped was a pleasant, nonthreatening manner—and things had improved somewhat. But where Fletcher was concerned she had learned to ask a lot of questions and make sure she got complete answers.

It wasn't easy being a woman in a male-dominated and -controlled profession. But it *was* challenging.

Fletcher watched her walk away from him, her long slender legs, the subtle curve of her ass under her skirt. Annie Jefferson always dressed in an elegant professional manner, usually wearing tailored suits that displayed her trim body to perfection without flaunting it. She had great legs. Her breasts—which he'd once caught a glimpse of through a sheer blouse on a hot day—were to die for. And her face was lovely. Clear blue eyes, looking surprisingly innocent for a woman who had been married for several years. Something sensual about the mouth. A straight nose with tiny nostrils that flared occasionally, when she was angry or upset about something, although she was too cool ever to let any negative emotions register for long on her face.

Ever since he'd first met her, he'd wanted to fuck her. Just that. He didn't want a relationship with her. He didn't *do* relationships. He fucked—and rarely the same woman twice. He didn't need the hassle of a woman in his life, didn't want the inevitable conflict, the jockeying for control, the complaints that he was inattentive or unfaithful or unable to commit.

He also didn't want any woman poking into his past.

He just wanted to fuck as many females as possible. Preferably the good-looking, submissive ones.

Annie fascinated him. She was cool on the surface, but he

fantasized that underneath that elegant control was a woman who shared his own dark passions.

He had to be careful, though. Fucking female colleagues was not smart. These days you could get hit with a lawsuit for even seeming *interested* in fucking female colleagues. His real heyday had been years ago in the singles bars, where the women were so eager to get home for a quick roll that he barely had to do a thing. His looks had been good enough—and they'd loved his well-toned, muscular body.

But the bar scene wasn't the same since the advent of HIV. Especially here in the City of Fairies. He had his best luck these days in the gym where he worked out. Women were into weight training these days. And there in the exercise room in front of the full-length mirrors that adorned every wall, he could check them out and they could check him out and it could all be arranged hardly without saying a word.

Trouble was, Fletcher didn't go for the hard-body type. He liked his women soft. He wanted to run his palms and fingers over soft juicy breasts, not hard pecs. He didn't want some bitch who could wrestle and pin him. He wanted one who was fluttery and helpless in his arms. He wanted a shy, reluctant lady, not a muscle-pumping bull dyke.

Despite the fact that she worked at least part of every day in a hard-hat construction site, Annie Jefferson always looked like a lady. She dressed like a lady, too, in suits and blouses and shiny shoes with little heels and matching handbags. She wore pale lipstick, and her perfect little fingernails were always painted soft pink or beige, never harsh and red. She was sweet and gentle, with a well-modulated voice and a patient smile even when things weren't going well. She was all woman. She was everything he'd ever wanted.

He loved to picture it—Annie Jefferson's slim, elegant body naked under his, straining and thrashing, a lovely sheen of perspiration rising on her honey-gold skin, her head tipped back, her eyes wide with passion—or, better, with fear—and her soft lips widening in a scream. . . .

One night.

It was all he wanted, all he needed.

One night that she would remember forever.

Chapter Five

Darcy laid out the tarot deck and pondered the cards.

"I wish you wouldn't do that around me," Annie said.

Darcy looked up, blinking. "I thought you didn't believe in it."

"I don't. Well . . . I don't think I do," she added with a smile. "But you always look so serious, and I find myself half expecting some gloomy death and disaster card to show up."

"There've been a lot of those gloomy death and disaster cards lately, it's true," Darcy said cheerfully. "But I've also seen some good cards for you. A strong, exciting man. Passion. Romance."

"Now that's the sort of thing I want to hear—good cards, predicting wonderful events and summoning handsome, sensitive, capable-of-commitment men!"

Darcy giggled. "Hey, they're my cards—I've got dibs on those guys, if they exist."

She and Darcy had gotten together for supper, as they often did on weeknights after work. Tonight was Annie's turn to cook, and she was tossing a salad while Darcy read the tarot.

"So what do you see in store for yourself?" Annie asked as she popped a loaf of San Francisco's famous sourdough bread into the oven.

The lower level of the house was open space, without walls separating the living, dining, and kitchen areas. Annie could see Darcy glaring at the latest spread on the coffee table before scattering it with her hands.

"Trouble," she said glumly. "Why'd I ever take up this New Agey stuff anyway? It's depressing as hell. You'd think I'd be resigned by now to being a dull person leading an uninspired life."

"Nonsense!" said Annie. "You are by no means a dull person. Everybody adores you, Darcy."

And it was true, she thought. She wasn't just complimenting her best friend. Women liked Darcy because she was unpretentious, lively, and empathetic. Men liked her because she was easygoing, friendly, logical, and quick with her hearty laugh.

"Well, I hate my life," Darcy said. "I wish I could be more like you. You're so polite to people, so diplomatic, so ladylike, so serene." Darcy idly picked up the remote control and flicked on the TV. "Don't you ever just feel like boiling over?"

Annie bit her lip and smiled. Did she? Certainly she *used* to feel like boiling over. She'd spent the first half of her life, in fact, doing just that.

Born to a single mother who was sent to prison for armed robbery when Annie was three, Annie was shuffled from one foster home in the Los Angeles area to another. She had adored her mother and could not understand why the police had taken her away. She'd hated the police after that.

Anger and grief over losing her mother came out in disruptive behavior, and by the time she was seven, Annie was notorious in the Department of Social Services for "acting out" and "recalcitrance." Foster parents couldn't deal with her. She was rude, combative, and a major behavior problem in every elementary school she was sent to. Despite placing well above average in intelligence tests, the various social workers who were assigned to her case reported that she appeared to have little interest in learning.

There were a few dedicated teachers who worked hard to get through to her. One of them used to take Annie home with her after school, feed her milk and cookies, and tell her wonderful stories about heroes and villains, gods and goddesses. The teacher even gave Annie a book of her very own with myths and legends in it. It was too hard for her to read, but she loved to look at the color plate of Perseus with his mirrored shield and his mighty sword fighting Medusa. And the one of Eros rescuing Psyche, who was chained to a rock over the sea, waiting for a dread monster to come and devour her.

The foster family she was living with at the time were strict born-again, evangelical, Word-of-the-Lord Christians. When her foster father found Annie trying to spell out the words in the book of myths one evening before supper, he took the volume from her, leafed through it, and declared it impious and sacrilegious. He burned her precious book in the fireplace, unmoved by Annie's screams of protest and rage, and then he whipped her soundly with his belt.

Annie ran away, swearing that she would kill herself if they tried to send her back. Instead they sent her to a group home with other difficult-to-place children. By the time she was ten years old it was clear to Annie that nobody wanted her . . . and nobody ever would.

She took to thieving the next year. Various social workers and foster parents had drilled it into her head over the years that she was a thief's daughter, so she figured she might as well live up to her heritage.

She stole, and she lied about stealing. She did it less out of need than out of rage. Everything that had ever mattered to her had been stolen from her.

By the time she was thirteen she'd been arrested three times and was well on her way to proving the curse of her genes.

With her blond hair, her pretty, waifish face, and her angelic turquoise eyes, Annie's best scam was to mimic a scared child from a good home who had somehow gotten lost in the city. She could spot a bleeding-heart sucker a mile away. She'd squeeze out a few tears and whimpers, mixed in with an occasional melting smile, and the marks would buy her food and clothing, ice cream, taxi or bus fare "home." When she'd taken them for all she could, she'd disappear, usually with their wallets as well.

It worked fine until the day she tried her game on Charlie Jefferson, then a college student, who proved to be not as soft a touch as he looked. Annie was fourteen by this time but small for her age. She hid her breasts under a baggy shirt and tried to look ten.

Charlie gave her a five-dollar bill on her first appeal, but she'd caught a glimpse of his wallet, which looked thick. So she distracted him—or tried to—and went for the wallet, but he was quicker than she was. He got a good grip on her wrist, and all her squirming, kicking, and yelling Robbery! Rape! and Murder! didn't unnerve him one bit.

He held her firmly until the cops came, and then, to her utter amazement, he told the officers that she was his kid sister who'd run away from somewhere in Orange County and he was taking her home. Because the officer in charge didn't know her, and probably because both she and Charlie looked so clean-cut, he'd turned them both loose. Charlie, whose grip on her arm hadn't for a moment wavered, then dragged her away to his car.

"You're a child molester!" she cried, resisting every step of the way.

"I'm a college student," he retorted. "My *parents* are child molesters. They collect incorrigible brats like you."

It turned out that his parents were educators who ran a progressive school for troubled adolescents. The emphasis was on individual responsibility rather than discipline, and one of the first courses Annie was offered was in Greek and Roman mythology. Even so, she continued to be rebellious, and it took the Jeffersons several months to win her heart and convince her that someone, at last, did want her.

She didn't see much of Charlie, who was away at school studying architecture, but she never forgot that he was the one who had rescued her. She was a beautiful young woman of eighteen when he came home to spend an entire summer. The mysterious chemistry that had initially drawn them together began working once again.

At first the relationship seemed doomed. When she tried to fit in to the Jefferson's social world, she felt completely outclassed. Although she had learned to behave herself, she had not learned the finer aspects of etiquette—the right things to say, the right forms of address, the right silverware to use, the proper way to dress, the correct subjects for polite conversation, the right way to conduct herself in every situation. "I'll never be good enough for you," she told Charlie, who laughed and reassured her. Anything she needed to learn, he would teach her.

He was a very persuasive young man. Like a hero from one of her myths, he had played Pygmalion to her Galatea, discovering within her intelligence, ambition, and a true hunger for learning. Annie flung herself into her studies. She vowed never, ever, to make him sorry for loving her.

With Charlie's help, she finished high school and enrolled in college. He taught her everything he knew and loved about buildings and encouraged her artistic side. For a while she had dreamed of following his footsteps into architecture, but eventually she had chosen interior design, and during the course of graduate school she'd shifted into corporate design.

And she and Charlie had gotten married.

Together, they'd founded Fabrications.

She hadn't realized how dependent she was on him until he died. Or how hard it was to make her way in a world deprived of magic and myth.

"Annie?" Darcy's voice brought her crashing back to the present. "Come here, and take a look at this." Darcy increased the volume on the television. "Looks like the jury's back in the courtroom. And they're smiling and making eye contact. Shit, I think that scumbag is going to walk after all."

Annie hurried into the living room area. She didn't have to ask "what jury?" The murder trial of Matthew Carlyle was one of the biggest crime stories to hit the country in recent years.

"You mean they've acquitted him?"

"They haven't announced the verdict yet, but it looks like the judge is about to say something."

The panel of eight women and four men were shown seated in the jury box, and the judge, a middle-aged woman who had been profiled by all the local and national TV stations and newspapers, was speaking to the bailiff. It had been a long trial, and every argument made by both the defense and the prosecution had been analyzed endlessly in the press. The closing arguments had been presented to the jury several days ago, and since then they had been deliberating.

Annie had had mixed feelings about the trial from the beginning. It was as if two completely separate processes had been inextricably linked to one another—the building of the cathedral and the trial of Matthew Carlyle. Because Francesca Carlyle had been the prime mover behind building the cathedral, her violent death and her husband's subsequent trial had thrown a pall over the project.

Ironically, as the cathedral had been slowly constructed stone by stone, Matthew Carlyle's reputation and credibility had been deconstructed in the same slow manner. There was no doubt about the outcome of Matthew Carlyle's trial in the press: In their view, he had already been judged and found guilty.

At least with the cathedral, something was being built rather than torn down.

The camera shifted to the defendant, who was sitting stiffly beside his attorney, his face was drawn, and there were visible lines around his mouth that Annie was sure hadn't been there that day two and a half years ago when he'd crushed her hopes of saving Fabrications. *How the mighty are fallen*, she thought.

According to the prosecution, it was Carlyle who had inflicted the heavy blow to Francesca's face that had caused her to fall and strike her head. Afterward, he'd thrown her unconscious body over the side of the yacht and in the Bay, where she drowned.

Carlyle's motive, said the district attorney, was simple: If Francesca had carried out her threat to divorce him, he would have lost half of his $4 billion fortune.

As Annie settled down on the sofa to watch the verdict, she focused on Matt Carlyle's face. She was amazed to feel a pulse of sympathy for him. How awful it must be to sit in a courtroom waiting to hear yourself judged by twelve strangers.

Dressed in a conservative dark suit and tasteful tie that his jury consultants had no doubt recommended, he sat upright, a model of restraint and self-control. His face was expressionless, but every now and then the camera caught a flicker of anguish in his eyes. It seemed to Annie that it was all the more vivid because of his efforts to hide it.

He doesn't deserve my pity, she reminded herself. *If I must feel sorry for someone, it should be for Francesca.*

"Has the jury reached a verdict?"

"Yes, Your Honor, we have."

Annie felt her heart rate accelerate. Had he done it? He was certainly ruthless enough.

"We find the defendant, Matthew Carlyle, not guilty," the jury forewoman said.

The courtroom erupted in pandemonium.

"You see, I told you," Darcy said with disgust. "A rich

man can get away with anything in this country. So much for the American system of justice. Francesca Carlyle lies unavenged in her grave because the law will always side with the members of the power elite."

Annie couldn't think of much to say. Essentially she agreed with Darcy, although she didn't think the verdict indicated a social conspiracy. "I guess that as far as the jury was concerned, the prosecution didn't prove its case. At least not beyond a reasonable doubt."

"Of course it did! Anyway, who else had any reason to kill her?"

"I don't know," Annie said. "Maybe the man she was having the affair with."

"*If* she was having an affair."

Carlyle's high-priced defense team had asserted that Francesca's behavior that night at her party had been an embarrassing but oft-repeated feature of a turbulent marriage. She was an alcoholic who frequently had affairs and threatened to leave, but when sober she always changed her mind. After the party had ended and all the guests had gone, she and Matthew had reconciled. Her death the next morning was a tragic and unexpected blow to her grieving husband.

The defense had further asserted that it must have been her lover who had murdered her, likely because he was enraged at losing the chance to marry Francesca and her $2 billion.

But the lover, if she'd had one, had never come forward, nor had the police ever figured out who he was.

Annie had wondered several times about Sid Canin, who had looked so possessively at Francesca on the final night of her life. Like everybody else at the party, he'd been questioned by the police, but there couldn't have been any evidence against him, since Sid had not been called as a witness at the trial.

Could a person have an affair without anybody ever finding out? Probably, Annie thought. No one had ever questioned *her* about what had nearly happened between herself and Matthew several years ago in England.

Abruptly, the cameras cut away from the analysts in the studio to the street outside the courthouse. Carlyle was emerging with his attorney. Annie expected him to be whisked away into a car, but instead the acquitted billionaire strode right up to the reporters whom he had been ignoring for months. They rushed to surround him, sticking their microphones in his face.

"I have a statement to make," he said over the voice of his attorney, who seemed to be about to say something himself. "I am grateful to the people of California for hearing my case and evaluating the evidence fairly. As far as I personally am concerned, justice has been done. But—" he paused for a second, looking intensely into the dozens of cameras pointed at his face, "justice has not yet been done on Francesca's behalf. She was brutally murdered. Her murderer is still at large. The San Francisco police, regretfully, stopped searching for him in their zeal to develop a case against me. I consider that a travesty."

He stopped speaking and was immediately assaulted with questions from the reporters, all of which he ignored. "That's all I have to say at this time," he said, then belatedly added, "Thank you."

He had sounded sincere, Annie thought. He had sounded as if he really thought that the killer was still out there.

Matthew Carlyle got into the waiting limousine and was driven away.

A free man.

That night, Annie could not sleep. Her mind kept replaying memories. She tried to focus them on Charlie and all the myriad joys of their life together, but memories can be wild horses, impossible to harness. And that night her memories were all of Matt Carlyle.

She had been flying to London for a meeting with a wealthy client who had hired Fabrications to design the San Francisco branch offices of his international corporation. The client had sent her first-class tickets and arranged first-class accommodations at the Dorchester Hotel in London.

Annie had never been to London, and she'd hoped that Charlie would accompany her, but Charlie had one quirk that he had never been able to conquer—he was afraid of flying. There was no way he would get on a plane and fly ten hours from San Francisco to London.

So she'd gone alone. And seated beside her in the first-class section was Matthew Carlyle, also traveling to London on business.

The dim interior of an airliner during a night flight to Europe can be a strangely intimate place. You meet a stranger, exchange a little personal information—no last names, of course—and sometimes something clicks. You end up saying things to the stranger that you would otherwise never say. In most cases, you're secure in knowing that after the plane lands, you'll never see your seatmate again.

But in this case, going first class all the way meant that

Annie and Carlyle were staying at the same deluxe hotel. And when he heard that she had hopes of doing some touring in London, he told her that it was his favorite city in the world, and he offered—no, he'd insisted—on showing her around.

Since they were both working during the week, they arranged to see the sights that weekend. They spent Saturday visiting Buckingham Palace, the houses of Parliament, the Tower of London, and the British Museum. Annie was impressed with Carlyle's encyclopedic knowledge of British history. He even knew the city well enough to take her to several lovely little historic pubs and coffeehouses for occasional breaks from sightseeing.

She felt the chemistry between them right from the start. But she'd been married for five years to a man she dearly loved, and it was a simple matter to convince herself that what she was feeling was just a silly kind of schoolgirl crush that the sophisticated Matt Carlyle was completely unaware of and absolutely immune to.

She didn't discover that he was not only aware but interested until Sunday afternoon, when they took a car trip to Stratford-upon-Avon, the birthplace of Shakespeare.

Until then she had seen him only in the most trim and proper business suits, but for this excursion he wore jeans, a casual shirt, and running shoes. Somehow this brought him down to earth, making him seem less like a wealthy captain of the computer industry and more like an ordinary guy. He'd rented a small MG for the journey, dismissing the limousine and driver who had been chauffeuring them around the city. Being within its close confines as they drove through the English countryside created an almost electric sense of intimacy.

The day had started out fine, and they'd explored both Shakespeare's birthplace and Ann Hathaway's antique thatched cottage under a fine August sun. But the weather had turned progressively gloomy, and when they'd emerged that evening from the theater where they had watched a stirring production of *Henry V,* they'd had to run back to the car in a downpour.

They were both drenched to the skin and laughing when Carlyle stopped fumbling with the door latch and simply pulled her into his arms, pressed her back against the steaming wet car, and kissed her ravenously on the mouth. Before she could give it a moment's thought, her arms had wrapped themselves around his shoulders, and she was entangling her tongue with his, matching his passion with her own.

Somehow they'd managed to get into the car, where the irresistible magic of hungry male and receptive female continued. She felt heady with desire as his heat, his touch, his scent combined to assault her senses. She'd forgotten who she was, where she was, what she was doing. All that mattered was the jagged-lightning rush of passion driving its arrows deep into her soul.

She'd thought often, later, that if they had been in the backseat of the limousine that they'd used for their touring of London, anything might have happened. But the rented MG was tiny, and there was a gear shift between them. Carlyle had finally broken off the embrace to whisper, "We passed a pub a couple of miles back. I'm sure they have a room, we can dry off and . . ."

The reality of what they were doing had penetrated her at those words. She was a married woman—what was she *doing*?

"No," she'd murmured. "No, please."

And he had held her in his arms and tried to convince her: *"Come with me. Don't think about it. Just come."*

"I can't. Please, don't ask me."

"You can. You've come this far. Some things are meant to be."

She had told him no. Finally and irrevocably.

But she had never forgotten the way he had made her feel; not during the days when she had hated him and blamed him for the loss of Fabrications, not even when he was accused of the brutal murder of his wife.

She hated him still; she blamed him still. But, ruthless though she believed him to be, she'd been unable to make up her mind about his involvement in Francesca's brutal murder.

Was Matthew Carlyle innocent, and justly acquitted?

Or had the state just freed a coldhearted killer?

Chapter Six

Matthew Carlyle sat in his corner office on the third floor of the new building that housed Powerdyme and stared out the window at San Francisco Bay. A crystal tumbler of the finest single-blend scotch stood untouched on the desk at his elbow. Faintly, he could smell it, but he left it alone.

The view from his office was magnificent, but the sun was too bright on his computer screen, and despite the climate control, the room was invariably hot. It was also cramped. And the floor-to-ceiling windows made him feel too exposed.

The new building was, in fact, a disaster.

He hated it, and his employees were none too happy in it either. And it was already too small.

Although sales and profits were up and Powerdyme continued to dominate its end of the software business, a recent survey had shown that job satisfaction within the company had declined, always a troubling indicator. But it was unclear whether that was due to the new building or to the economy or to the fact that the CEO had just spent more than a year in jail.

After the narrow confines of a stark cell in a correctional institution, Carlyle had figured he'd be overjoyed to be back in his sunny office. But the opposite was true. He hated it here, and he'd never been able to work productively in an environment he hated. This damn building had been wrong from the start.

Just like everything else in my life.

There are things you don't think about while you're locked up in jail, on trial for murdering your wife. You'd go crazy if you did. You don't think about the good times—those early days of courtship, surrender, and joy when he and Francesca had still been in love. And neither do you think of the bad times—the all-too-many days after she'd started drinking when you *did* want her out of your life. How could you persuade a jury to set you free if they knew that you had occasionally committed murder *in your heart*?

None of them could possibly know what it had been like to live with a beautiful but volatile woman like Francesca, whose very existence seemed calculated to make men crazy. She'd been a superb actress, and only the few people she'd allowed close to her recognized her for the controlling, manipulative, deeply insecure woman she was.

But you don't think about that—you simply couldn't allow yourself to remember all the torments she had put you through. And you especially don't dwell on the fact that your unfaithful wife was pregnant, and that DNA tests admitted as evidence during the trial by your attorneys had proven that you were the father of her child. The marriage had been in trouble, yes, but if he'd known she was pregnant, after so many years of trying to have a child, he'd have tried harder to hold things together. Much harder, dammit.

He was forty-one years old. As the tabloids had proclaimed during the trial, for the last twenty years he had "led a charmed life." He was the founder of one of the world's most successful businesses and was, journalistic hyperbole for once accurate, a billionaire. But, like many extremely successful people, he'd discovered that all the money in the world couldn't buy happiness, serenity, or peace of mind. Neither could it protect him from the slow-grinding wheels of the American system of justice.

His friends—what few he had left—had advised him to let it go. Put it behind him. Don't look back.

But his friends hadn't lived for a year and a half in a seven-by-nine-foot cell with a narrow bunk and a stainless steel seatless toilet, eating vile, fatty, unidentifiable food, and checked every fifteen minutes by a guard. They hadn't tossed in sleeplessness and despair, alive with the knowledge that twelve strangers could look into your eyes and judge your mind, body, and soul on the basis of the theories and distortions they heard in the courtroom.

Francesca was dead. But he was still alive, and now, finally, he was free.

Somehow, dammit, he had to get his life back.

Matthew picked up the phone and called someone he knew he could absolutely count on—the Reverend Barbara Rae Acker.

She was a wise and compassionate woman who, despite her friendship with Francesca, had been there for him throughout the trial. He was not a religious man, but that did not matter. Barbara Rae's goodness was not limited to believers alone.

Maybe she could help him figure out what the hell to do with the rest of his life.

"I love him," the teenager whispered.

Annie took the girl's trembling hands in both of hers. They were talking together in a private room at Barbara Rae Acker's Compassion of Angels youth center in the Mission district, where Annie volunteered two evenings a week. The youth center was just a block away from the cathedral construction site, so it was easy for Annie to stop by after work.

The teenager who had come in for counseling had an old, familiar story to tell. Paolina was seventeen, poor, and beautiful. Half Hispanic, she had unusual coloring—golden skin and natural blond hair that was so long it nearly brushed her hips. Her face was a perfect oval with strong, molded features and flawless skin that glowed like the finest polished marble.

The eldest of three sisters and three brothers, she had an intact nuclear family—increasingly rare, it seemed to Annie. Paolina's parents were very strict. Her father disciplined all his children with a broad leather strap.

Paolina had always followed the rules, she said, weeping. She had obeyed her parents, studied hard, helped out her mother with the little ones, cooked and cleaned and, for the past year, worked part-time as a seamstress to bring the family some extra income.

"I am not a bad girl," she whispered.

"Of course you're not," Annie assured her.

Paolina had never had a boyfriend, she said, until last

winter, when she met the young man she loved. She'd never met anybody like him. He followed no rules, respected no authority—although he did believe in and fear God.

"He told me what we were doing was wrong in the eyes of the Lord. So we tried to stop." Her dark eyes were glistening. "But I love him so much and when he touched me it felt as if God Himself was smiling on us. Do you know what I mean?"

Annie nodded. It had felt like that with Charlie sometimes.

"But how could He be smiling if this happened?" the girl asked, looking down at her swelling belly. "I feel so much shame!"

Paolina was four months pregnant. Despite altering her clothes in an attempt to hide her weight gain, she was starting to show. The preceding night her parents had found out, and her father had threatened to beat her with the strap. "Mama begged him not to, and Father beat her instead," the girl explained. "Then he told me to leave his house and never show my face again under his roof."

"Ah, Paolina, I'm so sorry. Perhaps when he is calmer, he will reconsider."

"No, he won't," Paolina said. "It's not just that I have shamed him, but who I have shamed him with. He hates Vico. He cannot forgive him. You see, Vico did something against the law. Then the police were looking for him, and he lost his job and now he has gone into hiding."

The entire story suddenly shifted into much sharper focus. "Wait a moment. Your boyfriend's name is Vico? Is that short for Ludovico? Ludovico Brindesi?"

"Ludovico Genese," the girl said. "But he is related to the Brindesi family, yes—Giuseppe Brindesi is his uncle." She looked at Annie apprehensively. "You have heard about him? From the police, maybe?"

Annie shook her head. "I know the people he used to work for, that's all." *And I approved his firing. . . .*

"He's not a bad man," Paolina said. "He's just a little wild, and he's made some mistakes."

"They're after him for a drug rap, aren't they? Does he use cocaine or other drugs?"

Paolina shook her head fiercely. "He thinks they're foolish. They rot the brain, he says. He would never use drugs."

But apparently he had no qualms about selling them to people who did use them. According to Barbara Rae, who had had several run-ins with him, Vico had been a troublemaker for years. He'd run with gangs since childhood.

And now he was on the run from the law. If Paolina was sheltering him, she could become an accessory after the fact. "Paolina, do you know where Vico is?"

She shook her head vigorously.

Annie sensed that she was lying. But when the girl broke down in sobs, Annie did the only thing that seemed appropriate—she pulled Paolina close and hugged her.

"Come, we'll talk to Barbara Rae. She'll know just what to do. Barbara Rae is very persuasive—she might be able to persuade your father to relent."

Although Annie spoke with confidence, she was filled with trepidation. She knew Barbara Rae to be an excellent mediator, and it was remarkable how often people changed their minds after she exercised her gentle art of moral persuasion. But she was not always successful. There was something strong, yet tragic, about Paolina, and Annie felt afraid for her.

They were getting up to go find Barbara Rae when, behind them, Annie heard a door slam.

"Where is she?" boomed a male voice, and Paolina's eyes went wild. She jumped to her feet, whispering, *"Madre de Dios,"* under her breath, then, "Vico!"

A dark-haired young man came striding into the room, and for an instant all Annie could think was: *Here he is, the young Hades, dark and wild, determined to snatch away the pale Persephone and bear her away to his private Underworld.*

He was as startlingly beautiful as Paolina. But he was dark, with shiny black hair falling too long over his neck and ears, in defiance of the latest teenage style. His face was classically Roman—a long arrogant oval with an aquiline nose and a determined chin. His eyes were black, with pinpricks of fire in their depths. He was of medium height, stocky and muscular, and he looked the way the still-handsome Giuseppe must have looked twenty years earlier.

Annie had seen him working on the construction site with his uncle, had overheard several of their flash-fire arguments. She had seen him stalk off, defiant, not caring what anybody thought of him.

He was seventeen years old.

Smarter than anybody.

Braver.

He knew what he wanted.

He wasn't going to let anything stand in his way.

Certainly not his pale, submissive girlfriend or the woman who had, along with Jack Fletcher, discharged him from the construction job that might have given him his one chance to make something of his life.

He walked straight up to Annie, the expression on his face coldly furious. Then he reached out for Paolina's hand, which seemed to be drawn to him, like iron to a powerful magnet.

"They said she was talking to a youth counselor," he spat. "Is that what you call yourself here?"

"I work as a volunteer, yes," Annie said.

"I'll bet you didn't tell her that you're the bitch who fired me from my job."

Paolina's eyes flew to Annie's face. Annie hardened herself. She knew his type, all too well. She knew intimately the extent of the betrayal he felt.

"And did you tell Paolina why you were fired?" she countered. "Or did you lie to her about selling drugs to children?"

Something flashed in those dark, mesmerizing eyes. "I do not lie, and I wasn't selling drugs," he said, and jerked Paolina's hand. "Come. We are leaving."

"She needs help, Vico," Annie said. "You're a fugitive from the police. They're looking for you, and eventually they'll find you. And when they do and you're in jail awaiting trial, what's going to happen to the mother of your unborn child?"

Ignoring her, he turned abruptly, and Paolina turned with him. She was bound to him as if by invisible cords.

"You want to be a man, Vico. You want the respect of a man. But until you learn to accept responsibility for your actions, you are still a boy, and a selfish one at that."

"Fuck you, Mistress Project Manager," Vico retorted. "You see nothing, you know nothing, and the people you work for are slime."

The door slammed behind them as he swept Paolina out of the youth center.

Annie sighed.

It was difficult to be judgmental. Vico reminded her too vividly of her younger self.

Chapter Seven

"Trouble?" a velvety voice inquired.

Annie turned. Barbara Rae Acker had entered the room. "Did you hear that?"

"The tail end of it," Barbara Rae said. "A very passionate young man."

"We fired him from his construction job at the cathedral."

"Annie, you had no choice. He's on the run from the police."

"He claims he wasn't selling drugs, Barbara Rae."

The minister shrugged. "I've heard that too, from some of the other kids on the street. They're saying the police have him confused with a pusher who looks a lot like Vico. It could be true. On the other hand, Vico has been in various kinds of trouble for years, and I wouldn't put anything past him."

"I was getting through to Paolina, I think," Annie said. "But when she found out who I was, she felt betrayed. We've lost her now."

Barbara Rae came up behind her and gently squeezed her shoulders. "We can't save all of them, Annie. You know that."

"Yeah, I know that," she agreed, but still she shook her head, wishing she could.

"Listen to me, honey. What you need is a nice big piece of girdlebuster pie."

"Please! I've been trying to lose five pounds for months!"

"Nonsense. You need to *gain* at least that much. Now, you come home with me tonight for a proper home-cooked supper. Gotta get some meat on your bones, girl!"

Annie smiled. "What exactly *is* girdlebuster pie?"

"Well, I'll tell you the ingredients, but don't ask me how many grams of fat it has, honey, or we'll both be too frightened to eat a bite!"

"I'd love to come, Barbara Rae," Annie said. "But I've really got to get back to the office tonight."

Barbara Rae sighed. "They sure keep you busy over at Brody Associates."

"No, it's me. I've turned into a workaholic."

Again, Barbara Rae squeezed her shoulders. Her back massages were heavenly. "You've had a lot of losses, honey. That'll do it to anyone. You need your security, and no one can blame you for that. I just worry about you, that's all. You're still young, and you're missing out on life's pleasures. A man, some leisure time, a piece of girdlebuster pie . . ."

Impulsively Annie stood and gave her a hug. Despite the ravages of age and a fondness for rich foods, Barbara Rae had a slim, sturdy body. At fifty-five, the indefatigable minister and shining light of the United Path Church congregation was vigorous and energetic, and she was rapidly becoming something of a legend in San Francisco.

Barbara Rae had a gift for reaching out to people and touching their hearts and minds. Her work among the poor, the sick, and the disadvantaged citizens of San Francisco had earned her the reputation of an American Mother Teresa, but she could be pragmatic and hardheaded when dealing with the wealthy and the sophisticated folks whom she approached for funds. Barbara Rae was one of those rare people who are charismatic in every stratum of society, projecting herself in a manner that made people blind to her sex, her religion, her race, and her class.

Annie had met her in the aftermath of Charlie's death and the loss of Fabrications. Early one morning, unable to sleep and feeling as if she was losing her mind, she had gotten up from her lonely bed and wandered the hilly streets of downtown San Francisco. She'd climbed Nob Hill and, panting from exertion, seen the gray stone of Grace Cathedral, an Episcopal church. She'd entered the huge old building, finding it nearly empty and very dark, the morning sunlight just beginning to brighten the magnificent stained glass. She'd sat in one of the pews at the back and tried to pray. But Charlie's death remained a bitter taste in the back of her throat, and she felt abandoned by God.

Barbara Rae Acker had sat down behind her, and later, when Annie rose, weeping, to stagger out of the beautiful Gothic church that, for her, was empty of the presence of God, Barbara Rae touched her shoulder gently and stopped her. "Before you leave," she said, "there's something I want you to try."

Annie looked into her face and thought that if God *did*

exist, He was looking out at the world through the wise, kind eyes of this tall, plain woman with kinky gray hair and thick, work-calloused hands. All the compassion in the world was contained in those chocolate-brown eyes; it shone through her like a beacon.

"Try what?" Annie asked.

Barbara Rae pointed to the floor on which they were standing. On it was a pattern, a massive circular design consisting of a large number of broken concentric circles. "The labyrinth," she said. "It's a reproduction of a similar ancient design in the floor of the cathedral at Chartres. It's a walking meditation. You simply enter the maze there, at the beginning, and follow the circular paths back and forth, around and around, until eventually you arrive at the center. It's not really a maze, since there are no false trails. Once you start, you will always find your way."

"Why?" Annie asked halfheartedly, wanting only to leave and lacking the faith for any serious attempt at meditation.

"Try it," Barbara Rae said gently but insistently, so Annie did.

Later, Annie had tried to understand what had happened that morning—why Barbara Rae had managed to reach her when God could not. Part of it was simply the serenity of the walking meditation. As she'd walked the narrow pathways on the floor, she'd felt a sense of connection with all the generations of people who had walked there before her, both in San Francisco and in Chartres where the labyrinth had originated.

And Barbara Rae was right in that the maze appeared to be complex and full of mysterious twists and turns and dead ends, but once you began walking, you saw that there was only one true path, and that it led, without fail, to the heart.

When she reached the center, Annie felt lighter somehow, as if her burdens had been lifted from her shoulders. She didn't see Barbara Rae when her journey was over, but when she left the church, the woman was waiting for her in the garden outside. "I come here often, although it's not my church," Barbara Rae explained. "God can be found in many places."

Impulsively, Annie had hugged her, and they'd exchanged addresses and phone numbers. It was the beginning of a friendship that had become central to Annie's life.

"It's going to be a fine cathedral, isn't it?" Barbara Rae said now, as they looked out the window of the youth center toward the towering building that had taken shape next door.

"It surely is," Annie said.

"A living symbol of heaven's beauty and our human striving toward the divine. Beauty touches us all; even those with the hardest of hearts can be moved by beauty."

Annie smiled. "No one has a hard heart around you, Barbara Rae. It's just not possible."

"There is some darkness in every heart," the minister replied. "Some of us are more resistant to it, so the evil remains nothing more than an unrealized potential. But the temptations of life are great, and, like young Vico, most of us have done something we sorely regret at some point in our lives."

Annie smiled. Barbara Rae was her moral barometer. "But not you. I can't imagine that an evil thought would ever enter your mind."

Barbara Rae shook her head sadly. "Ah, then, my child,

you do not know me. I assure you, the blackness of my soul seems at times to me darker than the hue of my skin."

Nonsense, Annie thought. "I just can't believe that."

But Barbara Rae looked serious and sad. "I found God at a time when I was just about as low as a body can go. Truly I died and went to hell, but somehow, through God's grace, I was born again."

Despite being a minister, Barbara Rae didn't usually use much religious imagery, but when she did she was utterly serious about it. Annie realized that she knew little, if anything, about Barbara Rae's life before she had found her calling.

She did know that she came from somewhere in the South, and she suspected, given her age and her race, that she had not had an easy life. But it was difficult to imagine that Barbara Rae had ever done anything that could truly be called evil.

"Well, I can sure relate to starting out wrong in life and then, through the grace of *someone*, straightening out," Annie said with a wry smile.

Barbara Rae nodded, then gave her a quick hug. She was one of the few people to whom Annie had talked about her past, one of the few people who knew that the well-educated, well-dressed, reasonably successful, and extremely competent architectural designer had once been as deeply troubled as any of the teenagers she counseled.

Charlie had saved her, and she in turn was determined to extend that same helping hand to others.

Surely there was something she could do for Paolina and Vico.

∗　∗　∗

Annie stopped at the supermarket on the way home that night. When she got to her apartment, she set the bag of groceries on her kitchen counter and began flipping through the day's mail.

The letter looked perfectly ordinary—a business-size envelope with her name and address printed in block letters. There was no return address, and it looked like a piece of junk mail. It was the sort of thing anyone else might have tossed, but Annie was meticulous about opening all her mail.

Inside was a single sheet of 8 ½-by-11 paper, printed, like the envelope, in large block letters. At the top it read: THE WORK OF THE DEVIL.

> *It is a SIN in the eyes of the Lord to build a monument to human GREED and PRIDE. All those millions should have gone to help the poor and the sick, not to this puffed-up Babel of vanity.*
>
> *Stop the building. Tear it down and feed the poor. If you fail to heed the command of the Lord, behold, the Tower will crack, tumble, and crash to the earth as the God of Hosts strikes down evil-doers.*
>
> *Take heed that it fall not on ye, Mrs. Anne Jefferson, ye harlot of Satan.*
> > *Jehovah's Pitchfork*

Wonderful, Annie thought. Threats, misogyny, religious mania. *And* he knew her name.

Chapter Eight

"You're awfully quiet Sam. Is something the matter?" Darcy asked.

She and Sam Brody were sitting in a small restaurant in Sausalito, with a view of San Francisco Bay. Darcy had chosen the restaurant carefully, for its excellent food and its romantic atmosphere.

She'd hoped it would be a perfect dinner, followed by a leisurely evening of long, slow lovemaking. She wanted to re-create the mood of the first night they had spent together, just two months ago.

Sam had called her that evening and invited her to go for a drive over the Golden Gate Bridge to Sausalito; he had suggested doing a little shopping at the shops along the water-front there, a proposition that amused and delighted Darcy. How many men actually invited a woman to go shopping? It was irresistible.

He'd taken her to a romantic seaside restaurant for dinner,

and afterward, as they'd walked back along the shore road listening to the lapping of the gentle waves, Sam had pulled her into his arms and invited her to come home with him.

She'd made a token protest: "Sam, if something goes wrong—"

He had taken her hand lightly, his warm fingers caressing hers. She had felt the pull of his calm and confident sensuality. It had been easy to imagine how his hands would feel on her naked skin. . . .

"You feel it too, don't you?" he'd asked.

She'd admitted it.

"So what do we do, then? Repress the attraction? Ignore it? Pretend it doesn't exist?"

"That would probably be wise, Sam. I like working for Brody Associates, and God knows I need my job." But even as she spoke, she had allowed her body to melt against his.

He had laughed in that lighthearted, joyous, delighted way that was so often heard around the office and said, "Hell, Darcy, I've always had trouble being wise." Then he had bent his head to take her lips.

So it had begun. The most wonderful, passionate, and just plain fun love affair of her life.

But tonight Sam was in a strange, uncharacteristically quiet mood.

She reached out and gently stroked his hand. "What's wrong? Tell me what's worrying you."

He looked at her and slowly shook his head. "Jesus, Darcy." He sounded miserable.

She heard alarm bells in her mind. She'd never before seen Sam in a bad mood. "This isn't like you, babe," she said.

He looked at their coffee cups, the silverware, his own

hands—anything but her face. Several moments passed, then he shook his head again and raised his eyes to meet hers. "Look," he said. "Oh, hell. It's over, Darcy."

Over? "What do you mean?" Her brain had absorbed his words, but her heart refused to heed them.

"I just can't do this anymore. It was a mistake from the beginning. You work for me. We both know how foolish it is to mix the personal with the professional."

"I've told you, Sam, it's not a problem for me. I can separate those parts of my life."

He sighed softly. "Well, I guess I've come to realize that I can't."

You're the one who was so quick to overcome my objections about that at the start! she thought, but she managed to stop herself from blurting out the words. It never did any good to point out to a man his blatant inconsistencies.

"Listen, you've been under a lot of stress lately," she said soothingly. "We all have. It's not the best time to be making decisions. Let's go home and talk about it—or . . ." she gave him her sexiest smile, "let's forget about it and see how we feel in the morning."

Instead of responding in his usual lighthearted manner, Sam looked at her and shook his head. He reached across the table and took one of her hands gently in his and squeezed it. He smiled at her sadly.

It was then that Darcy realized he was serious. She knew that sad, regretful, guilty look—she'd seen it in the eyes of other men: *It's over, babe. I want you out of my life*.

Darcy felt something shrivel inside her. Jesus! She'd had no warning. None. Two nights ago they'd been together and it had been wonderful. She quickly cast her mind back, searching for any little thing she might have said to put him off, anything that might have scared him into thinking that she wanted a commitment from him or that she was making demands. Men were so wary about that. One false move, and they were out the door.

But she honestly couldn't remember making any false moves. She'd gone by the book on this romance, being warm and approachable, but independent; sensual, but not too eager; self-confidently assertive, but never in the least bit demanding. She wanted Sam, and she'd planned her campaign very carefully. She couldn't believe that she'd failed.

"I'm sorry, Darcy," he said. "I feel awful about this. But I can't help how I feel. It's just not working out."

The hope inside her shriveled further. Shit! It was really over.

No, dammit, it *couldn't* be.

Sam was perfect for her! She'd run his birth chart over and over, thoroughly analyzing all his angles against her own. They were well matched. Their charts combined into one of the most harmonious unions of planets she'd ever encountered. She didn't just enjoy him as a lover, she was *serious* about Sam Brody. And she'd been hopeful, at least, that she could gradually lead this confirmed bachelor into taking her seriously, too.

Goddammit!

Darcy knew she wasn't very good at hiding her feelings, but she also knew instantly that she had to try. There was nothing more disconcerting to a man than an overly emotional woman. She had to work with Sam, see him every day. She couldn't afford to let him know that he'd just knocked her planets out of orbit.

Besides, if she stayed in control, she still had a chance. There was no reason yet to believe that his decision was irrevocable.

From somewhere deep within her, she summoned a smile. "Okay, Sam," she said lightly. "I'm disappointed, of course. But if it's not working for you"—she shrugged—"there isn't really much more to say."

He looked relieved, and she knew her strategy had been the right one. Most men hated to deal with disappointed women who made a big production over the ending of a love affair.

A cool, calm, independent woman, though—that was something else again. That was the type of woman they often ended up missing.

And wanting back.

Chapter Nine

Standing outside the room where the monthly meeting of the United Path Church building committee was in progress, Annie heard a burst of applause. She found it surprising, because things at the cathedral site weren't going *that* well.

The door opened and a smiling Barbara Rae appeared. Her face was unusually animated as she said, "Come in, Annie. We have some exciting news."

She sensed that something dramatic was going on. Mystified, she looked around at the six members of the building committee—all pillars of the community and dedicated members of the UPC congregation. As always, the office was badly lit, and everyone's face was shadowed. Annie was vaguely aware that seven, not six, faces were looking at her. And that one of them was set slightly apart from the others. . . .

"After months of floundering in the wake of Francesca Carlyle's death," said Barbara Rae, "we're delighted to announce that we once again have a dynamic leader to take charge of this committee. You've met before, I believe, Annie," she added as the seventh and newest member of the committee stood and extended his hand. "This is Matthew Carlyle."

Somehow Annie managed to maintain her composure as his firm hand briefly enveloped hers. *A murderer's hand.*

How many other people here thought the same thing when introduced to him? she wondered.

She had last seen him in person on the night of Francesca's death. Since then she had seen him a thousand times on television. Then, he had been a businessman, well known in the computer industry. Now, he was infamous all over the country.

He was not conventionally handsome—his features were too strong and craggy for that—but he could still be called a good-looking man. He was tall and slender, with high cheekbones and wavy black hair. Most men at his age were either balding or going gray, but Carlyle had only a slight feathering of gray around his temples, and his hair was still plentiful and thick. His face was lined a bit, especially around his mouth and his eyes, but his flesh was firm and he moved gracefully, indicating that he exercised and was fit.

Probably lifted weights in prison, Annie thought wryly.

His green eyes were a lot more piercing in person than they'd looked on television.

It struck her that there was something different about his looks now that'd he had been through the hell of the murder trial. He was harder somehow. His face, always angular, had an etched-in-stone quality to it now. She could imagine his long, slim body of hard bones and tough muscles carved into one of the marble frescoes in the cathedral. Not a saint, though—oh no. There was a ruthlessness in his eyes that a sculptor would never be able to capture. And it would be impossible to freeze in marble the mobile sensuality of his bottom lip.

Chairman of the United Path Church's building committee? That was the post his wife had held before her death. If he'd killed her, the appointment was a travesty.

Stop it, Annie! He had been acquitted. They'd been unable to prove him guilty, at least not beyond a reasonable doubt.

"Congratulations," she said.

His eyes bored deeply into hers. "Thanks," he returned, with a faint ironic edge to his tone.

A memory flashed. A rainy night, a warm, dry car, two bodies burning . . . burning. She had never told Charlie about it. She'd rationalized that telling him was unnecessary since she hadn't gone through with the affair. But that was something of a technicality, she knew. In her heart, she had been unfaithful.

Thank God she hadn't actually slept with him! It made her stomach lurch to think that she had nearly made love to a man who might be capable of murder.

Barbara Rae was explaining that the building committee had lacked direction ever since Francesca's death. It was true that the committee needed a strong leader. The position was important because the building committee oversaw the construction of the new cathedral. Although they usually rubber-stamped Annie's decisions, they were fundamentally responsible for the project—everything from the raising and allocation of the funds for the cathedral to the approval of any change orders that came during the construction process itself.

For whatever reason, none of the six people left on the

committee had been able to fill Francesca's shoes. Without
her dynamic, energetic force, the group had deflated. Barbara
Rae had been managing it herself for the past year, but she
had far too many other demands on her time.

"As his phenomenal success with his own company proves,
Mr. Carlyle is an expert manager," Barbara Rae said. "We
are very fortunate to have him devote even a small portion
of his inspirational energy to us."

When he thanked her, Annie thought, *I don't believe this.
I'm actually going to have to be polite to Matthew Carlyle!*

When the meeting ended and everybody had shaken hands,
Annie tried to slip away quickly. But Carlyle waylaid her in
the corridor.

"There's a lot I don't know yet about this project," he said.
"I'm counting on you to fill me in on everything I need to
know."

"Of course."

"I'd like to set up a meeting. You and I need to sit down
together and discuss this as soon as possible."

"Fine. I'll have my secretary call yours."

He reached into his pocket and pulled out a small leather
notebook. "That won't be necessary. Let's set something up
now. I've got my calendar right here."

Annie was tempted to say, Well, I don't! but she ordered
herself to get over it. It no longer mattered what she thought
of him. The building committee had voted him in, and that
was that. She had to learn to work with him, like it or not.

She opened her handbag and rooted around inside for her
address book/daily calendar. She didn't hurry. *Let him wait.*

"I've got some time at the end of next week," she said.

He smiled. "Sooner. How about a lunch meeting?"

"My schedule is tight," she said truthfully. "I have no free lunches this week."

"Dinner, then." He was eyeing his own schedule. "I'm free Thursday evening. Would that work for you?"

Thursday evening was a big blank on her calendar, and before she could come up with something that she absolutely had to do that night, Carlyle leaned over and noted the virgin white space.

"Thursday evening," he said decisively. "That would be excellent. The sooner the better as far as I'm concerned."

She sighed. "I'm really trying to carve out some personal time for myself. But, okay, Thursday. Might as well get it over with."

"You're not exactly thrilled about this, are you?"

"I'm sorry if I've given you that impression," she said quickly.

His mouth twisted upward at the corners. "Are you?"

She sighed. "It was unexpected. The situation may take me some time to get used to."

"What situation? Working for a murderer?"

His voice was bitter, and there was a tiny muscle twitching on his cheek. Annie flushed, ashamed. Whatever her feelings were, it had been impolite to let him see them.

"Look," he said before she could apologize, "the fact is that as the project manager for the cathedral, you are ultimately responsible to the owners. And now that I'm chairman of the building committee, that means you are ultimately responsible to me."

Annie wanted to argue, but there was nothing she could

say. He was absolutely right. She worked for the architectural firm, but the architectural firm worked for the owners.

Matthew Carlyle was, essentially, her boss.

It was nearly midnight when Barbara Rae's next meeting, the Vigil Against Domestic Violence, finally broke up. With less speed and energy than usual, Barbara Rae folded the chairs and stacked them against the wall of the rec room. To think that in a few months this wouldn't be necessary. No more squeezing into basements the way they'd had to do ever since her former church had been torn down to make room for the cathedral. No more making do with a table for an altar and the bare floor for kneeling and Styrofoam cups for after-service coffee. Instead she would be blessed to celebrate her faith in that beautiful and sacred building with its adjacent parish hall. A sacred place where the light would beam down upon her from the magnificent stained glass panels overhead.

And the light . . . what would it reveal?

If the light truly penetrated her heart, her soul, could she bear to examine what it found there?

"You look pensive," said a voice near the door.

Annie. Barbara Rae turned to her and smiled. She too had stayed on after the meeting, counseling troubled teens.

"I'm thinking on my sins, hon."

"I still find it hard to believe that you've ever committed any sins, Barbara Rae."

"We're all sinners in the eyes of the Living God."

"And we're all forgiven, too, if I understand my Christian theology correctly."

"Indeed it is so, if we truly and wholeheartedly repent."

"And how about the person who murdered Francesca Carlyle—could he repent and be forgiven too?"

Barbara Rae shook her head heavily. "I know it's hard to fathom. But we're told that God forgives all."

"Do you think a sin can come back from the past and haunt us in the present?" Annie asked.

Barbara Rae sucked in a deep breath. *Get out of your own mind*, she told herself. If Annie wanted to talk—as so many did—she considered herself obliged to listen and to empathize.

Especially with Annie. She was one of Barbara Rae's favorite people. Warm, hardworking, generous, always quick with a kind word and a hug, Annie was the sort of woman Barbara Rae would have liked to have had for a daughter if things had worked out differently in her life.

Like so many of the people she counseled, Annie had known sorrow and hardship in her life. Her childhood had been one horror after another. The death of her husband—a solid, trustworthy man—had shaken Annie deeply. But she had come out of it. Of her own volition, she had crawled, blinking and trembling, back out into the light. Annie had never discussed what had happened inside her, but Barbara Rae knew all too well the silent struggles of the human soul. Some people went through their entire lives without digging deep into the darkness of their own hearts; others made the terrifying descent and emerged chastened and pale, but no longer afraid.

"Sins from the past?" Barbara Rae repeated. "Yes, they can haunt us, if we're sensitive enough." She paused. "It's awfully late, Annie. Why are you still here? Is there something you need to talk about?"

"I hate to burden you with more of what you hear all day long. I should be helping you relax after a long day, not turning to you for counsel and advice."

"It's not a burden," Barbara Rae said honestly. "It's my life."

Annie smiled. "Okay, here it is. It's not a huge sin, anyhow. That is, the sin was far more in the thinking-about-it stage than in the committing-it stage!"

Barbara Rae smiled.

"It's about Matthew Carlyle."

Barbara Rae nodded. "That man sure does get around. It seems everybody has a story to tell about him."

"Mine's probably a pretty typical one," Annie said ruefully. "It happened several years ago, while Charlie was still alive. I met Matt on a flight to London. We hit it off so well that when we landed we agreed to get together. We were both alone in a foreign city, and—"

"I think I understand," Barbara Rae interrupted.

"Nothing happened. Well . . . some kisses, caresses—but we didn't make love. He wanted to, of course. *I* wanted to. But I loved Charlie, and I couldn't understand it—I felt as if my body was betraying me." She shook her head. "In a way, afterward, I hated myself for that."

"It is perfectly natural and human to experience temptation. We're not responsible for what we feel or even what we think. We're only responsible for our actions."

Annie nodded. "I know that now. But for a long time I couldn't help wondering whether Charlie's illness—diagnosed so soon after that trip to London—was some sort of punishment. A 'be careful what you wish for because it might come true' sort of thing. Not that I ever in a million years could have wished for Charlie's death. But for a couple of days, in London, my body wanted to pretend he wasn't in my life."

Barbara Rae touched Annie's arm gently. "Hard thoughts, but not uncommon in a situation like yours. When someone we love dies, and we're left alone without them, we try to find an explanation. But God's mysteries are beyond human logic and human guilt."

"You're right, I know. But it's been so hard to forgive myself for what happened. And I know I haven't forgiven Matthew Carlyle."

Barbara Rae nodded. "He's not an easy man."

"I realized today that I'm still attracted to him," Annie confessed.

"And he, I suspect, to you."

Annie looked at her. "You sensed that?"

"Absolutely. He can't look at you without his eyes softening in a caress."

"Do you think he's a murderer? Oh, I know what the jury said and all that, but you know something of him and you certainly knew his wife. What do you think?"

Barbara Rae shrugged. "I think the jury was probably right. But despite my profession, I've learned that I'm no expert in seeing into another human being's secret heart and soul. Someone killed Francesca Carlyle. I have the unhappy feeling that it was probably someone we all know.

"And that disturbs me, Annie. It disturbs me very much."

* * *

After Annie left, Barbara Rae went to the small makeshift bedroom that she was using while the new rectory was being completed and put on a light sweater. Then she went back downstairs and took the old underground passageway through the basement of the youth center and former nunnery to the construction site next door.

Barbara Rae began and ended each day with prayer and meditation. This was not because she regarded herself as exceptionally pious. On the contrary, she sometimes felt that she was just as much of an addict to her prayers and meditations as other people were to pills or drink or sex. If she missed a prayer session, she felt nervous, edgy, and short-tempered.

During the past few months, since the basic structure of the cathedral had been completed, Barbara Rae had developed the habit of praying in the spot that she had already begun to regard as her heart's new home—the sanctuary where the marble high altar had just been installed.

She slipped into the dark shell of the cathedral. From her purse she removed a slender pocket flashlight and turned it on. The construction workers typically left all sorts of debris from their work on the floor at night and she didn't want to trip and fall.

She always felt a hush come over her spirit when she entered the cathedral. All the more so because, like many places of worship, it was being built on an ancient holy site. Excavations for new churches often turned up previous churches or chapels. This site had previously been used for a Roman Catholic church. Before that it had been a Spanish mission—one of the oldest ones in the city, destroyed by the great earthquake of 1906.

Before the mission, who knew? But every time she entered the cathedral Barbara Rae felt that the area was imbued with power. She knew herself to be sensitive to such forces. If the power was ancient, it was probably pagan—power that came up from under the earth, the power of the earth renewing itself and sweeping away the dead. The gods who were named to symbolize that power were unimportant, really. It was the power that remained, interpreted through whichever set of symbols were dominant in the culture.

Barbara Rae had never had any problem reconciling such beliefs with her Christian tradition. She believed in her heart that the outward signs and symbols of her faith were metaphors for a simpler inner truth. Ritual was only a means of establishing the connection, bridging the chasm. There were many different paths, but only one Source.

She reached the scaffolding in the transept aisle directly beneath the sanctuary steps. The scaffolding was high and solid; the workmen who were hanging the stained glass panels had been using it, as had various other workers. She shone her flashlight up toward the vaulted ceiling, picturing the drawings she'd seen of the finished building. The light from the sun would be filtered in through the stained glass, shining gently and beneficently on the congregation beneath.

Suddenly, without warning, Barbara Rae felt ill. There was a weakness in her knees and the sense of wind rushing past her head. It was a feeling she recognized, and hated.

It's a vision, she thought. *The Sight*. Since childhood, these visions had come upon her at times.

She couldn't breathe. She opened her mouth to cry for help, but no sound emerged. A mist crept up from the floor. It rose over her calves, her knees. It was deathly cold. She shut her eyes, but she was unable to fend off the terrible cold rising around her—up to her thighs now, her hips, her waist, squeezing her, freezing her.

She looked up high overhead where the mist hadn't yet reached and realized that she could see the stained glass panels arching over the nave of the cathedral. The glass was dark; no sunlight shone through. So dark. And then she saw something swirling down from above—heavy and sharp as an ax. . . .

As she flung herself out of the path of the hurtling object, she thought she could smell the coppery tang of blood.

Silence reigned. The mist had cleared. Trembling, Barbara Rae looked everywhere for the falling object that had mercifully missed her head by inches.

But there was nothing there.

Nothing at all.

Chapter Ten

The next threatening letter was delivered to Annie at her office at Brody Associates. Again, her name was printed in block letters on the envelope.

> *You have been warned. But the Tower of Babel continues to rise. The eyes of the Living God are upon you. Everywhere you go, His footsteps will follow. Heed not the beckonings of Pride. Beware the wrath of the Lord.*

The signature was the same: *Jehovah's Pitchfork.*

Feeling a bit shaken, Annie went down the hall to Darcy's office. "Take a look at this." She handed over the letter. "It came this morning."

Darcy, who had been staring out the window at the Transamerica Pyramid, turned and took the letter. Annie noticed that her nail polish was chipped—highly unusual for her.

She read it over quickly. "Yikes!" she said.

"Nice, huh?"

"This is scary! Have you got the envelope?"

Annie showed it to her. "San Francisco postmark—with no return address, of course."

"Well, I suppose it's just some religious crank," Darcy said. "It's unpleasant, but this sort of thing *does* happen occasionally."

Annie wished it hadn't come today. She was already feeling edgy. She had a meeting this afternoon at the site to introduce Matthew to the construction crew, and this evening, Thursday, she was scheduled to have dinner with him—an engagement she was alternately looking forward to and dreading.

"It's not the first one," Annie said. "I got something similar at home a few days ago. I probably should have saved it, but my instinct at the time was to file it directly in the wastebasket. It was the same sort of religious imagery, with the same complaint about the cathedral costing too much money. And the signature was the same, 'Jehovah's Pitchfork.' "

Darcy shook her head. "Jehovah doesn't have a pitchfork. He has a lightning bolt or something. The Devil's the one with the pitchfork, right?"

Annie nodded.

"On the other hand," Darcy added, "sometimes it certainly *seems* as if God has a pitchfork. And He's just kinda prodding us along."

"Darcy, are you okay?" Annie asked. It struck her that Darcy hadn't been acting like her normal self all week.

"Who, me? Hey, no worries, mate."

But Annie wondered. Darcy was avoiding her eyes, which was unusual. "Sure?"

Darcy shrugged. "Maybe I'm getting my period."

"No, seriously, I mean it. I've been worried about you."

"Thanks for asking, but I'm fine. A little tired maybe, that's all."

"Well, d'you have any advice as to what I should do about this letter?"

"I'd make copies and give it to everyone on the site—well, the important people, anyhow. Security, too. It's probably just one of the usual harmless nuts, but there's no point in taking chances. Hell, it's a threat. I might even show it to the police."

As Annie headed back to her office with the poison-pen letter, Darcy helped herself to a cheese Danish from the tray in the office kitchen. Normally she stayed away from the rich breakfast pastries, but today—what the hell. She needed something to brighten her dark mood, and if sugar and fat would do it . . .

Annie was too damn intuitive, she thought. It was hard to hide anything from her.

In truth, the past few days since Sam had broken up with her had been utter hell. She couldn't sleep, she'd been eating all sorts of things she didn't usually touch, and she hadn't been doing any of her exercise routines.

Her work was beginning to suffer too. She couldn't concentrate. Even though she had several very important things to attend to, she kept pushing them out of her mind. All she wanted to think about was how she could change Sam's mind and get him back in her arms.

She'd been obsessively comparing their birth charts. There

were some communication conflicts—perhaps that's where the trouble lay. Sam was more secretive than she was. He was lighthearted on the surface, but he was motivated by deep wells of emotion. A lot of water in his chart. Scorpio and Cancer—strong emotions tenaciously held.

She'd also been consulting her favorite tarot deck two or three times a day, and the spreads there confirmed the astrological findings. All indications continued to be favorable for a lasting romance between herself and Sam.

What had happened, she hoped, was that Sam had entered the distancing period of the classic approach-avoid syndrome. He was, after all, a single man in his early forties, a man who had avoided commitment all his life. He probably panicked every time he felt himself getting seriously involved with a woman. All Darcy had to remember was not to panic in response.

Being supportive and understanding was the key. Let him feel separate. Let him begin to miss her. Let him realize what he was losing. And leave the door open so he could easily come back.

She knew that in a situation like this, she was lucky to be working in such close proximity to the man. He could hardly forget her when he saw her every day! Despite her agitation and sleeplessness, she had been taking extra care every morning with her clothes and her makeup. She had to look her best and act her best. Inevitably he would compare her behavior with that of all the other women he'd broken up with and realize that she was special, one in a million.

And once he realized that—she had him.

Darcy wished she could tell Annie. But Sam had insisted on keeping their relationship secret. The architectural design industry was small and full of gossip, and Sam had been very firm about keeping his private life entirely private.

Even so, Darcy mused, that shouldn't have stopped her from telling her best friend. After all, women told each other a lot of things that men never dreamed they told. . . .

But she'd kept the affair secret from Annie for another reason altogether. For some time she'd suspected that Sam had a bit of a thing for Annie. There was no sign that Annie reciprocated, but Sam was an attractive man. And if he had broken up with her because he wanted to start seeing Annie . . .

God it didn't bear thinking about.

But if such a thing did happen, Darcy hoped she could be civilized.

A true, unselfish friend.

But, dammit it, she wasn't sure she could stand it.

Chapter Eleven

Sidney Canin stopped by Annie's office later that morning, while she was on the phone with a prospective client. His face was long and gloomy as always. He signaled her from the doorway, pointing to the hold button on her phone.

Sidney rarely interrupted anything. Usually he was content to wait until she was free. She put the caller on hold.

"I need to talk to you," he said, coming into her office and shutting the door behind him.

"Sorry. I'm right in the middle of an important conversation."

"This is more important."

"Can you wait a few minutes? This is a prospective client I'm talking to."

Nodding, Sidney crossed his arms over his chest. He clearly intended to wait right there in her office, leaning against the wall and scowling.

Exasperated—she didn't like Sidney and was beginning to

wonder if she would ever get away from him professionally—
Annie ended her phone call as quickly and as gracefully as
possible.

"Okay. What's so important?"

"The cathedral."

"What about it?"

"There's a problem."

According to Sidney, there was always a problem. "What's
wrong?" she asked.

Before he could tell her, Annie's phone rang again. She
could have let voice mail answer it, but Sidney's demands
irritated her. She picked up the phone while her colleague
glared at her.

"Hello, Annie," said Matthew Carlyle.

At the sound of his deep, husky voice, she felt something
stretch and curl in the pit of her belly. At the same moment,
she was conscious of Sidney watching her. Two impossible
men . . .

"We still on for dinner tonight?" he asked.

"Yes. And don't forget the site meeting at one-thirty."

"I'll be there. About tonight—"

"Do you mind if I call you back in a little while? I've got
someone in my office."

He gave her his number, and Annie wrote it down and hung
up.

"Who was that?" Sidney asked.

"Matthew Carlyle. He's the new chair of the UPC building
committee, which means, essentially, that we're all working
for him now."

The scowl on Canin's face was erased by what appeared
to be an expression of pure shock. It turned, quickly, to anger.

"Are you telling me that that murderer is taking Francesca's place on the committee?"

"Yes. Ironic, isn't it?"

"It's worse than ironic! It's *sick*. Jesus Christ, has the entire world gone mad?"

Annie was surprised for a moment by the intensity of his reaction. Then she remembered that even before the murder there had been no love lost between Sidney Canin and Matt Carlyle.

"It's going to be difficult, I suppose, but we'll all have to live with it," she said. "Whatever we may think of him personally, he was lawfully acquitted."

"That was a foregone conclusion even before the trial. Billionaires kill with impunity. They never go to jail."

"Well, you might be right, but even so, we're going to have to work with him. I'm having dinner with him this evening, as a matter of fact, to try to forge some sort of working relationship—"

"You're having dinner with him?" Sidney interrupted.

"Yes. Why shouldn't I?"

"Why shouldn't you?" he said scathingly, as if the question were the stupidest one he'd ever heard.

"Is there some personal animosity between you and Matthew Carlyle?" she asked. "Seems to me you didn't like him even before Francesca died."

"No, I didn't," he said hotly. "I liked Francesca, and Carlyle never treated her right. Her marriage was a torment to her, and just as she was about to escape it, he killed her."

Annie decided to ask the question she had long wondered about: "You weren't her mysterious lover, were you, Sidney?"

"Don't be ridiculous!" he snapped. But the color rose in his usually pale face. "I was her friend and her confidant. That's all I was."

"Well, do you think she had a mysterious lover? Or was that just an invention of the defense attorneys and the press?"

Canin strode to the door and whipped it open. "I don't know and I don't care. She's dead. To hell with it. To hell with everything. To hell with the fucking cathedral."

He slammed the door behind him.

Great, thought Annie. What a day—threatening letters, strange behavior from Darcy, crazy behavior from Sid, and now, to top it off, she had *two* meetings with Matthew Carlyle.

At the cathedral that afternoon, Matt insisted on seeing everything. And he had about a thousand questions. They were intelligent questions, though, about technical matters of architecture and design, and Annie could tell that he had done some research. Apparently he was taking his responsibilities very seriously.

She introduced him to Jack Fletcher, who appeared suitably impressed to meet such a notorious man. Carlyle shook hands with the subcontractors' crews that they met during their tour of the site. All of them knew who he was, and several of them took the opportunity to congratulate him on winning his freedom.

Annie thought that there were some workers among the crews who hated Matthew Carlyle for his wealth and his business success, but if so they kept their feelings to themselves. Carlyle lacked the easy charm that Sam Brody possessed, so he didn't exactly create a sense of instant camaraderie, but he didn't piss anybody off either. He grinned and freely shook hands with dozens of people, and the buzz, she sensed, was positive.

It was positive for her as well. Walking beside him, both of them wearing hard hats as required on the site, Annie felt both conspicuous and oddly comfortable. On several occasions he touched her, once to help her mount a ladder to some low scaffolding to examine the marble facing applied in the exquisite Lady Chapel in the apse, and another time he touched her under the elbow as they clambered over some cans of paint on the floor.

On the second of these occasions, he looked down and caught her eye. She smiled at him, and something sparked. Chemistry. It had been there all those years ago in London, and it was still beating between them now.

So how did it work, she wondered, that strange confluence of shoulders and limbs and eyes and mouth and those mysteriously undetectable pheromones that somehow drew one human body to another? Was it all chemical and biological? Was destiny charted in the hormones? Why, knowing all that she knew about this very dangerous man, did these nonverbal messages still have such power?

The last person they encountered was Giuseppe Brindesi, who was high on the scaffolding at the east end of the transept aisle. Matthew wanted to meet him. In fact, he had actually started up the scaffolding ladder when Giuseppe yelled that he'd be coming down.

"Have the two of you met?" Annie asked as the master craftsman stepped off the scaffolding. She nodded from one man to the other. "Giuseppe Brindesi, Matthew Carlyle."

Matthew put out his hand as he had been doing all afternoon. "No, I don't believe so. Pleased to meet you."

Giuseppe hesitated a moment before shaking his hand. "I knew your wife, sir," he said slowly. "Please accept my condolences."

Matthew looked blank, so Annie added, "Giuseppe is the stained glass expert whom Francesca recommended to us. He did some work in the old UPC church before it was torn down, so I thought you might have met."

Matthew's expression changed—he seemed to grow more alert. But he shook his head and said, "No."

"I regret I was in my native Italy when Signora Carlyle died," Giuseppe said. "After that I was in England, doing restorations. I have only recently returned to this country."

"I remember that she spoke of you," Matthew said. Annie thought she detected an edge to his voice, but his face was once again under careful control, and she had no inkling of what he was thinking.

"A beautiful lady," Giuseppe said gently. "She is missed."

"Thank you," Matthew replied.

He was polite, but there was an audible finality to his words. It was clear that he did not wish to discuss his dead wife.

They spoke briefly about the stained glass, and Giuseppe seemed somewhat preoccupied as he explained what he was doing. Then he turned to Annie. "May I speak to you a moment?"

She stepped aside with him. "I'm having a few problems installing the largest panel," he told her. "I'd like to come into your office tomorrow and have a look at the blueprints."

"Of course, but don't you have your own copy of the latest CAD file?" she asked, referring to the computer-aided design software that all architects and designers used to assist in modern blueprint preparation.

"Alas, I seem to have lost a page of the blueprints," Giuseppe said. "I'd like to see the original file, if you don't mind."

"You'll have to come to my office at the firm for that," she said.

"That's fine. Tomorrow, perhaps?"

"Okay. I'll be in by nine."

"Good," he said, and with a polite nod to Matthew he climbed back up the scaffolding and resumed his work.

"Anything wrong?" Matthew asked.

"I don't think so," she said.

As they left the cathedral, Annie noticed that Jack Fletcher was leaning against a column only a few yards away, half hidden in the gloom.

Chapter Twelve

"I don't know why I'm so nervous about this meeting tonight," Annie said to Darcy as she changed her dress for the third time.

"Hey, I'd be nervous too, having dinner with a murderer. Jeez, Annie, at least you could have insisted on meeting him in a restaurant! Going alone to his house doesn't sound very smart."

"It's really not fair to keep referring to him as a murderer."

"He did it—I know he did. I have a strong intuition about these things. Besides, the potential for violence is clear in Carlyle's chart."

Annie raised her eyebrows. She didn't agree with Darcy's beliefs that everything had a cause or an explanation in the stars.

"How does this one look?" she asked, slipping into a black sheath with short sleeves and a V neckline. She and Darcy regarded her reflection in the full-length mirror in Annie's bedroom.

"That's good. Sexy and sophisticated but not too wild."

"I don't want to look sexy."

"Honey, all women want to look sexy. We want men to think we're sexy, too. We just don't want them to actually do anything about it—at least not while we're having a business dinner."

"You're right, I should have insisted on a restaurant."

"Billionaires don't meet people in restaurants. They order you to come to their mansions and be tended by their servants and fed by their cooks. But I wouldn't worry *too* much. He can hardly rape you in front of his entire household staff."

"Whatever he's thinking," Annie said tersely, "it's too late."

"You're still mad at him for saying no to you about Fabrications, aren't you?"

Annie shrugged. Her feelings about Matt Carlyle were, at best, mixed.

"I just read a book on male friendships as compared to female friendships," Darcy said. "Just goes to show—men are so different from us!"

"Ain't that the truth."

"We think of our best friend as someone we can talk intimately to. A man's best friend is someone he can *do* something with—you know, hunt, fish, watch football. And even when they do have a conversation, they rarely listen and empathize the way women do."

"They're too busy giving advice," Annie said ruefully.

"Right. They even define the term *friend* differently than we do. Maybe they haven't seen or talked to someone for twenty years, but because they were on the football team together in high school and swore an eternal pact of friendship, they still feel loyal."

"Whereas for us, friendship is more day-to-day, in the present."

"Exactly. Women are more practical about friendship. You and I haven't known each other very long, for example. But we're close friends."

"Absolutely."

"Compare that with the long and old friendship between a couple of men. For example, Sam and your date for the evening, Matt Carlyle."

"It's not a date!"

Darcy grinned. "They don't socialize very often, as far as I can tell. But Sam testified for the defense at Carlyle's trial. He risked alienating all sorts of people by standing up in court on behalf of a man whom everybody thought was guilty."

"I would have done the same thing. Wouldn't you?" Annie asked. "Surely both men and women are loyal to their friends when the chips are down."

Darcy shrugged. "If you asked Carlyle, I'll bet he'd say that most of his friends abandoned him in his time of need."

"Well, maybe they did. But *I* was never a friend of his, Darcy."

"Still, he's bound to be angry and bitter. Watch out for this guy, Annie. I'm serious. You want me to come with you —as another representative of the firm?"

Annie shook her head. "No. I can handle it." She smiled wryly. "I guess I've got to prove that to myself."

Their eyes met in the mirror, and Darcy nodded solemnly. "You can handle it."

* * *

The first thing she thought when she arrived at the secluded, gated mansion was that she must have made a wrong turn somewhere.

Surely this dark Gothic horror could not be the home of one of the wealthiest and most sophisticated CEOs in the nation. It looked like something out of a Stephen King novel.

Carlyle lived in the traditionally upscale area of the city known as Pacific Heights. From the tops of the hills residents had a fantastic view of San Francisco Bay, with the Golden Gate Bridge to the left, the village of Sausalito across the Bay, Alcatraz Island looking deceptively picturesque out in the blue waters, and the shores of Berkeley to the right.

Carlyle's home was situated on a hilly lot, with high walls and terraced gardens surrounding it. A steep, winding driveway led up to the house from a security gate constructed of tall cast-iron pikes of the sort that, in ancient times, were used to impale the heads of one's enemies.

The mansion was a four-story monstrosity of "eclectic" style. The architect must have been either drunk or mad, Annie thought with some amusement as she pulled in and parked. He had combined Georgian ponderousness with a Gothic sense of the bizarre, and crowned it all with ornate Victorian touches. There were crenellated towers and rooftop galleries that resembled battlements, and the square, solid walls looked thick enough to withstand the siege of Troy.

Keeping guard over a front doorway, that was tall enough to admit a giant on stilts, were three horrific stone gargoyles that looked as if they should have been guarding the gates of hell.

What a perfect place for a wife killer to live, Annie thought with a shiver.

She parked her car in the half-moon area directly in front of the main entrance and climbed the wide stone steps that curved around the front of the house to the gigantic door. She saw no doorbell, so she raised the heavy knocker (the roaring head of a lion) and released it. The sound of the bronze striking its metal plate was like a gunshot. Startled, Annie felt little fear-devils chasing themselves up and down her spine.

"Get a grip," she ordered herself.

She was expecting a lugubrious butler dressed like Boris Karloff to open the door, but all that happened was that dogs began barking inside. After thirty seconds or so she knocked again. She heard the sound echo through the house. Still, no one came.

This is odd. She began to wonder if she had the right day, the right time. She was sure his instructions had been clear, and that she had carried them out precisely.

She was lifting the knocker one more time when Carlyle himself opened the door. "Sorry for the delay," he said with a smile. "I was locking up the dogs, and my housekeeper, Mrs. Roberts, has the night off." He stepped back and showed her in with a flourish. "Welcome to the ugliest house in Pacific Heights."

She smiled. "This *is* quite a place," she said, crossing the threshold into a large foyer with a vaulted ceiling and a black marble floor.

"Yes, isn't it. As an architectural designer, you might be interested in knowing that the man who conceived and built it ended his days in a psychiatric hospital."

Annie laughed. She remembered his dry sense of humor

from London, but she hadn't seen much sign of it since then. "It's certainly a mad mixture of styles."

"That's for sure. Francesca and I moved in just a couple of months before her death. She thought it had 'possibilities.' She was going to have it completely redone, of course. But then she died."

The inside was perfectly in keeping with the outside—with high-ceilinged rooms and a seemingly infinite number of odd angles and small nooks and crannies. The walls were either painted in dark colors or hung with gloomy wallpaper that had seen the passage of several decades. The furniture was well made and expensive, but if any attempt had been made to choose the right piece for the right room, Annie couldn't discern it.

The interior of the house had no soul. She wondered if this indicated a similar lack in its owner.

"In a way, I like the gloominess of the place," he said, staring at her as if he guessed what she was thinking. "Its ponderousness and darkness seem appropriate to me somehow." He came to stand beside her. "Have you ever been afraid of the dark, Annie?"

She took a step away from him. "Well, yes, actually, I still am. I'm a bit claustrophobic, especially in the dark."

"I used to be terrified of the dark. As a kid, I'd curl up in bed and cover my head with the blankets, tense as a board, knowing—absolutely sure of it—that there was a monster waiting to consume me there. I used to pray very hard to God to protect me, back when I believed in God."

"Imagination can be a terrible thing, can't it?" she said lightly.

"So can reality."

There was nothing she could say to that. She remembered that his reality had included living in a small, dark cell for more than a year while his trial droned on. She would have gone crazy, locked up like that.

She glanced at him. His expression was closed, his features like granite. A man who was in supreme control of his emotions. Yet she remembered the way he had appeared on television in the courtroom on the day when the verdict had been announced. The look in his eyes had revealed his inner turmoil.

Not so tonight, though. Tonight she had no idea what he was thinking.

They stared at each other for a long moment, then he turned away and said in a normal tone, "Come, I never use this room. There actually is a more pleasant place. Let me show you the garden."

Sliding doors led from the living room outside to a small intricately laid-out Japanese garden. Here, clearly, a landscape artist had been at work. There were flowering plants of all sorts, their vividly colored blossoms dancing in the breeze. There were trees, both natural and exquisitely small bonsai trees, and flowering shrubs. Through the middle of the garden wound a flowing stream that opened into a fish pool where Annie saw the coppery gleam of carp.

"It's very beautiful. Almost a fairyland."

"I'm not a very visually oriented person, so I probably don't even appreciate some of the finer details, but I do know that I feel at peace here," he said. "When I come out and walk in the garden, sit quietly, feed the fish, the rest of the world seems, briefly, to slip away."

"Yes, I can see why."

He turned to her, and she noticed that he was very close. Self-consciously, she took a step back.

"I'm getting the distinct feeling that you're uncomfortable here with me," he said.

She met his eyes. "Yes, I am, a bit." She was comparing the way she felt with him with her feelings about some of the other men she knew. Sam Brody, for instance. Or Charlie. With Charlie she'd felt a pleasant zing of combined friendship and attraction—the sort of feeling that blossoms into love, companionship, and trust. But with Matthew Carlyle she already felt the beginnings of the same wild and sweeping lust that had gripped her so strongly that weekend long ago in England.

It was a strong, earthy, passionate attraction, based purely on sexual chemistry. The sort of thing that did nothing but cause trouble in the people who were foolish enough to romanticize it.

"So what's the source of your unease?"

Annie wasn't about to say that she was fighting a strong and abiding attraction to him! As she fumbled for words, his expression darkened. "I presume you believe, along with so many other people, that the jury acquitted a guilty man?"

Of course he would think that. Yet, oddly, despite her conversation with Darcy, she hadn't given any thought to the murder since she'd arrived. The danger she sensed from him was of another variety entirely.

"No," she said quickly. "I believe the verdict was fair. And I remind you that my own conflicts with you go back a lot further than your problems with the state of California."

He stared at her for a long moment, then he smiled. "You're right, of course. I've reclassified my life into two periods—

Before Francesca's Murder and After Francesca's Murder. Anything falling into the Before period seems like ancient history to me, but of course that isn't necessarily true of other people."

Annie felt a tiny bit ashamed as it occurred to her that if he had *not* murdered his wife and if he *had* loved her, he must have suffered far more deeply even than she had when Charlie died. She had been consoled by friends; her grief had been respected. Carlyle's grief, assuming he'd felt any—the inevitable qualification—had been discounted.

"Forgive me," she said.

He blinked. "What for?"

She shrugged. "Insensitivity. Most people our age don't know how it feels to have to cope with the death of a spouse. I do."

He shrugged. "So it appears that you and I have something in common after all."

Darcy pulled past the house, looking for a parking place. Damn San Francisco! There was never any place to leave your car.

She drove on up the next block, then pulled into a driveway and turned around. Coming back down the hill, she stopped on the sidewalk a few doors from Sam's house in the Russian Hill district. She was blocking the entrance of somebody's driveway, but it didn't matter. She'd only be there for a few minutes, and she wasn't getting out.

Fool! You shouldn't be here at all. What if he sees you? What if you get caught?

She would die of embarrassment, she knew. There wasn't

much that embarrassed her, but being caught skulking around after Sam Brody would do it.

This was crazy. There was absolutely no point to it. It wasn't going to help, and besides, it was pure emotional torture. Especially on a night like tonight. Sam had a date. He was seeing a blond woman who, from a distance, looked remarkably like Annie. In fact, if Darcy hadn't known that Annie was out this evening with Matthew Carlyle, she would have thought Sam's date *was* Annie.

They had enjoyed a romantic dinner in a restaurant downtown, and now they had returned to his apartment. They'd each come in their own cars. The blonde had parked hers just down the street on the left, lucking into an empty slot. She drove a little red Mercedes, and Darcy glared at it balefully, wanting to come up behind her at a stoplight and ram the shit out of that trim little rear end.

Sam had held the blonde's hand as he'd led her up the stairs to the front door. By now he was probably kissing her and coaxing her toward the bedroom, where he would make love to her with that careful blend of tenderness and passion that made him such a skillful lover.

Stop it! This is crazy and self-destructive! He's not worth it! Have you no pride, no dignity? Why can't you stop obsessing over this jerk?

Darcy stared at the light in the front window of the old Victorian. Sam lived in one of the "painted ladies"—a beautiful restored Victorian from pre-1906 earthquake days. The lights were easily visible from the street, and Darcy couldn't count the times she'd driven by, at all hours of the day and night, just to see if his lights were on. No matter where she had to go in the city, she chose a route that took her by his house. Frequently when she started out she would resolve *not* to drive anywhere near his house, but some demon would take over, directing her hands on the wheel, and she would find herself on his street.

It didn't matter whether he was home. In fact, it was often better if he was away. Because he could *come* home while she was waiting, giving her a glimpse of him. Seeing him in person was better than simply seeing his lights, although it increased the risk that he would notice her and wonder what she was doing there.

For some bizarre reason, this obsession did not bother her during the day at work. She could deal with seeing him then. It was as if he were a different person during the day, in the office. There, she was in control.

But when she got away from work her control broke, and she was at the mercy of her unruly emotions. Sometimes they frightened her so profoundly that she thought she was going insane.

Over and over she'd told herself that this would pass, that time would heal her, that she would forget about him and exorcise this cancer from her soul. Sam Brody didn't love her. He didn't even want her. There was nothing she could do to change that fact, and she'd damn well better get over it.

Especially now. There were problems at work, things to think about, things to worry about. Things she had to do. She couldn't afford to waste her evenings like this. It was beyond stupid—it was asinine.

Tonight was chillier than usual, and Darcy began to shiver. It was always a problem to decide whether to leave the motor running. Once the police had driven by as she was idling in front of a driveway. She'd hurriedly jerked a map out of the glove compartment and pretended to be studying it as they'd signaled to her to move on.

This is sick. It's got to stop! At this rate I'll soon be boiling bunnies!

The light in the front window went off. Darcy felt her heart twist. They must be moving into the bedroom. She imagined Sam and his date in bed, their naked limbs entwining, and her hands began to shake. Jerkily she turned the key to start the engine. She had to get out of there. No one in her right mind would torture herself this way.

She started to head for home, but one of the new impulses that were so difficult to control made her turn instead down the road that would take her once more around the block past Sam's place.

Maybe someone would be leaving and she would spot a parking place. . . .

Chapter Thirteen

Annie was surprised at how pleasant her dinner with Matthew Carlyle turned out to be. They ate in a candlelit dining room at a mercifully small table set in front of a roaring fireplace. The food, served by an unobtrusive staff, was delicious.

They spoke in more detail about the progress of the work on the cathedral. She found him to be a quick, intelligent conversationalist, good both at talking and at listening. After some initial reticence, she began to open up, and he appeared to do the same.

"One thing I'm not sure I understand," she said. "Having lost the last year and a half of your life, there must be a lot of things you need to do, a lot to catch up on. Why get involved with the cathedral? You mentioned earlier that you don't believe in God."

He shrugged. "That's true, but I do owe something to Barbara Rae. And, as you probably know, I've been peripherally involved in the cathedral from the start because of Francesca's interest in the project." His expression was intense as he added, "The fact that you were involved was a major factor, for me at least, when it came time to write a check to the building fund. Frankly, I admired your work."

"I'm astonished to hear that," she said. "And I'm not sure I believe it."

He blinked. "Why not?"

"You'd refused to engage Fabrications the previous year."

"I told you the reason for that. Everything I predicted came true."

Her chin went up. "Everything you predicted came true because we didn't get the Powerdyme job. If we had, Fabrications might have survived!"

"Temporarily, perhaps. In the long run, no. You were too small. And, apart from you, the company didn't have the talent. Your work, personally, was terrific, but after Charlie died—"

"Let's not rehash this now," she said testily.

"Okay, but I think I'm just realizing something that I've never understood before." He paused. "You blame me for the demise of Fabrications, don't you?"

"No, of course not," she said, but she could hear that her tone was unconvincing. It was irrational to blame him, she knew. Fabrications had failed for many reasons; probably mainly for the same reason that most small businesses fail— they simply aren't well known enough to get the contracts to keep them out of the red. The economy had been bad as well. Even big companies like Brody Associates had suffered during those years.

Still, it had been much more comfortable to have a villain

to blame. And Matt Carlyle had fit the bill very nicely for a while. "What I blame you for, I guess, is blasting my hope. Fabrications was all I had left after my husband's death. I desperately wanted to believe I could keep it going."

She looked at him, expecting a lecture on the risks and the realities of entrepreneurial ventures. But instead he said, "It must have been a tough time for you. I'm sorry if I made it worse. My first company failed too, so I know how it feels."

Annie was amazed at the congeniality of this statement. She never knew what to expect from this man! "You had a company that failed?"

"Yup. One of the first computer game companies. If things had worked out, my life might have turned out quite differently." He shook his head. "Sam Brody's life would have been different too. He and I were partners. Did you know that?"

"I knew you were friends. Roommates in college, right? But Sam's an architect. What would he have had to do with computer games?"

"He's also a talented illustrator. And in those days he had no desire to go into the family business. He and I were going to change the world together."

Instead, she thought, he'd started a software company and changed the world alone.

"I don't really know all that much about Sam's personal life," she said.

"Well, when we met, he was the sophisticated, wealthy private-school boy who took me under his wing. I was poor but smart—a typical math and science geek. Sam used to call me the human computer—which wasn't exactly a compliment at the time, since computers were awkward, clunky things that took up an entire room."

His manner was low-key and self-deprecating, which Annie found very appealing.

"Since Sam was so affable and well connected, he was the front man for our company," he went on. "I didn't know how to market a product properly, and, what's more, I hadn't the slightest interest in doing so. Pretty ironic, isn't it, considering what I do today. Back then I didn't own a three-piece suit, and my idea of sophisticated marketing was to candidly tell people not only the strengths but also the weaknesses of our products.

"Anyhow, we failed, and poor Sam was pretty disgusted with me. Can't really blame him, in retrospect. It took me a few more years to learn the lessons about business that I needed to know."

"You and he are still good friends, though, right?"

"Oh, yes, absolutely," he said warmly. "Sam was one of the few people who stood by me during the trial. He never doubted that I was innocent."

"It's good to have a friend like that."

"Yeah, it is. Sam is one of the few people in my life whom I know I can always count on, no matter what." He paused, then added, "I'm glad things have worked out so well for you at Brody Associates. Sam's previous design manager was incompetent. And the timing was perfect—he had just gotten rid of her when I told him about you."

Annie blinked. "When you told him about me?"

"I called Sam on your behalf, yes. He'd heard of you, although he knew your husband's work better."

"You mean Sam asked you for a reference when he was deciding whether or not to hire me?"

Matt shook his head. "Never mind. It's not important. I'm just glad it all worked out."

"No, wait." Annie was so astonished at the implications of what he was saying that she couldn't just let it go without explanation. "Are you telling me that you were the one who put Sam onto me in the first place? He called me initially, you know."

He nodded. "Right after that meeting we had when I told you I wouldn't be hiring Fabrications. I mentioned to Sam that you were a top-notch designer and might soon be looking for a job." He hesitated for a moment. "Sorry if that sounds patronizing, but I respected your work and wanted to do something to help."

All this time she'd seen him as a villain—when in fact she owed her current job to him!

"I don't know what to say. I had no idea." She felt herself blushing. "I guess I owe you a belated thank-you."

He shrugged. "All I did was make a phone call. You did the rest yourself. Sam never would have hired you if he hadn't been convinced of your talent."

"He never told me," Annie said.

"No reason why he should have."

Looking at him, Annie reminded herself that Matt was a skillful businessman who never did anything without having a clear-cut strategy. "Is there a reason why you're telling me now?"

He looked directly into her eyes. "The most egotistical reason, I suppose." His expression darkened. "I've just spent more than a year deprived of my freedom. The public has reviled me, most of my friends have abandoned me, my enemies have gloated.

"I know I wasn't guilty of the crime of which I was accused. But I must have been guilty of something—some lack of charity or sensitivity or kindness toward others, perhaps. I must have done harm, or surely I wouldn't have been as thoroughly hated."

Annie made a sound as if to stop him, but he continued anyway. "I've seen that dislike reflected in your own eyes— and I hate it because it's so different from what I once remember seeing there. Somehow I lost your respect, your affection. No doubt I deserve whatever feelings you hold toward me. But for my own sake, I think, I need to remind myself that not everything I've done with respect to you has been thoughtless or selfish or cruel. There was at least one generous act."

The raw emotion beneath his words was so powerful that Annie was moved nearly to tears. She suddenly got a very clear and dramatic sense of what it must have meant to be Matthew Carlyle for the past year and a half since his wife had been killed.

It must have been hell.

She felt deeply ashamed. All this time, she realized, she'd been judging him . . . and finding him wanting. Yet it was all due to one stupid reason—that she'd believed he hadn't found *her* good enough and had wanted to take some sort of petty revenge.

On that matter, at least, she'd been wrong about him.

Looking directly into his deep, burning green eyes, she said, "I owe you an apology."

He shook his head. "No, you don't."

"I wish there were something I could do to—"

"Just relax, Annie. Right now I can't think of anything nicer than simply having the pleasure of your company."

She smiled. That much she could gladly give him.

Annie wasn't sure when the tone of the evening changed. At some point a moment came when she ought to have risen from the table and said, "Thank you very much, but I think it's time to go."

The words were right there. Why couldn't she speak them?

Instead, she allowed the fine red wine to relax her. The warmth from the fire seeped into her, and she luxuriated in the smoky scents of hickory logs, fine wine, gourmet foods, and the faint tang of hearty masculinity that imbued the entire place.

By the time the flourless chocolate cake arrived, they were laughing and gently flirting with each other. They agreed on a shared love of dark chocolate . . . that it was heavenly . . . life's second greatest pleasure. . . .

He fed her the last bit of the scrumptious dessert from the tip of his own fork.

This is crazy, she thought, as he rose from the table and took her hand. She walked with him into a room that had probably been used as the parlor to which the men retired after dinner for cigars, brandy, and males-only conversation. The room was dark, lit only by another low-burning fire. Like an old English manor, this house had a fireplace in every room.

He led her to a long sofa with soft, buttery leather uphol-stery, and they sat down. His right thigh was touching her left one and his right arm encircled her shoulders. She let her head fall against his shoulder and closed her eyes. Her heart was thumping wildly in her chest, yet at the same time she felt strangely calm and centered, as if anything that happened would be okay.

The wine, she thought. She'd never been much of a drinker.

Nonsense. She'd had less than one glass, and such a small amount of wine had never affected her like this before.

It wasn't the wine; it was Matthew himself. He'd mesmerized her in London, and he was doing it again now. His body felt as cozy and familiar to her as if they had been lovers for years.

When he turned his face to hers it seemed a perfectly natural movement. His mouth approached hers and she turned hers up in readiness. His kiss felt wonderful. He was both tender and teasing, full of sensual promise. Her passions, unexpressed for so long, built swiftly as his arms tightened and his tongue began to probe. It felt lovely and very sweet.

But as she relaxed in his arms, he backed off. He leaned away from her and caught her eye. He gave her a pleasant, lazy smile and said, "Thanks, Annie."

Bewildered, she said, "What for?"

"For not skittering away like a frightened rabbit. You're the first woman I've kissed or held in my arms since the night Francesca died. I know that you don't trust me, and who could blame you? You probably think—like so many others—that there's at least an even chance that I'm guilty. But you came here alone, and you've shown every sign of loosening up in my company. I'm not egotistical enough to think that's any tribute to my charm. It's your goodwill that deserves notice." He paused. "You're a nice woman and good soul, Annie Jefferson."

Several emotions jagged through her. The strongest felt like disappointment. "Thanks, I think. But is that why you kissed me? As some sort of test?"

He looked at her. Something leapt in his eyes. He shook his head and muttered, "No."

She knew she shouldn't push it, but she couldn't stop herself. "Then why?"

"You drive me crazy," he said slowly. "You always have, from the night we met on that airplane when we were both still married."

Her mouth went dry. Something heavier came into the room with his words. Something darker. She'd unleashed it herself.

And this time she did back away from him.

"I should go," she said.

For a moment she thought he would try to stop her. Or at least tell her in detail why she ought to stay.

Then she felt him also stiffen and disengage. "You're right. You should."

"We'll be working together," she said. "There's some question about professional ethics here, and—"

"The cathedral is going to be finished soon," he cut in. "That's a lame excuse and you know it."

"There's no point in arguing," she said softly. "It's just a—a bad idea, for several reasons. As you say, you just got out of prison and you haven't been with a woman for all that time. I could be any woman. You'd feel the same no matter who it was."

"No. You're wrong. That's not it. That's not why."

She met his eyes. "Of course you would say that."

His expression darkened. "I don't lie," he said sharply.

"Everybody lies. To themselves if to nobody else. None of us is completely conscious of our motivations."

He nodded. "Okay. And what about you? Are you running away because you think there might be a conflict of professional ethics or because you're not sure that these same hands"—he held them up—"that could tease and caress you into pleasure might also be capable of closing around your slender throat and squeezing the life out of you?"

Annie caught herself staring at those hands, marveling at their strength and their beauty, and remembering how they had felt that weekend in England, skillful and hot against her bare skin.

"Are you?" he snapped. "Is that what you secretly believe?"

"I don't know," she whispered.

His mouth twisted in a bitter smile. "The irony is that I occasionally did think about killing her."

She blinked. "What?"

"Haven't you ever thought about it? Ridding the world of someone you hate? Or someone you're angry with or jealous of? Someone who deserves punishment for some evil they've done, but who manages to escape with impunity over and over again?"

"I don't sit around and plot people's deaths, if that's what you mean," she said with a shiver.

"Well, maybe it's more common among men," he said. "I don't think there's any doubt that we're generally more violent and aggressive than women are. But I'd be surprised if most men hadn't occasionally fantasized about killing an enemy or a rival. Certainly I have. Although that's not the sort of thing one admits to a jury," he added dryly.

"So you're admitting that you did at least *think about* murdering your wife?" she said nervously.

"I'm admitting I'm human, yeah. Francesca could be a very difficult woman to live with. Temperamental, demanding, controlling, excessively critical. The only time I was ever tempted to be unfaithful to her was that time with you in England, but she was unfaithful to me frequently. In fact, our marriage had been crumbling for years, and if it hadn't been for her pregnancy, I'd have been perfectly content to let it die. We'd been trying to have a baby for years, and I'd pretty much given up. I wanted that child, Annie, even though I couldn't be absolutely certain it was mine. I suspected her of having an affair, and I figured the baby could just as easily have been sired by the other guy."

"*If* there was another guy," Annie said.

"There was. There's absolutely no doubt in my mind about that." He was cold again now. He'd controlled the impulse that had threatened for a moment to sweep them both into a landscape where restraint was impossible.

"She admitted her affair to me that night—the night of the party, the night she died. She told me he'd been pressuring her to leave me . . . that she was so confused . . . that she'd been drinking again because she was so stressed out by his demands." He shrugged. "Not being able to prove it at the trial was frustrating. But there was no reason for her to lie. I knew her better than anyone on earth. Francesca was telling the truth."

"But she didn't tell you who he was?"

"She refused to tell me." He paused. His jaw tightened, and Annie saw a tiny muscle jumping over his cheekbone. "But I think she was ambivalent about him. Because what happened that night was no different from her usual pattern—drunken rages, then a desperate attempt to reconcile. A lot of wild talk about a divorce, then her insistence that she loved me and would love me forever." He sighed. "It was a rollercoaster, and I'm not sure how much longer I could have endured it if it hadn't ended when it did. My guess is that she drove the other guy just as crazy as she drove me."

"And so he killed her?"

"It's the best explanation I can come up with, Annie. He murdered my wife and he murdered my child. And that's something that will haunt me forever."

Chapter Fourteen

Annie left Matt's house a little before eleven o'clock. By the time he walked her to the door, they both had themselves under control. He didn't touch her again, even after she put her jacket on and turned, awkwardly, to face him at the door. Would he kiss her?

He did not. He walked her out to her car, though, and he stood there with his hands jammed into the back pockets of his jeans as she got in and started the engine.

"Thanks for the fantastic dinner."

"Anytime."

Well, shit. She opened the window and beckoned. Looking puzzled, he leaned over, his face near hers. She stuck her head out quickly and dropped a kiss on his lips, then pulled back and grinned.

"Bye!" she said and sped away.

* * *

After Annie had left, Matt sat alone in a leather recliner in his dark and gloomy house, staring into the dying embers of the fire. His thoughts were clearer than they'd been for months, and he needed to follow them through.

It was good that Annie had hesitated . . . and that he had controlled himself. The last thing he needed, or wanted, was to heedlessly fling himself into any kind of intimate involvement. What he had to do now was focus on getting his life back together. He had a business to run. He had relationships to reestablish. He had work to do.

Things changed very fast in the computer industry. Powerdyme had always been on the cutting edge, largely because of his own visionary talents. Granted, as Powerdyme had become increasingly successful, he had been able to hire a lot of talented people, and they'd proved their mettle by keeping the company thriving during the time that he had been wrestling with the state of California. But now, once again, they needed his leadership.

That was where he had to focus. He really couldn't allow himself to be scattered about by the winds of his emotions.

And yet . . .

Being jailed for eighteen months changes a man.

He'd had to face the possibility that he might never be free again.

He'd had plenty of time to think about all the things he regretted, all the things he'd done wrong. And now that he *was* free and life once again expanded out to the horizon, he had to make some decisions about how he was going to live.

Unfortunately, his thoughts on the matter were fairly contradictory. He knew he wanted a family, and children. He swallowed hard as he remembered everything he'd lost. Dear God, yes, he wanted another chance to have a child!

But he didn't want to fall in love too quickly with a woman, commit to her without first getting to know her well enough to be sure they were compatible.

He'd made that mistake with Francesca, acting rashly in the flush of new love, remaining blind to her faults until well into their marriage. The last thing he needed to feel was that passionate pull of body to body, soul to soul. It was too easy to be deceived, too easy to overlook the details that would loom in later years and fracture the relationship. Desire is a powerful force, but it takes a deeper kind of compatibility to join two disparate souls.

He wished he didn't feel such a strong desire for Annie Jefferson. He'd learned to distrust desire. Wonderful though it was, it was no basis for a permanent relationship. And its very power often served to mask the areas in which two lovers were *not* compatible.

He liked Annie. There was a great deal about her character and her temperament that would suit him very well. But there was no need to rush into anything. How much wiser it would be to take things slowly and find out if they were indeed compatible in other ways.

Her kiss, though, he knew would haunt him.

Her sweet, sweet lips . . .

Darcy woke suddenly, feeling stiff and disoriented. For a few seconds she had no idea where she was or why she was sitting up, feeling cold and cramped instead of lying stretched out in a cozy bed.

Sam.

Oh shit!

She'd fallen asleep in the car, parked on the street outside his house.

Had he seen her? What if he'd walked by, peeked into the car, and seen her curled up here? What would he think? That she was crazy? That she was stalking him? Would he call the police? Call a shrink? Fire her from her job?

Shit, shit, shit!

It was still dark out. She looked at the clock—4:11A.M.

What had happened to the blonde? she wondered. Had she spent the night? Was she still there, naked and satiated, lying pressed to Sam's beating heart?

The pain arrowed through her middle.

Stop it! She glanced at the clock again and felt a moment of panic. How could she have fallen asleep given everything she had to think about, everything she had to do?

Jesus Christ, Darcy, you're really skating on the edge this time.

Her fingers felt numb as she struggled with the car keys. Falling asleep in a car while spying on an old lover. It was sick. Sick. And it was stupid.

As she carefully started the car and pulled out of her parking slot her eyes checked out the opposite side of the street for the blonde's little red Mercedes. It was no longer there. There was no sign of it anywhere on the street.

Well, that was something, at least. He'd obviously kicked her out before morning. Maybe the blonde had been a lousy lay. Maybe he wouldn't want to see her again. Maybe there was still hope. . . .

Oh stop with that crap, Darcy! He doesn't want you, and

*if you had any sense, you wouldn't want him either—the
bastard!*

*And you certainly wouldn't waste your valuable time and
energy on this obsession.*

She glanced again at the tiny clock on the dashboard. It
was now 4:13.

Dammit.

Chapter Fifteen

Chapter Fifteen

Barbara Rae always rose a few minutes before the dawn. This was a legacy from the days when she had worked in the fields, mindlessly picking whatever fruits and vegetables were ripe and ready for market, and grateful for the work, back-breaking though it was. There in the fields amongst the ripening fruit, she would raise her face to the brightening sky and seek answers to the questions that had tormented her from childhood: Why is life so full of suffering? Is there anything to hope for? Why, oh why, do I feel such pain? How can I relieve the sufferings of others?

It had been many years before she had received any answers, and more still before she had dared to believe them.

At night, before sleep, she had no questions. Her nighttime prayer was silent, meditative. In the darkness she was receptive—she kept very still and listened in case God had something to say to her.

But in the mornings she questioned God. Interrogated Him sometimes.

On Friday morning, she rose slightly later than usual. Her limbs felt stiff and heavy as she got out of bed, and there was a faint humming in her ears like the echo of a distant wind. She dressed quickly and simply, as was her habit. She would shower later.

The morning was chilly, so she slipped into a jacket before she walked down the sidewalk to the cathedral. She hurried because she knew that a few of the workers arrived very early in the morning, to catch the first light.

Although the sky was still dark, there were signs of a brightening in the east. Barbara Rae treasured each dawn, and thanked God each morning that she had lived to see another. The world was surely a marvelous place! Despite all the sorrow of life—and all the evil that lurked in the human heart—the endless richness and variety of the world never ceased to delight her. It was so very *exciting* to be alive!

As she quietly entered the construction site through the south transept entrance, the humming in her ears grew louder. She shook her head, wondering if she was getting a cold.

As soon as she was within the walls of the cathedral, however, Barbara Rae began to have the eerie feeling that, despite the early hour, she was not the first one to arrive this morning. She stood silently, letting her eyes adjust to the pervasive darkness. Although nearly blind in the unlit structure, she felt her other senses grow more acute. "Hello?" she said softly. "Is someone there?"

A great hollow silence engulfed her.

* * *

Annie was awakened by the *trilling* of the phone. She groped for it. "Hello?" she said groggily.

"It's me, Sam."

She squinted at the clock. No, she hadn't overslept—it was just a couple of minutes after seven. Her alarm didn't ring until seven-fifteen.

"Hi, Sam. It's a little early."

"Yes, I know, I'm sorry," he said in a clipped voice that was very unlike him. "I've just had a call from the police. There's been an accident at the construction site. One of the workmen has been killed."

"Oh no!"

"Apparently he fell from the scaffolding to the cathedral floor, some eighty feet below. The cops are there now, and they want to talk to the people in charge. Since you're one of them—"

"Sam, for God's sake, who was it?"

"I'm afraid it's the foreman of the crew of craftsmen we brought over from Italy to install the stained glass."

"Not Giuseppe?"

"Yes." There was a slight pause. "Annie, I'm so sorry. I hate to wake you with such awful news."

"Dear God," she whispered. She leaned forward, clutching the phone in one hand and wrapping her free arm around her suddenly aching middle. "When did it happen? How?"

"No details yet. But you'd better get over there. The police will want to talk to you—well, to all of us." Again he paused. "When someone dies suddenly . . . you know how they are."

"I'll go immediately," she said. "Has his family been

notified? He has a sister here, and Ludovico, the nephew, who used to work for us—"

"I believe the cops are taking care of that now. They have some questions. I'm on my way down there too—to the site, I mean."

They have some questions. "Sam, it *was* an accident, right?"

"What else could it be?"

Right, Annie thought in confusion. *What else could it be?*

She dressed rapidly feeling numb. Giuseppe dead? That talented, vital, friendly man? God. What a waste!

Had Sam called Darcy? she wondered. She didn't hear any sounds from next door. She went out onto the front porch and rapped on her friend's door, but Darcy didn't answer. She hadn't been home last night, either. Annie had stopped by after getting home from Matt's to assure her that she hadn't been raped or murdered after all.

She shivered. No, *she* hadn't been murdered.

But a wonderful man was dead.

Chapter Sixteen

Annie arrived at the construction site just before eight o'clock and found an ambulance and several police cars parked with the construction trailers. Several workers in hard hats were standing around, talking nervously to one another and smoking cigarettes. Yellow crime-scene tape had been used to cordon off the entire site, and a policewoman prevented her from entering the cathedral.

"Sam?" she said shakily. "What's going on?"

He was talking to a police detective outside the south transept entrance. As soon as he saw her, he held out his arms. She went into them and he hugged her convulsively. Then he stepped back, shaking his head sadly. He looked exhausted. His golden hair looked dull, almost gray.

"I'm so sorry, Annie. I know how important all these workmen have been to you, and Giuseppe in particular."

She moved back into his arms and for a moment clung to him. "Do they know how it happened?"

"I'm not sure, but it looks like they're treating it as a crime scene, at least until they have evidence to the contrary. I guess they have to make sure that Giuseppe wasn't pushed off the scaffolding or something. The medical examiner is in there now," he added, nodding at a coroner's van parked at the curb. "The cops have been in there making perimeter searches for physical evidence."

"Who would *push* somebody off the scaffolding?"

"Shit, Annie, I don't know. I assume they're just being cautious, doing their jobs, all that sort of thing."

He looked so distraught that Annie laid a gentle hand on his arm to comfort him.

"Does anybody know exactly what happened?" she asked. "Were any of the rest of the crew working with Giuseppe?"

Sam shook his head. "It was too early. Apparently he was here alone."

Annie nodded. Giuseppe typically arrived earlier than the rest of the crew.

"I think Barbara Rae was here, though," said Sam. "Praying or something. Or maybe she's the one who found him. She's in there." He pointed to one of the trailers. "They're interviewing her now."

As he spoke, the trailer door opened and Barbara Rae emerged looking grim and tired. The police detective, a tall, expressionless woman, pointed to Sam. "You next, Mr. Brody, please."

Annie rushed to Barbara Rae Acker's side. The older woman embraced her. "The poor man," she said in her deep contralto. "He was a master craftsman and a good family man. It is a heavy loss."

"Barbara Rae, what happened? Did you witness the accident? What time did it happen?"

"I didn't see him fall, but I did discover his body," she said. "I came here to pray. I thought I was alone."

"You were praying in a construction site? I know it's going to be a church—your church—but still . . ."

"I know it sounds a little strange, but I come here often to pray. I think of it as, well, nurturing the sacredness of the place right from the start. Asking God to come here and feel at home, as it were. Making it a comfortable place not only for humanity but also for the divine."

Well, maybe God hadn't shown up yet, Annie thought. Letting somebody die in the construction process didn't seem a particularly wise or generous gesture on the part of God.

Don't even think such things, she ordered herself. Her faith had been sorely challenged when Charlie died.

"The worst thing is, I had a premonition about this," Barbara Rae said. She was looking off into the distance, and her voice was low, barely audible.

"A premonition?"

Barbara Rae shook her head slowly, back and forth, back and forth. "I get them. It's the Sight. My mother had it too. She called it a gift, but it's always been hard for me to see it that way. The premonitions, when I have them, are always bad, and no matter how much I pray, I don't seem able to avert what's going to happen."

"You mean you see, in advance, when some tragedy is about to occur?"

"Not always, no. It's very rare—for which I'm thankful. And I don't see the actual event. I get just a hint of it."

Annie nodded, not really understanding or believing in

premonitions or visions. That sort of thing was more in Darcy's line. "What sort of hint did you get about this?"

Barbara Rae folded her arms around her middle. "It came on one evening when I was in there praying. Darkness. A sense of something falling from a great height. The scent of blood."

Annie found herself shivering. There was a commotion near the door as two men began rolling out a metal stretcher, the body hidden from sight in a black zippered bag. Annie turned away as it was loaded into the back of the ambulance.

Poor Giuseppe!

Barbara Rae turned toward her and they moved into a hug. Annie could hear Barbara Rae murmuring something, and little by little her voice got louder until Annie recognized the words: " 'Yea, though I walk through the valley of the shadow of death, I will fear no evil, for Thou art with me . . .' "

Sam came out of the trailer the police had commandeered and joined Annie and Barbara Rae. He looked dispirited and sad. "I think they want to talk to you now," he told Annie. He gave her hand a squeeze as she went in.

There were two detectives, Catherine Sullivan, the businesslike one, a tough, no-nonsense woman with graying brown hair and glasses, and John Foster, a middle-aged man with a paunch and a thick smell of cigarettes. Sullivan asked most of the questions, while Foster tapped his fingers on the edge of his laptop computer.

How well had she known the deceased?

What, exactly, was his job?

Did she have any idea why he had come to work so early in the morning?

Did he have any enemies?

What did she know of his family?

Who had access to the construction site during the night?

Who had access to the scaffolding and how many people understood how construction scaffolding was put together?

At some point as she struggled to give satisfactory answers to their questions, Annie asked, "You sound as if you're considering this a suspicious death. You surely don't believe that this was anything other than an accident?"

"We're not excluding any possibilities at present, Ms. Jefferson," Sullivan said.

"But do you know what happened? I mean, no one seems to be able to give me any clear information. Did part of the scaffolding collapse? Is that why he fell?"

"That's what we're trying to ascertain, Ms. Jefferson."

"You see, as the project manager and the interior designer, I'm in charge of the interior as well as the entire construction site. If there's a safety issue here—"

"Yes, I'm sure you're concerned about your liability. Mr. Brody expressed a similar concern," Sullivan said in a somewhat sour tone.

Annie flushed. The possible legal ramifications had not yet occurred to her. What she was thinking was that if there were dangers, she didn't want any of the other workers to take any risks.

Projects like the cathedral did have inherent dangers, no matter how much planning and effort went into trying to reduce them. Construction workers suffered one of the highest rates of occupational hazard of any profession. People did occasionally die on such massive projects.

But until this morning she had been satisfied that everything possible had been done to reduce the risks associated with this job. And it was important, both for Brody Associates and for McEnerney Construction, to affirm that they had done their best to provide a safe working environment.

Therefore, the cause of Giuseppe's death was vitally important. If he'd fallen because the scaffolding was faulty in some way, somebody would likely be hit with a lawsuit.

"It has come to our attention," said Detective Foster, "that the deceased, Mr. Brindesi, had a nephew who used to work with him on this project."

"Yes. Vico. I think his full name is Ludovico Genese."

"And is it also true that this young man—this Vico—was fired recently from his job?"

"I'm sorry to say that he was."

"For what reason?"

"He didn't show up for work, and it was our understanding that he had been accused of a crime and was a fugitive."

"And do you know the whereabouts of this fugitive, Ms. Jefferson?"

She shook her head and said, "No." She wondered if she should mention that she had seen Vico at the youth center with Paolina, then decided to wait and see what else they asked her. She wouldn't lie to the police, but she didn't feel inclined to get Vico and Paolina into worse trouble than they were already in.

"Did Vico have any problems with his uncle?" Detective Sullivan asked.

"Well . . ." She hesitated. "They argued a lot. Giuseppe

was trying to straighten the boy out, but Vico is proud and very stubborn."

"So there was conflict between them?"

Annie stared at the two detectives. Her head was beginning to ache. "What are you suggesting?"

"We're not suggesting anything, Ms. Jefferson. We are merely trying to establish a few facts."

"Is there something suspicious about Giuseppe's death?" Annie demanded. "Are you looking for someone to blame it on?"

The cops exchanged glances. Sullivan nodded, and Foster said to her, "We're looking at some possible sabotage of the scaffolding in there, yes. Three of the pins that hold the pipes in place under the wooden platform where your workman was standing have been removed. The thing was bound to collapse, killing whoever was standing on it at the time. So, yeah, we think Giuseppe Brindesi was murdered."

Chapter Seventeen

With the cathedral closed down and the site surrounded by crime-scene tape, Annie had no choice but to return to her office at Brody Associates. There she found people standing around in small groups, talking and speculating. The news that Giuseppe's death had not been an accident spread fast.

By eleven o'clock the press had arrived, trying to get some footage to put on the noon news. Annie declined to talk to them. She knew that as the project manager, she would have to talk to them sooner or later, but she was damned if it was going to be now.

At a few minutes past twelve, Matt Carlyle telephoned. "I heard about your workman's death," he said. "How are you holding up?"

Annie was touched. Except for Sam and Barbara Rae, who were always thoughtful, Matt was the first person to ask about her state of mind instead of peppering her with questions about what had happened at the site.

"I think I'm in shock. I knew him and liked him very much, but I haven't had a moment yet to focus on the fact that he's gone."

"Can you escape for a few minutes?" he asked. "I know what it's like over there—but can you meet me for lunch?"

"I don't—"

"I'm concerned about this too, Annie. After all, I am the new head of the building committee. And I was introduced to this poor man yesterday, just a few hours before his death. I thought of coming directly to your office, but I'm sure you're getting enough publicity as it is without the zoo that would result if the infamous Matthew Carlyle showed up in the aftermath of another suspicious death."

He was right, of course.

"Where do you want to meet?"

He gave her the name of a small pasta restaurant in Union Square just a few blocks from her office. "They know me, and they're discreet."

"Okay. I'll see you there in twenty minutes."

Annie slipped out the side door and walked briskly up Post Street to Union Square, the heart of the city's shopping district. Macy's, I. Magnin, and Neiman-Marcus rose over the small park, and she longed to head into one of them and lose herself in a whirl of what Darcy called "retail therapy." And where *was* Darcy? she wondered. She hadn't seen her all morning.

A cable car chugged up Powell Street. It stopped in front of the park to take on passengers—most of whom were tourists clutching cameras and maps—then continued up the hill. It would go over Nob Hill and Russian Hill, then descend to sea level on the other side of the city at the Cannery near Fisherman's Wharf. Annie wished she could join the tourists and forget her troubles. Just be a visitor here, without anything greater to worry about than which cable car to squeeze onto.

She found the restaurant tucked between two stores on Geary. She descended into a dimly lit cellar, which was filled with a few small tables with green and white checked tablecloths. Matthew had already arrived. He was wearing a beautiful dark suit and tie that fit perfectly over his broad shoulders and that spoke, discreetly, of his great wealth and excellent taste.

He stood as the waiter led her to his table in the corner, and Annie thought, *I keep forgetting how tall he is.* She knew that she was deliberately trying to forget how magnetic he was.

She felt a thrill go through her when he took her hand. Mentally, she rebelled against it. *I don't have time for this. And it's just not right, with poor Giuseppe lying dead. . . .*

"You look pale, Annie. Sit down. Have you eaten anything today?"

"I don't think so. I had some coffee at the office. Too much coffee, probably."

He signaled the waiter. "Do you mind if I go ahead and order for us? I have a feeling you're not going to be able to concentrate too well on that menu. Is there anything you don't like?"

"I don't eat much meat," she said. "Fish or chicken is okay."

He ordered hearty salads and their catch-of-the-day special, to be served with plenty of pasta. Crusty bread and red wine showed up almost immediately, and Annie forced herself to taste a bit of both.

Matt kept the conversation going with pleasantries of various kinds, and Annie relaxed and allowed the sound of his husky voice to help to center her. He ordered tea instead of coffee after the food was cleared away, and as they sipped it, he finally asked about the tragedy.

"I've already heard rumors that he was murdered. Is there any truth to that?"

She nodded wearily. "That's what the police told me when they interviewed me. They said it looked as if the pins had been removed from some of the joints just underneath his platform on the scaffolding."

"Pins?"

"Construction scaffolding is made of metal cylinders that slide into one another," she explained. "It's similar, in a way, to an erector set. The joints are secured with metal pins about a quarter of an inch in diameter . . . maybe a little thicker than that, actually. If the pins are pulled out or loosened, the wooden platforms they support can't take a man's weight. The police wouldn't allow me inside, but from what I can gather, that part of the scaffolding collapsed, and he fell to his death."

"So somebody sabotaged the scaffolding? When? During the night?"

"Presumably. Giuseppe gets to the site very early every morning. Just after dawn, usually, so I suppose it must have been done during the night."

"And do you think Giuseppe was the intended victim, or were other people using the scaffolding?"

Annie had been wondering about that too. Giuseppe did have men helping him, but he was notorious for insisting on doing the lion's share of the work himself. And because Giuseppe was the first to arrive and the last to leave, it was difficult to imagine that anybody else could have been the target.

She explained this and added, "I think the police are focusing on his nephew. Vico is already on the run from the law. He and Giuseppe were at each other's throats—Giuseppe was so disappointed in the boy."

"Just because two people are in conflict doesn't mean one will murder the other," Matt said with an edge to his voice.

"I didn't say I suspected Vico, just that I got the impression the police do."

He made a gesture that showed exactly what he thought of the police.

"On the other hand," she said, "if the scaffolding was sabotaged in the manner the police described, it suggests that whoever did it is familiar with construction techniques. In other words, he would have known what to do."

"So would anybody else who worked there," Matt pointed out.

She nodded. Losing Giuseppe was bad enough, but the thought that the fiery young Vico might have killed him just made things worse. When she thought about Paolina, his pregnant girlfriend, she felt a kind of despair settle over her.

"If the boy and his uncle fought, and one of them killed the other, I should think it would be a crime of passion, not premeditated murder," said Matthew. "Sabotaging the scaffolding is a devious, cold-blooded act. Is this kid likely to do it that way?"

"You're right," Annie said slowly. "No, I can't imagine him doing it that way. If Vico killed, he'd do it in your face, with a gun or a knife."

"*Is* there anybody else that you know of who might have wanted to murder the guy?"

"Maybe." She told him about the threatening notes she'd received. "They appear to be aimed more at me than at any of the workmen, though."

"Have you shown them to the police?"

She shook her head. "No. I probably should have mentioned them this morning, but I think I was in shock, not thinking straight. . . ."

"Don't worry. You'll get another chance. I'm sure the cops aren't through with you yet."

She sighed. "I'd better get back to the office. There will be all sorts of ramifications. The press is there, and OSHA will undoubtedly turn up demanding an investigation. It's going to be messy." She met his gaze uneasily. "You know what the press is like. Somebody will zoom in on the fact that there's been a murder in the cathedral within a few days of your being elected chairman of the building committee, Matt."

"I know," he said grimly.

"I'm sorry. You'll probably be in for more nastiness."

"It's not your fault. Murder seems to be dogging my footsteps lately. Like a curse."

Chapter Eighteen

That afternoon in Sam's office there was a tense meeting of everyone who was working, or had worked, on the cathedral project, including Sam, Darcy, Annie, a couple of Brody Associates structural engineers, Jack Fletcher, and Paul McEnerney, the general contractor.

Sam was more belligerent than Annie had ever seen him before. He'd told her briefly before the start of the meeting that the more he thought about what had happened to Giuseppe, the angrier he got. "Look, Paul," he said now, "you assured me the site was safe. You also assured me that there wasn't going to be any trouble. Now we've got a man down—murdered, for chrissake!—and the press is swarming all over the place like a cloud of locusts."

"Take it easy, Sam," McEnerney said. "Sit down. You look like shit."

"I feel like shit. I've been answering questions from the

cops and the press since six o'clock this morning. We've got tabloids declaring that the site is cursed and the Devil is determined to throw down the work of the Lord."

"A real epic battle, huh?" McEnerney said. "Don't worry, Sam. The Lord always wins these things."

Sam shook his head. "Look, a man—a good man, an artist whose work is respected all over the world—was killed while working on my project. I want to know why. I want to know, for example, if this has anything to do with union/nonunion trouble."

"You mean because Giuseppe was nonunion? I doubt it. The unions all know that we have to hire these guys for the esoteric work like fine marble carving and stained glass."

McEnerney glanced at Fletcher and added, "My job superintendent here hasn't noticed any union/nonunion troubles, right, Jack?"

"Right."

Sam turned to Annie, "Do you agree with that, Annie? Have you seen any evidence of union-related conflict on site?"

She shook her head. "We have a lot of subcontractors on site. The workers all have different skills, and my impression has been that they respect each other. Giuseppe and his men kept pretty much to themselves, and I never witnessed any trouble."

"Except from the nephew," Fletcher put in. "Vico and his uncle were at each other's throats."

"So this kid is the prime suspect?" McEnerney asked.

"It's beginning to look that way," Annie said reluctantly. "But it's really hard for me to imagine that Vico would murder his uncle."

McEnerney shrugged. "Maybe he wanted money and his uncle refused to give it to him, they had a fight—who knows? People kill each other for all sorts of stupid reasons."

Sam ran a hand through his hair, and Annie felt a rush of sympathy for him. This killing had taken a toll on everyone. Every time she thought of Giuseppe's family, her heart seemed to squeeze in her chest.

"All I know is, the cops are tearing up the city looking for the kid," he said. "And I hope to God they find him. Soon."

Darcy spoke up for the first time: "Are there any other suspects? Any other reason why somebody might want Giuseppe Brindesi dead?"

Sam's eyes locked with hers. "None that I know of," he said. He glanced at Paul McEnerney. "I certainly hope it doesn't turn out in any way to be a job-related killing."

"You worry too much, Sam," McEnerney said.

Sam sighed heavily. "Somebody's got to. By the way, the cops want to fingerprint everybody who works at the crime scene or was there during the last few weeks. Apparently they're processing an area that's full of prints, and if the killer's are there, they want to find them."

"*All* our fingerprints will be there, Sam," Annie said.

"Of course they will. Doesn't mean any of us is under suspicion. Just that they want to identify all the prints they can, and see what they have left."

Doesn't mean any of us is under suspicion.

Maybe not, Annie thought. But if Vico didn't kill his uncle, who did?

* * *

That night Annie went as usual to the youth center to volunteer. It seemed odd to be so close to the cathedral and yet not able to enter the site. The police crime-scene tape was still in place.

For once, there was no one to counsel. The activity of the police so nearby was keeping them away, Barbara Rae speculated.

Annie didn't stay long, since Barbara Rae was in the middle of preparing a eulogy to deliver at Giuseppe's funeral.

Annie had left her car parked among the trailers in the construction lot adjacent to the cathedral. Two police cars were still there, and there were lights in the back of the cathedral and crime-scene tape around the east end. The west end, however, was dark and quiet. No police, no tape. All the activity was down by the altar.

So, Annie was startled to see a slight figure tiptoeing in the shadows near the west entrance. She caught a glimpse of long blond hair as the figure slipped into the west entrance of the construction site.

Paolina. Vico's girlfriend.

What was she doing here? Looking for Barbara Rae? Sneaking inside to pray for her missing lover and her unborn child? She must know, surely, that the cathedral had been closed down as a crime scene. She must know that Vico's uncle was dead and that Vico was being sought for questioning in the murder.

What was she up to? Didn't she know that there were police cars parked at the other end?

Annie hurried to the west entrance and followed Paolina inside. There was a pile of bricks by the opening to the area, and, in the dark, she stumbled on them.

"Damn," she whispered. She felt in her purse for the pencil flashlight she always carried with her. She switched it on, noting from its dim light that it would soon need new batteries.

She felt a shiver of pure fear. As she had told Matt the other evening at his house, she had a lifelong fear of being shut up in dark places. She assumed that it had something to do with one of her experiences in those awful foster homes as a child, although she must have repressed the exact memory.

It wasn't exactly claustrophobia, since she could ride in subways and elevators and fly in planes without feeling as if she had to tear at the walls. But if she was in an elevator and it stopped and the lights went out . . . she was sure that she would rapidly devolve into a candidate for the psychiatric ward.

"Take it easy, Annie," she muttered. "There's nothing small and confining about this place."

She directed her light toward the extreme west end of the nave. For the moment, she didn't see Paolina. Nor were there any lights in the front of the church near the altar. Maybe the police investigators had finished up their task and left.

Most of the inside walls of the building were lined with scaffolding, used by the men who were working on the walls, the electric connections, the masonry, and the windows. But Annie squinted down at the scaffolding that had failed. From a distance it looked much the same as usual, which surprised her. There wasn't enough light in the cathedral for her to see the part of the structure that had fallen.

Poor Giuseppe! She imagined how it must have been to fall for endless seconds through the dark, knowing that when the falling stopped, so would your life. Falling through darkness. It was like a terrible dream.

She forced her mind away from that. Dammit, where was Paolina?

A bright movement at the corner of her eye alerted her. Paolina was in one of the side aisles, gliding silently toward the east end of the cathedral. With her long blond hair and her dark flowing dress she looked more like an apparition than a teenage girl.

Annie hurried after her. She was about six feet behind her when Paolina turned, her face white and scared.

"Shh, it's all right, nobody's going to hurt you," Annie said. "What are you doing here?"

The girl shook her head wordlessly.

"If you'd like to pray, I'm sure Barbara Rae will pray with you, but this is a construction site, and it's not safe. You can't be in here, Paolina. Especially now. The police are here."

Paolina gasped and looked around wildly.

"Paolina, do you know what happened to Vico's uncle?"

The girl looked at her, and Annie wondered, for an instant, what was wrong with her. Was she on drugs? She seemed vague and confused, as if she was high on something. Dear heaven! She was pregnant. She damn well ought to know better!

But Paolina's eyes cleared as she looked at Annie. "Yes, I know. He's dead."

"And Vico? If you know where he is, please tell him to come forward. The police are searching for him."

"They've been searching for two weeks," Paolina said disdainfully. "They won't find him."

"Yes, they will. The stakes have gone way up. Before, he was just another punk who sells drugs. Now he's a suspect in his uncle's murder."

Paolina's eyes widened. "He's a suspect?"

"Exactly that. Vico and his uncle had some problems. The cops are afraid that—"

"No!" the girl cried. "Vico did not do it! The scaffolding broke apart and Giuseppe fell! Vico would never hurt anyone, especially his uncle." Her tone was passionate and insistent. "I know they argued sometimes, but Vico loved him!"

A flashlight snapped on in the apse of the cathedral and they heard a man's voice call out to another. The anguish in the teenager's eyes changed to panic. She pushed past Annie and fled along the north wall of the cathedral.

Annie rushed after her, retracing her steps toward the door they had both used to enter the construction site.

"Hey, where d'you think you're going?" a man exclaimed as Annie careened into him in the darkness. He grabbed her arm and pulled her to a stop. As she whirled to face him, he quickly let her go. "Annie?" he said.

It was Jack Fletcher.

"Please, let me pass. There was a girl in here—she said something important."

"I didn't see a girl," Fletcher said. "I've seen a lot of cops hanging around, but no one else."

"Jack, I was just talking to her, dammit. She slipped past me and got away."

"Do you know who she was?"

"Yes, of course. Her name is Paolina. She's Vico's girl-friend. She says he didn't do it."

"Well, of course that's what she says."

"I know, I know, but it was more than just a lover's denial, Jack." What was it Paolina had said? *"Vico did not do it! The scaffolding broke apart and Giuseppe fell!"* It sounded as if Paolina had actually seen it happen. As if she had been right here in the cathedral at the time. "I think, from what she said, that she may have been a witness to Giuseppe's death. Perhaps she and Vico were both witnesses."

"Yeah, like she witnessed *him* doing it," Fletcher said.

Annie shook her head. Of course he wouldn't believe her. Neither, she was sure, would anybody else.

But Paolina had sounded so sincere and so passionate.

"What was she doing in here anyway?" Fletcher asked.

"I don't know." She looked at him. "What are *you* doing here? Isn't the site still off limits to all of us?"

"To hell with that," Fletcher said. "It's my construction site, and I damn well want to know exactly what happened here last night."

"Yes, well, so do I."

"We're well away from the crime-scene tape," he added. "It's not like we're tromping through the evidence."

Somebody shouted at them, and flashlights were beamed their way. "Even so, I think we're about to be nailed in our own building," Annie said with a sigh.

"You'll have to tell the cops about the girl," Fletcher said.

"Mmm." Annie was already wishing that she hadn't told Fletcher.

Had Paolina been here last night?

Had she witnessed Giuseppe's death?

After the police grilled them and finally let them go, Fletcher walked Annie back outside to her car. She was clearly preoccupied, and she didn't seem to notice how close beside her he was walking, or even that he took her arm once to help her around a pothole in the razed lot they all used as a parking area.

"It's late," he said in as gentlemanly a manner as he could muster. "Would you like me to follow you home, make sure you get there okay?"

She blinked at him, obviously puzzled by the question. "Thanks, but that's not necessary."

"I guess you're pretty brave, huh?" he said.

"What do you mean, brave? Why am I brave?"

"Well, here you are at a construction site in the middle of the night . . . just after someone's been murdered. That takes guts, I think."

"Does it? You're here," she pointed out.

"Hey, I'm a guy."

She gave him a freezing look. "I guess that explains it."

Stupid idiot! he raged at himself.

She frowned but said nothing more about it. A second or two later, she started up her car. "See you tomorrow, Fletcher," she said, and pulled away.

Fuck. Fletcher got into his car. He thought about following Annie home anyhow but decided not to risk it. One mistake per night was enough.

He wondered about the girl in the cathedral. Paolina. Vico's girlfriend. He'd seen her hanging out at the site when the kid was on the job. Blond girl—a real looker, all right.

Annie had not mentioned her to the police. Why had the girl been hanging around the cathedral? And what was Annie trying to hide? Could she be trying to protect Vico?

God, he'd love to get something on Annie. He needed some way to get her under his thumb.

Fletcher picked up the cellular phone in his car. He was

proud of that phone. Made him feel like a big shot to be talking on the phone while waiting for a red light to change.

He dialed Sam Brody's private number. It was late, but what the hell. There'd been a murder on the site, for chrissake. Anyhow, Brody liked him to check in on a regular basis. Sometimes he felt like he was working more for Brody than for McEnerney Construction. Especially since McEnerney was such a prick.

"Mr. Brody, you know that kid—Giuseppe Brindesi's nephew? The one the cops are after?"

"What about him, Jack?"

"He had this girlfriend. Blond chick. Very good-looking. When the kid was there she used to hang around sometimes, encouraging him. You remember her?"

"Sorry. I don't know anything about her. Why?"

"I was wondering if you had any idea how to find her. An address? A phone?"

"First I've heard of her, Jack."

"Well, she was lurking in the cathedral tonight. Annie seems to think the girl might know where Vico is. She could even be some kind of witness. Annie thinks she and her boyfriend may have been around when Giuseppe got frosted."

There was silence on Brody's end for a couple of moments. Then: "Annie?"

Fletcher pulled it in a couple of notches. "The Jefferson babe."

"I'd hate to see her reaction if she heard you calling her a 'babe,' Jack. Women are very sensitive to that sort of thing nowadays."

"Sorry," Fletcher mumbled, clenching his fists.

"As I said, this is the first I've heard of Vico's girlfriend."

"I'd like to find her. Ask her a few questions."

"So will a lot of people, especially if she or the boy was a witness. Still, isn't that the sort of thing we should leave to the police, Jack? They'll find Vico and the girl, if necessary, much more easily than you or I will. At least, that's what we pay our taxes for."

"I suppose," Fletcher said.

They said goodbye and hung up. But the more Fletcher thought about it, the more he believed that the blond girl was the key. The key to Annie. If he could find her and find out what she knew, he could take it to Annie. She'd be grateful, he knew. Very grateful.

He drove home, fantasizing all the way. What he wanted, he decided, was a combination of grateful and scared. Grateful so she'd have to come to him. Scared once she was in his hands.

Annie was brave, and it was starting to get on his nerves. He wanted her nervous. Tense, fretful, a little upset. Briefly, when the cops had confronted them, she'd looked as if she hadn't known quite what to expect or exactly how to handle herself. She'd been wary, perhaps a little frightened, and Fletcher had loved it.

That was the way he wanted her to look just before he fucked her. Vulnerable. Scared.

That was the hard part, for him. If they were willing, they usually weren't scared. Made him want the ones who *weren't* willing, but that raised a whole other set of problems. He'd learned the hard way that unwilling women could be real nasty about things afterward.

No, the women he got were usually the sluts who couldn't wait to get on with it, and most of them were just too damn aggressive in bed. And the demands they made—Christ, what a pain in the ass! Not only would they expect to be given an orgasm—or several orgasms in the case of some of these broads—but they'd dictate how to do it and when to do it and where to touch, precisely, and how long and how hard.

Then there were the ones who didn't make any demands but expected you to read their minds. They were a bit better, but not much. If you didn't figure out what they wanted and how they wanted it, they didn't scream at you and flounce into their clothes and out of your house—no, they sulked. Or, worse, they cried. He hated that. Crying women reminded him of his bitch of a mother, who'd been a whiner and a crier all her life. She was gone now, and good riddance. He'd always wanted a soft, warm, loving mom, but instead he'd had a harpy who'd terrorized and beaten him bloody when he was a child, then whined and cried because he didn't come round to see her as an adult. .

Annie, though—Annie would be different from all the other women. She was a lady, with all the class his loudmouthed mother could never in a million years have possessed. He'd never heard Annie mouth off at anyone—she was too elegant, too smooth. He just couldn't see her picking up his finger and depositing it on the precise spot on her clit. She had better manners than that. She would wait for him to make the move, and if it wasn't exactly what she wanted, she'd be far too polite to say so.

No, Annie would behave. Annie would do as she was told. And if she didn't . . . Well, there was a remedy for that as well. His mind slipped into a fantasy of Annie, naked, spread-eagled and bound to the frame of his king-size bed, her beautiful long limbs straining and her body arching as she struggled to get free. That was how he *really* wanted to fuck her.

And before he fucked her, he wanted to watch her expression. He wanted to see her fear. She'd look vulnerable then, by God. She'd look nervous and worried and sexy as hell.

Fletcher recalled with great pleasure the last time he had tied a woman up. Actually, she'd suggested it. Said she was into it. Said it excited her and to do it, do it please.

He'd never tied a woman up before then, although he'd certainly fantasized about it often enough. Having a taut female body arching helplessly beneath him while he fucked her was one of the sexiest things he could imagine.

And it had been wild. He'd gone with his instincts and blindfolded her as well. She hadn't expected that, and he'd seen the wariness come over her face as he was tying the scarf over her eyes. Before that she'd looked almost too eager, but with the blindfold he got her back under his control. She didn't know what he was going to do. She wasn't absolutely sure she could trust him not to hurt her. What a turn-on!

And he *had* hurt her a bit. Slapped her a few times, pinched her nipples. Oh, he'd been careful about it. He'd been real careful about keeping his head and staying in control. At one point she'd complained about some numbness in her fingers, so he'd untied the numb hand and massaged it and made sure the rope was looser when he bound her again.

By then she was relaxed enough to get into it. So he'd hurt her a little more, and then he'd fucked her, and they'd both come, screaming.

Yeah, it had been wild. In fact, she was the one woman he'd actually *wanted* to see a second time. But then, she'd been the one to say, no thanks, no way. Once was all you get, kid, back off.

Not nice of her.

Not nice at all.

Fletcher forced his mind back to thoughts of Annie.

This time he'd do the bondage thing right. He'd learned a bit from the first experience. He'd learned he could push them a lot farther, a lot closer to the edge. That pain and arousal got mixed up in a woman's mind. That as long as you did a couple of things to calm them down and set their minds at ease, you could get away with stuff that most men would never even dare dream about.

Maybe he'd tease her for a while first. Maybe he'd caress her inner thighs lightly until she became excited lying there. He wouldn't let her get too excited, though. He wouldn't want her to come. No, he was going to take his revenge against all those feminist bitches who'd given him instructions on how to maximize the quantity and quality of their orgasms. Annie wouldn't be *permitted* to come. He wasn't fucking her for her pleasure. He was fucking her purely for his own.

Someday . . . Fletcher thought.

He got a hard-on just thinking about it.

Someday soon.

When she got home that night, Annie found another letter. This time it had been tucked under the front door. Annie recognized the block writing on the envelope as soon as she saw it.

He was here, she thought, shivering. *The person who's doing this might be outside right now, watching the house.*

She slammed the door and locked it, then drew all the curtains and pulled all the shades. Next she went through the entire house, checking to make sure that no one had broken in, that all the doors and windows were secure. Only then did she open the envelope.

A single page of paper slipped out. It was short this time. And it was written in the form of a mock obituary:

> *Entered into rest, Anne Jefferson, designer of church interiors. Suddenly. Crushed by the weight of her own prideful vision.*
> *R.I.P.*

Below that, in larger letters, were scrawled the words, *Watch out—you're next.* And then the signature; *Jehovah's Pitchfork.*

Chapter Nineteen

"I probably should have shown these to you before, Sam," Annie said the next morning, pulling out photocopies of the three threatening letters and handing them to him. "Besides poor Vico, there's somebody else who appears to have some sort of hostile intent toward the cathedral. That's the latest one I've gotten," she said, pointing. "Last night I turned them over to the police."

Sam read the letters, his expression growing increasingly grim as he read. By the time he got to the most recent one he was looking very angry indeed. " 'You're next'? My God, Annie!"

"The hostility toward me in particular has been escalating," Annie said dryly.

"I'll say," said Sam. "Jesus. It's been one thing after another lately, hasn't it?" He looked up at her. "How do you feel about this?"

"Not great."

Sam muttered a curse, unusual for him. He shuffled the letters, handling them gingerly. "Do you have any idea who might have sent them?"

She shook her head. "I've been assuming it's some random nutcase. But now that there's been a murder, I'm wondering if there could be any connection between the killer and these letters."

"When did they start arriving?"

"Recently. Just a few days ago, in fact."

"What about that kid Vico? He may be the murderer. Could he also be your poison pen?"

Poor Vico, Annie thought. Everybody was so quick to blame him. "I doubt it, Sam."

"You don't believe he's a killer, either, do you?"

"I don't know what to think."

Sam rose and took a turn around his office. He stopped in front of the windows and rubbed the back of his neck, ruffling his golden hair. Then he turned to her and said, "Look, this is tough on all of us. But after seeing those letters, I'm realizing that it's probably toughest on you, Annie. I'm really sorry about that."

His voice was gentle, and Annie felt her eyes tear up. She bit her lip. Much as she liked Sam, she didn't want to betray an oversupply of emotion. She couldn't forget Charlie's lectures on the subject: Women cry too easily. It's unprofessional. If a woman is going to be accepted to work alongside a group of men, she has to adapt to their style. Men don't cry.

Control yourself, Annie.

"I'll be fine," she said quietly. "A good night's sleep will help a lot. I'm planning to go to bed very early tonight."

"I'm worried about these letters," he said. "I don't want to scare you, but they sound really sick to me."

"Well, the police know now. Presumably they're doing something about it."

"Have they offered you any kind of protection?"

"Well, no . . . but I didn't ask for it."

Sam reached for the phone. "Dammit, I'm going to get you some. This is ridiculous. A man has been murdered, nobody seems to have a very clear idea why, and now you're being threatened—"

"It's funny, but in spite of what's happened, I don't feel as if the letters are really a threat to my life," she said slowly. "It's more as if—this is just my intuition, of course—but it's more like somebody is just trying to frighten me."

His hand paused on the receiver. "What do you mean, frighten you? Why would anybody want to do that?"

"I'm not sure. Maybe for the simple reason that I'm a woman, and it's not all that common for women to be in charge of twenty-million-dollar construction projects." She paused. "Sam, if you hadn't put me in charge, who would have gotten the project manager's position?"

He shrugged. "It would have depended on the owners, of course. It didn't have to be one of us. In fact, it wouldn't have been at all unusual for them to hire someone from outside, someone who knows the construction business better than you do, in fact."

"Somebody like Jack Fletcher, perhaps?"

Sam's eyes narrowed. "You suspect him of being involved in this somehow?"

"Oh, God, I don't know." She *had* wondered about Jack Fletcher, because there was something about him that always made her feel a little uneasy. But it was just a gut feeling and very vague. "I don't like him much, that's certainly true. But that's unfair of me, I know. I'm getting paranoid, I think. I'm starting to suspect everybody!"

"Well, actually, if you hadn't been chosen as project manager, there's somebody else in this firm who would have been perfect for the job. And that's Darcy."

"Darcy?"

"Sure. As an architect, she already knows some of the technical details that you had to learn on the job. And she's worked with contractors before—in fact, I believe she did some sort of summer internship with Paul McEnerney back when she was still in architecture school. She lacks your know-how on interior fittings of churches, though. But in other areas she is your equal, if not your superior."

"Well, that's a relief," Annie said with a smile. "The one person I don't suspect of trying to frighten me out of my job is Darcy!"

"Listen," Sam said slowly. "I want you to let me know if this begins to get too nerve-racking, okay?"

"Uh, what exactly do you mean?"

"Simply that a lot has been going on—a lot of unexpected stuff. Being a project manager isn't supposed to involve getting mixed up in a murder investigation or having your life threatened."

Annie felt her anger rise. Was he suggesting that she wasn't tough enough to deal with these things?

She quickly told herself not to overreact—Sam was only expressing a sincere and legitimate concern for her. But what he could never understand, as a man, was that a woman in this business was always nervous about being thought incompetent.

Murder and threatening letters probably brought out the macho in most men. Men under fire were supposed to tough it out and fire back. But women under fire were expected to wilt with the pressure.

I'm not wilting, dammit!

"I can handle it, Sam," she assured him.

"I know you can. You've been great on this job, and you know it. I'm immensely proud of the work you've done."

She relaxed a little. "Thanks."

"But I promise you, I'm not going to allow you—or anyone else, for that matter—to risk your life because of a construction project. I don't care how many millions it's bringing in. I'm going to have a little chat with the detectives on this case. If they think there's significant danger to any of my people, I'm going to pull everybody back for a while."

"But, Sam, the construction schedule—"

"The hell with the schedule. The cathedral is close to completion, and a few more weeks aren't going to make all that dire a difference. If the building has to sit empty with no work going on while this crime is investigated and this killer caught, fine. I don't want to go to any more funerals, Annie." He paused. "Especially yours."

As Annie left Sam's office, Sid Canin brushed by her and went in. He took no notice of her. In fact, ever since the other day when he'd exploded in her office about Matt Carlyle's involvement with the cathedral project, Sidney had been exceptionally rude.

Annie had brushed it off as an irritation not worth fretting about. Besides, Giuseppe's murder made everything else seem even more trivial.

Now, though, she noticed that Sidney began yelling at Sam as soon as the door closed behind him. She couldn't make out what he was saying, and she wasn't going to hang around and eavesdrop.

As she walked down the short hallway that led back to her office, she heard Sam yell back.

About an hour later, Darcy popped her head in. "More trouble," she said. "Sam fired Sidney."

"What?"

"Yep. Apparently it's one of those 'clean out your desk and don't darken my doorway again' sort of things. Gloomy old Sid is out."

"On what grounds?" Annie asked.

"Sam's not talking. Rumor has it they had a tear-up, rip-roaring fight. Supposedly Sid is saying, screw this business, screw this city, he's going to chuck everything and go live in New York, just like he'd planned a couple of years ago."

Annie shook her head. "Everything's changing," she murmured. "And it's all happening so fast."

"Everything sucks," Darcy agreed, "but it can't change fast enough to suit me."

Chapter Twenty

Darcy began crying during Giuseppe Brindesi's funeral and couldn't stop. People hugged her and offered soft words of consolation; others seemed surprised and touched that she was so upset by the death of a workman whom she hadn't really known very well.

Darcy felt like a fraud.

She had known and liked Giuseppe, but her grief, she knew, was not entirely for him. She was mourning in part, for herself.

Things were falling apart on all sides. She had made no headway whatsoever with Sam. He didn't seemed to be at all interested in resuming their love affair. None of her tactics were working.

Meanwhile, Sid Canin's summary dismissal had rattled everybody at Brody Associates. Although Darcy was not particularly sorry to see Sid go, she didn't like not knowing *why* he'd been fired. What had he done or not done? What had he said? If Sam had found fault with Sidney's work, what was to stop him from examining her's? What if he found some flaw in her work that he could use as an excuse to send her packing too?

Everything depended on her keeping her job. Shit, and she'd slept with the boss! She couldn't believe the risk she had taken. Or the new risks she kept taking every day.

And of course Giuseppe was dead—a good man, a fine craftsman, his life cut short. It was so wasteful, so unnecessary.

God, what a world.

Entering the church with the other mourners, Darcy had exchanged a hug with Sam—the same friendly, comforting hug she had exchanged with everybody. Except it seemed that Sam had held her a little closer this time, and for longer than was strictly necessary.

Or had she imagined it?

She could tell that he too was very upset by the murder. He was one of the speakers during the service, and his words about Giuseppe were so warm and so emotional that he'd had most of his listeners in tears. At one point he'd choked up as he'd read a short selection from John Donne: "No man is an island, entire of itself . . . any man's death diminishes me, because I am involved in mankind."

Listening intently, she'd been moved by his words, and proud of him.

Dammit, she still loved him so much!

She wondered about the blonde. Had he seen her again? Would he see her again soon? This coming weekend, perhaps? Or would he use the blonde and cast her off as casually as he had done with her?

Darcy felt a confused surge of anger.

She tried to convince herself that she knew Sam's type—

wealthy, sophisticated, single, and unable to commit to one woman. He was forty years old and had never married. In San Francisco, that would usually suggest he was gay, but she knew better—she'd heard too long a litany of Sam's cast-off women.

Yet, somehow, his romantic elusiveness didn't seem to fit with his great personal warmth and friendliness. How could someone who was so empathetic with people he barely knew not be all the *more* so with the people who were close to him?

Was there some blockage there? Some deep-seated inability to commit to an intimate relationship? Or was it merely a case of keeping his private life separate from his professional life?

She reminded herself that Sam was close with Matt Carlyle; in fact, she'd just seen the two of them exchange a warm handshake and slap on the back as they'd met in the church. Like many men, they might not hang out with each other on a daily basis, but they were obviously old, trusted friends.

It's just you he doesn't want to be close to, Darcy, she told herself.

Dammit! Why d'you want him anyhow? Just because he's more of a challenge to you than any of your previous lovers? If he were as wild for you as you are for him, how long would your own interest last?

Maybe you want him because he's like you.

You're warm and friendly too. But look at your own wariness about trusting people. You tell your friends the frivolous things, the superficial things about yourself, but you keep the important things private. Annie, for instance, probably thinks she knows you. But she'd be amazed if she could see the things that are really in your heart.

Amazed and disgusted.

As she watched the coffin being wheeled down the center aisle of the church toward the waiting hearse, Darcy realized for the first time that she was grateful for her obsession. If she concentrated all her thoughts and energy on Sam Brody, she didn't have to think about the death of Giuseppe Brindesi. She could lay it aside and pretend it hadn't happened . . . pretend he was still alive. . . .

She slipped to her knees and prayed.

Annie was surprised to see Matt at Giuseppe's funeral. The press was there—they were all over the story—and she had expected Matt to avoid any risk of an encounter with the journalists who had haunted him during his trial.

She was already seated in a crowded row when he entered, and she wasn't even sure if he'd seen her. He sat down with Sam, and the two of them plunged into an animated conversation. Annie tried to get their attention but failed.

Sidney too was in the church. She smiled weakly at him across the pews, but he looked right through her as if he didn't see her. His face was set and grim, and she noticed that at one point he left his spot in the pew and went over to have a brief talk with Catherine Sullivan, the homicide detective, who stood impassively at the rear of the church, watching everyone who came to pay their respects.

As the church emptied after the Roman Catholic service, Matt shook hands with Sam, then came over to Annie. "Hi there," he said.

"Hi there, yourself."

"As I was pulling up to the church, I saw you arrive with some of your colleagues from your office. I was wondering if you might consider leaving with me?"

"All right," she said, then smiled at his look of surprise. "Thought I'd say no, huh?"

"Annie, where you're concerned, I never know what to think."

They ducked out one of the side doors in an attempt to avoid the crowd of reporters. Matt had a limousine waiting next to the one reserved for the family. The police were all over, looking for the one member of the family who had not shown up. Despite the extensive police search, Vico had not been found.

"Not exactly inconspicuous, is it?" she said as his chauffeur opened the door to the limousine.

"Actually, there's nothing more inconspicuous at a funeral than one more big black car. Shall we go to the cemetery?"

She shook her head. "I don't think I can deal with it. What I'd really like is to just—I don't know . . . Could we drive around for a while?"

"Sounds good to me," he said, and instructed the driver to head down toward the Embarcadero.

As she settled back into the luxurious seat with Matt just a few inches from her, she thought, *It's silly to pretend that something isn't happening between us.*

He draped an arm around her shoulders. When she didn't resist, he pulled her in, gently, until she was leaning against him, her head falling against his shoulder.

There was a CD player in the limousine, and he put on

Mozart's *Requiem*. Then they both leaned back to absorb the music.

Annie loved Mozart, and the *Requiem* had been the major piece of music played at Charlie's funeral. The Mass, so beautiful and so tragic—Mozart had died before finishing it—had always made her cry. But this was the first time she had listened to it since Charlie's death, and when the beautiful strains of the Lacrimosa began, she lost it entirely as the memories poured over her in waves.

Matt moved even closer and put both his arms around her. Annie buried her face against his shoulder and wept.

He just held her, soothing her with gentle hands in her hair. Brokenly, she tried to explain why the music was affecting her so, and he apologized for playing it. "Shall I take it off?" he asked, but she shook her head. She both needed and wanted to hear it.

Annie appreciated his kindness and his understanding, but when the Mass was over, something had shifted into clearer perspective in her mind: Charlie was gone, and that part of her life was over. She needed to move on. Life was fragile, as Giuseppe's death reminded her.

"I know this is a helluva moment for me to say this," Matt said slowly. "But I want you, Annie."

She didn't answer. What could she say? *I'm yearning to be with you, too? I think of you first thing in the morning when I wake up, and go to sleep at night with fantasies of you unwinding in my head?* It was true.

So why not? she asked herself. *Why not, dammit?*

"I don't think I'm ready," she heard herself say.

He took her chin in his hand and turned her face so that he could look into her eyes. "What will it take, Annie? Time?

Seduction? Long-suffering patience on my part? Or a little more in the way of romantic roguish aggression?" He smiled a little. "Give me a hint, okay?"

She smiled back. "You're doing fine, believe me. I like you, Matt. A lot more, actually, than I expected to."

"But . . .?"

"But I've been through a scary time, and I'm realizing now that I'm not completely out the other side of the tunnel. When I lost Charlie—" She put up her hands in a helpless gesture. "Some things are impossible to describe. I clung to Fabrications both for the security it offered and because it was something my husband and I had created together. We'd wanted a child, but it hadn't happened yet. Fabrications was our baby, in a way, and when it died too I felt for a while as if I had nothing left to live for."

He was shaking his head, and she touched his hand in reassurance. "Then Brody Associates came along and gave me back my professional competence and pride. That, at least, I was able to rebuild and rediscover. And right now it's all I have. I can't do anything to jeopardize it. We have a crisis going on. It's very tempting to try to push it out of my mind. But I can't do that. I need to focus. Someone committed a murder in my cathedral and I don't understand how, or why, and until I do . . ." Her voice trailed off.

"Okay," he said. "I hear you. And believe me," he laughed shortly, "I understand."

They sat in silence for a moment. The CD had finished and the only sound was the smooth flowing of the pavement beneath the limousine's tires.

"Along those lines, Annie, there's something you should consider," he said slowly.

She looked into his eyes, which were grave.

"The cops haven't contacted me yet about this murder, but they will. They're going to be looking at me, just like they did when Francesca died."

She blinked. "Why?"

"Because they will find—if they haven't already—my fingerprints all over the scaffolding from which your workman fell."

She and Matt at the construction site . . . him meeting the workers and shaking their hands . . . her calling up to Giuseppe . . . Matt starting to climb the scaffolding . . . Giuseppe coming down to talk to them in the nave instead.

"It's all right," she said quickly. "Everybody knows what you were doing there. There are witnesses—"

"They'll say I went back later, knowing from my experience as a murder suspect that the perfect place to leave trace evidence is a place where I had an innocent explanation for leaving that evidence."

"But even if they said that, you were just meeting Giuseppe for the first time. You had no reason to kill him. Fingerprints or no fingerprints, why would the police focus on you?"

He shook his head slowly. "I don't know, Annie. But my instincts tell me that if there's the slightest excuse to harangue me, these guys will do it. Call it the paranoia of a falsely accused man."

He was probably right, she realized. For him, murder was a nightmare that never ended.

Chapter Twenty-one

Darcy and Annie were sitting in Annie's living room, in front of the roaring fire that Annie had built when she arrived home after Giuseppe's funeral. There was something very comforting about a fire dancing on the hearth, and she built one whenever she could, summer or winter. San Francisco weather was rarely too hot to discourage it, and tonight it was downright chilly.

Despite the fire, though, Annie was shivering. She and Darcy were eating take-out sushi from their favorite Japanese restaurant, and Darcy had just advanced her latest theory on who had killed Giuseppe.

"It was Matthew Carlyle," she said.

"Darcy, please. I'm *dating* the man!"

"Yeah, and you shouldn't be. Look. I've been thinking about this. There's a connection. Francesca Carlyle was responsible for Giuseppe and his workers being here, if you remember. She's the one who originally put us in touch with them. She knew Giuseppe well. And vice versa." She paused to let a piece of raw eel slide down her throat and to wash it down with a sip of sake. "Giuseppe was last here, in this country, just a few days before Francesca's death. Now look at the chronology: Right around the time of Francesca's death, Giuseppe left the country for his native Italy and had been abroad ever since. He missed the investigation; he missed the trial. I doubt very much that he was ever questioned by the police. But what if he knew something, something that he was never able to tell? Something that would nail the case against Francesca's husband."

"Something like what?"

Darcy shrugged. "I don't know. Maybe he actually saw the murder. Maybe he was scared—that would explain his suddenly leaving the country."

"Darcy, he didn't suddenly leave the country. He had a job to do on a church in Verona."

"Well, what if he left early for Verona? How do we know exactly when that job was due to start? All I know is that he vanished right around the time that Francesca died—maybe even the very same day."

"How do you know that?" Annie asked.

"He told me himself. He said the story was big enough to make the Italian newspapers and TV news, and he'd heard it in Italy after he'd landed."

Annie shrugged. Giuseppe had never mentioned this to her.

"Maybe Giuseppe was her mysterious lover, Annie. Sam and I were talking about that today after the funeral. Think about it. Giuseppe was a good-looking man. Maybe he had a thing going with Francesca and he fled out of fear that Carlyle would murder him as well."

"Oh, come on, Darcy—"

"No, listen. Giuseppe flees and stays away for over a year. Meanwhile Matthew is arrested and is on trial for murder, and Giuseppe probably thinks it's safe to return. So he comes back. But Carlyle is acquitted. In fact, he's suddenly in charge of the cathedral project, as the new chairman of the building committee.

"So Carlyle goes to the cathedral, and he and Giuseppe meet. Carlyle knows instantly that Giuseppe is a danger to him. He's gotten off scot-free, but Giuseppe can change all that. He's got to kill him to keep him silent, and he's got to do it fast. He hadn't realized that Giuseppe was back in town, but now that he knows, he's got to act. So he does act, the very next day. Think about it. Carlyle meets Giuseppe, and less than twenty-four hours later, Giuseppe's dead."

Annie shook her head. "You're forgetting double jeopardy. Even if an eyewitness showed up and claimed that he'd seen Matt murder his wife, the state couldn't try him again for it."

"No, but an eyewitness could talk to the tabloids and revive the public's interest. Remember, Carlyle is desperately trying to restore his reputation so he can keep his business alive. He certainly wouldn't want a witness running around. And when you've gotten away with one murder, it's probably a lot easier to do the second. . . ."

"Well, it's a theory," Annie said dryly. "I guess it isn't any more outlandish than some of the others I've heard."

Darcy looked as if she was about to protest, then she grinned and shook her head. "Anyway, it is curious the way all the principal players in the Francesca Carlyle murder case seem to be the principal players in this one as well. Including Matthew Carlyle." She sipped more sake. "On the other hand, maybe Barbara Rae did it. She's very mysterious at times."

Annie raised her eyes toward the ceiling. "Maybe I did it, Darcy. Maybe *you* did it."

Darcy choked on her sake. "Maybe we should stop speculating and let the police figure it out."

Annie couldn't sleep that night.

It was something Matt had said to her in London, and she had never forgotten it. They'd been talking about his work, and he'd mentioned a battle he'd had with another software company about a product.

"Basically, they hired away two of our top program designers and stole our architecture," he'd said, using the term *architecture* in a manner that was new to her and had, she knew, nothing to do with buildings. Apparently the same word was also used to refer to the construction of computer programs in code.

"It was unethical and it would have set us back about nine months—an enormous disadvantage in the software industry. I couldn't let it pass. I don't forget and I don't forgive. Sooner or later, I even the score."

The rest of the story detailed how he had later torpedoed the rival company by working his people overtime until they produced a product that was superior to the one that had been stolen. But that was not the part that had stuck in Annie's mind. The words she kept hearing now were: *"I don't forget and I don't forgive. Sooner or later, I even the score."*

Francesca, his wife, had been unfaithful to him. Perhaps that in itself would not have been so great a sin, since Matt himself had nearly strayed from his vows in England. But if there had been any other such occasions, he'd been discreet, since Annie had never heard any rumors that he played around. Certainly he had never publically humiliated his wife the way she had humiliated him on the night of her death.

Annie remembered the way Francesca had behaved that night—drunk, mocking, laughing acidly at what she described as their sham of a marriage. It was a pattern he was used to, Matt had claimed. But that didn't necessarily make it any easier to cope with. Annie knew from working with her on the cathedral project that Francesca could be difficult. There had been a couple of times when *she'd* felt like hauling off and smacking her. Carlyle, for all his self-control, was, she knew, a man of deep and passionate feelings. Could he have snapped, finally, and killed her?

"The irony is that I occasionally did think about killing her."

Matthew had said that, too. He'd admitted having fantasized about killing his wife.

"Haven't you ever thought about it? Ridding the world of someone you hate? Or someone you're angry with or jealous of? Someone who deserves punishment for some evil they've done, but who manages to escape with impunity over and over again?"

That night at his monstrosity of a home, Matt's account of what had happened on the night of his wife's death had sounded honest and convincing. She wanted to believe him, to trust him. But she didn't yet know him well enough to see into the corners of his soul.

Anyone could kill, Annie believed, if circumstances combined to drive them over the edge.

Matt Carlyle was no exception.

Chapter Twenty-two

Chapter Twenty-two

Annie found the next note on the windshield of her car.

She had spent most of the week at an interior design convention at San Francisco's Moscone Center on Howard Street. There on the huge show floor she'd seen exhibits and demonstrations of every imaginable kind of interior fitting, from ventilation pipes and electrical wiring to New Age furniture and fabric. She had also attended seminars and had lunches and dinners with prospective clients.

She had parked in an open lot a couple of blocks from the convention center. It usually had space if she got there early. On the final day of the convention, when she returned to the lot, she saw the large square of paper under the driver's side windshield wiper. She thought it was an advertisement until she noticed that the paper was covered with a handwritten scrawl.

Annie felt a jolt of fear. Another note from the poison pen? Was he following her?

Grabbing the paper, she jumped into her car, and locked the door. She started the engine, then switched on the overhead light. The note read: "Tonight, 8 P.M., Coit Tower." There was no signature, but scribbled in someone else's handwriting at the bottom were the words: "PLEASE come. P."

She felt relief. This note looked nothing like the work of the poison-pen writer. The "P," she decided, stood for Paolina.

She glanced at her watch. It was now 8:30, and it would take her at least ten minutes to drive over to the other side of the city and up Telegraph Hill. Would Paolina wait that long? Would she have Vico with her?

Annie paid the attendant and pulled out of the parking lot. She drove across Market to the heart of the city, up and down the hills of San Francisco, wondering what sort of wild goose chase she was on.

This wasn't a very private spot, Annie thought as she drove up the winding road that, during the day, was usually clogged with tourists. Even at this time of night there was some traffic. The 210-foot Coit Tower, at the top of Telegraph Hill, was one of San Francisco's most famous landmarks. Named after a well-known philanthropist, the tower was a monument to the firefighters who had battled the blazes that struck the city in the wake of the 1906 earthquake.

The site also commanded a stunning view of San Francisco. On a clear night the city was spread out in a mass of twinkling lights set like jewels against the velvety darkness. Tonight, though, the sky was cloudy, the visibility poor.

Annie parked in the lot at the foot of the tower and looked around. Seeing no one, she got out of the car and leaned against the door. Almost immediately she heard footsteps behind her. She turned to see a young woman in jeans, a peasant blouse, and Doc Martens walking toward her. Despite a fragile body, she was a bit thick around the waist. Her condition was starting to show.

Annie bit back the impulse to simply put her arms around Paolina and hug her. She didn't want to do anything that might spook her. "Are you okay?" she asked. "No one's been able to find you, and we've all been worried."

The girl nodded. She cast a glance over her shoulder toward a beat-up old Chevy parked on the far side of the lot. Was Vico hiding in that car?

"Where is he, Paolina?"

The girl pressed her hands together and rubbed nervously. "Who?"

"Look, no more games, okay? I'm here to help you, but please, you've got to be honest with me."

She nodded slowly. "We don't know what to do." Her eyes darted about. "He is very upset. Giuseppe raised him, you see. He was like his father. Vico's real father died when he was a small boy."

"I'm so sorry."

"And now he is angry as well. He is frustrated because he must hide instead of taking action, taking revenge."

"Revenge for what?"

"For the murder, of course! He says it's his duty to kill the person who murdered his uncle."

"Paolina, the police think he did it himself."

"Well, that's a lie!"

Annie's head was spinning. She was also cold. The city's famous fog was rolling in from the Bay, and the moist, cool air seemed to envelop them both. "Let's get into my car, where it's warmer," she said. "How are you feeling, Paolina? Are you taking care of yourself and of the baby?"

The girl nodded. "I'm fine now. I felt sick at the start, but that has passed. I'm not worried about myself."

"So where is Vico?" Annie asked again when they were settled in the front seat with all the windows rolled up.

Paolina avoided her eyes. "I can't say where he is. But he's safe."

"And you've been with him? Or did your father let you come home?"

She hung her head. "He let me. My mother convinced him, I think. But I don't stay there much. Vico needs me."

"Paolina, are you aware that he's being hunted by the police? He must give himself up. If he's innocent, his name will be cleared."

As she said it, she thought of Matt. He'd been a wealthy and highly respected businessman when he'd been accused of murder. How much more likely to be charged was a young troublemaker like Vico?

"He can't give himself up!" The girl said passionately. "He doesn't want to die like his uncle did!"

"And how *did* his uncle die? Paolina, please. You know what happened, don't you?"

She shook her head, looking panicked now. "I can't talk to you. Vico said I could find some way to contact you as long as it wasn't while you were at work, so I followed you this morning and left the note. But he insists on talking to you himself."

Annie nodded. That was fine with her.

"But first you'll have to give me your promise that you

will not betray us. Vico says his life will be worthless if anybody finds out what he knows."

Annie considered what she knew about Vico. During the several times they'd met, he'd struck her as a very intense young man. She had a clear image of his dark brown eyes, which seemed to burn with deep and powerful emotion.

As for Paolina, she was angelic, and her delicate skin was lightly dotted with tiny freckles and skeins of strawberry blond hair. There was something ethereal about her, and Annie could understand why these two young people were attracted to each other.

"I'd be glad to talk to him," she told the girl. "And I give you my word that I'll tell no one of his location. But please keep in mind that if Vico has evidence of a killing, he'll have to go to the police at some point. And if, heaven forbid, he is responsible for Giuseppe's death, then I'm sorry, but he must answer for it."

Paolina shook her head, obviously daunted by the prospect of explaining this to Vico. "He won't talk to the police. He can't. Somehow you've got to fix things to keep the police out of it. Can't you do that?"

"I don't think so," Annie said. "I work for an architectural firm. I don't have any influence with the police."

Agitated, the girl started to get out of the car. Annie put a restraining hand on her arm. "No, wait, please. I'm trying to be honest with you, but that doesn't mean that I won't do everything I can to help you and Vico. Paolina, you were in the cathedral when Giuseppe died, weren't you? Do you know who the killer is?"

The girl bit her lips and looked away, squeezing herself

with her thin arms. "I don't know. But Vico does. Now I've got to go. Don't try to stop me." With that she ducked out of the car.

"Damn!" Annie flung open the door on her side. "Paolina, please, listen to me!" She was afraid that if Paolina got away without telling her where Vico was, she'd never hear from the girl again.

The fog was even thicker now, and Paolina melted away into it. But Annie could dimly see the old Chevy there in the parking lot, possibly with the boy hiding inside. . . .

As she approached the car it started up with a roar and careened rapidly around the parking lot. As it whipped past her Annie saw two people inside, one of them a dark-haired male.

Annie jumped into her car. She wasn't sure what possessed her—maybe it was the night itself, dark and wet and secretive with fog. It was the kind of night when strange things happen. She tried to tell herself that this wasn't her business—that she ought to forget about it and let the police find Vico—but she felt compelled. She *had* to know what Vico knew. If Paolina was telling the truth, he must have seen the killer.

They couldn't get too far ahead on the hilly road that wound down from the Coit Tower. Heavens, how fast could he go?

Fast, she realized. Very fast. *Let me just keep them in view. He's got a hideaway somewhere, and if I keep up with him, he'll lead me to it.*

In her concentration, Annie didn't notice that the only other car in the Coit Tower parking lot nosed into the street behind her. As Annie chased Vico westward through the city, she was followed by a gleaming dark sedan.

* * *

The fog lifted suddenly, as it was wont to do, but the improved visibility just encouraged Vico to drive faster, and at some point Annie realized that she was no match for a macho teenage driver. Vico took risks with that old car that she would never have dreamed of taking—risks that chilled her, considering the condition of his passenger. Maybe it was better just to let them go.

At this rate, the impetuous Vico would either crash that car or hit a pedestrian or attract the attention of the very police that he was trying to avoid.

As they roared into the Pacific Heights district, she fell back deliberately. Let them think they had lost her. Maybe they'd slow down. Maybe she'd catch up with them if they did. And if that didn't work, well, maybe Paolina would get up the nerve to approach her again. She and Vico couldn't hide forever.

The houses in Pacific Heights were large and lovely. Here, overlooking San Francisco Bay, were the stately homes of some of the city's wealthiest residents. Matt lived around here somewhere, she remembered. On the night she'd come, she'd approached the area from the other direction. His place was on a cross street, no more than two or three blocks away. . . .

Damn, she'd lost them. She came to an intersection and had no idea whether to go straight or to turn.

On pure instinct, she hung a left and accelerated. At the next intersection she turned left again, and up ahead of her she saw taillights that looked like the ones on the Chevy.

They were moving more slowly now. The street they were on sloped steeply down toward the Bay. Annie fell back even farther. Ahead, the taillights flashed bright red and remained that way. She slowed to a crawl. She saw the car turn abruptly into a driveway in front of one of the houses in the next block and vanish, presumably into a garage.

Annie stopped, confused. She wasn't entirely sure that it was still Vico's car she'd been following. But if it was, whom could a poor boy from the Mission district possibly know in Pacific Heights?

She started looking for a place to park. Parking was always a problem in San Francisco. Street parking was almost always reserved for residents, and many of the smaller houses had tiny driveways that only the owners were allowed to block.

It seemed that all the residents of this district were at work, their cars jamming the streets, driveways, and even the sidewalks. But then a new set of red taillights up ahead alerted her to the possibility that somebody might be leaving. She depressed the accelerator, her adrenaline rushing like a hunter's. A parking place. *Yes*!

Annie pulled up behind the exiting car, her left blinker flashing as she waited for the spot. Expertly, she parallel parked in a tiny spot with only inches to spare, got out, and locked her car.

She walked along the street as the black mirror of San Francisco Bay reflected placidly at her from the bottom of the hill.

She was looking for a house with a short driveway that, presumably, led to a garage. There were several that fit the description, but it was difficult to judge distances in the dark. They didn't seem to be quite as far away as the place where she thought Vico—if it had been Vico—had turned in.

She saw several cars parked in narrow driveways, but no

elderly Chevys. Had she lost Vico on one of the turns and ended up following some innocent resident of Pacific Heights?

Damn! It was a good thing she wasn't trying to support herself as a private detective! She certainly hadn't acquitted herself very well so far.

Annie wasn't sure, afterward, what had alerted her. The neighborhood was generally considered safe, so she wasn't paying quite as much attention as she would if she'd been walking in a rough area south of Market. But as she was standing there, puzzled, a chill touched the hair on the back of her neck, and she whirled around to see a dark sedan coming down the street toward her. Then the car accelerated, heading straight at her.

The street was narrow, and Annie dived to the side. But the cars were parked so closely together that there was no clear way through to the sidewalk. And there was no time! The dark car was coming too fast. . . .

Annie threw herself at the obstacle in her way: an ancient, round-hooded Volkswagen. Some miraculous spurt of adrenaline lifted her up and over its hood just as the dark sedan roared by with only inches to spare. Annie's momentum kept her going and she rolled off the VW and landed hard on the sidewalk. She heard the screech of brakes. He had missed, but he was coming back!

Stumbling, she jumped to her feet. Her hip and thigh, which had taken the worst of the impact of her fall, were crying out in agonized protest. The dark sedan had reached the end of the block, and its white back-up lights were illuminated. He was turning around. He was going to make another pass at her. Perhaps this time he'd get out. . . .

Panting, Annie darted between two parked cars and

streaked across the street. Adrenaline was controlling her now, and without stopping to think, she ran headlong into a narrow alley between two large houses.

The alley was lush with window boxes and flowers. Annie slowed up a little, her common sense reasserting itself. The alley was too narrow for the car to enter. But the driver could certainly follow her on foot.

Someone was trying to kill her.

Or at least to frighten her badly.

Goddammit! Who? Vico? Had he swung around and gotten behind her somehow? Or someone else? Had somebody been following her while she followed Vico? What if it was the crazy person who'd been writing the threatening letters?

"Entered into rest, Anne Jefferson, designer of church interiors. Suddenly."

We'll see about that, she thought grimly. She was operating on instinct now. And memory. Those long-ago days when she'd lived on the streets and survived with her quick thieving fingers and her fists came surging back to her.

That's what they don't know about me. They think I'm some clueless interior designer who's liable to faint at the thought of violence. They don't know who they're dealing with here.

The guy in the dark sedan—who was he?

A friend of Paolina and Vico?

An enemy of theirs?

The poison pen?

Or Giuseppe's murderer?

Annie jogged to the end of the alley, then warily checked out the street ahead of her before venturing forward. It looked very much like the last one—neat rows of luxury houses on both sides, and cars taking up every parking space. There was no sign of the lethal speeding car.

"Damn," she muttered.

To the left she saw a gloomy bank of overhanging trees on the edge of a larger-than-usual property lot. She stopped, staring. She knew this spot. She was standing outside the grounds of Matthew Carlyle's home.

Situated on the top of a hill, his home was slightly above her. There was a five-foot-high wall on the south edge of his property, and a set of brick steps leading up through the garden to the house.

Annie was suddenly conscious of the increasing pain in her left side and thigh. She must have hurt herself more than she realized when she'd landed on the sidewalk.

Matt would help her. He had to.

Chapter Twenty-three

Annie was limping up the garden steps to Matt's house when she saw headlights approaching slowly down the street. Still jumpy, she squatted behind a shrub until the car had passed the house.

She heard a faint whirring sound near the end of Carlyle's driveway and realized that it was the metal gate, opening. The car from the street turned into the driveway and proceeded up the incline toward the house. He'd been out, obviously. He was returning home, thank goodness. Good timing.

She was about to stand up and wave to him when something about the headlights niggled at her. Headlights were headlights. Two bright bulbs, widely spaced—they all looked alike. Well, almost all. These were unremarkable. The headlights on the car that had tried to ram her had been unremarkable.

She stayed down.

From her position she saw the car pull past her. There was another whirring sound as the garage door was activated, probably from a remote control inside the car. She recognized Matt's profile as the floodlights in the front garden shone on his face as he pulled the car into the garage.

The car was a dark, late-model, two-door sedan. She couldn't swear what make or what model, but she could swear that it looked very similar to the car that had just attacked her.

"I don't forget and I don't forgive. Sooner or later, I even the score."

Crouching, Annie turned and ran back across the small square of lawn that led to the steps. She felt thoroughly spooked and very vulnerable. She wasn't sure what was going on, but this wasn't the time or the place to try to figure it out.

Was Matt Carlyle a killer after all?

Had he just tried to kill *her*?

Her heart rejected the idea, but her mind kept throwing up contradictory fragments—things he'd said, things other people had said about him. Could she trust him? How well did she really know him? Suppose everything he'd told her about himself had been a lie?

The streets were safe now, surely. He and the car were home. She'd get back to the street and find a phone or pound on some neighbor's door or simply scream as loudly as she could until somebody called the police. That's what she should have done in the first place—screamed. To hell with this trying-to-be-brave nonsense. To hell with self-control.

The fog had rolled back in and now shrouded the small garden. For a moment she was disoriented, unsure where the staircase started. The steps had been slippery, she remembered;

she shouldn't run, shouldn't rush—she didn't want to fall and be stuck here. He didn't know she was here. He'd given up, at least for tonight.

Annie had just found the top of the stairs when she heard growls and then loud insistent barking. He must have let the dogs out. The furious barking stopped abruptly, followed by an ominous silence. She remembered a stray scrap of information: Attacking dogs do not make a sound. . . .

Stressed out and totally confused about who were the good guys and who were the bad, Annie did the worst possible thing. She ran.

She knew that she couldn't outrun attack dogs, but she had seen a tree just a few yards back—thick and sturdy, and with branches low enough to climb.

Annie stumbled and fell as she reached the tree and grabbed at the lowest branch. She let out an involuntary cry as she cracked her head on the tree trunk and her knee on something hard. As she heard the whoosh in the bushes behind her, she knew that the dogs—which Matt had locked up the last time she'd been here—were almost upon her.

Annie's palms were sweating as she clambered to her feet and snatched at the branch overhead. With a powerful heave, she pulled herself up just as the dogs burst out of the brush behind her. Seizing the next branch, heart hopping, she climbed another few feet and then another, hugging the tree trunk as two enormous hounds from hell—or so they appeared in the fog—barked and leaped against the bottom of the tree.

So much for escaping quietly.

It was only a couple of minutes before she heard him coming. First was the blinding beam of a powerful flashlight, then the low voice she recognized. He spoke to the dogs, which, with obvious reluctance, backed away from the tree. As they vanished into the fog, Annie heard the jangle of chains.

"Okay. Get down," he said in a voice that was clearly accustomed to being obeyed.

"The dogs . . .?"

"I have them under restraint."

He was at the base of the tree now, peering up at her. "Jump down," he ordered.

Annie stumbled as she landed and ended up sprawled at his feet. He was wearing running shoes, she noted. Black running shoes.

His legs were clad in jeans. A billionaire in jeans. *Absurd*, she thought, *the things you notice when you're scared to death*.

Looking up at him, blinking against the light, she felt her terror shift to humiliation. What must she look like—scruffy and wild, her clothing torn, her hair wild, her body still trembling with exertion and adrenaline and fear. . . .

He made a sound. Recognition. Real or fake, false or true? Even if he had been the driver of the dark sedan, he would be surprised to find her here. He wouldn't have expected that.

The worst of the bright light moved, sliding on down her body, and she could see him once again as she lay there looking up, a tall, dominant figure silhouetted against the night sky. He held the two dogs on short chain leashes. They were panting, drooling, still looking as if they'd like to rip her to shreds.

"Annie?"

He sounded truly surprised. And no wonder. If he *had* tried to run her down, he must have been cursing himself for missing her, and now here she was delivering herself directly into his hands.

She saw that he was holding an automatic pistol. Dear God! Her fear took a giant leap. With the gun in his hand, he looked more like a desperado than a wealthy, sophisticated businessman.

As they stared at each other, gazes locked over the gun he held, the skies opened and the rain came pouring down, its swift and sudden violence plastering Annie's hair against her skull. She closed her arms around her body, shivering, even as she expected at any second to feel the violent impact that would end her life.

"Christ!" The word exploded out of him. "What kind of stupidity is this? I took you for a burglar. You're lucky I didn't shoot you."

He reached down and hauled her to her feet. She stumbled, feeling as if her legs wouldn't hold her weight. The surges of adrenaline that had sustained her so long seemed now to have been exhausted. She felt as if she was crashing, unable to fight any longer, unable to do anything more in her own defense.

Matt ran the flashlight over her again. "Shit," he said softly. "You're hurt."

Annie looked down and saw the blood on her knee. It must have happened when she fell against the tree. "It's just a scrape," she whispered.

He released the dogs, who were docile now that their master obviously knew the intruder. Matt shoved the gun into the pocket of his jeans and took Annie's hand. "Come with me."

He pulled her along behind him as he started back up the stairs. She made a token attempt to free herself, but he was too strong. When she stumbled again, he stopped, turned, and shifted his grip on her, then picked her up in his arms. He carried her the remaining few steps to the back garden of his mammoth house.

With rain pouring down on them and thunder growling in the distance and an occasional flash of lightning piercing the fog, Annie felt as though she were entering an unreal world. Her brain felt sluggish, but all her senses were alive. She could hear each individual raindrop as it struck the earth and the stones underfoot. The rustle of leaves, the sighs of the flowers as their stems bent in the wind. The combined smells of herbs and grasses, Matt's faintly musky, masculine scent, a lemony whiff of her own perfume.

He was holding her, carrying her, straining a bit—she could hear it in his breathing; but he was strong and fit enough to do this—stronger than she was—male, ruthless, indomitable. He had just tried to kill her. Now he was taking her inside his huge house, where the rooms were gloomy and the walls were thick and he would be able to do anything he wanted to her. She wouldn't be able to stop him any more than she could stop the storm.

She closed her eyes, letting her head rest against the hard flesh and bone of his shoulder. She could feel the steady, if slightly rapid, beating of his heart. It reminded her of another day, another time. London. The rain. His arms around her, his hands sliding under her clothing to find her hot, slippery skin. Yearning. Pleasure. Need.

I must be totally out of it, Annie thought vaguely, because for some reason, she wasn't afraid.

* * *

Matt Carlyle had no idea why Annie Jefferson had been darting about his property, dashing precipitously down his garden steps. It was one more mystery among too many. But he didn't know, and didn't care.

The point was, she was here.

He had her.

Her body was wet and slick, and by some miracle she felt as light as feathers as he carried her. He knew that tomorrow, surely, he would ache all over from this madness. But that didn't matter. Where Annie was concerned, he'd been aching all over for years.

No more. The chase had gone on long enough. This would be the night that ended it. He was going to settle things between them once and for all.

He reached the house and shouldered his way in through the half-open door. The dogs followed, still excited, still uncertain about this stranger and what was going on. He kicked the door shut, snapped on the lock. The woman in his arms shivered at the sound, and he knew she was as confused as he was.

That didn't matter, either. The confusion would soon end. There was one way to end it, and he should have done it long ago.

He carried her through the dark kitchen, through the pantry and the dining room, out into the hallway and up the grand staircase to the second floor. He was breathing hard now; his heart was straining. His arms and back felt numb with stress. She was far smaller than he, but she wasn't *that* small. He figured that she weighed about 120 pounds.

He carried her directly to his bedroom, elbowed the door

shut behind them, crossed the huge room, and laid her down gently in the middle of his unmade, king-size bed.

She lay still for an instant, her eyes shut, apparently trying to absorb what had happened and where she was. Her entire body was tense and stiff, but beautiful. The rain had pasted her clothes to her. He could see the rise of her breasts, the flat of her belly, the beguiling curve of her hips. Her legs were long and well shaped. Her wrists were delicate. Her blond hair, drenched, looked darker than usual, and strands of it clung to her cheeks and neck and shoulders. She looked helpless and vulnerable, and he wanted to comfort and soothe her. But not as much as he wanted to take her, conquer her, make her his own.

He knelt beside her on the bed and put his face close to hers. She turned away, but he gripped her chin and turned it back to him.

With his lips brushing hers he told her, "Annie, I'm going to take off your wet things. Then mine. Then I'm going to make love to you. Right here, right now, while the storm rages outside."

She opened her eyes. The expression in them was half dazed, half wild, like that of a forest animal trapped in a hunter's beam.

But he held her gaze, and slowly her expression calmed. Her limbs unstiffened and her body relaxed.

"Why?" she whispered.

"Because I can't stand it anymore."

She nodded. The look in her eyes now was dreamy and mysterious—eternal womanhood, the creature he could never in a million years understand. He hadn't understood Francesca, and at the moment, Annie seemed even more subtle a mystery.

"Okay," she said.

That was it. *Okay.* Consent. It wasn't exactly a ringing endorsement, but *okay* was good enough.

Annie was beyond surprises now and far beyond fear. *It wasn't his car*, she was thinking. *It was dark. All those cars look alike. It couldn't have been his car.*

Another part of her was thinking, *I don't even care if it was his car. It doesn't matter what almost happened, because this is more powerful than that.*

He was stripping off her clothes, a little roughly, but efficiently. Her leaden hands tried to help him but he pushed them away. His were faster, and quickness mattered, quickness *mattered.*

A button on her blouse popped and flew across the room, and then it was open, pushed away to the sides, and his hands were on her breasts. She sighed as he caressed her, squeezed her, brushed his fingers over the tips of her nipples. Fire arced between her breasts and sped down to the pit of her belly. He bent his head. His mouth took the nub of one breast and his tongue darted over it and then he sucked. Annie arched her back and moaned. She felt the slickness between her legs as her body responded to his.

He felt so familiar. The years washed away. Her body *remembered* him. Remembered and accepted him in a manner that her rational mind never could.

But her rational mind had shut down. She couldn't hear its

warnings. There are things known in the heart, known in the bone, that the mind has no conception of.

His hands left her for a few moments and she heard him pulling off his shirt, shoes, jeans. While he frantically worked, she unzipped her skirt and pushed it down over her hips. Her panties, too. His hands came back and tore them away.

He fumbled for something in the drawer beside his bed, and she realized that his mind was operating better than hers, for despite this onslaught of passion he was protecting her with a condom. Would a man who had just tried to kill her care about using a condom?

It wasn't his car, couldn't have been his car.

When he came to her she closed her eyes and simply felt the sensations—skin against skin, muscle against muscle, flesh against flesh. His arms enveloped her and he rolled them both on their sides. His legs meshed with hers, his knee against her mound, one hand caressing her back, the other her breasts.

Her hands, in turn, explored his strong arms and shoulders, delighting in the springy feel of sinew smoothed over bone. He squeezed her nipple hard enough to elicit a gasp, and she could feel his smile against her mouth as he kissed her deeply, the smile fading as his tongue penetrated and teased and probed.

"Annie," he murmured as his fingers slipped between her thighs to touch the soft slick petals, so damp, so sensitive. She moaned and pressed herself against his hand. As he strummed her there she quivered and cried out with the sweet simple pleasure of it, and the yearning, and the need.

His tongue deep in her mouth, he flipped her onto her back and with his knees pushed her thighs apart. She opened to him gladly, eagerly. He continued to caress her wickedly between her thighs, and Annie moved against him, frantic now, desperate. She was climbing toward the peak when he stopped. She moaned in protest, and he reared up over her and thrust inside her, penetrating her fully with one masterful lunge.

Together, frantic, on fire, they rode out the storm.

Chapter Twenty-four

No sooner was it over than Annie pushed him away and rolled to the far side of the bed. She sat up, pulling the sheet around her like a toga. She could feel herself trembling.

"Annie," he said, moving toward her.

"Don't touch me!" She leaped from the bed, dragging the sheet with her. Keeping her eyes on him, she backed away until she came up against the wall.

His face darkened. "You don't know how it makes me feel to look into my lover's eyes and see that deep inside her, there's a shadow of doubt whether I'm a killer."

The bitterness in his tone stabbed her in the gut, but she ordered herself to be strong. Even though all it took from him was a single look, a random touch, to reduce her body to liquid, she had to resist. She had to clear this up. She had to. Oh, please God, she had to!

"It's more than a shadow," she whispered. "Someone tried to kill me. He lured me to this neighborhood, then tried to run me down with a car. I eluded him—or so I thought. Then I came to you for help. But when you pulled into your driveway, your car looked identical to the one that had tried to hit me. So I fled."

His green eyes were burning. "I see. Once a murderer, always a murderer?"

She pulled the sheet more firmly around her. "What about Giuseppe?"

Matt sat up in bed, leaning back against the headboard, unabashedly naked. "What do you mean, 'What about Giuseppe'? I didn't even know the man."

"Francesca did. In fact, she was the one who originally recommended Giuseppe and his fellow craftsmen to me."

He shrugged. "Francesca knew a lot of people. Very few of them were folks whom I bothered to get to know."

"Giuseppe and your wife were great friends. He was a sweet man who loved to play paternal admirer to any beautiful woman. He used to treat my friend Darcy with the same affectionate indulgence that I remember seeing him express with Francesca."

Matt stared at her as if to say, *So*?

"He left the country on the same day she died. He was abroad during most of your trial, then he came back, and now he's dead. In fact, you might just have been one of the last people to see him alive."

The hostility level in his eyes intensified. "What the hell are you implying?"

"You say you didn't know him. But you surely haven't forgotten that I introduced you to him that afternoon when you came for your first tour of the cathedral. He died that same night."

He stood up suddenly, startling her. He strode around his bed and came up close to her—too close. She remembered these intimidating tactics from long ago—the first business meeting she'd had with him, when Fabrications still existed . . . before he had refused to hire her. As always when she remembered, she felt her spine stiffen. She stood her ground. This man would *not* intimidate her again.

"Are you suggesting that I killed him?" he asked in a quiet yet dangerous tone.

"I was just wondering if the police had drawn any conclusions—erroneous ones, of course. I know you have no respect for the police in this city. They hounded you before, you say, and I wondered if they were hounding you again."

"Hounded me? Is that what you'd call it? They did an incompetent and lazy investigation of a brutal murder, pinned it on me, and tried me for my life—and all it sounds like to you is *hounding*?"

"If you think about what hounding originally meant, it's pretty accurate, I guess."

He touched her arm, and she found that she could not pull away, either from him or from the powerful gleam in his eyes."And now? Who's hounding whom now?" he asked her.

She swallowed. "Look, I just—"

"You're getting scared, aren't you? I'm getting too close to you and you're shying away."

"That's not it!"

"What, then? Five minutes ago you were howling out your passion in my arms. Now, suddenly, you're throwing my wife's murder in my face."

"Actually, I was throwing Giuseppe's murder in your face," she said softly.

His hands were on her shoulders now. ''And what I don't understand, dammit, is why?''

Annie remembered Darcy's theory. ''Well, what if Giuseppe knew something that could incriminate Francesca's killer? He may even have been your wife's lover.''

Matt stared at her. Then he threw back his head and laughed.

''It's not funny.''

''Dear Christ, it's hilarious!''

She stared at him, fidgeting with the sheet, while he howled with laughter. It wasn't good laughter, however. It retained that bitter edge.

''Francesca was a snob and a social climber. She would no more lie down with a construction worker than she would with a woman.''

''Giuseppe wasn't a simple construction worker. He was a master craftsman, an artist.''

''Trust me, Annie, if he made less than a quarter of a million a year or dressed in anything other than Armani, she wouldn't even have looked at the guy.''

''He was handsome, too. An older version of Vico—and trust me, Vico is a hunk.''

''Vico is also your killer, Annie, not me.''

''I just can't believe that. I think Vico *saw* the killer, but I don't think he *is* the killer!''

Matt shook his head. ''You don't know what you think, Annie.''

His voice was weary now, and something in it got through to her. She sank down on the foot of the bed and bent over, putting in head in her hands.

What's the matter with me? she asked herself. *I just made love to this man. Why can't I trust him?*

What are you afraid of?

Maybe he was right. Maybe she was afraid.

"Look," he said. "This conversation is going nowhere. I'm going to go downstairs and make us some coffee." He nodded toward her clothes, which were flung all over the floor. "Why don't you get dressed. Take a shower first if you want to. Maybe you'll feel better if you wash yourself clean of me. What just happened between us was obviously a mistake."

She moaned as though he had struck her. She felt him hesitate as he moved past her, headed for the bedroom door. She lifted her head and met his eyes . . . and saw his pain.

"Wait," she whispered. "Matthew. Matt." She reached out her hand to him. "Wait a minute. Don't go."

She thought for an instant that he was going to turn his back on her, and she realized that she wouldn't blame him if he did. But the moment passed. He sighed, came closer, and took her hand. She squeezed his fingers, and the current arced between them again. Shaking his head, he sat down beside her on the bed.

"I'm sorry," she said softly. "I don't know what's the matter with me. I'm stressed out, I'm nervous, I'm feeling at the end of my rope. And someone tried to kill me tonight. Then suddenly you were making love to me, and it was so amazing, so good. . . ." She slid closer, turned her face to his shoulder. "Help me, Matt. My head is swimming and I don't know what to believe about anyone or anything."

His arms came around her, hard. She felt his lips against the side of her head. "Annie, I swear to you on my life, it wasn't me who tried to run you down. I didn't kill Francesca and I certainly didn't kill Giuseppe. As for you . . . I'm crazy about you. I'd never hurt you, never, Annie. I need you to believe that. If you can't believe it, we're dead in the water. We'll never get off the ground."

She nodded against him. She understood exactly what he was saying, what he was feeling. After all he had been through, he needed her trust, just as she had once needed Charlie's.

But how could she give him what she didn't yet feel?

"Come back to bed," he said.

She lay down beside him and he pulled the covers over them. She could feel his heart beating against hers.

"I'm sorry," she whispered.

"Listen." His voice hardened. "If someone tried to run you down, I'll catch the bastard. If it's the same man who murdered Francesca, I'll tear him apart."

Again she nodded against him. She believed him. She *did*.

She tried to turn onto her side, but he pressed her down on her back. He threw one heavy thigh over hers, holding her in position. "Your body trusts me, Annie," he said. "Sooner or later, your mind will follow."

Sometime during the night, after another bout of passionate lovemaking, he said gently, "Okay, let's think about this together. Are you absolutely sure that the driver was trying to hit you?"

Annie forced herself to think back over the earlier events of the night. Had she overreacted? Had the car simply been speeding and a little out of control? A drunken teenager, perhaps?

She shook her head. "I don't know if he was actually trying to hit me. But he was trying to frighten me, I'm pretty certain about that."

"Tell me exactly what happened. From the beginning."

Starting with the note on the windshield of her car, she described the rest of the evening's events.

When she'd finished, Matt said thoughtfully, "So there are two possibilities—either Vico got around behind you, and, annoyed at being chased by you, tried to scare you off."

"Vico was driving a different kind of car."

"Okay. How about this, then? Somebody followed you to the meeting with Paolina and Vico and continued to follow you afterward. While you were concentrating on your pursuit of the teenagers, you didn't realize that somebody was pursuing you."

"But who? And why?"

"Well, the obvious suspect is the person who's been writing you the threatening letters."

"But he sounds like a crazy person, some sort of nut."

"Well, suppose for the sake of argument he's not a nut, but someone whose purpose is to frighten you into—Into what? Quitting your job?"

"I've been asking myself the same question. Is there somebody who wants me off as project manager? Is that it? And if so, why? Does somebody else want my job? Sam said that if he hadn't given it to me, he'd probably have given it to Darcy. But it can't be Darcy—she and I are close friends . . . and why would she want the job anyway?"

"Who else besides Darcy?"

"Well, there's Jack Fletcher, whom I've never really trusted. I keep getting the feeling that there's something strange about him. But he's the contractor's job superintendent, which is a pretty good job in itself. He probably has more power on site than I have. So unless he just can't stand working with me, it doesn't make sense that he would be trying to get rid of me."

"Maybe he can't stand working with a woman."

She shrugged.

"Or maybe it has nothing to do with someone wanting your job. Maybe it's because you represent a threat to someone."

"What sort of threat could I represent?"

"Annie, you're not naïve. It could be something connected with the job itself. Some sort of fraud by the contractor or one of the subs. You've been the project manager for months, and maybe you know something that you don't realize you know. Maybe somebody wants to get rid of you before you figure it out."

He had a point, Annie thought. Paul McEnerney, for example, struck her as the type of guy who wouldn't hesitate to get his hands dirty if the profit was high and the risk low. And then there was Sidney Canin, whom Sam had fired without telling anybody why.

"Last, let's not forget that a man was just murdered," said Matt. "The killer and the poison-pen writer could be one and the same."

"It's giving me a headache to keep thinking about it," she said.

"I know the feeling, believe me. The last thing I need in my life is another murder."

"Oh, Matt, I'm so sorry!"

He smiled. Then he leaned over and kissed her. "If you're really sorry, I can think of several ways for you to show it," he said.

Playfully, she struggled against him while he held her down. The night had been so intense that there had been no time for lighthearted sensuality. Now, for the first time, she realized that Matt could love her in a way that was both pleasurable and fun.

No, *fun* wasn't exactly the word, she thought wryly a few minutes later. It was far too mundane a term for the passion that gripped them both.

Chapter Twenty-five

"Annie, you look a little pale. Are you feeling all right?" Fletcher asked the following evening. They were in the choir loft at the west end of the cathedral, watching the installation of the pipes for the great church organ. It was quitting time, and the workmen were leaving.

"I'm fine," Annie said. "I'm leaving shortly. Will you close things down tonight for me, please?"

"No problem."

Annie was in a hurry to get home because she had a date with Matt. She'd been thinking about it all afternoon, alternately nervous and excited. He'd called at lunchtime, and he'd made no pretense of talking about the project or the murder or anything else. "I need to see you," he'd said, and the intensity in his voice had spoken volumes about a very private need.

"If you wait a few seconds I'll walk you out to your car," Fletcher added.

"Thanks, but you really don't have to."

"I know, but considering the murder and those threats you've been receiving, I figure you could use a strong man's company, especially after dark."

Not yours, Annie thought. Then she checked herself. She was being unfair to the guy. He'd never been anything but polite to her, and at the moment he seemed sincerely concerned.

"Well, okay, thanks," she said.

They walked together to the elevator that had just been installed in the south bell tower. The cathedral was dark and gloomy, filled with shadows. Annie remembered what Barbara Rae had described of her premonitions and had to suppress a tiny shiver. Ever since Giuseppe's death it had seemed that a pall lay over the cathedral. Instead of a place of beauty and divinity, it seemed to her a place of pain.

It was working, Fletcher thought as he accompanied her to the elevator. The method had been crude, but he liked the results. Annie was not quite as self-assured and cocky as she'd been a couple of weeks ago. She was frightened, and her fear softened her, making her even more feminine.

Of course, he would have to be careful. No more threatening letters now that the cops were on the scene. Too dangerous. He certainly couldn't afford to take any chances.

And as for following her by car—no more of that, either. He remembered the sharp thrill of stalking her, and the even sharper thrill of hurtling down the dark street toward her. Scaring her. Hell, he had scared himself. It had actually crossed his mind: What if he struck her, sent her lovely body flying, left her crumpled and broken in the street and unable to torment him any longer.

God, you're crazy, man, he said to himself. He didn't want to hurt her, really. Hurting her was a weird, sick fantasy. He knew the difference between fantasy and reality—the therapist had drilled that into him in prison.

He just meant to scare her.

And so far the scare campaign was going fine. Although an anonymous phone call might be in order. He'd have to make it from a pay phone, of course. That was the only safe way. You never knew, nowadays, who had caller ID.

The best time to make it was the middle of the night. An hour or so after she had gone to bed. She'd be asleep, yet not so deeply that she wouldn't hear the phone. She'd be groggy when she answered, and her natural defenses would be down.

He wondered if she slept naked. He imagined her rolling over, her body bare and fluid in the darkness, reaching for the ringing phone. When she answered, he wouldn't say anything, of course. But she would feel the connection—the intimate connection—with another living, thinking, dreaming mind.

Maybe he should get one of those electronic voice distorters so he could speak to her without her recognizing his voice. He wanted to speak to her in the darkness. Tell her what he was going to do to her when he had her alone. He would demand her complete surrender. Whatever resistance she had within her, he would methodically strip away. When he finished with her, she would be totally and irrevocably within his control. His for one night, his to do whatever he wanted to. And what he wanted . . . yeah, he wanted everything.

He'd bet it would turn her on too. Make her hot, make her

wet, even though she was scared. It was there inside her—he could tell. She was yearning for a man who could take her outside herself, drive her to her knees, make her plead for the wild dark passions that only he could give her.

But first he had to make her vulnerable to him. And to do that he had to scare her so profoundly that she would turn to him for protection. He wanted her crying out her submission to him. He wanted her damp with it.

Late this afternoon he had used his knowledge of electronics to adjust the switches in the newly installed elevator. When he hit the button for the ground floor, it would descend instead to the lowest level, underground to the basement of the south tower.

When they stepped into the elevator, Fletcher let Annie push the button herself. Didn't want her to think he'd had anything to do with the result.

They began to descend. The elevator was small, as was necessary in the narrow bell tower. The choir loft was only the second stop. It could ascend all the way up to a small room directly beneath the bells.

He loved being so close to Annie. He could smell her perfume, and the scent just about drove him wild.

The elevator passed the first floor and continued to descend. Fletcher shot a glance at Annie and saw that she was paying no attention to the control panel. She was staring straight at the door, her mind obviously a thousand miles away.

He wondered what she was thinking. What was responsible for that soft, dreamy look on her face?

The elevator stopped and the door slid open. Annie started to step out, then stopped abruptly. Fletcher was right behind her, so when she caught herself, she bumped into him. He felt her ass against the front of his thighs for a moment and it made his blood boil.

"This isn't right," she muttered.

"Looks like the basement," he said. "Must have skipped right by the first floor."

"I'm sure I pressed the right button."

"Must be a malfunction," he said, fiddling with the control panel. He pulled a wire he'd left loose earlier, and the dome light in the ceiling of the elevator went out.

Annie gasped. Then she stepped out of the elevator and into the equally dark basement. "The light! Turn on the light," she said, and Fletcher felt a surge of lust as he realized that she was *really* scared.

"It's not working. Damn electricians must have fucked up during the installation." He banged around with the control panel, trying to make it sound as if he were attempting to fix it. "Shit, nothing's working now," he said as he followed her out into the bell-tower basement.

It was a small area, he knew. Both bell towers had basements, but the nave of the church was built on dirt and bedrock, with only a crawl space underneath it. Up at the far end, the east end of the church, there was a much larger basement under the sanctuary, but this space was small. It was also unfinished, with nothing but a thin concrete floor and cement block walls.

He could easily corner her here. If she screamed, no one would hear.

"Dammit, Jack, there must be a light in here," she said, her voice rising in panic. "Don't you at least have a flashlight?"

"No. Sorry."

"I've got this childish fear of the dark."

He exulted. She sounded terrified, and he was thrilled. "There's a lightbulb overhead somewhere," he said, moving toward her voice. But in fact all there was was an empty socket. He'd removed the bulb earlier.

"There's a door somewhere, too," she said, and he heard her moving her hands against the wall, searching for it.

Maybe he'd just do it. Do it now. Why wait, why plan? This was perfect. He had her. Seize the moment. The moment was now.

He heard her fumbling with something and then suddenly his eyes burned as a beam of light stabbed them. Shit. *She* had a flashlight. He should have thought of that.

"Oh, there you are," she said, sounding very shaky. "I found it in my purse. Now, where's the door to the stairwell? There. I see it, thank goodness."

He was tempted just to grab her and get it over with, but she was too quick for him. She had no sooner located the door than she had dashed to it and flung it open. A second later she was clambering up the spiral staircase to the main floor.

Fuck. *Fuck.*

He raced after her. His erection felt like a fire hose hopping at full pressure. He caught her at the bell-tower exit. "Sorry about that," he choked out. "I'll make sure that elevator gets fixed first thing tomorrow morning. Come on," he said, taking her arm. "I'll walk you to your car."

She shook off his hand and ran to her car, unlocked it with trembling hands, jumped inside, and locked the door. Her wheels kicked up gravel as she sped out of the lot.

So. He'd spooked her.

Good.

∗ ∗ ∗

Annie drove home feeling sick and constantly checking her rearview mirror.

The elevator *could* have broken down.

These things happened. Hell, in new construction, they happened all the time.

It wasn't fair she knew, to suspect a man just because she didn't like him. Look how unfairly she'd treated Matt in that respect.

Jack Fletcher hadn't done anything threatening. He hadn't so much as touched her. And the terror she'd felt when the lights went out was an old one; it would have hit her just as strongly if she'd been down there with someone she liked and trusted.

Even so, she couldn't stop shivering.

At gut level, she was convinced that she'd just had a very lucky escape.

Chapter Twenty-six

"What is this place?" Annie asked as Matt turned up a long driveway. A heavy rain was pelting the car and the windshield wipers could barely keep up with the demand. Matt was driving slowly and carefully, squinting through the windshield to see the pavement ahead.

Annie, seated beside him in the Porsche, concentrated on the grace of his body as it went through the simple motions of driving. His long legs pumping the brakes and the clutch. His well-shaped hand, encased in a black leather driving glove, skillfully manipulating the wooden-handled gear shift. His profile in the dimly lit car, so calm, so intent, so . . . well, so handsome.

Jeez, I'm really hooked, she thought. Look at me. I'm acting like a lovestruck teenager.

"It's a beach house I own. Actually, it belonged to Francesca. It was part of her estate."

The estate that he was now entitled to. If he'd been convicted of her murder, he would not have inherited it. Who, she wondered, would have?

"Matt, did Francesca have a will?"

"I know it's ridiculous, but no, she didn't. I have one, of course. And I asked her many times to make one. I even made appointments for her with our lawyer, but she refused. She was superstitious about wills."

"Why?"

"Because her parents were killed in a boating accident the week after they executed their wills. One of those freak things. But she was convinced that making a will was bad luck, and she even tried to prevent me from making mine. She was afraid I'd die as soon as I signed it." He paused. "This all came out at the trial."

She looked at him. "I didn't follow the trial that closely," she admitted.

"I'm glad. It was awful, sitting there in court and hearing the story of my life told to strangers, presented as truth, having only a shadowy resemblance to my own perceptions."

"I guess truth is subtly different for all of us."

"The prosecution wasn't even trying to present the truth," he said bitterly. "All they cared about was making up a story that convinced people I was a heartless killer. They did a pretty good job of it, too."

He stopped the car in front of a dark structure. No lights were on in the place, although a couple of floodlights shone on the perimeters. From what she could see through the driving rain, it looked glassy and airy, an usual and striking piece of architecture.

"What was the extent of Francesca's estate?" she asked.

"Compared to the average American, it was substantial," he said. "This house is worth a fair amount, and the land has value. She also had a respectable portfolio, much of it inherited from her parents and wisely invested."

"I don't remember her estate's being much of an issue in the news during the trial."

"No, it wasn't, because her separate holdings were negligible when compared with mine. No one ever thought I murdered her for her money."

"No, they figured you murdered her to prevent her from divorcing you and getting half of *your* money."

"Exactly. We were married for twenty years—the entire period of my building of Powerdyme. We had no prenuptial agreement, and with California's joint property laws, she would legally have been entitled to half my fortune. Two billion dollars, in other words."

Annie laughed a little shakily. As a motive for murder, two billion dollars was hard to refute. No wonder the prosecution had been so determined to nail him.

"So, instead of that, when she died, her entire estate went to you?"

"Actually, I gave her money to charity. It's what she would have wanted done if she'd *had* a will. She spoke of it often—she wanted Barbara Rae and the United Path Church to be her beneficiaries. Francesca loved Barbara Rae." He paused then added, "I think everybody at the church was pretty shocked to learn that Francesca hadn't made a will. They were relieved when I turned the money over to them anyway."

"So the cathedral building committee benefited from Francesca's death?"

"Actually, it benefited a lot more from her *life*. She raised most of the building funds herself."

And a substantial portion of it, Annie knew, had been raised from Matthew's own pockets.

"You're a generous man, Matt."

He shrugged. "It's easy to be generous when you're as rich as Croesus. I have far more money than I know what to do with."

"What, exactly, are we doing here?" she asked as she trailed after him through the empty house. It was kind of spooky. What furniture remained was covered with white dust sheets, creating an array of odd, ghostly shapes. In the library, Annie stood by the French doors looking out over the Bay, where waves were crashing against the rocks.

Matthew came to stand beside her in the dark. She hadn't realized he was so close, and at his touch on her shoulder, she jumped.

"You're nervous, aren't you?"

She hadn't told him yet about what had happened in the bell-tower elevator. That was for later. She hadn't wanted to dampen the fire that was running between them.

"There's someplace special I want to take you tonight," he'd said when he'd picked her up at her house. He'd shown up driving the Porsche instead of the dark sedan, and she'd laughed because it was the third different car she'd seen him in. The limousine he'd used after Giuseppe's funeral didn't count, he told her, grinning. That had been hired.

"Yes, I'm a little jumpy, I think," she admitted.

"Why? Because you're alone with me in a deserted spot?"

It was going to take him a while to believe that she trusted him. But that was okay, she told herself. Trust *should* come slowly.

She tipped her head back and smiled archly at him. "Yes, indeed. I feel like a maiden from the distant past. And you, dark lord, have abducted me to your fortress by the sea."

His eyes gleamed. "I can get into that."

"Can you?"

"Absolutely." He grasped her wrists and pushed them behind her back. "Lock your hands together, wench, and keep 'em that way, on pain of some very nasty punishment if you break position."

She obeyed, holding still for him while he ran his palms over her breasts, then, slowly, unbuttoned her blouse and pushed it back off her shoulders. She wore no bra, and his eyes admired her breasts for a long moment before repeating his caresses on her soft, naked skin.

"You look very vulnerable like that," he whispered.

"I feel very vulnerable."

He bent his head and touched her lips. "I like it. It's giving me a kinky surge of power." He grinned. "Now I know why abducting maidens used to be so popular."

She smiled back. Was it a game . . . or a way to show her trust in him? Either way, it seemed to be working!

"Kneel," he ordered.

She gulped. *Kneel*?

His fingers lightly tugged on one nipple, then tightened.

"Ahh," she gasped, then giggled.

"Don't think about it, wench. Just do it."

She knelt, trying hard to be graceful while still holding her hands behind her back. She looked up at him and saw a kind of bemused pleasure on his face, as if he couldn't quite believe this was happening but was thrilled about it anyway.

"Wow," he said. He dropped to the floor beside her and pulled her into his arms. "I'd take you into the bedroom but I don't think I can wait that long."

She laughed joyously as they tore at each other's clothes.

Annie saw a different side of Matt that night in the isolated beach house. The first night they'd been together, he'd been beside himself and nearly out of control with passion, but tonight he was very controlled, very demanding. He showed her what a master of sensuality he truly was, and how helpless she was to resist him.

That night she started to feel that anything he demanded of her, at least in the bedroom, she would willingly do. Kneeling, she soon learned, was just the beginning.

There was an edge to him that was so commanding that it seemed unthinkable to thwart him. He swept her away. He didn't ask, he laid claim. She could no more have refused him than she could have prevented the sun from rising in the morning sky.

She gleaned that he liked to rule in the bedroom and that he relished her trust and her surrender. And yet, he was deliciously attentive to her needs and her desires. In a low, sexy voice, he ordered her to tell him her fantasies, to tell him things that she had never said to another living soul. Not even Charlie had known the contents of her most erotic imaginings. She'd been too embarrassed to discuss with him scenes and images of forbidden activities, some of which seemed too dark ever to discuss with anybody.

But nothing, she quickly learned, embarrassed or startled Matt Carlyle. Indeed, his own dreams and yearnings, as he described them to her, were every bit as wild and outrageous as hers. "I want your honesty," he said, his voice low and intense. "No, more than that. I demand it. It's what I ought to have insisted on with Francesca. No secrets. Nothing hidden. You lie naked before me, but it's not enough. I have to see your naked heart, your naked soul."

"You ask too much," she whispered.

"I know. But I will have what I ask for, just the same."

"I'll give you all I can."

He swooped over her, pinning her with his hard, bare body. "And I'll take everything you can give."

"Look," she said to him sometime during that endless night. "Did you see that?" Rising, she went to the window that looked out over the cliff on the north side of the house.

"What?"

"I thought I saw a flash of light."

He joined her at the window and peered out, trying to see through the fog and the slashing rain.

"Probably just lightning," he said.

He pulled her slowly into his arms. His big hands moved

sensuously over the muscles of her back and shoulders. His head came down, and he kissed her on the mouth.

Annie responded warmly, but her feeling of unease persisted. The flash had looked like headlights, from a stationary vehicle, coming on and then immediately being doused. She pulled back a bit and whispered, "I have the most eerie feeling. As if we're being watched."

He smiled. "Even if you were right, there wouldn't be much for anyone to see. Too dark and too foggy." He kissed her more deeply, his tongue tangling with hers. "Relax, Annie. Relax."

Matt dreamed that he was out on the coast road, looking up toward the house, which was a vague, ghostly mass in the fog and rain. In the dreamscape he saw a dark, late-model sedan begin, slowly, to close in from the shadows. Its engine purred too quietly to be heard above the noise of the storm, and its headlights were not on.

The driver was staring up at the house and vowing that Matthew Carlyle would never be happy again.

That he would suffer.

That he would lose everything that had ever mattered to him.

That he would die.

Matt tossed restlessly in his sleep. He was with Annie. He *was* happy again.

The driver didn't like that. It wasn't supposed to happen this way. It didn't fit the plan.

The plan was to destroy Matthew Carlyle.

And if someone else—like Annie Jefferson—interfered with the plan, she too would have to die.

He woke with a start, his heart pounding. He pulled Annie close and held her very tight.

Chapter Twenty-seven

The following afternoon, back at his Pacific Heights estate, Matt was enjoying cooking somewhat mangled pancakes for his laughing new lover when he heard the front door bell. He glanced up at the clock on the wall. Two o'clock on a Saturday. Who the hell—

Mrs. Roberts, the housekeeper, came into the kitchen, her face impassive as always but her eyes alarmed. "Sorry to bother you, sir," she said, trying not to look at Annie. "There are two people at the door who say they're detectives with the San Francisco police."

Matt felt the old familiar sinking in his stomach. He glanced at Annie and he could see the concern racing through her. She was empathetic, he knew—she had shown that to him over and over again last night. But she could have no real inkling of what it was like, to him, to hear those words.

Still, four months of sitting impassively in a courtroom under orders not to betray the slightest emotion that could influence the jury against him had trained him well. He was able to quiet the wild racing of his heart and nod calmly to Mrs. Roberts. "Show them in, please."

"Oh, Matt—" Annie began as the housekeeper left the room.

"Shh, don't fret. They were bound to get around to me sooner or later. As we said, they can put me at the crime scene. They've got my fingerprints all over the scaffolding, and I assure you, the San Francisco police have my fingerprints on record. Hell, they've probably got them in a special display case."

Mrs. Roberts reentered, two detectives in tow, a male and a female. Matt satisfied himself that he didn't know either of them. They hadn't been assigned to Francesca's murder.

They introduced themselves, and Matthew was polite. He was about to introduce them to Annie when she cut in, "It's okay. I've already met Detectives Sullivan and Foster."

Sullivan did most of the talking. "We're investigating the murder of Giuseppe Brindesi," she said. "Did you know him, Mr. Carlyle?"

Matt leaned back against the kitchen counter. "Coffee, detectives?" he said.

They both shook their heads, although Sullivan glanced eagerly at the steaming coffeepot. Both detectives looked as if they'd been up all night.

Matt thought with some amusement that he and Annie probably looked the same. But happier.

"Look, Carlyle," said Foster. "You know the routine. Let's not beat around the bush. We have your prints all over that scaffolding in the cathedral. You care to explain that for us?"

"Do you see my lawyer present, Detective Foster?"

"At the moment, we're not charging you with anything."

At the moment.

"So, what, am I expected to do my civic duty and have a friendly little chat with you outside the presence of my attorney while you and the DA's office try to put together another trumped-up case against me?"

"There's no need to be alarmed, Mr. Carlyle," Sullivan interceded quickly. "Several of the workmen on the construction site have already explained your presence at what's now become the crime scene." She glanced at Annie. "As did Ms. Jefferson, of course."

"Then it seems to me, Detective Sullivan, that even if my lawyer were present, there would be no necessity for me to answer any of your questions."

"We're trying to establish a time line and to understand various subtleties about the case," she said.

"Well, you certainly have my best wishes. I too would like to see the killer brought to justice as quickly as possible."

"That's why we were hoping for your cooperation, sir. Perhaps your insights will assist us."

Matthew felt his anger rising. What kind of an idiot did they think he was? These people—or others from their department—were responsible for the eighteen months of fear and misery he'd endured at the hands of the state. Whatever innocence he'd had in dealing with the American justice system had been blasted forever. They were damn lucky he didn't throw them bodily out of his house.

Before he could respond, Foster cut in, "It has come to our attention, Mr. Carlyle, that the deceased, Giuseppe Brindesi, master stained glass worker, may have been acquainted with your late wife, Francesca. Do you have any comment on this, sir?"

"Yes, I have a comment," he said slowly.

Both detectives leaned slightly toward him.

"This is my comment, detectives: My days of cooperating with the San Francisco police and/or the DA's office are in the past. If you intend to charge with me a crime, do so. I will then call my attorney, and any statement that I make to you will be made in his presence. Otherwise, I have nothing to say to you." He forced a smile. "I'm sure you understand."

The homicide detectives glanced at each other. Matt knew damn well that there was nothing more they could say or do. This wasn't—yet—a police state. They couldn't force anyone to talk.

They thanked him politely and left.

"I can't *believe* they suspect you!" Annie cried.

"Yes, you can," he said, pulling her into his arms.

He felt her tremble against him, and he wondered if she was still uncertain of him. What would happen when she was alone and had time to think? Would she turn against him the way so many of his friends and acquaintances had?

Why shouldn't she? he thought grimly. What was to stop her—the pleasures of sex? Sure, the chemistry between them was powerful here, now, but sex hormones often acted as drugs clouding the judgment. She might begin to see him very differently once she got home and those hormones stopped flowing.

All they had had together were two glorious nights.

Two nights to balance against all the negative images of a long murder trial and all the publicity associated with it.

It wasn't much to count on.

"Matt, I'm afraid for you," Annie whispered. "What if it turns out that Giuseppe was Francesca's lover?"

"I suppose it's possible. Hell, anything's possible. It was a little odd that they had so much trouble finding her lover at the time, but if he was out of the country—"

"It would give you a motive to kill both of them."

"Indeed," he said dryly. "The fact remains, however, that I didn't."

She looked up at him quickly. "I know that."

Sure, he thought.

"They'll have to prove it, though," he said, "and that's not going to be easy. God knows they tried to prove all sorts of allegations the last time. I'd be a lot happier if they didn't have my fingerprints on the damn scaffolding, even though they have a perfectly good explanation for that." He paused. "It's much too neat, you know."

"What do you mean?"

"The fact that my fingerprints are at this murder scene. It's just too fucking convenient—for the killer, I mean. Look at the situation it creates: Instead of looking for the real killer, the cops are all excited about what they suddenly think is a new way to nail the infamous Matthew Carlyle, who got away with murder."

"You think someone is trying to frame you, Matt?"

"I think someone has been trying to frame me from the start."

They both pondered the question that had tormented Matt for months:

Who?

"I won't let this happen to me again," said Matt.

"What do you mean?" Annie was frightened by the vehemence of his tone.

"I won't go through it again, goddammit! The shame and humiliation—the publicity—the rumors—the strangers' malevolent stares. If this is what my life has come to mean to everybody ..." He paused. "By God, I've never been guilty of murder before, but when I find out who the man is who's doing this to me ..."

"We will find him, Matt. We'll find him and we'll put a stop to this once and for all."

Chapter Twenty-eight

"May I come in, ma'am?"

Annie had just returned home from work the following Monday when Detective Foster knocked on her door.

"Please." She waved him inside. He smelled of cigarettes, and she hoped he wasn't going to light up in her home.

Foster pulled a small notebook out of his pocket and consulted it briefly, then he looked up. "We have a few more questions to ask you concerning Giuseppe Brindesi's death."

She stared at him. "I'm not sure that I should talk to you any further without consulting an attorney."

He smiled unpleasantly. "Maybe you're being influenced by your—er . . . friendship with Matthew Carlyle."

She flushed angrily and was tempted to ask him to leave. Matt had left for a two-day business trip to Washington, D.C., and had told her not to answer any questions about him from the police.

But then Foster added, "Actually, I'm pursuing another

angle at the moment. We've recently had occasion to speak with some of your colleagues, including Mr. Brody and a Mr. Sidney Canin. You are acquainted with Mr. Canin, I understand?"

"Yes. He used to work with me at Brody Associates." *Any* angle that led away from Matt was an angle she was willing to assist them with.

"And for you at your former place of business"—he glanced down at the notebook again—"Fabrications, isn't that true?"

"Yes."

"So you've known Mr. Canin for some time."

"Well, yes, but only in a professional capacity. I don't know him well in any other respect."

"He is an architect, correct?"

"Yes."

"Do you consider him a good architect?"

Anne hesitated. They must know that Sidney had been fired recently by Sam. "It's difficult for me to make that determination. I'm an interior designer. Although I work with architects, I'm no expert in their discipline."

"But in fact you are more than simply an interior designer, aren't you, Ms. Jefferson? You co-owned an architectural engineering firm that employed Mr. Canin. At Brody Associates, you are both the interior design manager and the project manager on several construction jobs, including the new cathedral. You have worked for, with, and above various architects for years, so you must have some means of evaluating their work. Isn't that correct?"

"Yes, it is," she conceded. "Okay, in my opinion, Sidney is a competent architect with a good head for details but very little creativity or artistic flair. He works best when partnered with other architects who are better at conceptualizing a project.''

''So is it fair to say that while you would not count on him to start from scratch and create an original plan for a new building, you would trust him more to attend to the minute details of a project, like the individual specifications about grades of steel, thicknesses of bolts, and things of that nature?''

''That pretty much sums it up, yes. He is good on structural details.''

The detective paused and once again examined his notebook. Where was he going with this? she wondered.

''Mr. Canin was recently fired from Brody Associates, correct?''

''Yes.''

''Do you know the reason for that firing?''

''Mr. Brody did not consult me about it, no.''

''As far as you know, had Mr. Canin's work been incompetent in any way?''

She shrugged. ''That depends so much on personal opinion. His inability to conceptualize is certainly a weakness. I had problems with him in that regard when he was working for me.''

''But are you aware of any specific reason why he was fired? Any recent job that he screwed up on, for example? Any particular problem that one could point a finger to and say, 'This guy is doing a lousy job'?''

She shook her head. ''No. I don't. But Sidney had some projects that I had nothing to do with. It's certainly possible that Sam—Mr. Brody—could have known of something like that. I suggest you discuss it with him, if you haven't already.''

The detective's expression was noncommittal.

Annie shifted in her chair. "If I might ask, what does this have to do with Giuseppe's death?"

Instead of answering directly, Detective Foster said, "What about Darcy Fuentes? How would you evaluate her expertise as an architect?"

She was taken aback. "Darcy? Why, she's terrific. She has a sterling reputation. She's won some of the most prestigious awards in the industry. Her work is creative, artistically beautiful, and supremely functional. She's one of the best."

If Foster was impressed he didn't show it. "Is there any truth to the observation that Ms. Fuentes is quite the opposite of Mr. Canin in terms of the attention she gives to the finer details of her projects?"

"What exactly do you mean?"

He closed his notebook, and his expression hardened as he said, "In short, Ms. Jefferson, it has been suggested by several people that talented though the woman is conceptually and artistically, she is not known for her attentiveness to detail. That when it comes down to actually drawing up the final plans and specifications for a project, Ms. Fuentes usually turns this work over to her associates. That on the occasions when she fails to turn this work over to someone else, there are problems. And that there are structural problems with the cathedral, a project that Ms. Fuentes designed largely on her own."

"That is nonsense," Annie said indignantly. "There are no structural problems with the cathedral—the work has gone remarkably smoothly all these months."

"Not according to Sidney Canin," Foster said. "In fact, it's his contention that Brody Associates rejected the suggestions he made for improvements in the engineering specifications at the time the plans were drawn up. There were several areas in which Canin felt that errors had occurred, but when he tried to convince anybody else at the firm of this, he was singularly unsuccessful."

Annie cleared her throat. "Detective Foster, please consider the situation from another perspective. You have to understand Sidney. He's generally a negative person, someone who sees in everything a disaster waiting to happen. He always exaggerates problems and never has the grace to apologize when he's proven wrong. Besides, don't forget, he was recently fired. He probably feels bitter about it, and this whole story may simply be vindictiveness on his part."

"At the time he was terminated, Canin claims to have been gravely concerned about the strength of the seismic connections in the structure where some large panels of stained glass were being installed," Foster said. "Giuseppe had mentioned to Canin his suspicion that the structural frame might have been underdesigned. That someone, in other words, had made a mistake."

Abruptly, Annie remembered Giuseppe's request to come to her office and examine the original blueprints. He hadn't told her why, and he'd been killed before he could do so.

"According to Canin, neither Ms. Fuentes nor anyone else was interested in discussing the matter. There were no problems with the building, everyone insisted. Canin didn't argue. As you say, he'd just been fired. *Let* one of the stained glass panels crash into the nave of the cathedral during a minor earthquake—that would teach the whole damn firm a lesson."

Well, that certainly sounded like Sidney, Annie thought. But her skin crawled anyway. The stained glass panels were huge and heavy. If one of them fell into the nave when the cathedral was crowded, there would be serious injuries, perhaps deaths.

Sid *had* burst into her office one day, she remembered, demanding to talk to her about a problem with the construction. But he'd gone storming off when he heard about Matt's involvement in the project.

"Canin says that he told Giuseppe he'd tried but failed to remedy the situation," Foster said. "Giuseppe seemed very concerned. He said he would speak to Ms. Fuentes about it himself.

"A day or two later, he was dead."

Foster looked at her expectantly as Annie digested what he was suggesting. The implication was clear: Giuseppe had been murdered and the killer—of all people—had been Darcy.

She rose from her chair. "You can't seriously believe this!"

"This is an investigation, Ms. Jefferson. I don't believe anything. I simply gather as much information as I can and turn it over to the district attorney."

"Look, detective, even if there *is* a problem with the structural framing of the building—which I seriously doubt—and even if Giuseppe was worried enough to talk to Darcy about it, that's not a motive for murder. Mistakes are made sometimes in construction work. Either the part is wrongly specified, or something about the design changes during the course of the building, or the original element specified is no longer available, or something comes on the market that would do a better job. Change orders get filed and adjustments get made, detective. Sometimes work has to be ripped out and redone. It's expensive and it slows down the project, but neither Brody Associates nor McEnerney Construction would cut corners that could result in an unsafe job. If a mistake is made, you fix it. You don't murder the person who brings it to your attention!''

''Not even if the project is a major one with an already inflated budget, every sort of publicity, and a strict deadline for completion?''

''Of course not! The idea is ridiculous! We're talking about someone's *life*.''

''Believe me, lady, people are murdered every day in this city for reasons a helluva lot sillier than that.''

''Well, I'm not convinced that Giuseppe was killed for such a reason. Especially since the cathedral is *not* underdesigned!''

''You may be right,'' Foster said mildly. ''But I've got an instinct about this one. And when a homicide cop has an instinct, there's usually something behind it—even if chasing after that instinct takes him down a few wrong roads.''

''Those so-called instincts can be devastating when you accuse innocent people of murder!''

The detective's eyes narrowed. ''If you're referring to the Carlyle case, he was guilty all right. He's a rich son of a bitch who beat the system. If I have anything to say about it, that ain't gonna happen again. I'm looking at this architectural angle today, but that doesn't mean I'm forgetting about Carlyle's fingerprints being all over the sabotaged scaffolding.''

''And I've explained to you how they came to be there, Detective Foster. No doubt you've confirmed what I told you with some of the numerous other witnesses who were there at the time!''

''We've also heard a rumor that Giuseppe Brindesi was Francesca Carlyle's lover,'' he said. ''That puts your boyfriend right back in hot water again, Ms. Jefferson, doesn't it?''

She stared at him, feeling sick. Was it true? Had they confirmed that?

"But, as I said, that's not the angle I'm working today," he went on. "There's not going to be any rush to judgment in this case—not if I have anything to say about it."

"Well, if you believe that either Matt or Darcy Fuentes had anything to do with it, you're on the wrong road this time, detective."

"Or the kid, either—Vico. You think he's innocent as well, don't you? Seems to me, Ms. Jefferson, you've got a habit of declaring everybody innocent, no matter how much evidence we have against them."

"Everybody *is* innocent, detective. Everybody except one person. So do me a favor, please. Do the people of California a favor. Get the right guy this time."

"We'll get him. Or her. Sooner or later I'll get to my destination, no matter how many wrong roads I take along the way."

After he left, Annie found herself pacing the apartment, her thoughts awhirl. Much as she hated hearing what Foster had said, she knew she would have to check into it. Because it certainly seemed that something was wrong here—it didn't take a cop's instincts to know that.

Annie was well aware that the San Francisco building codes were among the strictest in the nation, largely because of the risk of major earthquakes. It was pretty difficult to imagine anyone making a mistake about the seismic design. However, if a mistake was made, it would be caught long before the plans were approved. Before any construction could begin, the structural design had to be certified by the city inspectors.

On the other hand, she'd been in this business long enough to know that everything wasn't always done aboveboard. There were contractors who took a hefty profit out of every project. All contractors figured to make at least 15 percent profit and adjusted their estimates and their costs accordingly. That was the industry standard, and perfectly legal, of course.

But there were ways of increasing that profit margin, and it was something that both the primary contractors and the subcontractors might indulge in, depending on how unscrupulous they were. She wondered again about Paul McEnerney. She suspected that he wouldn't be above pocketing a few extra dollars if he had the chance.

There were many ways to cheat. And if the architects—or just one person at the architectural firm—were in cahoots with one of the contractors, cutting some sort of deal and splitting what they skimmed . . .

Mistakes? No way. But carefully planned and executed fraud? That was certainly possible.

But *Darcy*? The idea that she could be involved in something of that nature and then *killed* somebody to cover it up was ridiculous!

Even so, Annie couldn't get out of her mind the thought that Darcy had been behaving very oddly lately. She'd been jumpy and distracted, and people were beginning to notice. Annie had spoken with a client yesterday who had called to complain that Darcy hadn't returned his phone calls.

Clearly, there was something wrong with her. And whatever it was, Darcy didn't feel comfortable talking about it with her best friend in the world . . .

Christ, her head was aching! Ever since Giuseppe's death she had been tossed by one violent emotion after another, most of them engendered by her newly raised doubts about the people she cared most about.

She certainly didn't want to give serious consideration to any theory that would pin the murder on Matthew. But neither did she want to consider that Darcy could be capable of such a heinous crime.

But how well did she really know Matt? For that matter, how well did she know Darcy? If someone was a skillful actor and dissembler, was there any way to see into his or her heart?

Annie had always liked to believe that she had good instincts about people. But she couldn't be as good a judge of character as she had thought, because someone who was probably known to her had, with malice aforethought, loosened the pins on the scaffolding in front of the high altar, knowing that the next person who mounted it would fall eighty feet to his death on the stone floor below.

Chapter Twenty-nine

"If I understand correctly," said Sam, "it's Detective Foster's contention that Giuseppe had made some discovery about a catastrophic engineering error, confronted Darcy—the primary architect—and she killed him."

"Yes." Annie had gone straight to Sam's office the following morning to tell him about her talk with the detective. Sam had admitted that Foster had talked to him too.

"Well, I'm telling you what I told the detective," said Sam. "It's the most ludicrous thing I've ever heard."

"I agree with you. But if this idiot is serious, he could make all sorts of trouble for Darcy. He's already made Matt Carlyle's life miserable again."

Sam pressed his lips together and nodded. "They've been questioning me about Matt too. But setting that aside for a moment, think about it—if Darcy made some sort of error, then Sidney must have known about it, right? And if he allowed the building to go on without correcting it, then he too would be responsible. Ultimately, in fact, the entire firm would be responsible. Hell, I'm the one who signed and stamped the official blueprints. I'm the one who would be sued."

"And when you went over it, did you notice any errors?"

"No, but I admit I gave the final version a fairly cursory look."

"Sam, you don't believe there's any truth to what Foster said about Darcy's being no good with the fine details, do you?"

Sam shrugged. "'No good' is a blatant exaggeration. I don't think she likes the fine details, but she's a professional. I've certainly never seen any evidence that she cuts corners in any respect. You can't do that in this business, Annie, you know that. It's like the old proverb, 'For want of a nail, the horseshoe was lost . . .' For want of the proper flexibility of a seismic connection, the building fails its safety inspection. Or, worst case, collapses in an earthquake. There's simply too much money involved in these projects for anyone to risk their reputation on slipshod work."

"Just for the sake of argument," Annie said, "suppose a critical mistake was made in the design process, and no one caught it. Suppose the work went forward, all the structural work had been finished, and one of the experienced craftsmen at the site noticed that something didn't look right. Maybe he's wrong about it, actually. But he's stubborn and he clings to his theory, and he won't hesitate to tell others about it. Maybe he'll even go to the press. In other words, he could cause a lot of trouble."

Sam shook his head. "I don't know. I don't think I buy it. There are safety inspections to be passed—"

"You and I both know that some of the inspectors are, frankly, incompetent, and others can probably be bribed."

"Well—"

"And we've both been in the business too long to be naïve. There *is* corruption. Money does pass quietly under the table sometimes. Brody Associates and McEnerney Construction have worked together lots of times before; everything is very cozy, and with a project of this size, with so many millions of dollars involved, there might be a pretty big temptation for somebody to skim off a little money—"

His normally genial look disappeared. "Come on, Annie, think what you're saying here! Darcy couldn't be behind something as complex and dirty as that." He paused, seeming to reconsider, then shook his head. "I just can't believe it of her."

"No. No, of course not." Annie realized that she was getting nervous because Sam's tone, for the first time, was a bit uncertain. Hadn't he said something about Darcy having done an internship with McEnerney Construction a few years ago?

"Annie, look at me."

She raised her eyes. Sam shook his head gently, his eyes candid and serious. "Listen. I want you to stop worrying about this. As far as I know, there are no errors in the specifications for the structure of the cathedral. But I'll check into it. We'll run some tests, and if there have been any errors, they'll be corrected. We'll retrofit the entire place if necessary. Whatever it takes."

"Sam, listen, I—"

"What's more, as far as I know, Giuseppe Brindesi did *not* go to Darcy with any claims of that sort. But even if he did,

it's pretty hard for me to imagine that she would lose control—
or whatever the cops imagine—and murder him."

"It's pretty hard for me to imagine," he'd said. Not *"It's
impossible for me to imagine."* Dammit! She didn't want Sam
to believe it any more than she wanted to believe it herself.

"By the way, have you talked to Darcy about this?" he
asked.

"No. Jesus, how could I?"

"Good. Seems to me she's been a bit vulnerable lately. I
would hate to see her hurt by idle and totally unjustified
speculation." He paused. "How well do you two actually
know each other, anyway?"

"Very well," Annie said. "She's one of the best friends
I've ever had."

"Then you probably know that Darcy and I were lovers
for a short while recently."

What?

"No?" he said. "I thought she might have told you."

"No, she didn't." Annie was thoroughly startled. *Darcy
and Sam?* That was the kind of thing close women friends
tended to tell each other.

"Jeez, I'm sorry," Sam said, looking embarrassed. "Hey,
it was no big deal—a mistake, really, on both our parts." He
smiled wryly. "I probably made a lot less of an impression
on her than she made on me."

"I doubt that."

He shrugged. "Actually, in all honesty, I think it may have
been more difficult for her than she's willing to admit. I'm
afraid that she may have been a little more involved, emotion-
ally, than she let on."

That could certainly explain Darcy's strange moodiness

lately, Annie thought. What it didn't explain was why Darcy had never mentioned the affair.

"Anyhow," Sam said, "knowing her as well as I do, I sincerely doubt that there's any truth to what Canin had to say. Darcy's an excellent architect. And she's certainly not a killer." He shook his head. "At least, I don't *think* she is."

For the rest of the day, Annie turned the conversation with Sam over and over in her mind. She wished she could talk to Matt about it, but he was still in Washington. And in a sense she was glad that he was out of town, and safe, briefly, from being hassled by the police.

Little details kept haunting her: Darcy's recent and unusual skittishness; her attempt to convince Annie that Matt Carlyle must have been involved; the way she had seemed so totally distraught at Giuseppe's funeral; the fact that she hadn't been home on the night of the murder.

And there was something else that Sam didn't know, something that had happened on the day that Darcy and others from the firm had visited the site with Annie to observe the progress: Darcy had climbed up the scaffolding with Giuseppe. What had he said to her that day? *"You are the architect, are you not, madonna? Yes, please, come up, there are several things I would like to show you."*

Had he told her then that there was something wrong in the cathedral frame? Had she examined it, confirmed it, and decided then and there to kill him?

No, dammit! Not Darcy.

What would be the motive? Money? Darcy came from a poor family, and Annie knew that she aspired to far greater wealth than she had achieved so far. The men she dated tended to be affluent. Including, of course, Sam, whose high society credentials were impeccable.

Why didn't she ever tell me about that affair?

Annie thought, with some embarrassment, of the intimate details she had shared with Darcy about her relationship with Matt. She had always believed Darcy to be a very open person, someone who simply would not be able to keep a juicy detail secret. Now that she knew that Darcy had had an affair with Sam, Annie wondered what else she had been hiding.

And if, as Sam had hinted, he had ended the affair against Darcy's wishes, might her disappointment have been the proverbial last straw? Sam was exactly the sort of man whom Darcy would have hoped to marry. Rich, handsome, successful, charming, able to introduce her to a social circle far above the one to which she had been born. Losing Sam must have been difficult indeed.

What did it all add up to?

If Darcy was involved in some kind of architectural fraud, she couldn't do it without a partner. Someone from the general contractor's side. Someone with responsibility, someone in charge . . .

Jack Fletcher.

It had to be. Annie had sensed something wrong about him for months. He had control of the building schedule, kept track of the hours worked by the various subcontractors, and ordered the construction materials. If anybody could skim money, Fletcher would be the guy.

He was skimming, and Darcy was getting a substantial cut. In fact, maybe it was *Fletcher* who had tampered with the scaffolding. Annie still refused to believe that her best friend was capable of murder.

"*She's certainly not a killer,*" Sam had said. "*At least, I don't think she is.*"

Chapter Thirty

After work that evening, Annie drove to Sidney Canin's house in Cow Hollow. Hearing his story secondhand from the police wasn't good enough. In order to understand what he suspected, she had to hear it from him.

Although Sam had told her to stop worrying about it, she couldn't leave it alone. Sam was too easygoing. Sometimes she wondered if he had any concept of the evil that existed in the world.

Annie had been away from that evil for a long time. Charlie had pulled her from that morass of human greed, lies, and deception. She had been eager to leave it behind, to forget it. And she'd been especially eager to forget that she had once played a minor part in perpetuating it.

It was a grave mistake, though, to think that evil was confined to the streets. Greed, aggression, and the lust for power reached into bedrooms and boardrooms all over the world. These flaws knew no social, economic, or professional boundaries; they could turn up in anyone, at any time.

Even in the people you most liked and trusted.

Sidney's house was dark when she got there. Not a single light on in the place. This seemed odd, because Sidney was the finicky type who would always leave several lights burning to confuse prowlers. Sidney worried about everything and took precautions against every possible pitfall that life could offer up.

Annie parked illegally in front of a hydrant and climbed the five steps to Sidney's front porch. She rang the doorbell and heard it echo through the house.

No one came. He could be out, but again, why no lights? She felt an uneasy fluttering in her stomach. Sidney had told a story to the police that could, potentially, have changed the entire thrust of their investigation. He had suggested a conspiracy and had named Darcy as one of the possible guilty parties. If he was right, the last person who had attempted to blow the whistle on the scheme had been killed.

What if somebody had decided to take Sidney out of the game too?

There was a bay window to the right of the front door. Annie pressed her face against the glass and peered in.

There was nothing there.

No furniture, no carpeting, no pictures on the walls or knickknacks on the shelves. All she could see in there were a couple of folded cardboard boxes that had not been opened and an empty roll of packing tape.

Sidney loved his house, but apparently he'd decided that it wasn't in his best interests to stick around. He'd been talking for a long time about moving back to New York. It looked as if he'd finally done it.

Annie got back into her car and drove aimlessly through the city. Sidney Canin was a big question mark. She had an image of him at the party on Matt's yacht on the night of Francesca's death. Sid had rarely taken his eyes off the woman. He'd hurried solicitously to her side as soon as she'd made the startling announcement that she intended to file for divorce. He'd danced with Francesca. He'd held her close.

What if Sidney had been Francesca's mysterious lover? What if he'd loved her, expected to marry her, and then had killed her in a rage of passion and jealousy when he found out that Francesca wasn't ready to leave her husband after all?

What if Giuseppe, somehow, had known about Sid's affair with Francesca, making it necessary for Sid to kill him, too, to keep him quiet? What if, panicked that the police would figure it out, he'd invented the whole story about design flaws in the cathedral and told the police that it was Giuseppe who had been carrying on the adulterous affair?

The good thing about this theory, Annie thought with a sigh, was that it would take Darcy off the hook. Unless there was some sort of construction scam going on that was entirely separate from the murder. . . .

She ended up driving across Market, heading toward the construction site. She passed the cathedral, turned, rounded the block, and passed it again on the other side.

She noted that a light was on in one of the trailers in the

construction lot. Fletcher's. He spent a lot of time in that trailer. Didn't he ever go home?

Where did he keep his records? she wondered. If there was written proof of construction fraud, and he was in on the conspiracy, he might be the one to have it.

The police, she knew, couldn't get a search warrant without probable cause. She didn't know if the police even suspected Fletcher. And she had to admit that her own suspicions were irrational and intuitive: She didn't like him, so he must be the guilty party.

It was totally unfair and supremely illogical.

She wanted to search his trailer anyway.

Not being a law enforcement type, she couldn't get a search warrant. But then, she didn't need one. Breaking and entering had been one of the talents she'd acquired many years ago, on the streets.

She drove home and changed into a black warm-up suit and dark blue running shoes. Finally, she donned a dark knit ski cap to hide her blond hair.

Into the pocket of the warm-up jacket she placed a pencil-thin flashlight that had a strong, concentrated beam. From the bottom of a box that she had kept for over a decade—always securely locked—she withdrew a case of stainless steel tools that an old acquaintance of hers by the name of Top Floor Jocko had sold her for cheap. Lockpicks. She fiddled with them a bit to convince herself that she remembered how to use them. It was kind of like riding a bicycle, she thought, laughing nervously to herself.

She drove back to the cathedral area and circled the block. The light was still on in Fletcher's trailer. Damn. She didn't think he was the type to leave lights on to foil thieves. No, his car was still there in the lot.

She cruised past and headed down into the Castro district. She drove aimlessly, letting her mind wander. Darcy couldn't be involved, she told herself over and over. It must be Fletcher. There was nothing at all wrong with the architecture for the cathedral. What was wrong was that Fletcher was skimming. Fletcher was the one who had loosened the pins on the scaffolding.

Annie *really* didn't want it to be Darcy.

She drove past the construction site again. Twenty minutes had passed. He was still there. Dammit!

She was nervous but primed to act. She could feel the adrenaline shooting through her veins, and she was conscious of the hard feel of the lockpicks in her jacket pocket, vibrating to the rhythm of her pounding heart.

Come on, Fletcher. Go home!

It was after midnight when she finally gave up. The light in the trailer went out, but Fletcher's car didn't budge. He was obviously spending the night on the construction site.

Frustrated and demoralized, Annie shoved her housebreaking tools into the glove compartment and drove home to North Beach, where she fell wearily into bed.

Chapter Thirty-one

Annie had a dream that night about male and female friendship. She and Darcy were together in a room, laughing over a copy of *Men Are from Mars, Women Are from Venus.* "Our friendships are different," Darcy said. "We talk about real life problems, they talk about baseball statistics."

They both giggled wildly. Annie woke up in tears.

What she had to do was talk to Darcy. Nothing was fair until she did.

But her sense of frustration continued the next morning. Darcy had left the house next door to Annie's before Annie was out of bed. When she got to the office, she learned that Darcy would be in Oakland all day, checking out a building that Brody Associates was due to renovate.

Annie then went to the construction site, having decided on another course of action. She would try to get into that trailer during the day, while Fletcher was inside the cathedral. It was more risky, of course, but if caught she could always make the excuse that she'd wanted to talk to him, hadn't seen him in the building, and had come out to the trailer in search of him.

But after a couple of hours it began to seem as if nothing was going to go right for her. Fletcher spent most of the day either in or around his trailer. He was doing paperwork, apparently.

Dammit! She was going crazy. She didn't know whom to trust, whom to believe.

Darcy's car was parked out front when Annie got home around dinner time. Without even bothering to go into her own side of the building, she knocked on Darcy's door.

Darcy came to the door wrapped in a towel robe. Her long dark hair hung wetly down her back. "Thank goodness it's you. I just stepped out of the shower. Come on in."

Annie followed her back to the bathroom, where she continued combing out her hair. "Darcy, I've got to ask you a personal question."

"Okay. Shoot." She sounded totally unconcerned.

Annie took a deep breath, then blurted, "Did you have a short-lived love affair with Sam?"

Darcy's comb got stuck in a tangle of black hair. Her skin flushed, turning from olive to plum. "W-with Sam?"

"With Sam."

Her eyes met Annie's in the mirror. "Who told you that?"

"Sam."

"That son of a bitch!"

"You mean it's true?"

"Yeah," she said ruefully, "it's true all right. Actually, I'm surprised the whole world doesn't know, considering the way I've been mooning over him ever since.''

''Mooning? Over Sam?''

''Yes. He dumped me. First time I've been dumped in years. And maybe it's that I can't stand the rejection or something, but for some reason I've been obsessing over the guy.'' The words came rushing out. ''I mean, I've got it bad. I think about him night and day. It's really sick.'' She paused. ''You say he told you about it? Shit. Did he say anything about the way I've been hanging around his house?''

''No.'' So it was true! She'd half expected Darcy to deny it.

Darcy laughed shortly. ''You mean he didn't regale you with embarrassing stories about how I've been following him home at night and parking my car on his street, staring up at his windows, desperate for just a glimpse of him?''

Annie shook her head. She tried to imagine the irrepressible Darcy following some guy—any guy—around. It just didn't seem possible. Darcy had always struck her as extremely independent and self-possessed, especially where men were concerned.

''And this is *after* I see him all day at work, too. I mean, we're talking major-league obsessive behavior here. Fortunately it's not coupled with testosterone, or he'd probably be dead by now.''

''Jeez, Darcy!'' Annie shook her head, uncertain whether to laugh or to feel angry. ''Why didn't you tell me this was going on? We've been such good friends.''

''Annie, I swear to God, I wanted to tell you. But Sam was adamant that our relationship, while it lasted, be kept secret. And ever since it ended, well, I guess I've been ashamed to tell you. I mean, I've done things in the course of this obsession that I wouldn't want *anybody* to find out about. It's been that bad."

What sort of things?

Darcy laughed. "Telling you now sure feels like a relief! Shit, I wish I'd done it a couple of weeks ago."

"Why was it so important to Sam that you keep the affair a secret?"

"He's a very private person. And of course we were working together, which might have raised a few eyebrows, and not only in the firm. There's a lot of gossip in this business. You know that."

"Well, none of us even suspected. You and he must have been really circumspect."

Darcy shrugged. "If it had gone on much longer, I'd have probably told you, Annie. I'm pretty lousy at keeping secrets. Hell, that's probably one of the reasons he dropped me—because he knew I wasn't the discreet type."

"But you *were* discreet, at least about this."

"Yeah. That's a first. Maybe some of his discretion rubbed off on me." She paused. "Have you ever noticed that he never really talks much about himself? I mean, almost anyone can have a fine, long conversation with him, but I think that's because he's such a good listener. He encourages other people to talk, which most of us love to do. But he keeps still.

"Even with me, when we were going out, I thought I'd find out something more intimate about his life—you know, the things he cares about, the people he's close to, his interests and ideals. But it's weird, Annie. I found out nothing, or at least very little. And, in a way, I think that's been part of the attraction for me, part of the reason why I haven't been able to let go of my feelings. It's because he's so elusive. It's such a challenge."

"I wonder why he's so elusive," Annie said, musing. For it struck her that Darcy was correct about this. Sam was always warm and friendly, and yet she knew very little about his personal life.

Darcy brushed a long lock of black hair off her face. Her fingernails were once again long, red, and perfect. Annie figured that was a healthy sign.

"What are you getting at?" She asked.

Annie thought for a moment about what she did for a living. As a designer, she essentially had to take the shell of an edifice and outfit it from the frame inward, specifying and supervising the addition of Sheetrock, paint, wall coverings, carpets, fixtures, furnishings, and even such details as houseplants and pictures on the walls. But in order to understand her co-workers and friends, she would have to work backward—mentally dismantling all the outward decorations and furnishings until she could glimpse the true foundations of each person's soul.

With Matt, she felt confident that she was reaching inside him, seeing the truth of him, learning that although there were barriers, they were not hiding anything truly evil. With Darcy, there were quicksilver changes, moodiness, and perhaps some self-esteem issues, but again, nothing fearful, nothing dark. With Charlie there had been a combination of goodwill and tenacity, ambition and geniality, determination and stubbornness. A man with faults, as all people have, but essentially good. Such was the case with most of the people of her acquaintance. Once she got to know them, she usually had a clear feeling about what was inside.

But Sam was different. His exterior was so appealing that she'd never really bothered to look inside.

"You were Sam's lover," she said to Darcy, "but you're saying that you never really got to know him?"

Darcy shrugged. "I'm saying I didn't get to know him intimately. It was a short relationship."

Annie sighed. "Did you know that Sid Canin is alleging that there was a structural design flaw in the cathedral and that Giuseppe may have been killed because he found out about it?"

"What?"

"The implication appears to be, Darcy, that if this design flaw exists, you knew about it. That you may even have been responsible for it. And that, if so, you may also have been responsible for Giuseppe's death."

"You can't be serious." She turned away from the mirror and faced Annie directly. "I killed Giuseppe? Me?"

"Although Sam leaped to your defense when he heard this theory, the more we talked about it, the less certain he seemed."

"Well, shit, Annie." Darcy's face turned red, then, very slowly, white as the blood drained out of it. She shrugged and tried to laugh. "It figures. I always fall in love with the wrong guy."

After her talk with Darcy, who had passionately denied the charges and insisted that this was the first she'd heard of any complaints about the cathedral's design, Annie returned to the office. She let herself in with her key and identified herself to the night security guard. Everybody else had gone home.

She first looked at the CAD file for the cathedral, which was stored on her computer, then she got out the blueprints generated by the CAD software. She took these to the conference room, and spread them out on the table.

Giuseppe had asked to have a look at the architectural plans for the building. He had, in fact, asked for the originals. He'd never had a chance to examine them. He'd been murdered first.

She hadn't thought much about it at the time. But now . . .

Dammit, she wished she had more training in such matters as structural stress and load. Although she understood the technical issues involved, she didn't feel competent to assess whether there were any mistakes in the specifications.

Annie heard footsteps in the corridor outside the conference room. She raised her head guiltily. There was no reason why she shouldn't be examining the plans, but even so—

The door opened. It was Sam. "Oh, it's you," he said. "Saw the light and wondered who was working so diligently at this hour."

Go away.

"What are you up to?" he asked, coming farther into the room. "Those are the cathedral drawings, aren't they?"

"Yes. I was just having another look."

His eyes slid from her face to the blueprints and back. Annie felt herself flushing.

Sam sat down opposite her. "This is about Foster's theory, isn't it? Annie, I told you I'd checked the drawings myself." He frowned, and there was a reproachful look in his eyes. "What are you afraid of?"

She started to protest that she wasn't afraid, but the words jammed at the back of her throat. The truth was, in recent days she had begun to feel that everything in her life was shifting. She was in San Francisco, city of earthquakes, and the ground was moving beneath her feet. The accusations against Vico and Matt just hadn't rung true to her. But there was something about this idea of construction fraud that made her very uneasy.

"Look," Sam went on, "I've been following up on that discussion we had the other day. I've talked to the detectives and assured them that Sidney Canin is a troublemaker and a liar who bears the firm a monumental grudge. And I gave Darcy my backing, one hundred percent."

"Darcy's certainly not a killer. At least, I don't think she is."

"Thanks, Sam. I agree with you about Sidney, by the way."

"From what I understand about routine murder investigations, they have to explore all the angles. But I don't think that necessarily means that they take any one theory too seriously—at least not until they have some solid evidence." He paused. "For example, another angle that they ran by me is that Giuseppe's murder had something to do with the death of Francesca Carlyle."

Terrific. Not *this* again.

"It seems the police have a theory that Giuseppe may have been Francesca's lover. If so . . ." A moment later he added, "Annie, is it true that you've been seeing Matt on a personal basis?"

When she hesitated to reply, Sam quickly added, "I don't mean to pry into your private life. It's just that Matt has had a lot of trouble with the police, and if they're going to be investigating him again and you're involved with him, it will affect your life too."

"Sam, I thought Matt Carlyle was a good friend of yours!"

"He is, Annie. We've known each other for over twenty years."

"Well then, how can you possibly still think that he killed his wife, or that he'd be capable of murdering Giuseppe—"

"Annie," he said slowly, cutting her off, "we're not talking about my personal thoughts on the matter. It's the police who think he's the killer who got away. They couldn't nail him for the first murder, so they're hot to get him for this one."

"But they don't have any evidence! Sidney probably made up that story about Giuseppe and Francesca being lovers to cover up the fact that *he* and Francesca were lovers."

Sam shook his head. "Sidney and Francesca? Nah. Sid may have been hot for her—in fact, I know he was. Francesca was pretty amused by him, too, heartless flirt that she was. But he wasn't the one."

"You say that as if you know who was."

"I do. Francesca and I were friends for years, remember. Hell, I knew her even longer than I've known Matt. She never actually admitted it to me, but I knew all along that she and Giuseppe were involved. I saw them locked in a passionate embrace one day in the old church."

"My God, Sam!"

"I kept it to myself during Matthew's trial. I knew Giuseppe had left the country, so of course he couldn't have been the killer. But how could I come forward and admit what I'd seen? It wouldn't help Matt; it could only hurt him for that testimony to come out.

"So I kept silent. God, Annie, it's bothered me a lot, but Matt's my friend and I figured I owed him that much loyalty.

"Now, though, with Giuseppe dead . . . He was killed on

the same day that Matthew visited the cathedral and saw that he was back in the country. Then the cops find Matt's fingerprints on the scaffolding." He shook his head fretfully. "What am I supposed to think?"

"You know as well as I do how his fingerprints got there! I was with him. Matt didn't kill anyone."

"That's what I keep telling myself. Matt's just not the type to do something like this. There has to be some other explanation. It's been driving me crazy, trying to figure it out."

"Sam, you're not going to the police with this, are you?"

"No. No, of course not. I just wish they'd catch the guy. It's agonizing to have this suspicion on my conscience as one murder after another takes place."

She reached forward and gripped his hands in hers. "He didn't do it. Please believe that. He needs his friends now. Please don't turn on him now that things are once again looking black."

"He's very lucky to have found you, Annie," Sam said. "Don't worry. Matt's always been able to count on me."

Chapter Thirty-two

After leaving the office that evening, Annie drove back to the construction site. Her thoughts were whirling. The possibility that Matt had indeed had a solid motive to kill both his wife and Giuseppe made her all the more determined to prove his innocence. This time, she noted, the lights were off in Fletcher's trailer.

Without giving herself time to hesitate or think much about it, Annie drove two blocks past the cathedral, parked, and took her flashlight and her tools out of the glove compartment. Then she darted back up the street to the trailer.

Checking carefully to make certain nobody was around, she pressed herself against the door of Fletcher's trailer and knocked. With her ear to the door, she listened for any sound from within. She heard nothing.

She pulled out her tools and deftly set to work. She was amazed at how quickly and easily her fingers remembered. In less than a minute, she was in.

* * *

At his place in the Castro district that night, Fletcher was reminded of all the reasons why he hated his apartment. Location, location, location. The Castro was full of gays.

It was a nice neighborhood, clean and safe, but just down the hill was a commercial area packed with small shops—health foods stores, pharmacies, bookstores, hairdressers, and more. It was always crowded with weirdos who gave Fletcher the creeps. Men holding hands, sometimes hugging and kissing. Women dressed in tight leather miniskirts walking arm and arm with other *women*. Guys with brightly colored tattoos all over their bare chests and backs, girls with rings through their nostrils.

And the gym he worked out in—most of them in there were gay as well. Christ, he hated this city.

Hell, he'd like to leave, but Annie was here.

And all he seemed to think about these days was Annie.

He was mainly thinking that none of his tactics were working. He'd set out to scare her and bring her closer into his orbit, but what were a few anonymous letters compared to a murder? He'd tried to make those poison-pen letters sound really weird—like some nut with a God complex or something—but no one seemed to care much about them. The killer had stolen his thunder.

Maybe he needed to alter the game a bit. Or at least play by different rules. He'd planned to have Annie at least partially willing because things were less of a hassle that way, especially afterward. But the fact was, he wanted to possess and control her—to own her—so it didn't really matter whether she was willing. If she knew what was good for her, she'd submit, abjectly and fearfully. She'd bow to his will while he did anything and everything he wanted to her.

But in order for that to happen, he had to show her who was boss.

The thought aroused him.

He felt pumped, hot.

Ready to act. He *needed* to act. The pressures inside him were building up too strong.

The first time, though, would have to be by guile. She was a little nervous now; hell, she had to be. He remembered the terror in her voice when she'd found herself trapped in the night-black basement. The cathedral must be a scary place to her now.

So she was all the more in need of a man to rescue her. Save her from the dark demons of superstition that had come to haunt the place.

He had to get her back there, and it had to be night. That's when the claiming of Annie would take place.

And after that, well, then he could bring her to his apartment. The one good thing about the Castro district was that people minded their own business. Hell, he'd seen people walking in the streets with their hands secured behind their backs in leather wrist cuffs, guided along by their "masters." People were into some weird shit. He could probably lead Annie along the street with a dog collar and leash and nobody would even raise a single pierced eyebrow.

Yeah, he liked the idea. He'd claim her at the construction site and then he'd bring her here.

Despite the cutesy-cutesy atmosphere out on the street,

Fletcher's apartment was all man. He subscribed to several survivalist magazines, and every now and then he bought some of their mail order stuff. Some of the things you could buy through the mail were amazing. Of course, it wasn't always legal to own it. Fletcher had a couple of handguns and even an Uzi down in his basement, its various pieces carefully disassembled and stored in different cartons. He could assemble the thing in under two minutes flat if he had to, but its presence wouldn't be obvious to anybody poking through his things.

His favorite new piece of gear was his Desert Commando knife. He'd ordered it just a few weeks ago, and it had come in a plain brown cardboard package with some kind of computer software logo on it.

But the knife wasn't software. No, it was hardware of the most impressive kind. The blade was sixteen inches long and four inches across at its widest point. It was slightly curved, and sharp on both the top and the bottom edges.

It was the mother of all knives.

Fletcher pulled out the knife and looked at it, hefted it. He felt restless, and he knew he wasn't going to be able to sleep. He hadn't been sleeping so good lately. His brain was too busy plotting and planning; his head was full of fantasies.

Somehow he had to get Annie to come to the cathedral at night. That was the key. There had to be a way to do it. He had to *find* a way.

Fletcher put down his knife and grabbed his jacket. He'd come home tonight because he'd thought he might sleep better, but now he knew it wasn't going to happen. He needed to be at the site. He could plan better there. Besides, at the site, he felt much closer to Annie, even though it was several hours before he'd see her there.

He grabbed his knife as he was going out the door.

You never knew when a good knife would come in handy.

Annie did not feel good about herself as she snooped through the contents of Jack Fletcher's trailer. She told herself that she was doing this for a good cause—Matt's freedom—but still she felt sleazy.

Fletcher's home away from home was neat and orderly. He had a narrow cot, a small refrigerator, and a microwave oven. He also had a computer, which was sitting on a countertop that had been converted to a makeshift desk. Annie switched it on as she opened drawers and looked for papers, receipts, and correspondence. She didn't want to turn on the lights in the trailer, but the computer screen gave her a little glow.

In the drawer under the computer she found a set of hand-written supervisory forms on McEnerney Construction letterhead. Fletcher had been filling in the forms daily, detailing the activities of the various subcontractors and their schedules along with comments about their work.

There might be something here, she decided, sitting down in front of the computer to study the forms with the aid of her flashlight. She wished she had a Xerox machine handy. There were a lot of papers.

Fletcher was so intent on his fantasies that he drove right by the construction site without noticing. He went four blocks too far before he realized what he'd done.

It happened a lot while he was driving. He put himself on automatic pilot and just let his mind drift. Images were coming back to him. Memories were being unearthed—things so far in the past that he'd thought they were buried forever.

He'd always been good at blocking out the bad memories. His mother, stripping him naked and beating him with a metal curtain rod—his mind still shied away from those images, thank God. When she'd died of cancer, he'd actually been *glad*. He'd never gotten even with her because the cancer had finished her, and he resented that. Sometimes he thought the cancer had been too good for her.

But Annie inspired the good memories. Sometimes when he thought about her, his brain hyperlinked to other moments in time, and he found himself envisioning another girl . . . another blond-haired lady with buff-colored fingernails and some sweet perfume that smelled like summer wildflowers.

When he thought of her—that long-ago, long-buried girl, he felt it starting all over again. Those wicked, delicious feelings that he thought he'd conquered. Those feelings his counselor in prison had urged him to bury, bury deep. Bury them with the girl, the girl he'd kidnapped, the girl he'd mastered, the girl he'd loved day after day in the dark secret basement where he'd kept her, the girl he'd oh-so-adoringly choked because he'd read that the less oxygen she breathed while fucking, the deeper her sexual ecstasy would be . . .

He hadn't meant to choke her too hard. He'd cried and mourned and felt completely lost for weeks after her death.

They'd never gotten him for that.

They'd gotten him for the rape.

Anyhow, he wasn't *sure* he'd killed her. He wasn't sure if

it had been real, or a dream, or a nightmare fantasy. He wasn't even sure if he'd ever known her, ever touched her—if she'd even been real.

But Annie—she was real.

She was real, and she was his.

Annie's fingers froze as she heard the crunch of gravel under tires. She doused her flashlight and shut down the computer.

It had to be Fletcher, she thought. Who else would come there in the middle of the night?

She slipped the forms she'd been studying back into the drawer where she'd found them, then rushed to the door and cracked it open. She could see the sweep of headlights coming toward her. There was no place to hide in the trailer, she realized. She had to get out or she would be caught. But with the headlights shining directly at the trailer, she didn't dare open the door any wider. He would see her; he would know.

The headlights angled and turned, and she figured he was looking for a place to park where his tires wouldn't get stuck in the mud. The front of the trailer was dark now and she didn't think he could see her. But if he was parking so close, he'd be upon her any second.

Go! Go! she ordered herself. She eased the door open—it didn't squeak, thank God—and slipped out, forcing herself to move carefully, silently. She darted along the side of the trailer, keeping in the shadow of its dark hulk as she glanced uneasily at the bright moon. She heard a car door close at the far end of the trailer, and she slipped around the corner at the back just as his heavy footsteps approached the door where, seconds ago, she'd been standing.

The lock. She hadn't had time to relock the door behind her. Dammit, she had to get away from here now!

There was another trailer to the rear of Fletcher's, and she ran silently for it, taking refuge on its far side. The latch had been flimsy, and perhaps he'd simply think he hadn't locked it properly when he'd left. It happened. She occasionally made the same mistake with her own locks.

Beyond the next trailer was a dumpster, which she also put between herself and Jack Fletcher. Only a little bit farther and she would gain the street.

She glanced back and saw the lights in Fletcher's trailer come on. She hoped he wasn't fretting about the lock. She tried to remember if she'd disturbed anything. Would he notice that someone had been there? She thought she'd been very careful, but it had been years since she'd done this sort of thing.

And, given the way her heart was pounding, she was never going to do it again.

Fletcher was a little put out when he discovered that he hadn't locked the door. Shit! He was getting careless. It seemed like all he could think about was Annie, and thinking about Annie was messing up his mind. He had to stop thinking and start acting.

But as he lay down on his narrow bed, he felt that Annie was very close to him. He even imagined he could smell her scent. When he closed his eyes, she was all around him—

the heady fragrance of her body making him hot and dizzy and weak.

He had to have her. He'd go mad if he didn't take her soon.

He opened his jeans and took himself in his hand as he let his dark fantasies unfurl.

Chapter Thirty-three

Chapter Thirty-three

Matt called Annie from the airport the next evening and asked if he could come over. "I don't want to go back to my place. Mrs. Roberts tells me the cops are staking it out."

Why? she wondered. Could Sam have gone to the police and reported that he'd witnessed Giuseppe and Francesca making love? He wouldn't do that, surely.

"Don't worry. Matt's always been able to count on me."

She hoped so. God, she hoped Sam continued to be as good a friend as Matt had always believed.

While she waited for Matt to arrive, her brain continued its anxious spinning. She'd had a tense day at the site today, dreading every contact with Jack Fletcher, who had seemed sullen and threatening in the way he followed her constantly with his eyes. She just *knew* there was something wrong about him. If only she'd had a little more time to search his trailer. After her close call last night, she didn't think she'd ever try it again.

And yet, the more she thought about it, the less she could see Fletcher masterminding the alleged plot concerning some sort of fraud with the cathedral construction. Participating in such a plot, yes. Dreaming it up and implementing it, no.

Equally disturbing was the way her mind kept replaying her last encounter with Sam. When he'd caught her examining the CAD file, she'd actually felt frightened. She'd sensed a hint of something in him that she had never seen before. Either that, or her fevered imagination was working overtime again.

Darcy's words about Sam's elusiveness had come back to her several times. Until Darcy said it, Annie had never really thought of Sam as elusive. But her friend was absolutely right—none of them knew very much about Sam, despite his genial and seemingly open manner.

Now it struck her that instead of being able to see into Sam's depths, she felt as if she were always looking at the shiny glass of a mirrored surface, which reflected back to her whatever she expected to see. She couldn't get beneath the surface—it was one-way glass.

Had he really seen Giuseppe and Francesca making love? Why did she doubt his word? Had Sam, like everybody else she'd thought she knew and cared about, ended up on her not-to-be-trusted list?

Curiously, the only person she totally trusted right now was Matt. The accused murderer whom more than half the city's population believed had bribed his way out of the gas chamber was the only person whose story she fully believed.

"God, I've missed you, Annie," he said when he arrived. He pulled her into his arms and kissed her hungrily, as if her lips offered him salvation.

She had to do something to help him. She hadn't been able to save Charlie. Dammit, she wasn't going to sit back and watch another man whom she loved be unjustly destroyed.

"I've got some dinner ready," she whispered.

"Later," he said.

They still hadn't gotten around to eating when the phone beside Annie's bed rang. It was Barbara Rae. "I think you ought to get down here right away," she said in her firm, quiet voice. "Is Matthew with you, by any chance?"

"Yes."

"Bring him."

"Barbara Rae, what's happening?"

"I have somebody here who would like to talk to you."

"Vico?"

"Paolina. She's alone. I'm not sure how long she'll be here, so you'd better hurry."

Barbara Rae met them at the rear entrance to the youth center. Her broad, kindly face appeared troubled; there was a crease between her eyes, and she seemed unable to summon her famous smile. "Come," she said, ushering them through a dark corridor to a staircase that led to the basement. "She came to me after all, and I think I've convinced her to talk to you. I had the doctor come to see her. She was bleeding, but it seems to have stopped. She was terrified that she might be losing the baby, but it seems to have been a false alarm."

"What about Vico?" Matt asked.

Barbara Rae shook her head. "She still refuses to say."

They found the girl in a tiny but pristine room in the basement. She lay on a narrow cot, covered with blankets, her legs elevated to stave off further bleeding. Her lovely face was paler than Annie remembered, but her huge round eyes were dark and alive.

Annie and Barbara Rae went to her side. Matt hung back, leaning against the wall near the doorway.

When Paolina saw Annie she began to cry. Annie quickly sat down beside her on the bed and gave her a hug. The girl clung to her and sobbed.

"It's okay, it's okay," Annie murmured.

"I wanted to come to you, but I was too afraid."

"It's okay. Being afraid is something I understand very well." She held her for a while, despite what she read as impatience in Matt's eyes. When at last the girl was calmer, she said, "Paolina, you must know that people are looking for you. And for Vico. Lots of people, including the police."

"And the killer?" she whispered.

Annie shot a look at Matt, who was listening attentively. "You and Vico were in the cathedral, weren't you, when Giuseppe died?"

Paolina nodded, her eyes wide. "It was our meeting place." She looked guiltily at Barbara Rae, who was standing back in the shadows. "I know this was wrong, but we had nowhere else to go."

"It's all right," Annie said gently. "Everybody needs a meeting place."

"I didn't see what happened. Vico did. But he still won't talk to me about it. He says it's men's business and that women must not interfere in such matters." She made a helpless gesture. "It's part of his machismo, I think. He is very brave. But he is just a boy, really. I do not think he can fight this murderer alone."

"What happened that night, Paolina?"

"We went to the cathedral as usual, and stayed until early morning because Vico knew that his uncle would be the first on the job. He was always the first on the job, and everybody knew it."

The regularity of Giuseppe's habits had contributed to his death. The killer had known exactly where and when to find him.

"Vico needed money. He wanted me to have an abortion and his uncle was the only person he could ask."

Annie knew it would have been too late then for an abortion, but she didn't interrupt. No doubt Vico thought he knew best, and the girl had been too frightened of him—or too much in love—to argue.

"Then what?"

"We heard someone coming. Vico thought it was his uncle, and he didn't want his uncle to see me. So he made me hide in that room down the steps from the altar. The basement room."

"The sacristy?"

"Yes. Where they will keep the sacred vessels and the priests' clothes. I didn't see what happened. Vico went back up to talk to Giuseppe. He came down once to whisper that it wasn't his uncle we had heard, then he went up again. The next time he came down, he was crazy."

"Crazy? What do you mean?"

The girl was trembling, obviously from the strain of remembering an unpleasant experience. "He was crying. I have never seen him cry. He was crying and he was angry. I thought he was going to hit me he was so angry. He told me that Giuseppe was dead."

"Do you mean he left you down in the sacristy, and you didn't see him again until after his uncle had been murdered?" Matt asked.

"That's right."

Annie glanced at him, knowing what he was thinking. If the girl had witnessed nothing, how were they to know that Vico himself hadn't been the killer after all?

"You came back to the cathedral the following night," Annie said. "Why?"

Paolina looked confused. Then, slowly, she said, "I was frightened, and besides, there was my baby to think about. I didn't have the same hatred of the police that Vico has. I thought I should talk to them, maybe tell them that I, not Vico, had been in the cathedral, so they would know *something*, at least, of what happened on the scaffolding.

"I knew the police would be at the cathedral. But I also knew Vico would be very angry if he found out. I realized I couldn't do it. There would be too many questions. They would make me tell them everything. Vico would be caught and arrested and I would never be able to forgive myself. So I ran away."

"But later you tried to talk to me."

"You were so nice to me. I was afraid of the police, but I needed to talk to somebody. But . . ." She shrugged helplessly. "You had so many questions. It seemed to me that if I answered them, it would all unravel. And the biggest question of all I could not answer anyhow. I did not see the murderer. I cannot identify him."

"Vico has never told you who the killer was?"

"No. When Vico decides to be silent, he is a rock."

"But he knows?" Matt asked. "He recognized the killer?"

"Yes. He knows."

"So if he recognized the killer, it was someone Vico knew from the time when he was part of the construction crew? Someone he'd met here, on the job?"

Paolina shrugged. "I'm not sure."

"Can we be sure of this: Was the killer definitely a man?" Annie asked.

"I—I don't know."

"How does Vico refer to the killer?" Matt cut in. "Does he say 'he'?"

Paolina was silent. There were circles under her eyes and she appeared very weary.

Barbara Rae stepped forward. "I think you're going to have to leave any further questions until another time. Paolina has had a very difficult day. She needs to rest."

Matt nodded, but repeated his question. "Think, Paolina. Does Vico refer to the killer as a male?"

"I think so," she said slowly. "I'm not certain, but I think he does."

Barbara Rae stepped between Matt and the bed. She touched his arm gently. "That's enough now. Please."

"There's one other thing you should know," Paolina said softly.

Barbara Rae frowned, but stepped back. "Quickly then, child. I want you to sleep."

"Vico told me that his uncle was worried about two things, and that he thought they might somehow be connected. One was something to do with the stained glass panels that he was installing. But the other didn't have anything to do with the construction site at all." She glanced uneasily at Matt. "Giuseppe told Vico that he was going to speak to the police because he had some new information about Francesca Carlyle's death. That's why Vico is so afraid. He says it's all connected, like a great giant conspiracy, like who killed JFK."

Matt's expression turned to stone. He stepped forward and leaned over the girl. "Dammit. Where is Vico?" he demanded.

The girl stared right at him and solemnly shook her head. "I can't help you."

"*Won't* help us, you mean."

Her gaze was clear and unyielding. "I will not betray him any more than I already have."

"She'll go back to him," Matt said as they left the room.

"I'm sure she will. But not tonight. Barbara Rae said she was going to give her a sedative."

"As soon as it wears off and she feels safe, she'll go." He looked at his watch. "It's early. Not even eight-thirty. Even with a pill, how long will she sleep—six, maybe eight hours? At two, three, four A.M. she could be awake and on the move."

"Well, I hope she sleeps longer than that!"

"We can't count on it, though. We're going to have to watch her. That's the only way we'll find that kid. I propose we stake out this place and follow her when she leaves. Ten to one she'll lead us straight to him."

Annie sighed. Matt seemed so positive about the right way to do things. She wished she felt as sure.

"It seems like such a violation of trust. . . ."

"I'm sorry about that. But it has to be done."

He had that ruthless, implacable look on his face again, and Annie knew that there was no resisting him when he was in this kind of mood. It was the same mood he assumed when conquering other companies . . . and on the first night when he had so explosively made love to her.

"A great giant conspiracy, like who killed JFK."

An exaggeration, of course. But Annie knew that Matt, even more so now than before, wasn't going to let it go.

"Before we leave, let me just say a few words to Barbara Rae alone, okay?"

Matt nodded. He looked very tired, and he still hadn't been home. If he insisted on staking out the youth center tonight, he would have to sleep first. God knew, they both could use some rest.

She went into Barbara Rae's office and closed the door. Quickly, without going into all the details, Annie filled her in on the latest developments—Sidney's accusations, Sam's wavering support for Darcy, and now Darcy's firm denial of the charges.

When she was done, Barbara Rae gazed at her for a moment in silence. "There's something else, isn't there?"

Annie took a deep breath. "I told Matt to wait outside because I don't want to say this in front of him." She quickly explained what Sam had told her about having seen Francesca and Giuseppe in each other's arms. "If it's true, it's one more strike against Matt. And I'm not sure about Sam—he says he's not going to the police with this, but he seems a little uncertain. Barbara Rae, Sam is Matt's oldest friend. He's been betrayed by so many of his other friends that maybe there's nothing more that can hurt him, but I think this will. I really do."

Barbara Rae rose from her desk and went to the window. She stared out into the darkness, saying nothing.

"I don't understand what's going on around here, Barbara

Rae, but suddenly I feel as if I'm wandering in a fog. A man is dead, and the chief suspect passionately denies that he had anything to do with it. For some reason, I'm feeling more likely to trust and believe him—a teenage drug dealer—than I am to trust and believe my own co-workers and friends. But one thing I do *not* believe. I don't believe that Matt had anything to do with Giuseppe's death."

Still Barbara Rae said nothing.

"I think Sam lied to me," Annie said. She surprised herself by the words. But they were out there now, and she knew that she didn't want to take them back. "I think he tried to mislead me. I can't explain it exactly. It's as if I'm following the threads of a hopelessly tangled web. All I know for sure is that Matt still trusts Sam, whereas I suddenly don't."

Barbara Rae turned at last from the window. Her face was drawn and her eyes looked very tired.

"Are you okay?" Annie asked.

"I guess so. There are some things I have to think about, that's all."

Chapter Thirty-four

After Matt and Annie left, Barbara Rae finished up a few tasks at the youth center. She checked on Paolina, who was sleeping, and she wondered if she would still be here in the morning. Her bleeding had stopped, and she had refused to take the sedative Barbara Rae had offered. The girl was anxious to get back to her lover; when she woke, she would go.

Barbara Rae whispered a prayer for her. There was nothing more she could do. Paolina was stubborn and she was in love.

Barbara Rae went upstairs to her small, makeshift bedroom. She was alone on the second floor of the building, but not completely, never completely. She could feel and sense the powerful presence of God. He alone could see the secrets she held in her heart.

She went down on her knees at the side of her bed and put her face against the cold iron frame, feeling the rough rungs bite into her cheek. There she prayed, unmindful of the discomfort to her knees, her shoulders, her face.

"Dear Lord," she whispered. "Help me to choose the right path."

When at last she rose, long minutes later, she knew what she had to do.

Once again the temptation had been irresistible. It was nine o'clock at night, and Darcy had gone out to the convenience store near her house to get bread for tomorrow's lunch. But she'd ended up cruising Sam's neighborhood, and now she saw a precious parking spot only two blocks from his home.

As she stepped out of the car she felt the familiar rush of adrenaline. But it was something besides passionate obsession that was driving her tonight. She was angry. And the anger felt good.

She was outraged that Sam had told Annie about their affair. She might not have minded if he hadn't been so insistent that *she* tell nobody. God, what a hypocrite!

But she was even more furious to think that he would stoop so low as to suspect her of some kind of fraud on the cathedral project. Fraud, hell. He suspected her of murder!

She was going to confront him. She was going to tell him exactly what she thought of him. Not only for the way he'd betrayed her confidence but for the way he'd played with her emotions and then cut her off, leaving her yearning, hungry, starved for more.

She marched down the sidewalk toward his house imagining what she would say to him and how he would respond. What would he say to her charges? Would he deny them? Would he embrace them? Would he embrace *her*? Was there still a chance?

Maybe once she confronted him they would yell at each other for a while, then fall into each other's arms. Maybe—

Stop thinking about it, dammit!

There was a stiff wind blowing up off the Bay, and as she walked, Darcy felt cold.

This is so stupid. Why am I doing this? Why can't I stop?

She was within sight of Sam's house when she suddenly stopped walking. She realized that tears were pouring down her face and that she was about to break down.

Only you can stop yourself, said a voice inside her. Only you. And you *can* do it. But you have to try.

You have to set your mind upon reason and sanity. You have to say to yourself, Okay, this is it, this is enough, it's over. You have to say, I have a problem and I need help. Then you have to *get* help, Darcy. Therapy if that's what you need. You're not the only one who has these feelings. You are not alone.

Darcy leaned against a tree and let herself sob. "God, I sound just like Barbara Rae," she muttered.

She had no sooner thought this than she saw Barbara Rae herself walk down the street from the other direction, then head up the walkway to Sam Brody's house.

Jesus! At first Darcy thought she was hallucinating. But everything else around her felt firm and real. It was Barbara Rae, the physical Barbara Rae, going into Sam's house at nine o'clock at night.

Why?

The pounding in her head was the sound of her blood singing through her veins. Something was up here, something that had nothing to do with her own obsession. And it gave Darcy the courage to do what she had never dared to do before. As Barbara Rae entered the house, Darcy darted up the steps behind her and onto the porch. Crouching down to the side of the front door, she reached out and caught it just before it clicked shut.

"Sam, there's something I've wanted to talk to you about for a long time."

Genial as always, Sam offered her a drink, coffee, a cup of tea. But Barbara Rae wanted nothing. She just wanted to get this over with as quickly as possible.

"If it's a problem with your funding, you know I'll do what I can," Sam said.

"I know. You're a very generous man, and I thank you from the bottom of my heart. But it's not about funding, not this time."

Sam took the chair opposite her in the living room. He looked comfortable and casual, wearing a blue short-sleeved shirt and a pair of brown Levi's.

"Sam, because of my work, people talk to me about many different things. Sometimes these people just want an empathetic ear, sometimes they want advice. I try to listen and be supportive. I try to give them whatever it is they need."

Sam nodded and smiled. "And from what I hear, you're exceptionally good at it, too."

"Sometimes I hear things that are of a sensitive nature. Although I am not a priest, there are those among my congregation who regard me as one. They come to me as they would to a Roman Catholic priest, to make their confession and to seek absolution of their sins."

"Which is said to be very good for the soul," Sam said.

He leaned forward slightly. "What are you getting at, Barbara Rae?"

"Like a priest or a psychiatrist or a medical doctor, I feel that many of these conversations are privileged. What I hear is subject to the silence of my own personal confessional. It is my sacred duty to keep confidential discussions private, even when revealing them might seem to serve some higher ethical purpose."

Sam appeared puzzled. He looked at her steadily but said nothing.

"The problem is that, unlike a Catholic priest, I am not sworn to the seal of the confessional, nor am I guided by church doctrine. In a way, this makes it more difficult for me to decide which way my moral responsibilities lie. I must also consider that whatever I am told may be only one side of a complex story. A person could, for example, reveal something to me that is not actually true. Perhaps they believe it to be true, perhaps they only fantasize it to be true. Perhaps it *is* true. But I cannot swear the truth of what I'm told. The best I can do is make my own judgments, based on what I know about the character of the people who talk to me."

"I'm with you so far," Sam said. "But I'm not sure what point you're trying to make."

"My point is that someone once confessed to me something concerning you, Sam. I don't know if it was true—in fact, I found it hard to believe at the time. Still, it was important, and it later became even more so. I've tormented myself for many months, wondering if it would have been better, in this instance, to break my rule of silence, and wondering if I should break it now."

Sam stood, he turned his back to her, and walked to the

window. When he turned around again a few seconds later, his expression was perfectly calm. "You'd better be more specific, Barbara Rae, because I don't have the faintest idea what you're talking about."

Spit it out, she ordered herself.

"Before her death, Francesca Carlyle told me that she was involved in an extramarital relationship that was causing her both anguish and guilt. And she identified her lover as you, Sam."

His eyes narrowed. "Me?" he said incredulously.

Barbara Rae noted his direct gaze, his steady hands, and his flush of surprise. Either he was conveying his true emotions or he was a very convincing actor.

"That's what she told me. She felt particularly guilty because you were her husband's oldest friend."

"I should think so." He sounded slightly defensive now, but Barbara Rae had to acknowledge that that would be the case even if the charge was a lie. "Matt and I have known each other since college. I knew Francesca even longer. For me to sleep with her would have been a betrayal of friendship of the vilest kind."

Barbara Rae nodded. "But we do have reason to believe that she was having an affair with somebody. And it's curious that the police were never able to identify her lover. One can understand why he chose not to come forward. Perhaps if he had, he would have been put on the list of suspects. But it is surprising that despite an extensive investigation, not only by the police but by Matthew's private detectives, no trace of her lover was ever found."

"Is it so surprising? I thought the prosecution argued pretty definitively in court that the reason no evidence of her adultery was found was that there was no adultery. She drank too much, as you know. And she had an active fantasy life."

Now that last point was something that a lover might know, Barbara Rae thought. But so might a longtime friend.

And it was true, of course. Barbara Rae knew from experience that Francesca had been a dramatic woman with a strong tendency to exaggerate.

Perhaps she had only fantasized about having an affair with Sam Brody. After all, she was not the only woman to be taken with this handsome, pleasant man.

"Annie told me that you believed Francesca's lover was Giuseppe Brindesi."

Some hint of emotion darted across his face. Surprise? Had he expected Annie to keep this information absolutely private?

"I'm not going to comment on that," he said.

"She said you claimed to have actually seen them together."

"Even if that were true, I would never admit to it in court," he said. "Particularly now that Giuseppe is dead and Matt's fingerprints were found on the scaffolding. He's my oldest friend."

"But it's not true," Barbara Rae said. "Giuseppe was gay."

Now there was definitely emotion on his face. Shock. Denial. Quickly, he turned back to the window.

"He too confided in me. He was exclusively homosexual all his life. He would never have children, of course. That's why Vico's future was so important to him—the boy was the son Giuseppe could never have."

"Well, intriguing though that tidbit is, it doesn't change the fact that Francesca was pretty tight with Giuseppe. Perhaps all they were was very close friends."

"Sam, I'm not a lawyer. I don't want to fence with you. But two people have died violent deaths, and the police seem to think that there's some connection between Francesca's death and Giuseppe's. I would never forgive myself if I believed that an innocent man had died because I didn't tell the police what I had heard about the possible identity of Francesca's mystery lover."

He turned back. "If you're suggesting—"

Barbara Rae cut him off as effectively as she cut off the teenager troublemakers she dealt with at the youth center. "Sam, please let me finish. I know I don't have any right to ask this question, and you certainly don't have any obligation to answer it. But I'm going to put it to you anyway: Weren't *you* and Francesca lovers?"

"Yes."

Barbara Rae felt her eyes open wider. She realized with a certain kind of shock that she had expected him to deny it even if it was true. Which meant, of course, that she *did* believe Sam Brody was capable of lying.

"Francesca and I were lovers for about six months, twenty-one years ago," he said. "In fact, that's how Matt met her. She was my girlfriend until he charmed her right out of my arms. It was a big deal for me at the time. I loved Francesca, or I thought I did at the tender age of twenty."

He paused to clear his throat. "It was a tough time for me, and it very nearly wrecked the friendship between Matt and me. But I got over it. I got over her. And since then, since she left me for Matt and married him and lived her life with him, never once were she and I sexually intimate again." He looked her straight in the eye. "I told Annie that I believed Francesca and Giuseppe were lovers because I saw them together, kissing. Now you tell me he was gay, and I'm left trying to figure out what kind of kissing I witnessed. It looked pretty passionate to me, but hell, who knows? Francesca was always playacting, particularly with men. When all the speculation began about her affair, I naturally assumed I knew who her lover was. But I never went to the cops about it because it would have been one more nail in Matt's coffin."

Barbara Rae nodded. So far, everything he'd said had been reasonable. "I have one more question. Sam, where were you at the time of Giuseppe's death?"

"You sound like a police detective, Barbara Rae. Isn't there a saying in the Bible, 'Render unto Caesar the things which be Caesar's, and unto God the things which be God's'?"

"Luke, chapter twenty, verse twenty-five."

"Yet you still ask me that question?"

"I ask it, yes. You don't have to answer."

"As a matter of fact, I was with a woman that night. We went out to dinner, then she came home with me and didn't leave here until morning. She was here when the call came in from the police. She will testify to that."

"Thank you, Sam." After a moment she added, "Forgive my suspicions, please."

He sighed. "It's a time of suspiciousness all around. Seems like it has been ever since Francesca died. The repercussions of that just keep going on and on and on."

"Yes. And they will, I imagine, until justice is done."

From where she was crouching beside the front door, Darcy heard the whole thing.

Was it true? Francesca and Sam?

He denied their recent involvement. But he was lying. He sounded totally sincere, but he was lying.

He sounded exactly the way he had when he'd whispered passionately to her in the bedroom. And that had been a lie.

She felt a little dizzy. *I've got to talk to Annie*, she thought.

Quickly, she backed across the porch and leaped over the railing to the ground. She landed in the shrubbery just as Barbara Rae came out. Pressing herself against the side of the house, Darcy listened to the pounding of her own heart.

There was something else, she realized. Sam had lied about his alibi for the night of Giuseppe's murder. True, he'd had a date, and the blond woman had gone home with him afterward. But the woman's car—a red Mercedes, Darcy recalled clearly—had left sometime before 4:11 A.M.

Sam's alibi was a fraud.

Sam Brody stood perfectly still in his living room. He felt exhausted and wrung out. Had he just blown it? He'd always been good at reading people, and he thought he'd seen a flash of distrust in Barbara Rae's eyes, although he'd done his best to counter her suspicions.

Had she believed him? Was it possible that Barbara Rae could *disbelieve* him? He had donated thousands over the years to the United Path Church and its many charities. That ought to make her stop and think.

Maybe he shouldn't have allowed her to leave. What if she went to the police with her story?

Shit. Things were falling apart.

Calm down, he ordered himself.

Sam could see his reflection in the living-room window.

Staring at his face, he reached deep inside him and pulled out a smile. It was a good smile. Genial. Warm. Sincere. It was a smile that had been perfected over the years. It even reached into his eyes, which he could make soft, understanding, empathetic. His eyes were surrounded by tiny laugh lines that seemed to indicate a perpetual lighthearted, easygoing state of mind.

Sam Brody, great boss to work for. Sam Brody, thoughtful and sensitive friend. Sam Brody, excellent architect. Sam Brody, good and decent man.

He reminded himself that he *was* all those things. And that, as far as he knew, nobody even suspected that he had a darker side. He'd been very careful, over the years, to hide it.

Because he'd feared the consequences of allowing anybody to get too close to him, he had deprived himself of what so many people referred to as the joys of human intimacy. No wife, no children, no close friends privy to the secrets of his heart.

The secret, singular, he corrected himself. There was only one real secret, one real sin to cover up.

Sam had realized long ago that in a highly dishonest world, an honest man could make an excellent impression on people. He had been scrupulous in all his dealings, sometimes so much so that he had lost business. But in the process he had established his reputation as an unswervingly honest man.

By now his reputation was so well established that it simply couldn't be contradicted. Everybody agreed that Sam Brody was one of the guys in the white hats, and 99 percent of the time they were right.

His mistakes had been few and far between. Of course,

there had been mistakes. Nobody was perfect. He had some of the needs for intimacy that all humans had. He had been tempted. Darcy had been the most recent temptation—what a wonderful lover she was! But so far, thank God, he'd always come to his senses in time.

Now, though, he had a problem.

Barbara Rae.

So Francesca had talked to her, had she? Goddamn Francesca. Goddamn Matt.

The knot in his belly tightened the way it always did when he thought about Matthew Carlyle. Sam wasn't sure exactly when it was that he had begun to hate his old friend. Sometimes he thought it must have started the day they'd met.

But more likely it had come later, when he had realized the unique destiny for which the fates intended him: His lot in life was to sit smilingly by while Matthew Carlyle stole from him everything that was rightfully his.

Sam was smart, but Matthew was smarter.

Sam's business was successful, but Matthew's was one of the most famous American companies of the second half of the twentieth century—truly a phenomenon.

Sam was wealthy, but Matthew was a billionaire.

Sam had loved only one woman in his life, and Matthew had married her.

It had been on that day—the wedding of Matthew Carlyle to Francesca, a ceremony at which Sam had stood beside Matt in the role of best man—that Sam had made to himself his own most solemn promise:

Someday, somehow, he would even the score.

Because with all his heart and soul, he hated Matt Carlyle. And for more than twenty years he'd nurtured his hatred and felt it grow, black and poisonous, inside him. With each additional success that Matt had achieved, Sam had known new envy, new rage. But he hadn't shown it. He'd kept on smiling. He'd sworn to hide his feelings even if they choked him, which they sometimes did. When he was anywhere near his nemesis, he literally had trouble getting air into his lungs.

But it was almost over now. He was close—so close—to accomplishing his goal. He wasn't going to allow anybody to stop him—not Barbara Rae Acker, and not Annie Jefferson, either.

Annie could prove to be even more of a problem than Barbara Rae. She too was suspicious of him. And she was smart, and in love with his enemy.

When he'd put Annie on the cathedral job as project manager, he'd thought that the choice was one of his more brilliant moves. She was essentially an interior designer. Her projects had been limited to corporations—the contemporary office building, mostly. Some retail-space designing. And for the most part she'd worked out of an office in a design firm. She'd spent little time on site, little time around contractors and their subs. She knew nothing, in practice, about managing a large construction site.

In other words, Annie Jefferson would be easy to control.

But, increasingly, it hadn't worked out that way. Annie had proved to be far more competent a manager than he'd ever imagined. She'd done a terrific job, and he'd been absolutely sincere on the occasions when he'd told her so. She'd really come into her own, and he was proud of her.

The tough part of all this was when you truly *liked* the people you had to destroy.

Chapter Thirty-five

When Annie heard the loud knocking on her front door, she was half afraid it might be the police.

"Don't answer it," Matt whispered, pulling her closer. They were trying to get a few hours' sleep before they had to check on Paolina. But so far neither of them had done much in the way of sleeping.

The knocking ceased, but about a minute later the phone rang. Annie let her machine pick up, and they heard Darcy's voice: "I know you're there, Annie. Please open up! It's me at your door. Sorry if I'm interrupting anything, but I've got to talk to you—it's urgent!"

Annie threw on a bathrobe and rushed to the door.

Darcy came in, breathless. She flung herself into the nearest chair, not even appearing surprised to see Matt Carlyle, in a pair of jeans but no shirt, standing at the threshold of the bedroom.

"Darcy, what's happened? What's the matter?"

Darcy's lip started to tremble. "Annie, you're so sensible. So responsible. You're not going to get all carried away with emotion the way I do. I need you to tell me I'm crazy. God! I feel as if my head is about to blow apart!"

"Darcy, for heaven's sake—"

"It's Sam."

"What about Sam?" Matt cut in. "Is he hurt? Dead?"

She laughed wildly. "Dead? Dear God, no! He's not dead, Annie. He's the killer!"

Matt stared at her.

"All this time he's been fooling us. He's got everybody convinced he's such a wonderful guy." She glanced at Matt. "I know he's your best friend and all. Shit, I don't expect anybody to believe me. I can hardly believe it myself. Sam Brody a killer? Impossible." She shook her head. "But it's the only thing that fits."

Annie swallowed hard. She thought of Sam and Matt. Old friends. One from a wealthy background, with all the advantages. The other from a broken home, with none of them.

One friendly and affable, with golden hair and a smile like an angel. The other shy and introspective, forced to adopt an outgoing style for business in order to survive.

One of them was everything that he seemed. And the other?

Yes, it fit. It was in line with everything she'd been telling herself for the past twenty-four hours. The other was a killer.

She sat beside Darcy and took one of her trembling hands. "I believe you," she said. She looked at Matt, who had gone all tight and self-contained, his face a mask. She was reminded of that day in the courtroom when the jury had come in to announce their verdict. He had steeled himself then to control all his considerable fund of emotion. He was steeling himself now.

Annie held out her other hand to him. He didn't take it. She shook her head and whispered, "You know the thing Sherlock Holmes used to say—after you've eliminated everything that's impossible, whatever is left, no matter how improbable, must be the truth?"

Matt nodded.

"Sam's being involved may seem improbable, but it's been haunting me. He told me while you were away in Washington that Giuseppe was definitely Francesca's lover. That he'd seen them together. That he'd suppressed it during your trial to protect you."

"He's lying," Darcy interjected.

"I think so too," said Annie. "I don't know exactly *why* I didn't believe him. It just hit me the wrong way. I felt as if I was being smoke-screened. But all of a sudden I started asking myself how much I really know about Sam Brody. And it occurred to me that I really don't know him at all."

"You've got good instincts, Annie," Darcy said with a shudder. "A helluva lot better than mine. According to Barbara Rae, Giuseppe was gay."

Darcy quickly related what she had overheard of Barbara Rae's conversation with Sam. "He didn't have a woman with him for the entire night, Annie. I know because I was stalking him at the time. I fell asleep in my car, as a matter of fact. When I woke up, it was well before dawn and the bimbo's car was gone. She's covering for him, whoever she is. In fact, now that I think back, I think maybe Sam's car was gone too at that point. I wasn't thinking straight—I had a breakfast meeting that day with a potential client down in San Jose, and I was upset because I knew I wouldn't have time to get any real sleep before driving down there. But now it seems to me that Sam could have gotten rid of his date, gone to the cathedral, and killed Giuseppe, but because I was sleeping I never even saw him leave!"

"But why?" Matt cut in. "What could Sam Brody possibly have to gain from Giuseppe's death?"

"If it's structural fraud of some kind, he had plenty to gain," Darcy said. "If he's charging the owners for work that was never done and materials that were never used, he could be skimming tens of thousands of dollars from the project. Hell, hundreds of thousands."

"Sam, stealing money from a *church*?" Matt's voice was scathing.

"Sam, stealing money from *you*," Annie said softly. "A lot of the funds to build the cathedral came directly from the contributions you and Francesca so generously made. And the rest were raised through her energy and efforts."

"You're not suggesting that Sam Brody, my closest friend for over twenty years, is out to get me?"

Annie considered carefully before she answered. *Was* she suggesting that?

Yes, dammit!

Matted added, "I just can't believe that Sam could be involved in some kind of complex conspiracy involving sabotage and threats and—"

"And murder?" Annie finished. "Why not? Everybody believed it of you."

* * *

Ten minutes later, Matt was still resistant. Annie could see that pressing him wasn't going to do any good, so she tried to change the focus of the conversation.

"Let's look at the situation from another angle," she said. "Suppose someone wanted to skim some money off a lucrative construction project. What would be the best way to go about it?"

"Cheat on the materials," Darcy said. "Use cheaper stuff than was called for in the specifications."

"Wouldn't somebody notice?" Matt asked. "There are a lot of people working on a building like the cathedral. If you deliberately didn't follow the plans and the specifications, a lot of people would know."

"You could alter the plans," Darcy said. "Change them on the CAD file—the computer aided design program that's in your computer. No one would know, then. They would assume the plans they were working from were the right ones."

"You could produce a second, inaccurate set of plans," Annie said, warming to the notion.

"Right. You make up an original set of architectural drawings, get it approved, submit it to the city for the building permit, have everything ready to go, and then redraw the plans," Darcy said. "That building was way overdesigned. I know, dammit—I designed it! The size, spacing, and detail of the seismic connections in the structural framing was significantly above the city's code. But I haven't looked at what they're actually *building*. If the blueprints that the contractor received and built from are not the same as the ones that were submitted to the owner and the city, I'm not sure anybody would notice."

"Well, wouldn't somebody check?" Matt demanded.

"I'm talking about changing tiny technical details," Darcy said. "But such details in the basic structure of the building are potentially very significant. As for the actual builders, well, you've got a set of plans, you assume they're the original ones, and you go from there."

"If the architect and the contractor were in collusion," Annie said slowly, "it could work. The architect redraws the plans to make the building less expensive. The head contractor knows he's not working from the original drawings, but he and the architect are in it together. They get the full sum they've agreed on with the owner, but they spend considerably less. Then they split the money they've skimmed."

"In a twenty-million-dollar project like this one, that could mean they each get a couple of million dollars," Darcy said.

Matt raised his eyebrows. "That could certainly be a motive for murder."

"If something like this has happened, we'll need proof," Annie said.

"Well, if the drawings submitted to the building inspector are different from the ones McEnerney is working from, we'll have proof," said Darcy.

"I tried to examine the original blueprints," Annie said. "But Sam interrupted me. I do have my copy, though." She went to her desk and took out the plans. Matt and Darcy spread the pages out on the coffee table and looked at them.

"This is a copy of the version that went to the city when we applied for the building permit?"

"Yes," Annie said.

"And it's also the version the builders are working from? Are you certain of that?"

"Well, I'm not *certain*. I've just always assumed . . ." She wasn't an architect. She'd assumed she was looking at accurate drawings.

Was that what Sam had been counting on all along?

"We'll have to check this against the drawings McEnerney is using," she said. "But if he's in on it—"

"The original drawings were generated by a CAD program, right?" Matt asked.

Annie nodded.

"On whose computer?"

"On the LAN network in the office."

"And where is that program now?"

"I'm not sure. Probably still in our computer files."

"Let me get this straight," said Matt. "You think that the original computer-generated plan for the cathedral was subsequently altered by Sam. If you're right, after he modified the original file, he replaced it with a new one. He then sent the amended file to someone at the contractor's office who was in on the scheme. Possibly McEnerney himself?"

"Yes," said Darcy. "But they'll deny it, of course."

"Still, if he did it—if he altered the CAD file—can we expect to find the new file somewhere on the LAN network, too? Are there likely to be two different files?"

"If we find two different files, we've got proof of fraud," Annie said. "Let's go to his office now and see."

"Break in to Sam's computer, you mean?" said Darcy. "Well, I'd love to, but he's a security freak. His office will be locked, and his computer is password protected."

"I can get us into his office," Annie said slowly. "Locked or not."

Darcy raised her eyebrows.

"We may be best friends," Annie said with a smile, "but there are a few things about me that you don't know."

"As for me," said Matt, "I'm not nearly as good as some of the teenage hackers around, but I can still break in to the average non-government-secured PC. Hell, you folks are probably using a CAD program Powerdyme designed."

Darcy grinned. "I knew you'd turn out to be good for something after all, Mr. Billionaire Software King."

Matt shook his head, looking a bit bemused. But at least he was animated now, and he appeared to be open to the idea that his best friend might be involved in this, after all.

As if he read her thought, Matt looked up and caught her eyes. "You really believe that Sam is capable of something like this?"

"I don't want to believe it. But it's the only thing that really fits." She slipped around behind his chair and began massaging his shoulders. His muscles were very tight. "You know him better than I do, Matt. As you say, he's your oldest friend."

"Maybe I don't know him as well as I thought," he admitted reluctantly. "Sam and I don't interact on a regular basis. Hell, for years we've hardly seen each other at all. I knew the old Sam. I don't know for certain what he's become."

"That company you started together, Matt—why did it fail?"

He turned his head and stared up at her. He ran one hand through his hair, then stared at her again. "I don't know."

"What do you mean, you don't know?"

"I mean just that. I don't know why our company failed. It was doing well. Sam was the business-minded one in those days. I was the technical genius. I left a lot of the operations details to him. Hell, *all* of the operational details. And when we went belly-up, I figured it was just one of those things. Eighty percent of all new businesses fail—no surprise." He paused, then added slowly, "But now that I think about it, that company was doing extremely well. Why *did* it fail?" He looked off into the distance. "Shit, Annie. I'm starting to get a bad feeling about this."

She rubbed his shoulders harder. Darcy got up and made herself scarce. Annie heard her heading quietly to the bathroom.

Matt was still staring into space, obviously deep in thought. She knew him well enough now to realize that if he wasn't talking it was because he was thinking something through, and that he needed to do it in silence.

He looked back sooner than she expected. His expression was grim. "Listen, Annie. You know how sometimes you know something on a deep level, but you don't know it yet in your conscious mind?"

She nodded.

"Then suddenly it's like the proverbial light bulb going on. Illumination comes and you can see a landscape with perfect clarity that only moments before was hidden in the shadows."

"Yes, I know what you mean."

"Sam Brody is a good-hearted, affable guy. But that's not all he is. As a college kid he occasionally showed another side. He could be very judgmental of other people. He could be cruel. He often lied to women to get them to go to bed with him . . . and laughed about it afterward. There was always another side. I knew that, dammit, but I conveniently allowed it to slip my mind. Why haven't I ever asked myself this question: *Whatever happened to Sam's less attractive side?*"

Annie didn't say anything. She could tell he hadn't finished speaking.

"There's something else you probably don't know. Francesca was his lover before she was mine. She left him for me, as a matter of fact. I haven't thought about that in years— hell, we were kids—but I felt pretty guilty at the time. If he was upset about it, he didn't show it, though. No big deal, he said. And certainly to Francesca it was no big deal. But then she never was the faithful type."

"Do you think he cared more than he let on?" Annie asked.

"It's possible. He hides his feelings. But he is very proud, and back in those days he was the dominant member of our partnership. Although we were the same age, he saw himself as some sort of mentor to me. Henry Higgins, in some respects. If it weren't for him, he believed, I'd still be tinkering in some garage."

"That's ridiculous!"

He smiled. "You don't agree, huh?"

"Of course not."

"Well, I don't underestimate what Sam did for me when we were young. He taught me a lot. But in all honesty, I think I would eventually have learned most of what I needed to know without him. I've always been a pretty determined person, and I've always known what I wanted.

"But now that I think about it, our company crashed a couple of months after I took up with Francesca. Sam couldn't get anybody to invest in us, he claimed."

"Maybe he wanted to sever all ties with you, Matt. Maybe he lied about the investors. Maybe he sabotaged the company as a way to pay you back."

"If he did, he must have regretted it later. If he'd stayed my partner, he'd be a billionaire now."

He looked up and their eyes met.

If he'd stayed my partner, he'd be a billionaire now.

"That's it," she said softly. "That's it, right there. He made one huge mistake in his life and he's regretted it ever since. That's why he hates you, Matt."

He put his face into his cupped hands.

Chapter Thirty-six

"I can't believe what I'm seeing," Matt said to Annie, who was on her knees on the carpet outside Sam's office, skillfully picking the lock.

"It seems to be a night for surprises," Annie said.

"Ain't that the truth. Where did you get those tools?"

"Bought 'em off Top Floor Jocko for really cheap."

"Jesus." Matt sighed. Darcy giggled. They were all getting punchy from stress.

One last, deft turn and she had it. The latch slid back. Matt went straight to Sam's desktop computer and switched it on. "If it's here, I'll find it," he vowed.

"What are you doing?" Annie asked a few minutes later as Matt's fingers flew over the keys. On the screen were a mass of symbols, none of which she understood.

"I'm talking directly to the machine." He pulled a floppy disk out of the drive and substituted another. "Sam's using an encryption device to block entrance to his computer. It's one of the commercial products, actually—a piece of software made by a competitor of ours." He tossed her a grin. "It's not *totally* Mickey Mouse, but it won't keep me out for long."

"So you're breaking the code?"

"With the aid of some of my own software, yeah. I had some disks in my briefcase. That's what I was in Washington for. It's kind of hush-hush, but suffice it to say I was meeting with a certain government agency, giving them a little advice about computer security." He paused, concentrating on the screen. "What? Oh, okay, okay, go ahead, do that." He was talking to the computer now, shaking his head. His fingers danced on the keys. The screen changed and he smiled. Colors came up and then all sorts of little icons. "Here we go. We're into the system. Now to find the file."

"Cool," Darcy said. "Breaking and entering and electronic invasion—you two are really on a roll. My friends, the white-collar criminals. I'm impressed."

Within seconds Matt had the cathedral CAD file on the screen. They studied it carefully. "That's the original one," Darcy said. "The officially approved version."

"But not the one they're building from?"

"Well, it's the one they claim to be building from. But no, this is a legitimate file. What we need to find is an amended version."

"There are a lot of files on the hard drive," said Matt. "This could take a while."

"There aren't that many CAD files," said Darcy.

"Okay, we'll try sorting the files by type. Meanwhile, some-one ought to be checking floppies and tape backups, not to mention having a look at the other computers in the office."

"How do we know he saved it?" Annie asked. "Wouldn't

it have been more sensible to erase it and not risk leaving any evidence?"

"Even if he deleted it, I might be able to get it back," said Matt. "The hard drive looks pretty fragmented, which means he hasn't performed any maintenance on it for a long time. There's all sorts of junk on here, but much of it's old. I don't see many new files, either. Doesn't look as if he really uses this computer all that much."

"Is that good?"

"If he deleted the file we're looking for and nothing's been written over it, I can probably get it back. So, yes, that's potentially very good. But it's still going to take a while to go through all this stuff."

"I'll make us some coffee," Darcy said.

That night, Fletcher went again to the construction site. He'd waited long enough. The time had come to figure out exactly how to lure Annie to the cathedral in the middle of the night. He couldn't wait any longer.

He decided not to park in his usual spot in the lot with the trailers. The murder of Giuseppe Brindesi was an open file, and there were bound to be cops cruising by on patrol. He didn't want to alert them to his presence. Not tonight.

Cops or no cops, he could get quietly into the place from the underground passage that connected the cathedral basement to the youth center next door.

The passage had been there before the construction had begun. It had linked the old church on the site with what had been the main residence of the convent. The tunnel, dug through firm bedrock and reinforced several times over the years because of earthquake concerns, had remained after the demolition of the old church.

Fletcher wasn't sure whether Annie knew about the passage. Most of the workmen didn't. The ones who were used to climbing high on the structure and doing their intricate work dozens of feet off the ground, buffeted by wind and seeming incredibly brave, were the same guys who wouldn't be caught dead underground. Foundation men were a helluva lot different from roofers. And the foundation guys had finished up and left the site many long months ago.

There was no sign of cops on the far side of the dark hulk of the cathedral. It should be an easy matter to break in to the youth center building. He was quiet, though, because he knew that the Reverend Acker often spent the night. She had a room up on the second floor.

He raised a window on the dark side of the first floor and entered. *Smart,* he thought. *Lock the doors and leave the windows unlatched.*

With the aid of a narrow-beam flashlight, he found the stairs to the basement. When he reached the bottom, he stopped short, sniffing the air. His nose was very sensitive. He got a whiff of what he was certain was Annie's perfume. He shook his head in confusion. Wasn't it the same scent he thought he'd faintly detected in his trailer last night?

Had she been down here tonight? Had she been in his trailer last night?

The thought transfixed him. The door to the trailer had been unlocked. Anybody could have wandered in.

Fletcher followed the elusive smell to a small, dark room at the rear of the basement. There was a bed in the room and a dresser and a small table lamp. The bed was neatly made.

The scent was definitely there, combined with the scents of several other people. Someone had been in this room. Recently.

He stared at the bed and thought, *I could bring Annie here. Annie. I'll capture her in the cathedral, then bring her back through the tunnel to this room, this bed. It'll be more comfortable for both of us.*

He briefly imagined what he would do to her on that bed. He felt himself harden and his mouth go dry.

He turned and left the room, flexing his muscles as he walked. He opened the cracked wooden door to the cold passageway and shone the flashlight ahead of him. He thought he saw a quick movement at the far end and beamed his light on the spot. Nothing. Probably just rats.

The tunnel was old and crumbling. Probably not very safe. On the other hand, it had lasted through several earthquakes. There was a smell in here too, and not a pleasant one—it was dank and musty. He was glad when he reached the other end.

He entered the cathedral through its northeast foundation. He wasn't being particularly quiet, but over the noise he made as he climbed over the construction rubble, he heard a choked-off sound. A voice. A female voice.

Annie? The perfume? Was she here already, waiting for him? Had she come to his trailer because she wanted him?

He followed the sound into the semicircular apse that would soon be transformed to the Lady Chapel. There was a pile of bricks by the opening to the area and, in the dark, he stumbled on them.

"Who's there?" a woman's voice asked sharply, sounding both weepy and frightened.

Annie? His blood beat in sudden excitement.

He jerked his flashlight up. As he peered into the chapel, the dim beam revealed a woman—a girl, really. Her hair was fair and so long that it nearly brushed her hips. She was clad in something dark and flowing, a cloak perhaps, and her face as she turned toward the light was lovely. He felt the hair rise on the back of his neck. She was in the Lady Chapel, and she looked almost like the Lady Herself. . . .

Then she moved and a soft sob issued from her throat. Silvery tears glistened as they rolled down the girl's perfect cheeks.

"Mi amore?" she whispered. "Is that you?"

Mi amore? "Hey, who are you?" Fletcher said.

At the unfamiliar voice, the look in the girl's eyes changed to one of panic. She gave him a firm shove—which momentarily surprised him. Then she whipped by him, leaping over the bricks at the entrance to The Lady Chapel and fled.

He rushed out after her, but the girl was fast. He saw a swirl of her blue cloak whip around the corner. Shit! She was getting away!

And yet he felt almost reluctant to follow her. As if she might not be real, but a spirit. Jeez. Working in this place was making him superstitious.

She had to be that girl Annie had been talking about. The one who had been in the cathedral the night after the murder. The one Annie had neglected to tell the cops about.

Paolina.

He could hear her scurrying ahead of him. There was all sorts of construction debris on the floor, and the cathedral was dark. He heard a crash and the girl cried out. Yes! She had stumbled over something and fallen.

She was scrambling to her feet when he grabbed her. She clawed at him, her eyes wild. He twisted her arm up behind her until she gasped and went limp.

"You Paolina?" he asked roughly.

She nodded, blinking up at him, terrified.

Fletcher felt the power rush through him. That was the way Annie would look up at him.

But—something weird was going on here. What the hell was a young girl, a teenager, doing in the construction site late at night? And not just once but twice?

"*Mi amore,*" she'd said. Were she and her lover using the unfinished cathedral as a trysting place? But her lover was on the run from the cops. It was her lover they suspected of murdering Giuseppe Brindesi. What kind of fool would come back to the place where he'd committed a murder in order to meet his lover?

Unless he'd never left . . .

Shit!

The cops were searching all over the fucking city for the kid. But Vico was here, hiding in the foundation, somewhere in the basements or the crawl space.

The kid had worked construction here, so he knew the place. He must have explored around until he'd found a nice little hidey-hole for himself. And the girlfriend probably sneaked in every night—just the same way Fletcher had—bringing him food and water and her pert little ass and breasts.

He'd found the kid Annie was looking for. Or at least he was about to find him. The girl would lead him to Vico, and pretty damn fast, if she knew what was good for her.

It was the way, Fletcher suddenly realized. The way to get Annie to come down to the cathedral at night. She believed that Vico was innocent. She wanted to help him. If he convinced her that Vico was here, she would come. Tonight.

He'd have her right where he wanted her.

At last.

In the meantime, he had the girl, who was moaning softly and trembling with terror. Fletcher's heart was pounding. His cock was hard. He was going to enjoy questioning her.

Chapter Thirty-seven

"I think I've got something."

Matt had been at it for over two hours, while Annie and Darcy took turns guarding the door. They were working in darkness to avoid attracting attention from the security guards. The only light came from the flickering computer screen. "It's a deleted file. I'm going to try to view it. It'll look a little different from what you're used to. Those are CAD formatting commands. Okay, ladies, what do you think?"

Annie and Darcy leaned over and squinted at the screen. "That's it," Annie said as the graphics came up. "It's the cathedral CAD file."

"But which version?" Matt asked.

"Jesus," Darcy said. She sat down and stared at the structural specifications. "That son of a bitch."

Matt looked at her. "Okay, tell us. We're out of the area of my expertise."

"He's arranged for the construction of a cheaper and much

lower-designed building than the one we all agreed on. The changes are in the structural framing. He's specified far fewer connections and spaced them much farther apart. He's changed the spacing of the columns and beams, the number of bolts, the quality of the seismic connections, everything." She looked at Matt and Annie. "Paul McEnerney must be in on this. No way the contractor could build this without realizing what was going on. Sam and he must be in it together. They're probably splitting the money they're skimming ... and if this is the design and specifications they're using, they're skimming a lot."

"Let's get a copy of this," Matt said, sticking a fresh disk into the floppy drive.

"Let's print it out, too," said Annie. She turned on the plotter, and soon the blueprints came rolling out.

"What we have here," Darcy explained, "is a cathedral that on the outside looks to be everything it was originally designed to be. But what we're seeing is that the inner structure has been greatly weakened. Possibly to the extent that the building isn't even safe. I'd hate to think what would happen in a major earthquake. The cathedral was originally designed to withstand a magnitude of 8.5 on the Richter scale. But this building—the one we actually have on our construction site— would probably sustain major damage with anything over 6.0."

Annie was stunned. Not only had it happened, it had happened on her watch. She suddenly understood why Sam Brody had appointed her project manager. It wasn't that he thought she was competent, it was that he thought she was *incompetent*. She wasn't an architect. She had no direct on-site construction experience. He had expected her not to notice, and she hadn't.

"Outward beauty and a rotten inner core," mused Darcy. "Tell me, folks, does that sound like anybody we know?"

"But is it proof?" Matt asked.

"We've got copies of both files," said Annie. "Of course, we still have to prove that the amended one is the one McEnerney's been using. I wonder if there's any correspondence between them about it."

They all jumped when Annie's cellular phone rang. She'd brought it in from the car.

She took the phone into a corner where her conversation wouldn't disturb Matt. "It's Fletcher," she said a few moments later. "He says he's knows where Vico is."

Matt looked up from the computer screen. "If that's true, it's damn important."

Annie got the details quickly, then hung up and explained them to Matt: "He thinks he's been in the cathedral all along. Hiding out there, probably in the basement or somewhere in the crawl space under the nave. It makes sense, Matt. Fletcher says he found Paolina in there again a little while ago."

"Jesus." Matt pulled up a new page on the screen to get a look at the basement area of the cathedral. "It's possible. Why didn't we think of that?"

"It would also account for his having witnessed the murder. The cathedral wasn't just a meeting place for the teenagers— it was Vico's refuge."

"So has Fletcher actually got the kid?"

"No, but he's got Paolina. She refuses to talk to him, he says."

Matt raised his eyebrows. "Figures."

"I'm going over there," Annie said.

"I'm coming with you."

"We can't go yet," Darcy broke in. "What if there's something more here? As Annie said, what we need now is some kind of correspondence that proves that Sam was in on this with the contractor."

"You keep working on it, Darcy. This kid is an eyewitness, and I want to talk to him before the cops throw his ass in jail."

"Matt, maybe you shouldn't come," Annie said. "The police might be looking to throw your ass in jail, too."

"Hell, if they get too close, I'll just hunker down with Vico in the crawl space. That kid is smarter than I thought."

Chapter Thirty-eight

Fletcher waited in the small room behind the high altar, which was being finished as the sacristy. In it would be kept the sacred objects for the communion service—the chalice and the plate, the candlesticks for the altar, the minister's vestments. At the moment, the dark room was filled with construction gear and debris.

He was wired. She was coming. He was finally going to get his chance with her. And this time he wasn't going to blow it.

He hadn't found Vico yet, but he had taken some precautions in that regard.

The kid was hiding somewhere in the foundation, and he'd been thinking about that. He'd been considering the ways into the crawl spaces and the possible ways out.

Except that everybody knew that once you went down into the earth, into the underworld, you didn't come out again.

The kid liked it in there, did he? Fine, because that's where he was going to stay.

Meanwhile, everything else was prepared. He had found several tall, thick candles and arranged them on the floor around the high altar. They bathed the area in soft yellow light. It was romantic. He hoped she would see it that way. What more romantic place could there be than the peaceful sanctuary of a church at midnight?

Fletcher hoped that Annie wouldn't resist him too much. Fear was fine. He wanted her to be afraid. But he also wanted her submission. He was hoping that the atmosphere of the place would overwhelm her and she would know that everything in her life had been working up to this moment. Surely she would recognize that.

But if she didn't, he was prepared. There would be no backing down, no going back. He had a duffle bag filled with supplies, including an automatic pistol he'd bought from a mail order house down South, chloroform in case she resisted (procured from a medical supply house), his Desert Commando knife, and several lengths of strong nylon climbing rope. The smooth marble altar, already completed, would make a creamy, lovely bed. Far, far better than the little one in the basement of the youth center.

He imagined Annie bound here, stretched out on her back on the altar, naked and writhing in the soft candlelight. What a magnificent sight it would be! What a luscious feast for his eyes. What a perfect sacrifice.

She was coming, and for the first time in a long time, Fletcher felt joy radiating through him.

Maybe he should kneel and give thanks.

* * *

"There's a patrol car cruising up the street. You'll have to have to wait in the car."

"Dammit, Annie."

"I'll try to avoid them, obviously, but I've got a legal right to be on the premises. If they really are looking for you, though, they could arrest you."

"After last time, they're damn well not going to arrest me without a helluva lot more evidence than they have so far. It's Sam's word against mine, and we've just about got him nailed."

"Yes, but until we do have him nailed, I think you should be extra cautious."

"I *am* being extra cautious, for crissake. Look at me."

Annie smiled. He was crouched down below the car window. This was difficult, for Matt was tall. "I love you," she said.

"I love you too, Annie." They both took a moment to register the fact that this was the first time they'd spoken those words—here, in a car, while trying to elude the San Francisco police.

Annie managed to squeeze into a parking spot on the far side of the youth center. After taking a careful look around, she said, "Okay, the cop car is gone. If you're coming, come now."

They got out of the car and ran into the shadows of the construction site. Annie led Matthew toward the south transept door.

* * *

When Fletcher saw Annie slip in through the south entrance, his heart lifted even higher. By the light of the candles he'd placed all over the front of the cathedral, she looked beautiful. She was dressed simply, in blue jeans and a cream-colored blouse, with her golden hair pulled back from her face and knotted at the nape of her neck. The severe hairstyle made her look virginal, untouchable. But she was here for him.

And then, right behind her, a man entered. Worse, he stepped forward rapidly and put his hand on Annie's shoulder to stop her progress into the church. Sounds carried in the cavernous building, and Fletcher heard his sharp whisper: "What the hell are all these candles lit for? Wait a sec. I don't like the look of this."

Annie stood still, and the man's arm came around her from behind, his hand passing over a breast, lingering caressing it.

Fletcher felt a hammer crash down inside his head. He recognized the man, both from photographs and from his visit here a couple of weeks ago. Matthew Carlyle. Annie already had a man. She had a fucking billionaire.

He ducked back behind the altar. Anger hardened like a knot inside his belly. He fished inside his duffle for the Desert Commando knife, but instead his hand found the automatic. He grew instantly more peaceful when he felt the cool walnut stock slide into his palm.

Another man? No. That was not allowed.

Annie and The Other Man advanced into the building, moving slowly along the south transept aisle. They stopped for a moment beside the stone baptismal font that had just been installed to the right of the sanctuary railing. There were now two baptismal fonts in the building, one in the front and the other in the rear.

They moved toward the spot where the transept aisle intersected the main aisle—the apex of the cathedral's huge longitudinal cross. They had to step around the scaffolding from which Giuseppe had fallen. Annie looked up at it and seemed to shiver.

She called out softly, "Jack?"

Fletcher slithered over the floor behind the altar and down the steps into the ambulatory. Crouching in the darkness, he moved rapidly in a semicircle to the left, around the high altar area to the steps of the pulpit, which curved up to the elevated pulpit behind a solid stone balustrade. He could hear them whispering just beyond him, their feet clicking on the marble-inlaid floor as they walked.

"He might be down in the basement somewhere, searching for Vico," Annie said to The Other Man.

"If Vico has hidden here successfully for this long, I'm not sure why any of us think we can find him," said Carlyle.

Fletcher hated his voice. So deep, so—so rich. So guilty. He was a killer. He deserved to die. Deserved to have his throat slashed and his blood poured out onto the sacred marble, like a pagan sacrifice.

Fletcher glanced down at the gun in his hand. Bad choice. Next time he would select the knife.

"Jack!" Annie called out, right beneath the pulpit, and Fletcher jumped. She sounded loud and insistent. She sounded impatient. She sounded like all the women whose voices had been giving orders, making demands. Starting with his mother, that loudmouthed bitch.

They were right beneath him now, rounding the corner overlooked by the pulpit, about to enter the ambulatory. . . .

He reared up, the gun held backward in his raised hand. Firing it, much though he would like to, would be foolhardy. There were probably cops on patrol nearby.

As Annie and her lover started, looked up, cried out, Fletcher brought his arm down hard. He felt the blow through to his shoulder as the butt of the gun connected with the top of Carlyle's skull, and watched him slump to the floor.

Hadn't the man's wife died after being struck in the head? *Let justice be done*, Fletcher thought, with sudden, shining clarity.

Annie threw herself to the floor with Matt, trying to rouse him, seeking a pulse, breathing, anything. His eyes were shut and his face had gone blank, and that blankness terrified her, because it reminded her of Charlie's face on that awful last day in the hospital. *Don't let it happen again, please don't let it happen again, please, I love this man, please, please . . .*

Hands grabbed her and tried to pull her to her feet. She fought them, sobbing. *No please, no please, no please!*

She didn't care what happened to her. He had a gun; she'd seen its cold dark metal. She didn't care, if Matt was no longer breathing. . . .

She jerked away from the invasive hands, and her head fell back upon her lover's chest. And there, wonder of wonders, she heard the slow, steady beat of his heart.

He was alive! Unconscious, but still alive. But he needed a doctor. He needed—

This time the hands were successful. She was pulled away from Matt, dragged at least a meter across the floor, then flipped over onto her belly. She felt strong knees and thighs straddling her, rippling with tense muscles. She felt a hand in her hair, tearing out the pins and loosening it until it spilled out over her shoulders.

"Why did you bring him?" a voice muttered. "You were supposed to come alone. You were supposed to come to *me*. I was waiting for you, Annie. I was prepared. Everything was ready. I've been waiting for you for so damn long."

She knew it was Jack Fletcher, and she knew he was crazy. It was no surprise, really. But she'd never guessed he was *this* crazy.

Nothing was as it seemed. Fletcher had seemed a little eerie, but competent and capable of functioning normally in society. And as for Sam—

Get your wits together, Annie!

She had to handle this. There had to be a way to handle this.

"Jack, I came here tonight because you told me you'd found Vico." She spoke slowly and clearly, trying to reach him. "We want to talk to Vico because we think he can confirm the identity of Giuseppe's killer."

Fletcher spat toward Matt's still body. "There's your killer."

"No. The killer is Sam."

Fletcher laughed, but Annie was heartened to see that he was at least listening to her. He must still be capable of some vestige of reason.

"Sam couldn't kill a bug that was crawling on the carpet."

"Sam's got you fooled just as he's fooled everybody else. We have proof. Sam changed the blueprints for the cathedral after they were approved by the city inspectors. He sent the altered version to the contractors. And to you. All these months, you've been supervising the construction of an unsafe cathedral. Sam hired you because he knew you could be fooled. He hired me for the same reason—I had so little construction experience that he figured I wouldn't ask the right questions. And he was right. I didn't."

"I don't know what the hell you're talking about," Fletcher said, dragging her to her feet. God, he was strong. He pulled her up as if she were made of silk and feathers instead of flesh and bone. She heard him grunt with satisfaction when he felt her legs respond.

He wasn't listening, but she had to try. She had to try *something*.

"Matt and I were just in Sam's office. We searched his computer until we found the altered CAD file. Sam had tried to hide it electronically, but it was there. Jack, do you hear me—*we have proof*. Sam was in collusion with someone from the construction company—probably Paul McEnerney himself. They charged the high costs of the first cathedral, built the lesser one for several million dollars less, and pocketed the difference.

"And who do you think they're going to blame it on? You, Jack. You and me. We're the scapegoats, Jack."

"I don't believe you. Sam Brody is a stand-up guy. You're trying to confuse me. That's what women do—they lie and lie and confuse all the men."

"I'm telling you the truth, Jack. We have proof. We have the two different versions of the CAD file and the blueprints."

"Women of lies," he muttered. "Women of cries." He gave a little smile, as if impressed with his cleverness, and added, "Women complies or else woman dies."

He dragged her up the marble side steps toward the altar.

She saw the candles on the floor and the ceremonial altar all polished and bare. And she saw the ropes.

"At last," he was murmuring. "At last, at last . . ."

He pushed her toward the altar, and she felt sick. She remembered all the moments when she'd turned toward him in the cathedral and seen his hot eyes on her. Had he been fantasizing about this all that time?

She could feel his hands on her breasts now, through her silk blouse. He was rough, squeezing one of her nipples until she gasped. She struggled to free herself, and as she squirmed she felt his erection pressing into her from the rear.

He liked her fear, she realized. He liked her struggles. He was a sadist and probably a killer as well.

Annie craned her neck to look back at Matt lying on the floor. Was he still breathing? How bad had that blow to the head been? She could still hear the dull sound of the crack, and it terrified her. Was he dying? Was he dead?

She felt something vibrating and knew her limbs were shaking. It was some sort of reaction, maybe shock.

He shoved her forward and she sprawled against the altar, half on top of it. Boneless, she slid down its smooth marble sides, slipping to her knees. She felt his hands ripping at her blouse, tearing it partway off her, and she cried out for help from God or the Goddess or whoever was watching over this place. This was the traditional place of sanctuary, the place where harm was not permitted to come to anyone who claimed the protection of God and the church. To raise your hand against someone who had sought sanctuary here was to raise your hand against God.

He pulled her up and flipped her over. Annie felt the flat cold, marble altar under the bare skin on her back where he had ripped her blouse. She looked into his face and saw that his expression was rapt and excited. On some level, she doubted that he even knew what was happening.

Jehovah's Pitchfork, she thought suddenly. That's who and what he was. The Devil usurping the House of the Lord.

She made one last-ditch try. "This is sacrilege," she said, deliberately pitching her voice low. "I have cried out for sanctuary. If you don't release me, the Lord will strike you down."

Fletcher laughed at her. "You don't think I actually believe that crap, do you?"

"Whether you believe it or not, how can you do this here on the high altar, in this beautiful cathedral, to a woman who's never wished you any harm and is innocent of any crime toward you?"

Something twisted. "There are no innocent women," he spat.

"Maybe not," she said, and jabbed her fingers into his eyes.

He howled and rolled away from her. Annie scrambled down from the altar and flung herself down the sanctuary stairs, racing toward Matt. She heard screaming and vaguely realized it was her own; she heard Fletcher moaning and scrambling behind her. She hadn't done it hard enough! Oh God, she should have jabbed harder, harder. . . .

He grabbed her ankles from behind and she tripped and skidded across the floor toward where Matt lay. Was he still breathing? But then Fletcher was on her, was pulling her hair, jerking her head back and she felt something cold and damp and acrid against her nose and mouth. Then the world darkened and the ceiling fell in on her.

* * *

Fletcher was panting with exertion and pain. Annie had tried to blind him! His precious Annie, whom he'd yearned for all this time! She was no innocent. She was no different than all the rest of them.

The pain in his left eye, which she had jabbed the hardest, was intense, frightening. His right eye ached but it was nowhere near as bad. He could see, but his vision was blurry. He could see that Annie was unconscious, chloroformed like the other one, her piercing screams silenced at last.

She would wake up soon, though, and he would have two of the bitches on his hands.

He thought of dragging her back to the altar and tying her there and stripping her and taking her anyway, just as he had planned. But she was unconscious, and that would reduce his pleasure. He wanted to see her terror and hear her screams. More than ever, he wanted to punish her.

And he would, too. He'd take her somewhere where there were no other people for miles in all directions. Then she could scream all she wanted and no one would hear. Then he would savor the sound of her screams.

But in the meantime there were things to take care of. Get rid of the mess.

He dragged first Annie, then Carlyle, up the sanctuary steps, around the high altar, and down the stairs to the crypt. It was a large, roughly circular room with a cement block wall separating it from the rest of the basement. It would eventually be used as a burial chamber for a few special people—probably clergy—who were considered important enough to be interred in the cathedral. At present it was not yet finished.

The marble interior work was about two-thirds completed, and the stone floor was still being laid.

The ornate door to the crypt had been installed two weeks ago, though. It could be locked from the outside, and the big brass key to the lock hung on a hook beside the door.

He unlocked the door and pulled it open. The pain in his eyes had receded just a little, but his vision was still blurry. He was tense, ready once again to fight, for he had stashed the other girl in here earlier. She should be awake by now and was probably frantic to get out.

There was no light in the crypt, nor was there any sound. He shone his flashlight and vaguely saw the outline of the girl curled on the floor about ten feet from the door. Was she asleep or dead? He didn't give a damn. She'd been a disappointing bitch anyhow—cold and silent as stone. When he'd tried to get her to tell him where her lover was, she'd withdrawn into some kind of trance. Her pale face had looked as if she were a million miles away. She didn't beg, she didn't scream, and he'd lost interest in her quickly enough. She was nothing compared to Annie. Nothing.

Was there enough air in here for the two of them? Should be—the place was huge. Annie was still alive, and he wanted to keep her that way. At least until he had taught her better manners.

Five minutes later, Fletcher had not one but three prisoners in the cathedral crypt.

Now all he needed was a little help.

He went back to the pulpit, where he had left his cellular phone.

Chapter Thirty-nine

Barbara Rae woke with a start. Sweat was beading on her forehead and under her arms, and she felt a wash of coldness along the hollow of her spine. She'd dreamed of Giuseppe Brindesi, seeing him as clearly and vividly as she'd seen him in life. He was standing in the nave of the cathedral where the main aisle met the transept aisle at the intersection of the great longitudinal cross. He was saying something to her, but as he spoke there was a loud rumbling sound coming up from beneath the floor—not unlike the roar of an earthquake. She couldn't understand his words, although he seemed very anxious to convey his meaning.

Then the floor of the cathedral burst open and out of the darkness popped a tiny newborn baby, its face white, its eyes closed. . . .

Barbara Rae took several deep breaths, trying to calm herself. She sat up and reached for her dressing gown, which she kept on a straight-backed chair beside her bed. The dream was fading a bit, but the deep mental disquietude remained. Something was wrong.

She rose, pulled on the dressing gown, and headed down to the basement room to check on Paolina.

When she found the room empty, Barbara Rae wasn't really surprised. Either the boy had come for her, or she had gone to him. She knew full well that the two of them had been sneaking into the youth center for the past three weeks, to use the bathroom and to stock up on food and water and blankets to keep them warm in their cold, dark hiding place in the bowels of the new cathedral.

She had kept their secret because keeping secrets was her duty, her responsibility, and, yes, her passion. It was the debt she owed to the world in return for the one great secret that her parishioners had never discovered about her.

She saw the dream images again—the newborn with the still, white face—and she shivered. Many years ago, she, like Paolina, had fallen in love with the wrong man. Like Paolina, she had ended up pregnant, and like Paolina, she had been cast out by her judgmental father. And, all too soon afterward, by her lover as well.

In her despair and loneliness, Barbara Rae had abused her body. She had sunk into a netherworld of booze and drugs. She had sold herself on the streets. And the baby, when it came, had been born dead.

With the help of a compassionate priest, she had amended her life after that nadir, but the guilt had never left her. All her life she would bear the burden of knowing that if she had taken better care of herself, her child might have survived.

As for other people's secrets, perhaps she had been keeping

too many of them lately. Perhaps justice had failed because of those secrets.

She kept seeing Sam Brody's face as they'd talked earlier tonight. His great charm, his insistence that he was innocent.

"Matt and I have known each other since college. I've known Francesca even longer. For me to sleep with her would have been a betrayal of friendship of the vilest kind."

His marvelous skill at twisting the truth.

A great wrong had been done, and she had contributed to it. In the morning, she decided, she would put it right.

Wearily, Barbara Rae returned to bed. A few hours of sleep, she hoped, would make her spirit stronger.

As Sam examined an old blueprint of the Compassion of Angels youth center, looking for the most efficient way to break in, he contemplated his own escape. A contingency plan was always a good idea, even though he'd hoped never to have to use one. Long ago he'd stashed some money in a secret bank account in Grand Cayman and another in Zurich. If necessary, he could live very comfortably in Brazil for the rest of his life.

Not that he particularly wanted to live in Brazil. And he certainly didn't want to run. At least, not until he had finished what he'd started and brought Matthew down.

But depending on what happened tonight, he might have to move on. Too many people knew too much. Too many were suspicious. Now it turned out that Francesca had talked to Barbara Rae, dammit, and who knew whom Barbara Rae had talked to?

He intended to find out. He was going to pay her a surprise visit. And depending on the outcome of that, he would probably pay a similar visit to Annie and Matthew, whom he assumed were together.

The only loose end then would be Darcy. He'd already taken care of Sidney Canin, who had been the first loose end to unravel. Well, the first after Giuseppe, of course.

As for Darcy, he figured he could deal with her easily enough. Get her back in bed and she'd do anything he told her to do. She'd tried to hide it, but her lovesick gaze had betrayed that she still had feelings for him that he could capitalize on.

Barbara Rae, Matt, Annie, and Darcy. Shit. Things were definitely out of control.

Sam started at the sound of the phone. Who the hell would call him at this time of night? Should he let the machine pick up? No, always better to establish that he was home, just in case it was the police.

It was Jack Fletcher. Sam was in no mood to talk to him and was about to slam down the receiver when Fletcher said, "Are you still interested in finding Vico?"

"Vico?"

"Yeah. I caught his girlfriend in the cathedral. It's the second time she's been in there, and when she saw me, she thought for a moment I was her lover. That means he's in there. Hiding out. The damn kid's probably been hiding right under our noses in the cathedral all along."

Shit. Of course! "But you haven't found him?"

"He's underground. Somewhere in the foundation. There are basements and subbasements and crawl space under there. It's a maze, and he won't be easy to flush out."

"What about the girl?"

"She's here. I couldn't get her to talk, though. But with the right pressure I'm sure she'll lead us right to him."

Jesus Christ, Sam thought, I *forgot about Vico*. If the kid had really witnessed anything, he could prove to be more dangerous than all the others combined.

"Stay there," he ordered. "Don't make any noise and don't do anything more to alert him. I'm coming. Whatever you do, don't let that girl slip away again."

"Don't worry, none of them are going anywhere."

None of them?

"What the hell does that mean? You got somebody else there at the construction site?"

"I had a little trouble with Annie."

Fletcher's voice sounded tight, barely under control. The guy was right on the edge.

"What do you mean, Jack? What kind of trouble? Is Annie there?"

Silence. Then: "Yeah, Annie's here. She wanted to know about those kids, you see. She really wanted to know so bad."

"So you called her and told her before you called me?"

"I'm sorry about that. But it had to be done."

Sam bit back a furious response. Goddammit! That was the trouble with dealing with nuts like Fletcher. He was too damn crazy to do what he was told.

Sam knew more about Fletcher than Fletcher suspected. He'd thoroughly checked out his criminal history, psychiatric profile and all. Fletcher had been convicted of sexual battery nine years ago in Florida. He'd done six years in prison. His therapist had speculated that there may have been other violent episodes in Fletcher's past, but he had never been arrested for them. The records also stated that Fletcher had been "successfully rehabilitated."

Sam doubted it. People convicted of sex crimes had a very high rate of recidivism.

"So what was the trouble, Jack? Did she come down there? Has she talked to Vico? Where is Annie, Jack?"

"I had to lock her in the crypt."

"You did." Sam tried to keep his voice neutral. Long years of training himself to control his reactions were paying off. "Annie is locked in the crypt."

"Yes, she is. She was fighting me. I had to shut her up in there."

He was *over* the edge now. What had he done to Annie? Sam had been planning to take care of her himself.

"Jack. Listen to me. The crypt is where they put dead people. Is Annie still alive?"

He heard a strangled laugh. "Oh yeah, Annie's alive all right. She was screaming, Sam. But the door of the crypt is real thick, and it'll muffle her screams real well."

"Okay, Jack." Jesus! "Look, leave her in there, okay? Leave her there until I get there, then we'll figure out what to do."

"Annie's not going to be too happy in there, Sam, when she wakes up."

"No, I imagine she's not." She wasn't going to be too happy when she got out of there, either.

"She's afraid of the dark, and it's pitch dark in the crypt."

"Just keep her there till I come, Jack."

Had Fletcher raped her? Sam beat down a throb of sympathy for her. Yes, goddammit, he liked her. Liked her a lot, in fact.

But he couldn't afford to get sentimental at this point in the game.

Annie had to go. He'd known it for weeks now.

"Sam?" Fletcher's voice sounded tentative and uncertain. "Annie says you're the one who murdered the workman on the scaffolding."

"That's bullshit, Jack."

"Annie says that she and her computer expert friend broke in to your office and hacked in to your personal computer earlier tonight and found proof that you and McEnerney built the cathedral below code. She claims you put her on the job because you didn't think she'd ever figure it out, and you hired me because you knew I was crooked, and that if anybody ever suspected anything, I'd be the one who got nailed for the fraud."

He paused to draw a deep breath. "Sam, is any of that true?"

Somewhere in the middle of this incredible recitation, Sam had sat down on the edge of his desk. His legs didn't feel so good. Neither did his heart.

His voice sounded relatively normal—at least to him—as he answered firmly, "Not a word of it, Jack."

"She said there were two different sets of blueprints. She's got them both."

"She and her computer expert friend broke in to your office and hacked in to your personal computer."

Christ, if that was true . . . But he'd deleted the altered file from his computer. And he had a password-protected system, dammit. Annie had to be bluffing. Had to be.

Except that Matt Carlyle was the guy who'd invented the fucking computer software. If anybody could get past computer security, Matt could. And if anybody could recover files that had supposedly been erased from a hard disk, Matt was the man.

"She's lying, Jack," he said, trying desperately to stay calm. "Think about it. She and Matthew Carlyle are lovers. He did the murder, Jack. Annie knows it, but she's in love with the guy. She wants it to be anyone but Matt, and she'll go to any lengths to misdirect the police. That's why we need to find Vico. He saw the killer. He can confirm that Carlyle murdered Giuseppe."

"It's not true?" Fletcher repeated.

"No, Jack, I swear to you it's not. Annie will say anything to protect Matt Carlyle."

"She's been beguiled by him," Fletcher said. "He's twisted her mind and turned her against me. She hates me, Sam. I saw it in her eyes. I wanted to cut that hatred out of her. It's not smart, letting me see it, you know."

"Keep cool, Jack, okay? I'm coming over. I'll be right over. Don't do anything till I get there, all right?"

"He's here too," Fletcher said.

"Who?"

"Carlyle. I think I might have killed him, though. I hit him pretty hard."

I don't believe this. "Let me get this straight. Annie and Matthew are both there? And so are Vico and his girlfriend, right?"

"They're all here. You coming too, Sam?"

"Yeah. Sit tight. I'm coming."

Chapter Forty

Annie woke up feeling nauseated. She remembered the sweet-sickly smell of the chloroform and figured out what must have happened. But she had no idea where she was, except that she was in total darkness. The air was chilly and stale.

She rolled over and bumped into someone. She heard a groan. Her hands explored him quickly, feeling a pulse and a heartbeat. His body felt almost as familiar to her as her own.

"I feel like shit but I don't think this is a hangover," Matt mumbled. Annie flung herself onto him and hungrily kissed his face in the dark.

"I thought you were dead!"

"Nope. But I may be blind. My head feels like it's being drilled with a jackhammer, and I can't see a damn thing."

"It's pitch black in here." She shivered, trying to beat down her fear. Now that she knew Matt was alive, her other, less rational anxieties were growing. "I think we're in the crypt."

"Terrific. What makes you think that?"

"The floor is polished stone and the wall is marble. I designed this damn thing."

"So how did we get here? Somebody bashed me on the top of the head, obviously. Vico?"

"No. It was Fletcher." She could hear her voice shaking. "He was always a little off-center, but now he's seriously disturbed."

Matt rolled over and wrapped his arms around her. "What happened?" he whispered. "Did he hurt you? Are you all right?"

Annie steeled herself. "I'm fine." She wasn't going to think about it. This was not the time for it. She would deal with it later, when they were out of here.

If they got out of here.

"Did we find Vico?"

"Not yet," said a new voice in the darkness. Annie sucked her breath in sharply as she vainly sought out its source in the blackness. "But Vico has found you."

Introductions were quickly made by the light of a strong flashlight. Vico appeared just as cocky as always, although his skin was pale and his face was dirty. He seemed quite prepared to take charge of the situation.

"Come. There's a way out. I got Paolina out already. Now it's your turn."

"How?" Annie asked. "The interior walls of the crypt aren't finished, but the foundation walls for it were laid in months ago."

"When I was working here I was friends with the guys

who were doing the crypt," the boy said calmly. "They told me that most of the old churches and cathedrals in Europe had priest holes and secret passages. It was tradition, they said, for the stonemasons to leave small passages in certain places in the walls. They were making one in the crypt, and they showed it to me. It is a small and secret exit behind a loose piece of marble veneer. Later, when I needed places to hide, I remembered."

"So you've been living down here under the cathedral for the past two weeks?"

"Three weeks, actually," Vico said proudly. "Ever since the police first came after me."

"Does Fletcher know how to find you?" Matt asked.

Vico scoffed. "He has tried, but it was a joke. He'll never find me. Down here, I am king!"

Annie remembered the image that had gone through her mind when Vico had stormed into the youth center and seized Paolina—Hades abducting Persephone. The Lord of the Underworld. They were in his realm now.

Vico showed them the small square hole in the wall, just big enough for a person to wriggle through. He had disguised it behind one of the new marble panels, although there was so much construction debris in the crypt that a bit more mess and confusion was not likely to be noticed.

Vico was wearing heavy dark clothing and a hard hat with a miner's lamp. He carried a big flashlight and was obviously well equipped for subterranean living. When Annie questioned him about it, he told her that the church had had a program last year for inner-city kids to participate in Outward Bound. They had been taught some of the techniques of spelunking for a planned trip to a cave about two hundred miles outside the city.

Vico had missed that trip, but he had attended the classes and learned about caving techniques and equipment. Someday, he said dreamily, he would go to New Mexico. There were many wonderful caves there.

Under Vico's direction, Annie and Matt crawled out of the crypt through the narrow opening and found themselves in the larger darkness of the cathedral basement. Since they were under the elevated sanctuary area at the east end of the cathedral, the basement here was a full one, with a ceiling that was well above their heads. It was completely unfinished, though, and the floor was concrete poured directly onto the stony dirt of San Francisco.

At one end of the basement was the room that contained the cathedral's physical plant—furnace, water heater, oil tank, air-conditioning units, electrical panels, and telephone and data communication lines.

The rest of the basement area was storage space, as yet unutilized.

"We're not safe here. There's access to this part of the basement through the sacristy," Annie said, picturing the CAD drawings.

"For safety we must go into the crawl space under the main section of the church," Vico said. "It is vast and there are many good hiding places."

"I was afraid you'd say that." The thought of crawling around in darkness where the floor was dirt and the head room was unlikely to be more than two or three feet gave her the willies. There would be rats and other creatures living there. . . .

"It's fun," Vico said buoyantly. "It's like a live game of Dungeons and Dragons."

Annie thought of Jack Fletcher with his gun and his mad eyes. "This is not a game."

"No," Vico agreed, suddenly sounding mature and serious. "Not a game since they murdered my uncle, and now since they have tried to harm Paolina."

Matt and Annie exchanged a look. They would have to question Vico about the murder, but finding a place of safety was now the higher priority.

Vico handed Matt his flashlight and switched on the miner's light on his hard hat. Then he led them west through the main basement. The ceiling sloped sharply under the steps that led down from the high altar to the sanctuary. A little farther west, the ceiling sloped at a more gradual angle where, above, the stairs descended from the sanctuary to the area where the north and south transepts crossed the center aisle of the cathedral. There the basement ended and the crawl space began.

"Come," said Vico, dropping to his hands and knees. "I will take you to the place where I have hidden Paolina. We'll be safe there."

Matt must have sensed her reluctance, since he pulled her into a quick, hard hug. "It'll be okay," he whispered.

"There are rats," she said with a shudder. She didn't want to tell him she was deathly afraid, not of rats but of the yawning blackness itself.

"Don't worry—they'll be scurrying away as soon as they sense this group of lummoxes venturing into their terrain."

Calm down, Annie. Think of something else. "How's your head?" she asked.

"Hurts, but I'll live. Come on."

Annie crouched down and gingerly began to crawl after Vico. The dirt felt cool against her palms and knees. "I feel like Jean Valjean fleeing through the sewers of Paris," she muttered.

"Don't worry. That Fletcher character is no Javert."

Sam was driving to the cathedral when the cellular phone in his car rang. He grabbed it, expecting new information from Fletcher.

"You blew it," said a harsh voice in his ear. "The cops just paid me a call. They're suspicious. They're asking questions about how well we know each other and how often we've done business together."

Sam sat up straighter, holding the receiver. Outside, the world was still dark. "What the hell?" he muttered.

"It's over, asshole," the voice said. "I'm cutting you loose."

Cold as dry ice. Click. He was gone.

Sam sat hunched in the dark, the receiver still in his fist.

"It's over, asshole."

McEnerney. He never should have gotten into it with him. He was probably tied to the mob.

Sam thought about the conversation they'd had last week. Met at that Mexican joint that McEnerney favored. Watched him stuff tamale after tamale into his maw and wash them down with four bottles of Dos Equis. Four. Swallowed the stuff like tap water.

"It's starting to come down just like I was afraid it would," McEnerney had said, chomping and scowling. "Serves me right for getting mixed up with a fuck-up like you."

"Watch it, Paul."

"Fuck you, Brody." The words had exploded across the table. "I should known better than to do a deal with an amateur. You need somebody like that workman dead, you go to the people who know what they're doing. The experts. You don't try to take care of it yourself."

"There was no choice. It happened too fast."

"You let things get outta control, Brody. You *never* let things get outta control."

"Nothing's out of control," Sam had insisted.

"It better not be. You'd better take care of it. I'm not going down because of a pissant operation like this."

Pissant operation. A profit of $3.8 million split two ways wasn't what Sam would have termed "pissant." True, it wasn't the couple billion he might have snagged if he'd married Francesca, but two million was still a lot of money to most people.

Now Sam realized that their deal was nothing new to McEnerney—he'd probably been making similar ones for most of his career.

No matter how good you are, there's always someone better.

No doubt McEnerney had a plan for covering his own ass. And the first step in that plan probably involved hiring one of those experts.

He almost had to pull over. His face in the rearview mirror was haggard, and his guts felt like water.

He reminded himself that he too had a contingency plan. He had prepared for something going wrong, and going wrong big time.

If it happened, he knew what he would have to do.

But—hell. He was still hoping there was another way.

Chapter Forty-one

Fletcher waited in the pulpit for Sam Brody to arrive. He liked the pulpit. It gave him an excellent view of the entire breadth and depth of the cathedral.

All he could see tonight were shadows, since the light from the candles he had lit in the sanctuary didn't extend to the main body of the church. Out there, where the congregation would sit, the pews were cloaked in darkness.

He turned back to look once again at the high altar. Briefly, oh so briefly, he had spread Annie out there. It had been a glorious moment, but too short. He should have tied her hands first, of course. And her legs so she couldn't kick him. Next time he would do it right.

His eyes were still hurting. He could see pretty well now, though. Her jabbing hadn't blinded him. She had gained nothing but an increase in the torment she would suffer.

He had to kill her now. Now that she hated him, she would have to die. He had believed that her body and soul were his to master, but she had given them both to another man. If she couldn't be his, she couldn't be permitted to live.

"I knew nobody would ever believe me," Vico said. The four were nestled in a reasonably cozy spot under one of the chapels on the north wall. The ceiling—which was really the cathedral floor—was higher here because the tiny chapel upstairs was elevated four steps above the nave.

The space was warm because a heating duct ran along the north foundation wall. Vico had covered the dirt floor with a layer of insulation that he'd found somewhere in the construction site. Over it he'd laid blankets. He had a couple of battery-operated lanterns that Paolina had smuggled in for him. There were also several bottles of water and some food that he kept in a metal box to secure it from the rats.

Paolina was lying on a mound of quilts and blankets that obviously served as the young couple's bed. She looked serene and happy, despite all the excitement, and her fingers kept brushing Vico's shoulder.

"Sam Brody is the big boss. The architect. My uncle taught me that a construction project is like an oceangoing vessel. The builder and the craftsmen are the workers, but the architect is the captain of the ship."

Right, Annie thought. Sam would love that metaphor.

"Who would believe me if I told my story?" he went on. "I had been fired. I was a fugitive already, and the cops were after me. And Mr. Brody was a well-respected man. Everybody who worked on the building liked him. If I'd named someone else they might have listened, but not Sam Brody. It's like he was God."

"But it *was* Sam you saw that night?" Matt asked. "You're sure?"

Vico nodded. "It was Mr. Brody. I'm positive. He came into the church. He went directly to the scaffold. I was watching from the sacristy stairway and I could see everything he was doing. He climbed up there. He had a wrench, and I could see that he was working on something high up on the scaffolding. Of course, I never imagined that he might be doing anything bad. I figured someone had complained and something was loose and he was fixing it. The only thing I wondered about was why the big boss would be attending to it personally instead of sending in an ordinary repair guy."

"And then what happened?"

"Nothing. He climbed down. I figured he was leaving. I thought, well, maybe he couldn't sleep that night or something. People do funny things when they can't sleep.

"But he didn't leave. He started looking around, as if he was searching for something. Then he came right for the steps where I was hiding. I scurried down the stairs and tucked myself away into a corner. I figured he was coming down into the basement to get something. A tool, maybe. I waited and listened, but I didn't hear him come down the steps. So finally I snuck out again to see where he had gone, and I saw him crouching there, on the sacristy steps below the high altar. Right where I had been. He was peering out into the sanctuary."

"Like you, he found it a good place to observe what was happening," said Matt.

"Yeah. I thought that was very weird. But I didn't put it together. I didn't know what the fuck—excuse me—I didn't know what was going on. Didn't have a clue. I did notice he was wearing some kind of gloves, though. I stupidly thought he just didn't want to get his hands dirty."

Annie and Matt exchanged glances. Sam had worn gloves to ensure that everybody's fingerprints except his own were on the scaffolding.

"So he waited and I waited," Vico went on. "I just wanted him to go away and not find me. I didn't want him anywhere near my hiding places."

"And then what happened?"

"Nothing for a while. I was getting real bored. Then I saw him come alert, like. He tensed up, and it seemed as if he was suddenly watching very closely. I started to get a bad feeling about this. I mean, he was all excited and there was something up, I knew it. But I still had no clue.

"He was watching something that was happening in the cathedral, but I couldn't see it. If only I'd known what he was doing!" Vico's voice rose in pain. "If only I'd realized what time it was and that soon my uncle would be coming in to work. But it's dark down here and I was tired and I'd lost track of the time. And besides, he was the architect. What interest could he possibly have in a workman like my uncle? It just never clicked."

He paused, and Annie saw that sweat had broken out on his forehead. "I didn't know anything until I heard the scream." He shuddered. "There was this horrible scream and then a crash, and I didn't know—I couldn't tell whose voice it was, I was just watching him—Brody—and he waited for a moment after the scream, but only for a moment—like maybe he was afraid somebody else had heard it or would come running or something. He opened the door and he slipped out, and by this time I was shaking. But I followed him and got back into my spot where he had been and looked out." He stopped again, his face pale. For several seconds he coughed into his cupped hands.

"All Brody did was take one look. Like, to be sure he was dead. Then he ran to the north door and in a flash he was outta there."

"And you?"

"I—I went out. And I saw who it was. And I looked at the way the scaffolding had collapsed, and then I knew. He'd killed him, and he'd done it deliberately. And that was when I knew that I'd have to kill him, too. Brody. Vendetta," he said, his young eyes gone totally cold.

"I think you should let the police handle it, Vico," Paolina said, speaking now for the first time. "This is not Sicily. If you kill Sam Brody, you'll go to jail for the rest of your life."

"Besides, I've known him a lot longer than you have," Matt said grimly. "Sam Brody is mine."

"Where are they?" Brody asked.

Fletcher watched him walk up the main aisle of the cathedral, holding a big flashlight to light his way. He was still standing in the pulpit, looking out over an imaginary congregation.

"Are they still in the crypt? Have you checked on them? How badly injured are they?"

Fletcher stared at him. He was curious about Brody's hair, which gleamed as golden as the finest and most sacred communion plate.

"Jack? Are you okay, man?"

"I'm fine," he managed to reply. "You're here for Vico? Take him and go." He wanted to be alone—alone with Annie.

"Let's see who you've got locked in the crypt first, Jack, okay?"

Brody led the way across the sanctuary, around the high altar, and down the short set of steps to the crypt door. Fletcher followed slowly. He felt as if he were floating, his feet whispering over the marble floor.

He was in a nice, warm dream as he pointed out the key on the hook, the key to the crypt. The dream thinned a bit when he saw Sam pull a pistol from his jacket and hold it at the ready. He held it as if he knew know to use it, too, which was something Fletcher hadn't expected of golden-boy Sam Brody.

Maybe it was true, what Annie had said.

Maybe Brody had been lying to him all along.

Slowly, Brody unlocked and pulled open the heavy door. He directed the harsh beam of his flashlight into the crypt and around it, the gun raised, his finger on the trigger. . . .

Abruptly Brody turned, and this time both the light and the gun were directed at Fletcher. "The crypt is empty. What the hell kind of crazy game are you playing?"

"No!" Fletcher cried, ignoring the gun, pushing past it, rushing into the low, circular chamber. He darted his own flashlight from side to side, top to bottom. The construction debris was still there, but his prisoners had vanished.

Chapter Forty-two

Standing outside the cathedral a few minutes later, Sam stared at the magnificent building rising out of the mundane architecture around it, shaking his head over what he had to do.

It was sad, really.

Tragic.

But if Matthew and Annie really had the two versions of the CAD file, there was little choice. If he didn't destroy all the evidence of construction fraud, Brody Associates would be ruined. They would never recover from the scandal. And he'd lose all those lucrative plum jobs that the cathedral project itself had dropped into his lap.

Shit, he *would* have to go to Brazil. The thought depressed him. His life was here. Matthew Carlyle, his obsession, was here. For the first time, he wondered how he would feel when Matt Carlyle was no longer alive to plot and plan against.

He'd know soon.

He had left Fletcher standing guard at the main exit from the cathedral basement while he'd come outside to the construction trailers. Annie, Matt, Vico, and his girlfriend were all down there somewhere beneath the floor of the cathedral. He and Fletcher had found the secret exit from the crypt.

Armed with flashlights and guns, he and Fletcher had made a brief attempt to negotiate the crawl space under the main body of the cathedral. They'd heard scuffling sounds in the distance as the fugitives had scurried away like rats, but the area was vast. Flushing them out of there before morning would be just about impossible.

Locked in one of the trailers were some supplies he had placed there several nights ago. Checking carefully to make sure no one was watching, Sam slipped into the trailer and recovered a supply of explosives used in construction for blasting foundations and destroying old buildings. As an architect, he was, of course, familiar with explosives and how to use them. He had hoped he wouldn't need them, but he'd wanted to be prepared in case he did.

He loaded the explosives into a large sports bag. Then he pulled out his copy of the blueprints and unfolded them. With his flashlight he carefully studied the design to make absolutely certain he knew where to place the explosives in order to do the most damage. He made a mental note of the primary weight-bearing columns.

It was truly a shame to destroy something so beautiful, he thought as he glanced again at the graceful neo-Gothic walls of the cathedral. But it was the only way to take care of all his problems at once.

The people who were most dangerous to him—Vico, Paolina, and Annie—were in there right now. Any charges they might have made against him would be silenced by their deaths. As for Barbara Rae, he would take care of her immediately afterward. She lived next door, and he would make it look as if she too had been killed in the blast.

Best of all, Matthew was in there. The twenty-one-year thorn in Sam's side was about to be crushed and removed. If it wasn't exactly the way he'd thought it would happen, well, nothing in life ever was. He would have preferred to look directly into Matt's eyes as the end came. For years Sam had fantasized that his face would be the last thing Matt would ever see. The smile of his tormentor, the eyes of his judge.

This was better, though. Once the building was destroyed, it would be difficult for anyone to prove that there had been any discrepancies between the original CAD drawings and the actual construction. In fact, it was doubtful that anybody would even care. All the attention would focus on the fact that a work of architectural splendor and unparalleled beauty had been leveled by a madman.

Sam took his sports bag and darted over to Fletcher's trailer. It was locked, but Sam had all the master keys. He put on a pair of latex surgical gloves and went inside.

The place was neater than he'd expected. But there were a few odd things lying around. He took a quick glance through a copy of *Soldier of Fortune*. It was amazing what you could buy through mail order these days. Guns of all sorts. Knives. Materials that could be combined with others to make bombs.

Excellent.

He also saw a couple of pamphlets from some antigay organization called Heterosexual Nation. Antigay in San Francisco—the man was living in the wrong city.

He went to the computer and turned it on. He opened a

new file and, using as a model the copy of one of the threatening letters that Annie had received recently, Sam composed a similar one:

> *I have warned you but you failed to obey. Now*
> *it is TOO LATE. The Hand of the Lord will rain*
> *fire upon you. The House of Pride will fall!*

He signed it *Jehovah's Pitchfork*, then he turned on the printer and printed it out.

He then laid the paper on the countertop in front of the computer screen and got a fresh sheet. With exquisite care, Sam began to print in block letters, copying from the original. He did only six words, then put down the pen as if he'd been interrupted. He didn't want to press his luck on the handwriting analysis.

He shoved both the printout and the handwritten note underneath a newspaper on the desk. If Fletcher came back here briefly, he probably wouldn't notice it. When the police started investigating—which they would do almost immediately after a major explosion—they would find the note and the file and draw their own conclusions.

Stealthily he left the trailer and headed back to the cathedral, carrying his sports bag in one hand, still wearing the thin latex gloves. The entire scheme was risky, but with any luck, no one would ever suspect that anybody except Fletcher had been involved.

They would blame Jack Fletcher, exactly as Sam had planned from the start.

Jack Fletcher, who, unknown to anyone but Sam, had a prison record for sexual assault.

Jack Fletcher, who also had access to construction site explosives.

Jack Fletcher, psychotic and perfect scapegoat.

"It was like everything crystallized," Vico said, describing his feelings and actions after the murder of his uncle. "If I admitted what I'd seen, either Brody would get me or the police would. If it was Brody, I was dead. If it was the cops, I was in the slammer, probably for good. I was already wanted—they'd throw my ass in jail and I'd never get out."

"So you decided to hide out?"

"I had to. At first it was just to figure out what to do. And I was hoping the cops would get cracking and solve the case. And if they didn't, well, I knew the killer and that's all it would take, really. If the law didn't get him, someday I would."

"Well, we've got him now," Matt said. "We need you to come in and talk to the cops. We have proof tying him to a scheme to defraud the owners of the United Path Church for what appears to be several million dollars. We have a motive for Giuseppe's murder, and we have the computer evidence of the fraud. Best of all, we have you as an eyewitness to the murder. It'll be enough. Hell, it's a lot more than they had on me when I was arrested."

"He's not going in unless they make a deal to drop the drug-selling charges," Paolina cut in. She sounded fiercely protective. "He's hidden this long and he'll hide a few more days if necessary. If he helps the police, they've got to help him."

Annie looked at Matt. "Do you think they'll do that?"

"Probably, yeah. Deals like that are made all the time. I

agree he shouldn't surrender until the deal is actually made, though. I could get one of my lawyers to put something together with the prosecutor."

Annie shook her head. "It's still so hard for me to believe. Sam Brody killed your uncle because your uncle knew that the structure of the cathedral wasn't sound," she said, almost to herself.

Vico raised his eyebrows. "That's not the only reason he killed him."

Annie blinked. "It's not?"

"No. The day before he died, my uncle told me that he was worried about something. He had met Sam Brody on the day you brought him to the construction site. He recognized him. And then a few days later he met Matthew Carlyle." Vico glanced nervously at Matt. "He knew they were friends, good friends. But he knew something that he now realized nobody else knew. He knew that Sam Brody had been the lover of Mr. Carlyle's wife. The one that was murdered and dumped in the Bay."

"*Sam* was her lover?" Annie said.

"Yes. My uncle knew it because he had caught them together in the choir loft of the old church that Reverend Acker used to run. He'd seen them, naked. There was, like, no doubt."

"Oh, wow," Annie said.

"Later, Mrs. Carlyle begged him to remain silent. He gave his word of honor.

"Then she died. He was out of the country at the time; he didn't know the details of the murder trial here. It wasn't until he returned and Mr. Carlyle was set free and he heard some of the news coverage that he realized that no one had ever identified her lover, or even proved that she *had* a lover.

"So he asked me what I thought he should do. Should he go to the authorities and give them his information, or should he go first to Mr. Brody and tell him that he wished to be released from his long-ago promise? We both thought the honorable thing to do was talk to Mr. Brody first." He paused. "Neither of us could imagine that Mr. Brody could be a killer."

"So *did* he go to Sam?"

Vico nodded. "And Sam killed him the very next day."

Matt had been silent and motionless during this revelation. Now, though, Annie heard him heave a deep breath.

"Show me the fastest way out of here, Vico," he said.

"Matt, no!"

"This man was the best friend I've ever had. Or so I believed for over twenty years. I'm going to find him, and then, by God, I'm going to deal with him in a manner the bastard will understand!"

Chapter Forty-three

Darcy not only copied the files off Sam's computer onto a disk, she printed them out on the plotter. And then she reduced and photocopied them for good measure. Nothing was going to happen to these babies—not if she had anything to say about it.

When she was sure that the evidence had been properly copied and printed and backed up, she searched Sam's computer files for anything else that might be incriminating.

When she came to his electronic mail software she viewed the log to check his recent messages. She noticed a couple to Paul McEnerney, and she quickly called them up on the screen. But they were routine—nothing incriminating.

Then she noticed that Sam's "trash" file, where old, unneeded messages are stored, was set to hold one hundred pieces of "trash." That was high. Her own was set to hold twenty. When that number was exceeded, the trash was automatically dumped.

She tried to call up files listed in "trash." The software refused. They were no longer accessible from the e-mail program.

Remembering Matt's tricks, though, she exited the e-mail program and used DOS commands to examine the contents of the directory where the e-mail software was stored. Sure enough, the trashed files were still there. Apparently they didn't actually get deleted until the entire trash grouping was "dumped."

There were eighty-nine old messages in Sam's trash. Tedious though the process was, Darcy decided to go through them one by one.

She was about two-thirds of the way through when she found what she was looking for. An e-mail from a year and a half ago to Paul McEnerney with an attached file transfer: "I'm attaching my new version of the document. The utmost discretion is advised."

The file he'd attached was his fraudulent version of the cathedral CAD file.

"We've got him!" she crowed. "Sam and Paul McEnerney, we've got them both!"

Computers, she decided, were beautiful things.

She was about to close down the system and get out of there with the evidence when another file name caught her eye: "Fletcher.txt." She called it up and found a police record stating that one John Albert Fletcher had served a prison sentence in Florida for sexual battery. The prison psychologist had noted that he was subject to "obsessive-compulsive behavior, especially regarding women, and occasional delusional episodes." He also had "difficulty in controlling his aggressive impulses" and "episodes of homicidal ideation."

Fletcher had had some treatment in prison, and was described by the same psychologist one year later as "much improved and able to function in society."

Sam had hired the guy, keeping quiet about what he knew. At one time this probably would have inspired admiration in her, Darcy thought wryly. Good old Sam, what a fair and tolerant man.

Now all she could think was that Sam had known he could use these facts to his advantage. He'd hired a crook to manage a scam.

Meanwhile, Annie and Matt had gone running off to the cathedral in the middle of the night at the behest of a mental case. The more she thought about it, the less she liked the idea.

Darcy had a sudden image of the tarot spread the last time she had laid out the deck. The Tower had kept coming up, even though she did the spread again three times. The Tower exploding in a massive wave of destruction, with rocks and bodies hurled out with tremendous force.

Darcy hurriedly copied the file on Fletcher onto her floppy disk and shut down Sam's computer.

"There's another way out," said Vico. "If we crawl all the way down to the east entrance of the cathedral, we can enter one of the basements under the north and the south bell towers. From there we go up the stairs to the bell-tower vestibule and walk right out the west entrance door."

"How do we know Fletcher won't be waiting for us there, anticipating our plans?" Annie said.

"He can't be everywhere."

"Let's do it," Matt said. He was eager for action. Every time he thought of Sam's betrayal, his brain started to boil.

Ironically, the words he remembered most vividly were his wife's. It had been during one of those petty, sarcastic arguments that married people tend to indulge in, always knowing the truest ways of striking the other person to the heart. Matt had been reminiscing about his friendship with Sam—how old it was and how good it was to have one person he could always count on.

"How can you claim he's your friend when the two of you never talk and never spend any time together?" Francesca had asked. "I don't consider another woman my friend unless we chat on the phone at least once a week."

"I don't have to see Sam or talk to him often to know that I can count on him if I need him."

"How do you know that?" she'd persisted. "Just because you were roommates in college twenty years ago? People change."

"Trustworthy people never change," he'd said, somewhat acidly.

"You think so?" she'd said in an even nastier tone. "Then you're a fool."

Had she been making love to Sam at the time she'd spoken those words? Probably. Francesca had known that Sam's loyalty was false.

"Let's not get sidetracked on Fletcher," Matt said. "Much as I'd like to strangle him for what he did to Annie—" his eyes burned as he looked at her, "our real problem here is

Sam. I say we get out of here as quickly as possible and take Vico and the two versions of the blueprints to the district attorney."

"Follow me, then," Vico said. "I'll lead you out."

Annie really didn't want to do it. She was just beginning to feel comfortable in Vico's cozy little sanctuary under the chapel. Crawling again on her hands and knees through San Francisco bedrock and dirt—which was cold, so cold—made her think of the grave. She felt trapped in a tomb, rock overhead, black earth beneath, utter blackness all around her, surrounded by creatures that live in the dark. How could Vico have spent three weeks down here? The very thought of it made her want to start screaming and never stop.

"What's the matter, Annie?" Matt's voice was gentle.

"I'm not sure I can do this."

"I'm here. Right beside you."

"What if there's an earthquake?" She knew it was a stupid question. The remote possibility of an earthquake was the least of their problems now. "We'll be crushed."

"I know how you feel," he said soothingly. "When I was locked in that tiny cell day after day, month after month, I thought I'd start tearing out the walls with my bare hands. I was sure I was going insane." He paused. Annie couldn't see, but she could feel his hands squeezing her shoulders. "It's truly amazing what the human spirit can tolerate."

"Matt, I'm sorry, I don't want to let you all down, but I just don't think I can do this."

"I love you, Annie. With me at your side, I promise you, there's nothing you can't do."

His words uplifted her and gave her courage. *Okay*, she thought. *Okay, I'll try.*

With her heart in her mouth, she began to crawl.

It felt like the hardest thing she'd ever done, but somehow she made it with the others to the far end of the nave. She had grown increasingly disoriented in the dark, but Vico assured them that they were now near the north bell tower, where there was an exit into the bell-tower basement.

Annie's heart sank when she heard him say, "Shit. They've blocked it."

"With what?" Matt's voice was analytical, ready to problem-solve. He also sounded impatient. "Can we get through?"

"Feels like bricks and fresh mortar. No, it's solid. The damn stuff sets very fast. They're trying to trap us down here."

Oh God. Annie lay on her belly in the darkness and felt the panic wash through her. The crawl space was damp and musty, and her flesh crept at the thought of the various insects that were probably invading her clothing right now, attracted to the scent of her fear.

"Let's try the south-tower basement," Matt said.

"All right. No point in all of us going. I'll crawl over there and check it. If it's blocked too, I'll be back and we'll figure out another way."

"*Is* there another way?" Annie asked, trying to fight back her panic.

"At the east end of the cathedral there are a couple of other ways out," Vico said. "But it's also easier for them to catch us back there."

"Well, let's check the south-tower basement first," said Matt.

Vico was gone for ten minutes. Matt held both her and Paolina, whose voice was also sounding ragged. Annie tried to worry about the girl instead of herself. It certainly couldn't be easy to crawl through the foundations of the cathedral on a pregnant stomach. But Paolina, though she was tired, did not seem afraid. Her trust in Vico, she declared, was unwavering.

"He'll get us out, don't worry," she assured Annie.

"The same," Vico said shortly when he returned. "They're trying to trap us in here. We'll have to go back to the east end of the building."

We're never going to get out of here! Annie thought.

But Matt was right there, holding her, speaking soothingly into her ear. "It's gonna be okay," he told her, and she clung to that thought.

The long crawl back was almost unbearable. The smell of the dirt sickened Annie. The blackness pressed around her like a suffocating glove, and it was hard for her to get her breath. She remembered all the stories she'd heard during the excavation about human bones and evil omens. Some of the workmen had whispered that the site was cursed.

It's a holy place, she told herself sensibly. *It can't be cursed.*

At one point Matt's flashlight caught the red glow of eyes staring at them in the distance. Rats. Predators waiting in the darkness.

Vico heaved a stone at them and they scurried away.

As they once again neared the great cross of the cathedral, beyond which lay the cement-finished basements of the sanctuary area, Annie felt her terror begin to calm. Logically, she knew that this was ridiculous, since the basement was likely to contain the madman who had attacked Matt and very nearly raped her. But she found the thought of Jack Fletcher easier to contemplate than the thought of spending any more time belly-crawling in the foundation.

Gradually, the ceiling got higher and the air smelled fresher. The gloom lightened ahead, and the sight of it was such a relief to her that she began to crawl faster, eager to get to the light, eager to get *out*.

But Matt grabbed her ankle. "Wait. We left no lights on behind us. Are there electric lights in the basement area, Vico?"

"Bare bulbs hanging from the ceiling at intervals, yeah," he whispered. "Looks like they're on now. It's like I figured. They're waiting for us here because they know it's our only way out."

"No one's got a flashlight on, I hope," said Matt.

"We turned them off a ways back," Vico replied.

A small pebble suddenly jumped into the air about a yard in front of Annie. It was followed almost instantly by a loud report.

"Shit!" Vico hissed. "Get back. He's shooting at us!"

"Goddammit!" Matt said.

"I can hear you in there, crawling and scurrying like the rats you are," a male voice called out from the basement area. Annie recognized it: Jack Fletcher.

There was another *crack* and an explosion of dirt a few feet to the right of Matthew.

"Send Annie out," Fletcher ordered. "She's the only one I care about. The rest of you can rot under there."

Lying with her chest to the cold ground and tears pricking her eyes, Annie was horrified to realize that she was tempted to go, give up, surrender. Anything seemed preferable to spending another minute in here.

But Matt pulled her back with him, safely out of the range of the bullets. The four of them huddled together, and Matt whispered, "There's got to be another way out of here, Vico. What about heating ducts? Water mains? The ventilation system? Have you investigated the entire substructure?"

Annie forced herself to focus. Vico was no expert on the kind of thing Matt was asking about. But she was—at least, she should be.

There in the darkness, she concentrated, trying to visualize the engineering plans. *This is my building, dammit. I know it—or I ought to, dammit. I know it cold.*

Think!

"There's a small trapdoor leading into the crawl space along the south wall," she said slowly. "The water main comes in at that point from the street. In the old church, which was less than half the size of this one, that was the only source of water. But we're connected to the water mains on the other side as well, in the basement proper near the water heater."

She visualized the blueprints of the foundation area. "One of the primary water pipes runs along the south wall, and there's a cut-off valve in the crawl space where our pipe links with the city's. Plumbing access was necessary, so we have the trapdoor. It's in one of the side-aisle chapels."

"Wow. I never found it," Vico said.

"Unless you know plumbing, you wouldn't suspect it was there."

"We can get out, into the cathedral, through this trapdoor?" Matt asked.

"We ought to be able to, yes."

"Which chapel is it? How far along the wall?"

"I'm not sure. Somewhere toward the middle, I think. But

I'm totally disoriented down here. We'll have to search them one by one."

"Come on, then. Let's find the sucker."

Once back inside the cathedral, the first and most important thing Sam had to take care of was securing the various exits. He didn't want to be interrupted while he worked. And he needed to make sure nobody could get into the building—or out—between the time he exited and the moment he detonated the explosives by remote control.

From his sports bag he removed a length of chain and threaded it through the brass handles that had just recently been attached to the huge door at the west entrance. The doors were solid; nobody would get through them.

He secured the chain with a padlock.

He then attended to the north and south transept doors. He planned to exit through the tunnel in the basement that led to the youth center next door. He had parked his car several blocks away. With luck, it wouldn't be noticed.

Working quickly, Sam moved from pillar to pillar in the nave of the cathedral, planting explosives. He'd chosen six of the columns as the ones most critical. They were stone with a core of steel, and they were designed to withstand the force of a major earthquake. But the building was not designed to withstand the stress of powerful explosives going off simultaneously at all the greatest stress points.

The cathedral would fall.

And what a terrible destruction it would be. Had the church been completed, it would have been more than two years under construction. It would have been the largest cathedral built in San Francisco in modern times.

But it would take less than ten seconds to bring it down.

Chapter Forty-four

"Somebody is walking around inside the cathedral," Paolina whispered. She and Annie had finally located the right chapel and the trapdoor. Matt was checking one a few yards down and Vico was checking one up on the other side.

Unable to endure being in the crawl space for one second longer, Annie had pried open the trapdoor and hoisted herself up into the chapel. Paolina had followed, and now they were crouched behind a marble statue of St. Joan. "That doesn't look like Fletcher."

"There's a nightwatchman, but he usually doesn't come inside," Annie said.

"See for yourself," Paolina whispered. "Be careful. Don't let him see you."

At first Annie didn't see anything. Then she caught a glimpse of a dark figure, moving quietly but not stealthily. He seemed confident, capable, and not concerned about being seen.

He was standing back and looking at something at the base of one of the columns that held up the barreled arch of the roof. He approached the column, bent down, and examined something at its base. Then he backed up again and nodded. He lifted something from the floor and moved up the nave toward the next column.

It was Sam.

Annie's heart began to race. He was dressed entirely in black, even to the watch cap covering his bright hair. She knew him by his walk, by the way he stood, the way he tilted his head.

What was he doing? Whatever it was, he was focused and purposeful. Whatever it was, it was not good.

Annie ducked back behind the statue and thought for an instant. Paolina was looking at her, her eyes wide and frightened. "Is it the watchman?"

Annie shook her head. She had to find out what Sam was doing. But she had a sick suspicion in the pit of her stomach.

If those were explosives he was attaching to the columns, they were hiding inside what was about to become their tomb.

Sam walked back through the nave, checking his work. He looked up at the huge vault of the ceiling and the stained glass windows all around. The building was magnificent. One of the most beautiful, surely, that his firm had ever designed. Its destruction would be a tragedy that the city would talk about for months.

The explosives were set to detonate by a signal from the electronic device that Sam held in his hand. Now came the crucial part of the plan. The part for which he needed crazy Jack Fletcher.

It must, of course, be Fletcher who was blamed for the explosion. And since the detonation would have to be triggered from outside, Fletcher was the only other person besides himself who would leave the building alive.

Once outside, though, the mad bomber, Jehovah's Pitchfork, would meet with bad luck. A large piece of schrapnel from the blast would strike him down. He would die with the detonator in his hand.

Giuseppe's murder would remain unsolved. Vico, dead in the ruins, could remain a suspect. With finesse, Sam would be able to suggest that Fletcher's antigay bigotry was the motive for him to kill Giuseppe. Yes, with any luck, it would *all* be blamed on Fletcher.

He went up the sanctuary steps and around behind the altar to the steps that led down to the crypt. Time to get Fletcher out of the basement.

As soon as she saw Sam duck out of sight behind the high altar, Annie jumped out from behind the statue of St. Joan. "Get Vico and Matt. Warn them. They've got to get out of here instantly. Sam is going to blow up the building."

"What are you going to do?" Paolina demanded.

"I'm going to try to pull those explosives off the columns," she said.

"No! Are you out of your mind? Please, Ms. Jefferson, no!"

"Get them out of there, Paolina. *Now!*" she said over her shoulder as she ran to the first column.

These things were supposed to be handled gently, Annie knew. And when it came to explosives, that was just about all she knew. That and the fact that they were detonated from a distance, electronically.

If Sam was right now leaving the cathedral—which he would have to do before he pushed the button—she had time only to rip the damn things off a few of the columns and hope that the explosion, when it came, would not take down the entire building.

As she tore the tape off the stone and disengaged the first few sticks of dynamite—or whatever it was—it occurred to her that she was probably going to die. *No, not probably*, she thought. *Definitely*.

But since it was impossible to imagine being definitely dead, she just went right ahead and yanked the explosives off the pillar and laid them carefully on the nearest wooden pew. Then she ran to the next column and did the same thing.

"They're upstairs," Sam said to Fletcher. "Annie and that other girl. I thought you'd like to know."

"They can't be upstairs! I've got all the ways out of the crawl space blocked!"

"Well," Sam shrugged, "you must've missed something."

"Shit!" Fletcher cried. "There *is* a way!"

Chapter Forty-five

"Are you *crazy*?" Matt had seen madness before—and matchless guts and courage—but he didn't think he'd ever witnessed anything to match the sight of Annie Jefferson tearing live explosives off the huge stone columns of a doomed cathedral.

"Get out, get out!"

"Vico's getting Paolina out, Annie. Come with me! Quickly—before Sam blows the thing."

"He's not going to destroy my cathedral, dammit! Not after all our hard work!" She pointed up at the magnificent stained glass windows, shrouded now in the dark. "He played me for a fool, Matt. It never occurred to me that I couldn't trust the architect. Or that he would sabotage his own building— and his most beautiful building at that. Well, he may have killed Giuseppe, but he's not going destroy his art!"

"Annie, I know how you feel, but it's too late." *How long till it blows? Shit!* How long?

He grabbed her arms and lifted her bodily from the column—the third of six that Sam had wired. "I'm taking you out of here now. Hell, it'll be a miracle if we can even get out."

She sobbed as he pulled her away. The nearest exit was the south transept door, and he ran toward it, dragging her while she screamed at him to let her go. Vico and Paolina were already there, and Vico was struggling with the door.

"Dammit, Annie, it's just a *building* for chrissake! I've lost everything else—I'm not going to lose you too!"

"I can't, Matt! I can't let it happen! We've got to stop him!"

"The cathedral can be built again," he said, wrestling her toward the door. *How long till it blows?* "Life once extinguished is lost forever. I love you, Annie. Stop fighting me."

She sobbed and went limp against him. Thank God! He swung her into his arms and ran toward Vico, who *still* hadn't gotten the damn door open.

Just as he skidded up to the teenagers, Sam's voice rang out behind him:

"Stop right there."

Again, Barbara Rae woke up suddenly. This time she knew it was hopeless. A peaceful sleep tonight was impossible.

Then she realized that what had awakened her this time was a pounding downstairs on the main door to the youth center.

She struggled into her dressing gown and descended the stairs. Her limbs felt stiff. Age was settling into her bones, slowing her down.

She expected Annie or Matthew, but it was Darcy at the door. "Thank God you're here. I didn't dare call the police because of Matt and Vico, but maybe I should have. Have you seen Annie and Matthew? They came over here to the cathedral more than an hour ago."

"No, I haven't seen them."

"Sam's a killer and Fletcher's a psycho," Darcy said. "We'd better call the cops."

They made the call, then Barbara Rae led Darcy to the basement of the youth center, while Darcy breathlessly filled her in on what they'd discovered at Sam's office.

"There's a way into the cathedral from here," Barbara Rae explained. "We can get in there before the police can."

"Good. My instincts are screaming that we'd better get in there fast."

Despite all the evidence, Matt hadn't really believed it until now. Even though he had known for several hours that his oldest friend had betrayed him in the vilest possible manner, he hadn't permitted himself to feel it in his heart.

Now, though, face to face with his nemesis, looking into the cold, hard barrel of a gun, he finally understood that Sam Brody had hated him for years.

"This is between you and me," he said. "Annie's not part of it. Let her go."

"Sorry. She wasn't supposed to be involved, but she just couldn't leave it alone," said Sam. "I really am sorry, Annie." He looked truly distressed. "It's never a good idea to get caught in the crossfire between two old adversaries."

"Is that what happened to Francesca?" Matt demanded.

"What happened to Francesca was, believe it or not, unintended. She was leaving you. I still don't know what you did to make her change her mind, but whatever it was, it wouldn't have lasted. She and I were going to be together, husband and wife, just as we would have been if you hadn't seduced her away from me twenty years ago."

"If that's true, why did you kill her?"

Sam looked pained. "She phoned me that night after the party. I think she called from a pay phone, which is why no one ever suspected me. She'd left the yacht to call because she was afraid you'd overhear.

"She told me she wasn't leaving you after all. We argued. I told her to go back to the yacht and wait for me . . . I was coming to pick her up. But when I got there, she wouldn't leave. She told me then that she was pregnant and the baby was yours. I didn't believe her. I thought she was just making excuses again.

"She was hysterical, and it turned—" he shrugged, "violent. She came at me, actually, with those long fingernails of hers bared, and I knew from long experience how nasty they could be. Don't try to tell me you haven't had a taste of that yourself on occasion. I was in no mood to be mauled, so I hit her. She fell and struck the back of her head on the railing of the yacht. That's how she died—or so I thought at the time. She wasn't breathing. I got no pulse. I thought she was dead and I panicked. I was *sure* she was dead, so I pushed her body overboard."

Where she had drowned. Neither of them said it. But it had been proven during the trial that Francesca had been alive when she went into the water.

Matt was trying very hard to keep his emotions under

control. "That's not the way a man in love behaves," he said tightly. "Here's what I think. I think you wanted Francesca purely for the pleasure of taking her away from me. But even more than that, you wanted to marry her to get your hands on half of my fortune. And once that became impossible, you focused on skimming money from the cathedral instead, since that was, indirectly, a way to steal money that had once belonged to me. A *lot* of money, incidentally.

"You're not a tragic lover, yearning for the same woman for over twenty years. You're a greedy, bitter son of a bitch who's been nursing a grudge for decades because the kid you felt so superior to in college turned out to be your master in every way."

Sam smiled genially. "In every way but one. You've never learned the fine art of dissembling, Matt. I'm an infinitely better actor than you are, and this is a culture that values the performance, the drama, a lot more highly than they value the truth. And wisely so, because truth is elusive."

"I would have trusted you with my life! Anything you asked of me, I would have given you."

"I know." Sam shook his head. "You always were a senti-mental fool, Matthew." He made a motion with his gun. "Enough chitchat. Get over there—all of you. Up against that nice column there with the dynamite." He took a quick look over his shoulder. "Jack? You still got that rope? Bring it over here."

"What are you going to do?" Annie asked. Her hand had slipped into Matt's, and he could feel the perspiration on her palm mixing with his own.

"Well," said Sam, "I can't blow the place until I'm at a safe distance, can I? You and Matt and the kids are going to stay here and enjoy the last couple of minutes of the cathedral's short but glorious life. Jack and I are going to leave."

"Don't listen to him, Jack," said Annie. "He'll kill you too. The last thing he wants is a witness to the fact that Sam Brody isn't the man everybody supposes him to be!"

"Don't bother," Sam said. "Jack and I trust each other."

"Yeah, and you're not going to let him die in the explosion because you need him alive in the aftermath," said Matt. "Someone other than you has to be a convincing candidate for using that detonator. You'll survive tonight, Fletcher. Sam'll wait till morning to serve you up to the authorities as the perpetrator of all *his* crimes."

Fletcher's eyes flickered speculatively. He seemed dazed, and he was acting like an automaton, stiffly obeying orders from Sam. He brought the rope and, at gunpoint, grabbed Annie, jerking her away from Matt. Matt lunged after her, but Sam stepped forward and put the barrel of his gun to the side of Matt's head. Vico, standing protectively in front of Paolina, eyed the guns in both men's hands and wisely decided to do nothing for the moment. But his handsome face was set in rage.

Fletcher threw one arm around Annie's neck and backed away with her. "You can do what you want with the rest of them," he said to Sam. Now that he was touching Annie, his voice was more animated. "But Annie is mine." He wrapped the rope around her body, passing it lovingly over her breasts, her waist, her hips, while she struggled futilely to free herself.

"Fine," Sam said calmly. "Do what you want with her. It's her lover I'm interested in."

"Annie and I have worked hard on this cathedral," Fletcher said unexpectedly. "Now you want to blow it up. I don't think that's a very good idea, Sam. I don't think I'm going to help you do it, either.''

''You'll do what I damn well tell you!'' Sam said.

Matt focused on the feel of the hard round cylinder of Sam's gun against the side of his head. He kept a gun and knew how to use it, although he certainly didn't consider himself an expert with firearms. But he knew that if you had the gun, you should never press it to your victim's body, because your victim could reach out and grab it. At least half the time, he could deflect it before you reacted fast enough to pull the trigger.

Half the time. The other half, you got a bullet in your brain.

On the other hand, if you were about to die anyhow . . . And Sam's attention was on Fletcher, who was continuing his plaintive objections to the destruction of the cathedral.

Matt raised his right hand, grabbed the gun barrel, and wrenched at it. The noise of the gun going off was deafening, but he heard it, he heard it, and he heard Annie scream, so he must still be alive. . . .

The recoil tore the gun right out of his grasp, but out of Sam's as well. He heard it clatter as it hit the stone floor, and at that same moment he swung around and smashed his fist into Sam's face. Matt felt the shock reverberate through his own body.

Then, out of the corner of his eye, Matt saw Vico spring toward the suddenly distracted Fletcher. With a bloodcurdling roar bursting out of his young throat, he tackled Fletcher and knocked him to the floor, where they rolled over several times, wrestling wildly.

Matt got off another blow, but Sam took it standing. He backed up a pace and struck back. Matt felt Sam's fist glance off the side of his head as he twisted away from it. Gasping, he came back with a tight combination, two lefts and a right, the final blow catching Sam cleanly on the chin and driving him back against the scaffolding, which he grabbed and clung to, to keep from sliding to his knees.

Matt hadn't boxed since college, but Sam probably hadn't either. He felt pumped up, almost cocky.

Then Sam fumbled in his pocket for the detonator.

Shit! Matt dived to the floor, grabbed the gun, and pointed it at Sam. "You can't blow it now. You'll die too."

Sam laughed. "Stop me," he said. And, ignoring the gun in Matt's hands, he swung himself up and began to climb the scaffolding.

Great, thought Matt. *He's going to kill us all, and to hell with his own life.* "Stop right there, Sam," he shouted. "If you don't, I'll blow you away."

Sam looked back at him and laughed again. "No you won't," he said. "I know you, Carlyle. You're no killer. Now that's a perfect piece of irony, isn't it?"

The gun vibrated in Matt's hand. *Do it,* he ordered himself. *Just do it, for chrissake!*

He swung the gun instead at Fletcher, but Vico had him disarmed and subdued on the floor. Seizing a piece of the man's own rope, he trussed him up, pulling callously at the rope and ignoring Fletcher's cries of pain and protest.

"Nice work," Matt said. "Unfortunately, though, Sam is going to blow up the cathedral and all of us in it."

"He must be crazy," Vico said. "He has chained and pad-locked all the exits."

Could he shoot the padlocks off the chains? Matt wondered, as, from somewhere behind Fletcher, Vico produced a knife that was huger than any Matt had ever seen before. He used it to slice through the ropes that bound Annie. She ran to Matt's side, and Vico turned back to Paolina. The teenagers grinned at each other as if unaware of the danger still hanging over them all.

Matt glanced up at Sam, who was now high on the scaffolding—the same scaffolding, he realized, where Giuseppe had spent the last few moments of his life.

"You'd better shoot him before he gets out of range," Vico advised. He examined the explosives taped to the column. "That stuff looks lethal," he said calmly.

"Matt, if you shoot him and he falls with the detonator in his hand, it'll probably go off with the impact," Annie said.

"Maybe not," said Vico. "His body might cushion the detonator."

They all stared at Sam as if they had all the time in the world to contemplate the intricacies of the problem.

In fact, Matt knew they couldn't get out in time. Sam had the detonator, and he could use it the moment any of them made a move toward one of the chained doors.

The real question was: Was Sam willing to die?

If he was, there was little they could do. If he wasn't, perhaps they could talk him down, make him surrender, get a hostage negotiator in here or something. . . .

High on the platform above, Sam was watching them. Matt cleared his throat and called up, "Look, we can talk about this, Sam."

His answer was a chilling laugh that, aided by the building's superior acoustics, echoed through the building.

Annie pressed against Matt's side and he held her hard

against him with his free arm. He loved her, dammit. There had to be a way out of this.

"Annie?" a new voice called out, and Matt swung around, staring in confusion at the exits, all of which were chained shut. But somehow or other Darcy appeared, running up the steps from the sacristy and stopping short when she took in the scene. "Jesus Christ! What's going on?" she cried.

"No, Darcy!" Annie screamed. "Get out of here! Hurry— get out!"

But Darcy did not get out, and neither did Barbara Rae, who was right behind her.

"How did you get in here?" Matt barked at them.

Darcy didn't answer. She was staring up at Sam, high on the scaffolding, with the detonator in his hand.

"There's another exit," Vico said in a low voice. "It's through the basement. It's a secret passageway that leads to the youth center next door. That must be how they got in."

Thank God! "Take it, then. Get the women out. Hurry."

"Matt, there's no time," said Annie.

"There's time if he's afraid to die. And most of us, when faced with it, are." He gazed up at Sam, who looked, from this distance, like a golden-haired angel. "Give it up, old friend. Any chance you had of covering this up is gone. We made several copies of both CAD files. There's no way out for you except an honorable surrender."

"Do you seriously think I'd subject myself to a trial?" Sam shouted down. "After what *you* went through? I'd rather end it now and have the satisfaction of knowing that I've finally finished you too."

Not wanting to endure the agonies of a murder trial was something Matt could understand.

"Besides, you're all here now, aren't you?" Sam added. "Dear Darcy, and Barbara Rae as well. It couldn't have worked out better if I'd planned it. The only person who's not here is Sid Canin, but I've already taken care of him."

"You killed him," Darcy said, her voice flat as she stared up at the man she had loved to distraction.

"Regretfully," said Sam, "he too was in love with Francesca. He thought Matt killed her, of course, until he got wind of Giuseppe's suspicions about the structure." He smiled, as if remembering. "It may be a while before they find his body, though. He ended up in the foundation of one of our other projects, just before the concrete was poured. Only his furniture went to New York."

"Shoot him," Vico said. He raised the handgun he'd taken from Fletcher. "If you don't, I will."

"No!" Barbara Rae said, her voice low but insistent.

No! thought Matt. Vico was too young to have a man's blood on his soul.

Sam moved on the scaffolding. He laughed, sounding manic. "Let's all count down from three," he called to them. "Then we'll go out together. If there's an afterlife, I hope Francesca has learned how to make up her mind."

It's up to you. Decide.

"Three!" Sam yelled. "You ready down there? I'm gonna press the button on 'One,' folks."

Barbara Rae stepped to the foot of the scaffolding. "Whatever you've done, Sam, it's never too late to find the love and the mercy of God. Release yourself into the Almighty's hands. Feel His love."

Sam laughed wildly. "Two!" he shouted.

"You lousy bastard!" Darcy shouted. "Maybe God still loves you, but I sure don't!"

Matt raised the gun and took careful aim. He steadied his arm, he held his breath, and just as Sam was saying "One!" and Barbara Rae was saying, "No, Matt," he pulled the trigger.

As if in slow motion, Sam fell. Gracefully, like a diving bird.

And as he fell, something small and dark flew out from his body and fell also, arcing gently down to the floor of the cathedral. There was nothing to do in those few seconds— which seemed to stretch out forever—but watch and wait for the explosion that would kill them all and turn the house of God into a fireball.

Sam's body struck the stone floor only inches from where Giuseppe had come to rest.

The detonator landed perfectly and precisely in the newly installed baptismal font, and as it hit, a silver splash of water rose into the air.

They waited for the fire, thunder, an earthquake of violent sound.

They heard only silence and the drip of holy water from a font that, to Annie's knowledge, had never been filled.

Chapter Forty-six

Six Months Later

Annie slipped into one of the back pews of the cathedral and pulled down the kneeling platform. She sank down on it and folded her hands together on the back of the pew in front of her, and briefly she closed her eyes.

When she opened them, she let the full beauty of the finished building seep into her soul. It was radiant with color and light. The fresh paint gleamed. The wooden pews were polished to a high gloss. The magnificent altar cross glittered like gold, and the dozens of chandeliers over the nave and bright sconces on the north and south walls banished any hint of darkness. The sun slanted, muted, through the stained glass windows, creating a wondrous pattern of color directly down the center aisle. And above, the bells in the tower rang out joyously as the hour changed.

The cathedral now was a very different place from the dark

and gloomy unfinished interior that had almost been blown out of existence. It had opened officially last week for services, after Darcy had worked hard with a new contractor to reinforce the existing structure and resolve the safety problems. The building had been certified as structurally sound, and tomorrow it would be the site of a special celebration.

Annie heard a step behind her and turned her head.

"I figured I'd find you here," said Matt.

He came into the pew and sat down. Unlike her, he did not kneel. She leaned back and felt the comfort of his knee against her back.

To her knowledge, he hadn't been inside the cathedral since the day he'd fired a gun at his oldest friend and watched him fall to his death in almost the same spot where Giuseppe had died. Annie's memory of the events right after that moment were a little fuzzy now, but there was one exchange she recalled with perfect clarity:

"There was no gunshot wound on your friend," Detective Sullivan said to Matt. "Looks like he either fell, or jumped."

"What?"

"Yeah, Carlyle, you're a lousy shot. We recovered your bullet from the wooden platform above where the guy must've been standing. You missed by at least a yard."

That had been a mercy, Annie knew. Despite everything, Matt hadn't wanted Sam's death on his conscience.

"Are you going to be okay about it?" she asked him now.

"About tomorrow? Yes. This place has been finished beautifully, Annie. I'm so very proud of you."

"The shadows are gone, I think. I hope so, anyway."

"The shadows are gone."

"I love you, Matt."

"I love you too."

"Vico and Paolina will be coming. And they're bringing the baby!"

"Well, we went to their wedding, so they'd better show up at ours."

She rose from the kneeling platform and sat beside him on the red-cushioned pew. He slung his arm around her and pulled her close.

"I'm so happy, Matt."

"Mmm, me too." He kissed her hair. "Oh, by the way, now that this project is finally finished, there's something I've been meaning to talk to you about."

She looked up at him. He smiled. "It's about Powerdyme. I really hate that new headquarters we built a couple years ago. It was never quite what I wanted, and it's just not right. I was hoping that you and Darcy might submit a proposal for a new Powerdyme headquarters. Now that you've got Fabrications up and running again."

"Gee, I don't know, Matt." She gave him an impish smile. "Seems to me I tried that once before—and got royally rejected."

"I suggest you try again anyhow. I hear the CEO of Powerdyme has turned into something of a softie."

"A softie, huh?"

"Yup. The guy's getting married, having a big church wedding with Barbara Rae Acker officiating. They say he's got a lot better taste both in women and in architectural design these days."

She laughed and inclined her face to his. "Do you think anyone'll mind if we steal a prenuptial kiss in the cathedral where our vows will be spoken?"

He shook his head. "The way I figure it, this cathedral owes us its life."

As he took her lips, the setting sun slanted in through the great rose window behind them, bathing their bodies in light.

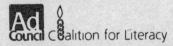